THE

SHINING
ROAD

THE
SHINING
ROAD

Carolyn Renfrew

Hastings College Press | Hastings, Nebraska

Introduction © 2022 by Hastings College Press

ISBN-13: 978-1-942885-70-2

This novel is produced from the author's typescript, which is housed at the Adams County Historical Society (Hastings, Nebraska).

INTRODUCTION

Carolyn "Carrie" Renfrew (1858–1948) achieved moderate fame as a writer in her lifetime, especially in her home state of Nebraska. Since her death, however, she has been mostly forgotten. She published six books—two collections of poetry, two collections of plays, and two novels—late in life. While she published her first poem around 1885 (and had a brief singing career in the 1890s), her first book was not published until 1923, when she was 65 years old. In addition to the six books she published in her lifetime, she left many more unpublished works. This oeuvre, which is currently housed by the Adams County Historical Society in Hastings, Nebraska, reveals that Renfrew was a much more prolific writer than her published works indicate. The Society possesses manuscripts and typescripts for seven novels, two poetry collections, ten plays, six music pieces, and twenty-four short stories, only some of which were published in Renfrew's lifetime. This novel, *The Shining Road,* is one of those previously unpublished works.

Renfrew's literary career was influenced by her life in Hastings, Nebraska. In fact, a small Nebraska town just like Hastings is the setting for many of her novels, which blend fiction with actual details from Hastings and Nebraska history. This novel, *The Shining Road,* is set in the years immediately before and after World War I and follows the disappointments and triumphs of Nadia Evertson, a young aspiring writer from Marshall, Nebraska. Like the real Hastings, Nebraska, the fictional Marshall is a small pioneer railroad town. The details of Nadia's life in Nebraska—from her family to the types of books she writes—are remarkably similar to those of the author's life, maybe uncomfortably close in some cases. *The Shining Road* is not an autobiography, but many of the details echo documented events in the lives of the Renfrew family.

The Renfrew Family and Hastings, Nebraska

Carrie Renfrew was born June 7, 1858 in Marseilles, Illinois, to parents Sylvester and Mercy (Clark) Renfrew.[1] Attracted by the prospect of cheap land in an up-and-coming state, the Renfrews—including children Alice (1854–1936), Myra (1856–1943), Carrie, Addie (1863–1941), Herman (1865–1952), Jennie (1869–1955), and Robert (1871–1879)—moved to Hastings, Nebraska in 1876.[2] Hastings had been officially incorporated just two years before, and the Renfrew family became one of its earliest and most respected pioneer families. In fact, the history of the Renfrews in this early period is intertwined with the history of Hastings itself. The fortunes and misfortunes of the family mirrored those of the town in many ways.

Carrie's father, Sylvester, began life in Hastings as a farmer, building a large house "some distance in the country" to the north of the village on property that in 1880 became known as "Renfrew's Addition" to the city of Hastings.[3] The family built a large home at 807 North St. Joseph Avenue around 1876, which, according to the Hastings *Daily Gazette-Journal,* was "for many years the largest house in Adams county."[4] In 1904, the editors of the *Adams County Democrat* recalled that the Renfrews' first home "was, for those days, quite a large and commodious house, but it was so far out of town that it was spoken of as 'the farm.'"[5] Sylvester bought quite a bit of land in Adams County and Hall County in the 1870s and 1880s, including large farms near Doniphan and Kenesaw that he leased to tenant farmers. His income came from selling land, collecting rent, buying and selling grain and stock, and lending mortgages—the family was considered one of the wealthiest and most prominent in Hastings.[6]

According to society columns and notices in Hastings newspapers, the Renfrew family was well regarded in the city and kept a busy social calendar from the 1870s to the first decade of the 1900s. The Renfrew siblings attended dances, wedding receptions, and card parties with the wealthiest families in town, and their comings and goings were reported on

RENFREW'S ADDITION to the City of HASTINGS

Filed for record June 30th 1880 at 9 o'clock A.M. R.B. Tussen

School Dist Add.

Renfrew's Addition to Hastings, 1880. Register of Deeds (Hastings, Nebraska).

regularly. The 1880s seem to have been an especially exciting time for the Renfrew siblings (and Hastings society in general). The Bostwick hotel, which opened at the corner of 2nd and Denver in 1885, provided a swanky location for many balls and wedding receptions the Renfrew siblings attended, and a "progressive euchre" craze swept Hastings, as evidenced by the many card parties thrown by Hastings' society women during this period.[7] The Renfrews also hosted fashionable parties themselves. The "Miss Renfrews" hosted a New Years Day open house in 1881, for example.[8] And the *Gazette-Journal* reported in February 1882, "We don't believe a happier time has been had by the little folks this winter [than] at the home of little Jennie Renfrew Monday evening. The occasion was her 13th birthday, and a house-full of friends had assembled to render the event a pleasant one. The evening was spent in dancing and in various games and frolics, and when the time came to go home, more than one wished that Jennie would have a birthday party every week."[9]

The Renfrew family was known for music and in the early decades often hosted musical gatherings at their home. The *Adams County Democrat* reminisced in 1904 that "The old settlers of Hastings were as fond of amusement and entertainment as are the people today." "Before any barn storming theatrical troupe had visited the city," the writer noted, "those early young folks would get home talent entertainment.... The home of Sylvester Renfrew was the scene of many a musical gathering.... the Renfrew family were all musicians and they loved to have the young people come to their home to play and sing."[10] In 1945, a few months before she died, Carrie received a surprise letter from Francis Kennon McLaughlin, a former acquaintance and Air Corps captain stationed in Guam, who wrote, "I really think of you and the many good times & visits I've had in your home with you. I also recall of the interesting evenings we used to have when a gang of us would come up to your home & gather around the piano for song and laughter."[11]

Hastings newspapers included dozens of accounts of Myra, Alice, Carrie, Addie, and Sylvester performing at church services, social events, and other meetings in the 1880s and 1890s. The members of the Burger family, another musical family in Hastings, were often mentioned in relation to the Renfrew family. The September 12, 1887 edition of the *Daily Gazette-Journal,* for instance, reported, "The choir at the Methodist church has undergone a complete change. Mr. Tyron Burger is now leader, with Miss Hutoka Poole as soprano, Miss Carrie Renfrew alto and Mr. German Burger bass. The organ is manipulated by Mrs. Burger [Myra Renfrew]." The short review continued approvingly, "The music furnished yesterday was of a very delightful sort and the audience both morning and evening seemed to drink in the pleasing melodies with a great deal of satisfaction."[12]

While the entire family was musical, the belle of the Renfrew family, according to Hastings newspapers, was Addie. An article in the May 18, 1884 *Weekly Gazette-Journal,* for instance, gave a glowing review of Addie's solo performance of

"The Ebbing Tide," which was "rendered by her in a manner to call forth well merited applause." The reviewer added, "we can truthfully say that we were pleased to hear so perfect a voice, that for some reason unknown … has been for some time withheld from us."[13] Her 1885 performance as Katish in a local production of Gilbert and Sullivan's *The Mikado* was an unqualified triumph. A review in the *Adams County Democrat* reported that "Misses Addie Renfrew and Laura Dilley were greeted with outbursts of applause at every appearance." "From the moment that Miss Addie's rich contralto and Miss Laura's clear and sweet soprano voices filled the auditorium," the reviewer continued, "if any doubt had been entertained as to their rare gift of song, and ability to grace the operatic stage, they vanished. They never appeared to better advantage."[14] The *Daily Gazette-Journal* reported a few weeks later that Addie had been invited to reprise her role with a traveling company based in Denver and that "if she should accept the offer, we have no doubt but that she could win many laurels."[15] It does not seem that Addie took the opportunity to join a traveling show, but she continued to be at the center of Hastings social life, attending parties and weddings, and performing at churches and organizations all around town. Addie was so popular that the *Hastings Weekly Gazette-Journal* announced her temporary, two-week job at the Nebraska, Loan & Trust Co. in October 1884.[16]

Although the Renfrew family flourished in the early decades of Hastings, their lives were not totally idyllic. The youngest sibling, Robert, died in April 1879 at the age of 8. The Renfrews thanked their neighbors and friends for their assistance and kindness in the April 11, 1879 edition of the *Central Nebraskan*, writing, "We desire to express our gratitude to the many kind friends who so freely tendered their sympathy and assistance during the late sickness and death of our little boy … Surely his young spirit is made happier by such manifestations of love and regard."[17] In June 1881 Sylvester bought an interest in a buggy and hardware business, Burger Bros., which "[kept] the largest stock of Buggies and Carriages and [sold] cheaper than can be got elsewhere west

of Omaha."[18] Peter Burger, one of the owners, was Sylvester's
son-in-law, having married Myra Renfrew in 1876.[19] It is likely
that Sylvester's infusion of cash into the business in 1881 was
a direct result of the disastrous fire in September 1879 that
destroyed many wood-frame buildings, mostly businesses, in
downtown Hastings. (Many people were injured trying to
save both the buildings and their contents, including Herman
Renfrew, who suffered a broken leg.[20]) Newspaper articles from
1880 to early 1882 chronicled the rebuilding of downtown (in
brick, this time) and advertised the businesses that reopened,
including the Burger Bros. store, now known as "Burger Bros.
and Renfrew," which reopened in its new brick building on 2nd
Street in January 1882.[21] Sylvester sold back his share to the
Burger brothers in 1883.[22]

Local Hastings politics got a bit heated at times, too, and
the Renfrews were sometimes in the thick of it. Sylvester ran for
several offices in Hastings and Adams County. In 1880 he ran
for mayor of Hastings, but lost the election despite the *Hastings
Journal*'s assertion that he "meets the approval of all with
whom we have talked" and that "He has all the qualifications
for a reliable, dignified and impartial executive officer."[23] A
1903 editorial in the *Adams County Democrat* on the history
of exciting municipal elections explained the 1880 mayoral
election as a battle between the raucous Western frontier and
the "enthusiastically moral element [that] appeared on the field,
and demanded to manage city affairs." This element "knew but
little of the life and habits of the frontiersmen. Coming from
the moral and civilized east, some of them were afraid of their
lives." The writer argued that "Hastings had many elements
of a western frontier town…. This being the largest town in
the western part of the state it was natural that cowboys and
freighters should drift here to purchase their supplies and as
they used to term it, paint the town." But, the writer continued,
the "ultra moralists" did not like the idea of a German, Fred
Forcht, being elected mayor: "When Mr. Forcht was named as
a candidate for mayor it became evident that a candidate with
different views must be put up against him or Hastings would

be turned into a 640 acre beer garden." Sylvester was nominated by the "ultra moralists" who did not approve of alcohol, but he lost the election.[24]

The Renfrews were, in fact, active with the temperance movement in Hastings. Proceedings of the local Temperance Alliance were published regularly in the *Gazette-Journal* in the early 1880s, with the Renfrews often giving short speeches and performing.[25] When Sylvester announced his desire to run for county treasurer in 1881, the *Adams County Democrat* wrote, "If the Hon. Mr. Renfrew cannot beat Fred Forcht for Mayor of this city, how can he expect to beat him for county treasurer, with the 'German vote in Fred's pocket.'"[26] A few months later the *Adams County Democrat* wrote, "The Hon. Sylvester Renfrew, the tall sycamore of the prairie, wants to be the next county treasurer. Sylvester, dear, thou art so near, and yet so far."[27] The derision of this comment is evident in the likening of Sylvester to a sycamore tree, which is native to the eastern United States but not to the Nebraska prairie. The Renfrews put considerable effort into the local elections of 1882, with the *Gazette-Journal* reporting, "We understand that Miss Alice Renfrew has secured a majority of the voters in the city to sign a paper agreeing to vote for none but temperance men for office."[28] In April 1882, as the election neared, the *Adams County Democrat* was explicit in its criticism of Sylvester's temperance stance, editorializing, "Once more it becomes our painful duty to chastise one of our best citizens and this time it is our honorable friend Sylvester Renfrew that draws our attention. Oh! Sylvester why doest thou bring thyself thusly into prominence?" The editorial's sarcastic, antiquated language implies that Sylvester's objection to licensing saloons (i.e., his advocacy for prohibition) was old-fashioned. "Your argument is very weak," the editors wrote, "and will have no bearing with intelligent people who are not blindly deceived."[29] Sylvester lost this election, too.

If the first half of 1882 was a stressful political time for the Renfrew family, the latter half of 1882 seems to have been even harder on their health—*The Gazette-Journal* reported that Alice,

Addie, and Carrie were all ill for several months. On August 10, the *Gazette-Journal* announced that "Miss Alice Renfrew was poisoned by some plant while at the Blue a few days ago. She is quite sick in consequence and her face is very much swollen."[30] She was not reported to be improving until the end of October.[31] On October 5, "Miss Addie Renfrew [was] very sick with the erysipelas," a bacterial infection of the skin.[32] And on November 16, the *Gazette-Journal* reported that "Miss Carrie Renfrew, who has been quite sick for some time past is rapidly recovering."[33] It is not clear from these reports whether the ill-fated trip to the Blue was the origin of all these illnesses or whether these illnesses were independent of each other. It seems certain, though, that this would have been a stressful time for the Renfrew family, especially immediately after the second failed election.

In 1887, the Renfrews built a new, larger residence, "adjacent to" the previous one, at 805 North St. Joseph Avenue. While the house was under construction, the *Daily Gazette-Journal* opined that it would "be one of the handsomest in the city and an ornament to that beautiful avenue."[34] The house and the family were known well enough in Hastings that in 1906 Mercy's decision to install radiators was important local news. The *Hastings Daily Republican* reported, "The contract for heating the residence of Mrs. M. Renfrew on North St. Joe avenue with hot water was awarded to Anson & Pratt. The Ideal boiler and American radiators will be used."[35]

Sylvester's death in 1888, just after the new house was built, coincided with the end of Hastings' first boom period. Lori Cox notes, "The boom collapsed in 1887, leaving Hastings residents somewhat chastened and the population of 13,584 in 1890 dwindled to 7,188 by the turn of the century."[36] The fortunes of the Renfrew family, so tied to real estate, took a similar turn. Starting around this time, the Renfrew siblings—all adults now—started looking to other horizons.

Myra was the first to leave Hastings for good. The Burgers, who lived next door to the Renfrews on North St. Joseph Avenue, moved to Denver in 1891, where Peter and his brother

The second Renfrew home, 805 North St. Joseph Avenue, Hastings, Nebraska. Photograph taken between 1960 and 1990. The lot on which the home stood is now a parking lot for Mary Lanning Memorial Hospital. Adams County Historical Society (Hastings, Nebraska).

Gamaliel were officers of the Denver Hardware Company at 1623 Larimer Street.[37] The business must not have been successful, though, because Peter is listed as a clerk for the Denver Stove and Hardware Company in the 1895 Denver city directory.[38] By 1899, Peter and Myra were living in Chula Vista, California, Peter's occupation being described in city directories variously as rancher, orchardist, and fruit farmer.[39] Their only child, a son named Clarence ("Clare"), died in November 1901 at the age of 20 from an apparent suicide.[40] Peter and Myra visited Hastings a few times, typically when a member of the family was ill, but they never lived there again. Hastings newspapers included several notices about Mercy, Carrie, and Alice visiting the Burgers in California, though. Mercy and Alice, for example, spent six weeks with Myra after Clare's death.[41] Mercy and her friend Elizabeth Babcock also wintered in southern California several times, staying with Myra in Chula Vista.[42]

Carrie turned her attention to a literary career around 1885, publishing dozens of poems in *The Woman's Tribune* and the *Chicago Inter-Ocean* in the next few decades. Many of these poems were syndicated in newspapers across the country. *The Woman's Tribune* was a national suffragist newspaper run by Clara Bewick Colby out of Beatrice, Nebraska. Although many of Carrie's poems addressed fairly non-controversial subjects such as love, death, and nature, a few were political. In February 1890, for example, Carrie published a tribute to Susan B. Anthony in *The Woman's Tribune* titled "In Commemoration of Miss Anthony's Seventieth Birthday":

IN COMMEMORATION OF MISS ANTHONY'S
SEVENTIETH BIRTHDAY

Friend and sister, helper, leader.
　　We would honor thee to-day.
As a brave, a gallant soldier;
　　One who never shirked a fray
When the cause of right demanded;
　　When the cause of truth had need
Of thy woman's strength of purpose;
　　Of thy woman's thought and deed.

Honor, honor to the courage
　　That had strength to dare and do;
To the ardent sense of justice
　　To the wide, progressive view,
Honor to the soul that, seeing,
　　Followed sight with action's wedge.
To the Self that turned from pleasure
　　And gave truth an earnest pledge.

'Tis by such that life has risen
　　To a higher plane to-day
And the upward growth moves onward;
　　Souls like thine to lead the way.
Weak'ning art thou, with thy struggles

> And the weight of seventy years?
> No! Still at the front we find thee
>   Ringing truths in deafened ears.
>
> Thou hast never bent to evil;
>   Thou hast never yoked with wrong.
> Yet the burdens thou hast carried
>   Would have weakened souls less strong.
> Bend thou now, O brave true spirit,
>   To receive our crown of praise,
> And our love, a grateful tribute—
>   Let them gild thy sunset days.
>
> Thou wilt need no shaft of marble
>   To perpetuate thy fame,
> For the happier lot of woman
>   Will do reverence to thy name.
> And that name will be recorded
>   In all future history
> In the foremost ranks, a chieftain
>   Of the nineteenth century.

The Renfrew women's interest in women's suffrage seems to be related to temperance. In 1890 the Renfrews supported a proposed amendment to the state constitution that would outlaw saloons. In a July article in the *Lincoln Evening Call,* Hastings business owners declared their stand on the prohibition issue, which was framed by pro-prohibitionists as a battle between "the home" and "the saloon," and "H. T. Renfrew, stock dealer" [Herman] is listed in favor of "Constitutional Prohibition."[43] The proposed 1890 amendment was unsuccessful. In April 1909, less than a year after the Hastings Brewing Company began operating, Mercy signed on to a petition, published in the *Hastings Daily Republican,* with over 800 women in Hastings, "call[ing] upon the men of Hastings to go to the polls Tuesday and vote to banish saloons from the city."[44] This vote was not successful either. In 1916, however, just a few years before national prohibition, Hastings voters did vote to ban alcohol in the city. No doubt the Renfrews, who had been fighting this battle for decades, rejoiced.

While the Renfrews carried on the good fight for temperance in Hastings after Sylvester's death, Carrie's national reputation as a poet started to rise. *The Magazine of Poetry and Literary Review,* edited by Charles Wells Moulton, featured a short but flattering biography of Carrie by poet John G. Clark in 1890. It focused not only on her career but also on her person:

> Carrie Renfrew resides in Hastings, Neb. Her progress in literary art and expression, though rapid, if not phenomenal, is evidently but the mere promise of what she is yet to accomplish, for she is still in the very morning of life, surrounded by every earthly comfort, a beloved member of a well-born, harmonious and happy family, who sympathize with her aspirations and rejoice in her success. Her mother, a rare and excellent woman, several sisters and a brother are still living, but her father, the late honored Sylvester Renfrew, one of the early pioneers of Hastings, died during the past year.
>
> Miss Renfrew was from childhood a thinker, dreamer and philosopher, but not, like most poets, an early rhymster. Her lack of training in the art of rhyming, while plainly visible in some of her first attempts, has its compensation in the higher and more essential qualities that characterize nearly all her recent efforts. It is scarcely more than five years now since the advent of her first poems in the *Inter-Ocean, Woman's Tribune* and other western papers.
>
> In temperament Miss Renfrew is a harmonious blending of the brunette and blonde types. She is of about medium size, has a graceful figure, an attractive manner and appearance, and a magnetic presence, and does not on acquaintance disappoint those who have

Carrie Renfrew, *The Magazine of Poetry and Literature Review*, 1890.

learned to love and admire her through her poetry. She has already endeared herself to a host of personal friends and to thousands who knew her only through her work. The world at large will know her better in the near future.[45]

The biography was accompanied by five apolitical poems—"Poetry," "Life," "Missing," "Before a Mummy," and "A Refrain"—and a photograph taken by a Hastings photographer named Townsend.[46]

In March 1893, notices in the *Nebraska State Journal* and the *Lincoln Herald* announced that Carrie had gone to Buffalo, New York, to edit a literary magazine.[47] We assume this magazine was *The Magazine of Poetry and Literary Review*, whose office was located in Buffalo. Her work for Moulton included writing biographies for Nebraska Women for an 1893 publication titled *A Woman of the Century: Fourteen Hundred-Seventy Biographical Sketches Accompanied by Portraits of Leading American Women in*

All Walks of Life. Carrie's own biography, probably written by herself, and portrait were included in this volume:

> Renfrew, Miss Carrie, poet and biographer, was born in Marseilles, Ill. She is a daughter of the late Silvester Renfrew, one of the pioneer settlers of Hastings, Neb., who died in 1888. She is one of a family of five children. She was carefully educated and reared in a refined and cultured atmosphere. She received all the educational advantages of her native town, and she has supplemented her school course with a wide course in reading. In childhood she was a thinker, a dreamer and a philosopher with a poetic turn of mind, but she did not "lisp in numbers." She waited until reason was ready to go hand in hand with rhyme, and then she began to write verses. She had not studied the art of rhyming, and some of her first productions showed the crudity to be expected where there was a lack of training in modes of expression. In spite of all drawbacks of that kind, she wrote well enough to attract attention, and her maturer work leaves nothing to be desired in the matter of form. In 1885 she became a contributor to the Chicago "Inter-Ocean," the "Woman's Tribune" and other prominent journals. In 1890 she began to contribute to the "Magazine of Poetry," and her poems have found wide currency. Her prose work includes a large number of biographies of prominent Nebraska women for this volume. She has written much in verse, and her work shows steady advancement in quality. She stands among the foremost of the literary women in Nebraska.[48]

It is not clear from newspaper accounts how long Carrie worked for Moulton, but this opportunity began an almost two-decade period of travel away from Hastings. We do not have a full timeline of her travels in the 1890s and 1900s, but newspaper announcements, city directories, and archival materials help to fill in the broad strokes. Lori Cox argues that Carrie began a "singing career around 1895 after studying music in Boston."[49] One unsourced newspaper clipping in Renfrew's personal papers notes that her "concerts received fine ovations … over the country before ending the tour because of frailty; she received an especially fine offer from a leading New York company to continue the tour."[50] A concert circular described Carrie as

> a soloist already well known and popular in the concert field and one who gives great promise of winning renown. She has a pure high soprano voice of wide compass, strong, flexible and sympathetic, with the dainty graces of the thorough artist. Her repertoire is large and varied, including the most brilliant florid music, oratorio and the simple ballads. Her singing is characterized by great intensity.[51]

In February and March 1895, Carrie was living at the New Sheridan hotel in South Bend, Indiana, and advertising for students in the *South Bend Tribune:*

> Miss Carolyn Renfrew, lately from New York, has decided to remain in South Ben [sic] and will take a number of pupils in singing. Will take either advanced pupils or beginners. Will prepare students for concert or church singing. Anyone wishing to consult with her in regard to vocal culture will please call on her at the New Sheridan hotel.[52]

She must have stayed in the South Bend/Chicago area for a few years because a January 1898 announcement in the *Hastings Tribune* announced that Jennie was planning to visit Carrie in Chicago.[53] In July 1898 the *Hastings Tribune* reported that Carrie and Jennie were back in Hastings from Chicago, "where they had a delightful visit during the past year."[54] Carrie did not stay in Hastings long, though, because the April 13, 1899 edition of the California paper *The Record* reports that she was visiting the Burgers in Chula Vista, where she gave a performance. Hastings newspapers announced her return home to Hastings in January 1900 and that she had been visiting California for her health.[55]

Around 1904 Carrie and Jennie left to visit friends in Kansas City and did not really return to Hastings until 1910. A blurb in the April 8, 1904 edition of the *Hastings Tribune* announced, "Miss Carrie and Jennie Renfrew are in Kansas City on an extended visit among friends."[56] In June 1905 Carrie and Jennie were living in Topeka.[57] From 1907 to 1910 Carrie and Jennie are listed in the Colorado Springs, Colorado, city directory as living at 523 N. Nevada Ave.[58] Their mother and Alice visited them in Colorado Springs in September 1908.[59]

While they were gone from Hastings, Carrie and Jennie missed several significant events, including their mother Mercy's broken hip in 1905. The *Hastings Republican* noted, "As Mrs. Renfrew is past 70 years of age this accident will go hard with her…. The friends and neighbors of this excellent lady earnestly hope she will recover from this accident."[60] When Mercy became ill in May 1910, the *Hastings Daily Tribune* announced that "Misses Carrie and Jennie Renfrew, of Casper, Wyoming, are in the city, having been called here by the illness of their mother, Mrs. Mercy Renfrew."[61] (We do not know when or why they moved to Casper, Wyoming.) Mercy's death in May 1910 proved to be the end of Carrie's and Jennie's wanderings.

Jennie's sudden marriage to dentist Fay Babcock on September 29, 1910, left Carrie to take care of their ailing sister Addie. Babcock was the son of Mercy's good friend Elizabeth Babcock[62] and brother to Frank C. Babcock, a prominent physician in Hastings. The wedding took place in Alice's home and, according to some newspaper accounts, was "a complete surprise to their friends."[63] Newspaper accounts from the previous years, in fact, give the impression that Babcock had been courting Addie, not Jennie. In a March 1910 listing of eligible Hastings bachelors in the *Hastings Daily Republican,*

Babcock was described as "very fastidious … has a beautiful trousseau with neckties, hose, handkerchief-borders and hat-bands to match."[64] Babcock's office was located at the State Bank Building (601 W. 2nd St.) for a few years and then at 822 W. 2nd St; the couple settled at 1103 N. St. Joseph Avenue, just three blocks from the Renfrew family home.[65]

Alice left Hastings in 1911 after the death of her husband, Robert Batty. "Bob Batty," as he was called in the Hastings newspapers, was a prominent lawyer and judge and had served as mayor of Hastings in 1878 and in the state legislature from 1878 to 1880.[66] He and Alice married in 1884 and were prominent in Hastings society, with Robert being heavily involved in local politics.[67] They lived less than two blocks from the Renfrew family home, at 619 North St. Joseph Avenue; Robert's law office was located in the German National Bank Building downtown.[68] While she was in California visiting Myra, Carrie would have missed the death of her niece Roberta Batty, "the pet and joy of the home," in August 1899 at the age of one year and three months.[69] After Robert died in 1911, Alice moved in with her two adult daughters (Alice and Elizabeth), who were students at the University of Nebraska at Lincoln.[70] When they graduated, Alice and her daughters moved to Chula Vista, California, to be near her sister Myra. The 1920 federal census shows that Alice and Myra lived next door to each other in Chula Vista, but the 1930 federal census shows that Myra and Alice, both widowed, were living together.[71] They likely joined households around the time Myra's husband Peter died in 1923.[72]

Mercy's death, Jennie's marriage, and Alice's move to Lincoln and then California in the years 1910–1912 left just Carrie, Addie, and Herman at the Renfrew family home. None of these three ever married and, in fact, they were each still living in the family home on North St. Joseph Avenue decades later when they died—Addie in 1941, Carrie in 1948, and Herman in 1952. The siblings lived on income from the family's farms, but Herman was the main source of financial support, carrying on with the family business after the death of their parents. His comings and goings were reported in Hastings and Grand Island newspapers for many decades. He traveled regularly as a grain buyer and often stayed at hotels in Grand Island, though the tongue-in-cheek tone of some newspaper snippets about Herman's trips seem to suggest that he had a reputation for not actually doing much work. The "Elite Eligibles" column in the March 12, 1910 edition of the *Hastings Daily Republican* referred to Herman as a "bachelor of leisure," who "occasionally interests himself in business affairs, but purely as a means of recreation." The columnist's further assertion that Herman was "rather of a speculative disposition" suggests that he liked to gamble.[73]

Increasingly ill health kept Carrie and Addie in Hastings for the rest of their lives. Newspaper accounts as far back as 1882 indicate that the two sisters were frequently ill. In June 1884, for example, the *Hastings Daily Gazette-Journal* reported, "Mrs. S. Renfrew has returned from a prolonged visit east, where she went with her daughter, Miss Carrie Renfrew. The friends of the latter will be glad to learn that her health is improving."[74] In September 1916 Carrie was so ill that Alice traveled from Chula Vista to Hastings to take care of her.[75] However, it was Addie—the former belle of Hastings society— who suffered the worst health. A September 3, 1921 blurb in the *Hastings Daily Tribune* announced that "Miss Addie Renfrew, who has been in ill health for a number of years, has gone to Rochester for treatment. She is accompanied by her brother and sister, Herman and Miss Carrie Renfrew."[76] It is not clear what caused Addie's long-term illness. She experienced a case of food poisoning in 1910 that was serious enough to cut short Jennie and Fay's honeymoon. Food poisoning this severe could have caused serious chronic side effects, such as kidney failure or brain/nerve damage.[77] She also suffered a broken hip in 1926 after slipping on an icy sidewalk, which could have led to permanent impairment.[78] Jim Fritzler suggests that Addie had a form of genetic hyperthyroidism that caused "breathing problems, nervousness, palpitations, hyperactivity, increased sweating, heat hypersensitivity, fatigue, increased appetite, and weight loss," and that Carrie and Herman suffered from this malady, as well.[79]

Whatever Addie's continuing illness was, Carrie apparently spoke of it often in personal and professional correspondences and seemed to resent having to be her sister's sole caregiver. Many friends who wrote to her alluded to these issues. In an undated letter (probably written in the 1920s or 1930s), for example, Vida F. Watson wrote to Carrie, "Your life has been spent in devotion and self-sacrifice."[80] In September 1929, Marie Herrin, who worked at the *Hastings Daily Tribune*, sent an encouraging letter that alluded to Carrie feeling "down hearted." "Life is hard to understand," she writes, "but somehow, sometime, things are evened up, I believe, and somehow, somewhere, you'll find a reward for the things you do."[81] An undated letter from a "Mrs. Dixon" is more explicit:

> I feel I still wish to tell you my heart is aching for you
> in your nervous condition and the care of ones that are
> ill beside the mental worry is undoubtedly the cause[.]
> I don't believe there is another thing that pulls on the
> nervous system like this and it is very evident to me
> from your letters Miss Renfrew that you are much
> in need of relaxing and owe it to yourself to do so at
> once, you will be able to carry the burden far easier to
> take care of your health and I hope you will set aside
> a time very soon for some one to relieve you and let
> you get a much needed rest. Please do so at once if
> you can. It may not be your choice but nessesity[sic]
> for the good of all about you as well as your own dear
> self.[82]

According to interviews conducted in 1984 by Hastings College student Lori Cox, Carrie, Addie, and Herman's final decades in Hastings were very different from the heady decades of the 1870s and 1880s. In fact, interviewees described the siblings as reclusive and strange. Margaret Young, who was Renfrew's neighbor in the 1920s, recalled that there were very

few visitors to the Renfrew home then. According to Young,
Carrie paced around a bush in the yard for hours everyday and
generally kept to herself.[83] Longtime friend Elmer Kearney told
Cox that "Addie was ill most of the time and the burden fell on
Carolyn to take care of her.… Herman was not willing to help
out and he and Carolyn did not get along."[84]

The more reclusive the siblings became in Hastings society,
however, the more Carrie's literary career took off. In 1923, she
won first prize in the Omaha Women's Press Club contest with
a poem titled "Hope."[85] This poem appeared later that year in
her first published book of poetry, *Songs of Hope*, published by
New York publisher Moffay, Yard & Co. The same publisher
also released Renfrew's *The Last of the Strozzi, and The Lure:
Two Plays* in 1923. Burton Publishing Company of Kansas City,
Missouri, published four additional titles: the novel *Footprints
Across the Prairie* (1930), the poetry collection *My Garden*
(1933), the novel *John Golding's Vision* (1938), and *Plays: A
Collection of Six Poetic Dramas* (1943).[86] All of these follow
her signature style: an adoration for nature; a focus on family,
dreams, and travel; and spirituality.

In her later years, as an established writer, Renfrew was a
minor national and Nebraska celebrity. A brief biography that
accompanied a review of her novel *John Golding's Vision* in 1938
notes that she was a member of "the Order of Bookfellows, the
National League of American Pen Women, the Poetry Society
of London, and the Poetry Center of New York." The article
also notes that she had been "honored by biographical sketches
in the 1932 edition of Principal Poets of the World, and the
1938 edition of the Biographical Dictionary of Contemporary
Poets."[87] A member of the Nebraska Writers Guild, she received
invitations and letters from all over Nebraska. *The Last of
the Strozzi,* for example, was frequently written about and
requested throughout Nebraska. Caroline Berg, a member
of the Pender Woman's Club (Pender, Nebraska) wrote to
Renfrew in October 1924 requesting a copy.[88] The Hastings
Women's Club dedicated a week to her accomplishments in
April 1938. The program included performances by Lillian Rice

of several of Renfrew's musical compositions, with Renfrew accompanying on the piano. Club members also presented a poetry reading and a play. To conclude the celebration, Renfrew was given flowers on a stage set as a garden from her latest book at the time, *My Garden*.[89] In May 1939, Edith King, the wife of the minister of the First Presbyterian Church in Hastings, thanked Renfrew in a private letter for sending a copy of *The Last of the Strozzi*, commenting that the play "has a remarkable resemblance to Shakespeare." King also notes in her letter that the many times she had read poems from Renfrew's *My Garden* at gatherings, "The various groups who heard me always expressed appreciation."[90]

In the late 1930s, Renfrew received many invitations from around the country but declined them all due to ill health. In July 1937, the *Hastings Daily Tribune* reported that Renfrew had turned down invitations to become "a corresponding member of the New York Woman's Press Association" and to attend "the drama festival at Leland Stanford University."[91] In 1939, she was invited to be a part of the public Poetry Week exhibit at the New York World's Fair in New York City. One of her poems was exhibited in "the largest book of poetry in the world and the panorama of American Poetry exhibited in the National Poetry center in the Communications building."[92] And in 1940, Renfrew declined an invitation to be "one of the directors at the National Poetry Day at the New York World's Fair."[93] Although she did not attend, Renfrew did take part in the "First Nebraska All Poetry Exhibit" in that same year by sending three of her works. One of the organizers, Mildred Dewcy, wrote in a letter that it was "very brave of you to bother sending them when you are not well and are so tired -- I WISH there was some way you could -- as I wrote before -- have a <u>vacation</u> from everything -- if you only could do that!"[94]

After many years of illness, Carolyn Renfrew died on July 6, 1948, at the age of 90, in Mary Lanning Hospital in Hastings, Nebraska. Her friend Lillian Rice sang at her funeral, and Renfrew was buried in Parkview Cemetery in Hastings. The Renfrew family plot includes parents Sylvester and Mercy, and siblings Robert, Addie, Carolyn, Herman, and Jennie, as well as Robert and Roberta Batty. Fay Babcock is buried in the same cemetery near his mother Elizabeth. The Renfrew home stayed in the family until May 1955, when it was sold to support the care of the last living sibling, Jennie, who died in December 1955.[95]

Autobiographical Influences on *The Shining Road*

The manuscript for *The Shining Road* is undated, so we do not know for sure when Renfrew wrote it, but the novel's timeline (the years preceding and following World War I) and pejorative references to the "jazz age" indicate that it must have been written in the late 1920s, maybe 1930s. Although the dates in the novel do not match Renfrew's life, many of the events in protagonist Nadia Evertson's life align with those of Renfrew's. Like Renfrew, Nadia is both a singer and a writer. As the second oldest child in a moderately well-to-do family of six siblings in the fictional town of Marshall, Nebraska, Nadia is called upon to put aside her musical and literary ambitions when her mother suffers a stroke and is unable to run the household. Because her selfish siblings refuse to help out, Nadia is forced to give up a decade of her life—her entire twenties—for housework and drudgery. The first half of the novel seems to be a fictionalized version of Renfrew's life in Hastings, with equal parts nostalgia and derision for the town and her family. In the second half of the novel, Nadia's circumstances change and she finds in New York City the material, literary, and marital success she desires.

The parallels between Nadia and Renfrew are so striking that the first half of the novel could be read as an expression of Renfrew's own personal and professional disappointments. Nadia's experiences in Marshall are often negative. While she and her sisters are gifted singers, the narrator tells us that their talents were not always appreciated by the town. "Sometimes our western towns, big and little, take pride in appreciating and recognizing their home talent," the narrator tells us. "[A]nd then again, sometimes, there will be a begrudging that would, alas, rather see some rare gift and worthy personality clouded and crushed than to see them spread their petals and open their bloom in the expanding light and warmth of fame" (31). Such is the case with Nadia, who finds fulfillment only when she leaves Marshall for New York City and, in fact, suffers a personal tragedy the first time she returns home for a visit many years later.

Nadia's literary career is very similar to Renfrew's. Like Renfrew, Nadia's career started with a "few worthy poems" and "one slight prize" (10). Nadia's first published book, a prairie epic in verse (74–75), is more ambitious than Renfrew's first book, a collection of poetry called *Songs of Hope* (1923), but they are published around the same time and both contain poetry. Like Renfrew, Nadia published poetry, drama, and novels (125, 132). One of the most disappointing events in her literary career also seems to parallel an event from Renfrew's life—a stolen movie screenplay. We do not know the details of Renfrew's experience, but she mentions a stolen screenplay in a 1927 editorial in the *Hastings Daily Tribune* in which she congratulates the editor of the paper on selling his "film play." She added at the end of the short editorial, "Though mine was stolen I am glad yours was not and is bringing you reward for your effort."[96] In *The Shining Road,* when Nadia tries to sell a screenplay to "one of the leading producers" of Hollywood, it is rejected, but a few months later, she sees a film by that producer that uses entire scenes from her screenplay. The narrator notes that "Only a year after that did she learn by carelessly, laughingly, relating the episode, that, had she kept her proofs and the name of the play, she stood a good chance, through the law, of obtaining damages; but even then was deterred, because she could not dare any expense in pushing the case" (138).

Also like Renfrew, Nadia has the opportunity for a singing career. The descriptions in *The Shining Road* of Nadia's singing match reviews and descriptions of Renfrew's singing in the author's personal papers. Like Renfrew, Nadia is technically proficient but due to her expressive performances prefers old-fashioned ballads. The narrator remarks that "Nadia had truly the gift of ballad singing, the lyric poetry of music. Her hearers loved her for the gift of expression that made their own heart strings quiver, soul speaking to soul, through these two avenues of words and music at their best" (201). Again like Renfrew, Nadia is offered a concert tour by a New York publicist. However, while Renfrew supposedly turned down the offer of an extended concert tour because of frailty, Nadia turns it down to focus on writing and to spend more time with her new husband.

Although Renfrew achieved modest success by the end of her life, she never gained the professional success of her fictional counterpart. In the second half of the novel, Nadia becomes a famous, best-selling author and lands a lovely and wealthy husband who is totally devoted to her. She stays in New York for the rest of her life. The second half of *The Shining Road* could therefore be seen as wish fulfillment—a fictional *what if?* What would it have been like to get away from Nebraska and family responsibilities for good and enjoy an independent and successful professional life? What would it have been like to have a loving domestic life with no financial worries?

The similarities between Nadia and Renfrew are not the only parallels to real life in the novel, though. It is hard not to see the real-life Renfrew family in the fictional Evertson family. Like the Renfrews, the Evertsons are a musical family: Frances, Nadia, Laurel, Carl, Jimmie, and Janice are all musicians. "Music," we are told, "was one of the drawing cards of their home and one of its mutual bonds of enjoyment" (12–13). Nadia and her sister Laurel are much like Renfrew and her sisters in the 1870s and 1880s—fixtures of local society, "centers of gayety and interest" (12), who are often called upon to share their gift of singing at parties and other gatherings. The novel tells us of the sisters, "Each one's atmosphere stirred a different chord in their admirers, yet they worked harmoniously together along the ways of every day life and their one special soul accord of music, for which both had a natural gift, achieving much on the foundational help given by father and mother, music lovers, without much from professional teachers" (12).

Also like the Renfrews, the Evertson family depends on the father's "real estate earning and income from his farm" (5). While outwardly wealthy, the family's income fluctuates with the health of crops and they live, according to the novel, modestly, always worrying about expenses, especially with so many children to support. When Mr. Evertson dies (90–93) and Mrs. Evertson subsequently suffers a stroke, the family is forced to economize even more because "[n]ow there was no one to earn" and "they must live on the income from the property alone" (95). That income is split up evenly between the siblings, which means that not all of it goes toward household expenses. This is exactly the situation the Renfrews found themselves in when Mercy died in 1910. And, like the Renfrew sisters, several of the Evertson sisters marry and leave the family home, which leaves Nadia to take care of the large household by herself, including the care of Mrs. Evertson and, later, the brother Carl, who is injured in the war.

Just as Renfrew expressed resentment at having to care for her invalid sister Addie, in *The Shining Road* Nadia resents having to care for her mother and the entire household. In many chapters, she expresses how selfish her siblings are in allowing her to carry all of this work by herself:

> Looking around on every side, Nadia beheld
> materialism, selfishness in the joy fields of life
> gathering its varied blossomings of desire, while she
> was shut in, bound to a narrow round of household
> tasks, of pinching economy, of aching hearts, and
> protest even if inescapable … All of the family but
> she and Carl were free to seek their own interests,
> desires, pleasures, and they were doing it according to
> their ability and opportunity…. She asked nothing,
> and little was given. All were so interested in their
> own affairs…. They did not mean, any of them, to be

> unkind. In their way they had always loved Nadia and
> Carl, but they accepted the conditions as an everyday
> fact. And the world only thought less of Nadia and
> Carl for being where and as they were. (133–35)

This self-sacrifice is mentioned by many characters as one of
Nadia's most appealing qualities, just as many of Renfrew's
friends commented in letters about her self-sacrifice.

If we ignore one of Renfrew's older sisters, the Evertson
siblings match closely with the Renfrew siblings. Like the
real-life Myra, for example, Frances moves with her husband
to Denver and is unable to help care for their mother. Like
Addie, Laurel is a society favorite in their hometown. Carl,
while garnering sympathy because he was injured in the war and
suffers from what today we would recognize as post-traumatic
stress disorder, does not help with the running of the household
and is the reason Nadia cannot afford to hire a maid. Though
Herman never served in the armed forces, he did sustain serious
injuries in a fire (1879) and an automobile accident (1920)
that would have made him dependent on family members for
a time.[97] Like the real-life Jennie, Janice makes a hasty marriage
decision that comes as a total surprise to her family. Jimmie, the
most affable of the Evertson siblings, gives a fictional second life
to Robert Renfrew, who died at a young age.

While the family is generally harmonious, Nadia and
Laurel have a difficult relationship. They are both gifted
singers and are close as teenagers, but the narrator describes
them as total opposites: "Laurel belonged more to the world
of the visible and its insistent calls, ready to answer and follow
after them. Nadia … had an inborn bias for the invisible,
the spiritual, developed into a ruling power by a love for the
literary and musical masterpieces" (12). These differences in
personality lead not only to disagreements, but also to betrayal.
Laurel's selfish, materialistic nature leads her to betray Nadia
several times, including taking Nadia's well-deserved spot at
the state university in Lincoln (leaving Nadia alone to take
care of their mother) and—spoilers ahead!—stealing Nadia's

fiancé. Is Renfrew's depiction of Laurel in *The Shining Road* an intentional criticism of her sister Addie?

While the novel seems to reflect Renfrew's frustrations with her family members, however, it also reflects the Renfrew family's expectations for civic and moral behavior. The Renfrews' long commitment to temperance and participation in civic life in Hastings is evident in the novel's Victorian approach to literature as a medium for moral education and improvement. In an 1882 editorial opposing the support of public schools through liquor licensing, for example, Sylvester Renfrew framed temperance in moral terms, arguing that "the liquor traffic" has a "known tendency to drunkenness, debauchery, crime degredation [sic] and misery." Even if saloons are "first class," he argued, they are still "hell holes," and every saloon, no matter how fancy, "deals the same poison and accomplishes much the same end." He concludes that public schools need to be managed by "men with higher nobler aims."[98] Although the *Adams County Democrat* chastised the Renfrews for their "ultra moralist" beliefs and Sylvester Renfrew was never elected to civic office, the Evertsons are depicted in *The Shining Road* as examples of moral leaders of the town. Despite the novel arguing that "the west never had drawn distinctions of class, either financial or educational, as noticeably, decidedly as the older east," for example, it nevertheless identifies the Evertson family as high "caste": "there was a strong touch of [caste] innate in Nadia and Laurel, and the family of which they were a part. That sometimes happens in families … an intellectual or cultural, or inborn social courtesy superiority" (26).

Nadia assumes that her duty as a writer is to improve the moral outlook of her readers and to achieve a noble, spiritual goal. The novel's title, *The Shining Road,* is a metaphor for Nadia's moral and spiritual aspirations. In fact, one of the central dramatic conflicts of the novel is whether Nadia, to gain material success, will forsake her ideals and write a book that capitulates to what she considers to be the moral degeneracy of the jazz age. Considering the association between jazz and nightclubs in the 1920s, Renfrew's distaste for this modern form of music may be an extension of her family's strong stance on temperance. The novel attributes the limited success of Nadia's first three books—an epic poem, a drama, and a novel—to the fact that her purpose is too high. When her second book is published, for instance, the narrator reports that "the jazz degeneracy of the following year, in both music and literature, was already beginning, and within a couple of years was to become rampant. From now on the finer things had a struggle to lift their heads above the horizon wherefrom they beheld the lesser, the houdoo productions moving easily on to victory by an advance processional acclaim" (125). At a dinner party later in the novel, the guests discuss the current state of theatre, and the narrator opines that the "theatre was, like music and literature, sliding fast on the downward grade. Idealism, spirituality was passe in all of them" (133). "[M]uch of the fiction and drama," the narrator continues, "had become as cesspools inoculating, degenerating the younger generations and adding to the lower tendencies of the supposed stronger mature element" (133). To become financially successful, Nadia is pressured "explicitly and implicitly" to "choose her heroines or heroes from the sensual ranks; make sex, not in its high but its low sense, the very god of all thought and purpose and action, with money getting and self gratification the boosters, demigods" (133). It is tempting to see the Renfrew family's long fight for temperance and moral authority in Hastings in Nadia's conscious effort to fight the tides of cultural and moral degeneracy in *The Shining Road*.

It is hard to say what effect the publication of *The Shining Road* would have had among Renfrew's friends and family if it had been published in her lifetime. We know from letters housed at the Adams County Historical Society that in the last few decades of her life, Renfrew complained to many people about the difficulties of caring for her sister Addie and Herman's unwillingness to help. How would family members have responded to a novel that represents these domestic issues with a very thin fictional veil? Likewise, how might the community of Renfrew's adopted hometown, Hastings, Nebraska, have responded to its less than flattering, fictional portrayal?

Literary and Cultural Influences on *The Shining Road*

Despite its clear autobiographical influences, *The Shining Road* is also a direct commentary on the larger cultural scene of post-WWI America. Renfrew shares with modernist writers of the early twentieth century a general sense of moral decay and rot, a diagnosis of the twentieth century's unhealthy emphasis on material culture. The first world war looms large behind the events of the novel. One anonymous character expresses the novel's general theme when he says that "Let us eat, drink and be merry for tomorrow we die," is the "slogan of today" (257). Unlike the modernist writers, though, Renfrew looks not ahead to something new, but backward to something old. The moralizing tendencies of *The Shining Road* place it squarely within the literary conventions of the nineteenth century. This may be the primary reason it did not find a publisher in Renfrew's lifetime. It probably would have seemed a bit old fashioned to publishers in the 1920s and 1930s. In fact, Nadia's struggles as a writer within the novel suggest that Renfrew was aware of this discrepancy.

Renfrew's literary influences for *The Shining Road* lean heavily toward the Romantic period. The novel's primary metaphor, Nadia's "shining road," demonstrates a deep influence of Romantic writers. According to Kathryn Van Spanckeren, these authors believed in "art as inspiration, the spiritual and aesthetic dimension of nature, and metaphors of organic growth" and that "[a]rt, rather than science … could best express universal truth."[99] The novel's title comes from Nadia's metaphor for the "desire, deep within me, to give something of value to the world, to leave some little—shining trail—because I—had—lived" (241). To seek the "shining road" is "[t]o be, to do, to achieve something for the mind, the spirit, the upward striving humanity" (188). This focus on the spiritual over the material is evident throughout the novel, but especially in

Nadia's continuing dissatisfaction with and alienation from the world around her. Just as Van Spanckeren argues that "typical protagonists of the American Romance were haunted, alienated individuals," Nadia is out of sync with most aspects of her life—the town she grew up in, her family, and American culture's materialism writ large.

The first few chapters, for instance, find a spiritual component in the landscape and echo William Cullen Bryant's famous 1832 poem, "The Prairies." The prairies in Renfrew's novel, "[t]hough so different from the mountains or valleys, … have a grandeur of their own, overwhelming sometimes, too, as the sea; the wild mad sweep of the winds is as though the ancient mystical gods were let loose in a frenzied ruthless rush, where the gentle breezes creep with tender caressings and whisperings" (1–2). The prairie-ocean metaphor—so common in nineteenth-century prairie literature—and the meeting of calm and frenzied winds in this passage echo Bryant's description of the prairie in his poem:

> The Prairies. I behold them for the first,
> And my heart swells, while the dilated sight
> Takes in the encircling vastness. Lo! they stretch,
> In airy undulations, far away,
> As if the ocean, in his gentlest swell,
> Stood still, with all his rounded billows fixed,
> And motionless forever.—Motionless?—
> No—they are all unchained again. The clouds
> Sweep over with their shadows, and, beneath,
> The surface rolls and fluctuates to the eye; (lines 4–13)[100]

Also like the speaker in Bryant's poem, Nadia imagines in a reverie the lost people of the prairies: "She could not help but people these plains with an ancient civilization, lost in an unrecorded past, whose phantom images and lives and builded walls, of homes and temples, still seemed to hover in a vague insistence over the land" (3). This ability of Nadia's to see beyond the material world not only sets her apart from her more materialistic siblings but also indicates her Romantic nature, her ability to touch the spiritual plane.

As with the Transcendentalist Romantic writers, such as Ralph Waldo Emerson and Henry David Thoreau, the landscape for Renfrew is a conduit to the spiritual realm. The meadowlark, for instance, is "[l]ike something linking heaven and earth. God or the angels must have dropped it from a higher sphere to touch a mortal soul to some new key in the great yet undiscovered realms of sound. Its poignancy of beauty rifts the listening bending sky beyond, where only soul can follow and words cannot transcribe" (2).

Nature run amok, particularly the sublime, is a defining feature of Romantic literature. Renfrew's occasional references to the sublime, while perhaps influenced by the real-life dangers of life on the prairie in the late nineteenth century, nevertheless signal a connection with Romantic writers. When Nadia and her beau Oliver are driving in the countryside, for example, they witness a lightning strike that reminds them of the sublime fury and unpredictability of nature. The narrator underscores the sublime character of prairie weather by noting that there is "grandeur indescribable in a storm on the great western prairies" (58). As Nadia and Oliver are driving along, they see a lightning bolt that flashes "from a distant clear looking part of the sky … like the sudden sword of some unseen angry god." The young people, along with Nadia's friend Robert Merrill, save several horses from a barn, which quickly becomes a "fiery furnace" (59–60). Hastings, Nebraska, newspapers from the 1880s and 1890s include many descriptions of similarly destructive storms on the prairie frontier, such as this poetic description in the August 7, 1878 edition of *The Adams County Democrat:*

> Last Friday a terrific thunder storm visited this section, the most violent of any experienced since the settlement of this county. For the space of a couple of hours in the afternoon the rain came down in torrents, when it slackened up until about dark and again, the water gates were withdrawn from the cloud reservoirs

and an almost deluge followed. The heavens were
fairly aglow with brilliancy, caused by the constant
electrical display, and some of the bolts took effect.
One man, by the name of Steele, while holding a span
of frightened horses, some miles south of town on
the new railroad, was struck and instantly killed, but,
strange to say, the horses were not injured in the least.
Three horses which were hitched a few rods south of
town were killed instantly, one of them belonging to T.
R. Lee, and it was a very superior animal. A house near
Juniata was struck, but without damage further than
tearing down a chimney. A stack of wheat belonging to
Mr. Renfrew was struck by lightning, and taking fire,
burned entirely to the ground. The streets were made
to look as rivers, and in places the sidewalks were
submerged.[101]

While Renfrew's description of the thunderstorm in *The Shining
Road* might be influenced by actual weather on the prairies,
this moment in the novel has more symbolic than literal
significance. A tragedy like this occurs at every turning point
in Nadia's life. In this case, the lightning strike is a supernatural
omen for her relationship with Oliver.

Readers familiar with Louisa May Alcott's 1868 novel
Little Women might recognize elements of Jo March in the
character of Nadia Evertson. Despite the selfishness of Nadia's
siblings, the Evertson family is described as warm and loving,
like the March family in *Little Women*. Nadia is very similar
to Jo March, both loosely autobiographical female characters
who want to become writers. Also, like Nadia, Jo struggles to
disentangle herself from her family to forge her own identity.
Renfrew's *The Shining Road* and Alcott's *Little Women* are both
coming-of-age stories defined by the protagonist's personal
struggle between loyalty to her past self and growing into the
best version of herself. Both Nadia and Jo feel responsible for
supporting their families, and both experience personal and
professional disappointments when their respective families

experience hardships, such as illness, death, and money issues. (Both novels also involve younger sisters stealing a love interest!) The primary difference between Nadia and Jo is that Nadia never returns to her family after leaving. Despite Nadia's rapturous descriptions of nature on the prairie, the town (and her family) are described as materialistic and selfish.

On the surface the novel has similarities with the early twentieth-century literary phenomenon Carl Van Doren identified in 1921 as "The Revolt from the Village." Van Doren argued that late nineteenth-century American authors created an unrealistic conception that small American towns were, "sweet innocence, an environment in which the best in human nature could flower serenely, a rural paradise exempt from the vices, complexities, and irremediable tragedies of the city."[102] This perception of "good society" was driven by authors who based their narratives in "fictive small towns," which were produced with reference to "the real small towns of their childhood."[103] According to Van Doren, in the first few decades of the twentieth century, authors revolted against these idealistic conceptions of small towns, preferring to depict rural life in more psychologically and socially realistic ways. Authors such as Sinclair Lewis and Edgar Lee Masters began to produce a "more realistic interpretation of the town, emphasizing its moral repressiveness and stultifying conformity, and protesting its standardized dullness."[104] Nadia's experiences in her hometown and the hardships she faced because of its lack of opportunity could be seen as prime examples of this more realistic turn in depictions of American small towns.

However, the writers in the "Revolt from the Village" movement typically complained about the moral repressiveness of small towns. In Masters' 1915 *Spoon River Anthology,* for example, characters reveal the hypocrisy of small-town life in first-person, posthumous epitaphs. Sherwood Anderson's 1919 collection of short stories, *Winesburg, Ohio,* shows how sensitive and lonely characters are crushed by the moral repressiveness of the town. *The Shining Road,* though it depicts a character who flees a repressive small town, does not argue that Marshall,

Nebraska, is morally repressive. Just the opposite. Nadia seeks a *more* spiritual way of life. "Realism," in fact, is the opposite of Nadia's desires as a writer. For Nadia, to write for realism means to "[c]ome down from the clouds of spirit to the realities of earth. Make sex and its abuses the all absorbing center" (135). Rather than follow the twentieth-century "Revolt from the Village" writers, then, Renfrew looks for another nineteenth-century inspiration.

If the first half of the *The Shining Road* could be seen as a twentieth-century version of *Little Women*, the second half could be seen as a twentieth-century version of Charlotte Brontë's 1847 novel *Jane Eyre*. Like the protagonist of Brontë's novel, Nadia is able to pull herself out of her oppressive situation through intelligence and hard work. Instead of a governess, however, Nadia becomes a successful writer. The success of her fourth book gives her the financial resources to move to New York City, where she finds a wealthy, brooding lover, Raymond Dexter, who is not dissimilar to Jane's brooding lover Edward Rochester. Instead of an aristocrat, however, Dexter is a hugely successful businessman. Like Rochester, Dexter pushes his young fiancée to marry quickly so that his hedonistic and mentally unstable first wife cannot ruin their plans.

The most poignant parallel between *The Shining Road* and *Jane Eyre,* the spiritual connection between the heroine and her lover, underscores Nadia's virtue and connection with the spiritual plane. Just as Rochester brings Jane back to him thorough a psychic call—"Jane! Jane! Jane!"—Nadia brings Raymond back from the dead by calling his spirit. As all the bystanders and doctors stand around helpless during this emergency, "With heart breaking intensity the cry went forth, 'Raymond, come to me. I need you. I need you, Raymond! Raymond!'" And Raymond comes back. The narrator identifies this episode as "the miracle of spirit calling to spirit, overcoming with its yea the nay of material bondage" (261).

In *The Shining Road,* Renfrew intentionally and explicitly turns away from twentieth-century literary conventions, preferring instead the sentimental and Romantic conventions of the nineteenth century, the spirituality of the nineteenth century over the materiality of the twentieth century.

Acknowledgments

We are indebted to the many members of the Hastings, Nebraska, community who have kept Carolyn Renfrew's legacy alive. The Adams County Historical Society in Hastings, Nebraska, currently houses and cares for Renfrew's many unpublished manuscripts and typescripts—we thank the Historical Society, particularly Elizabeth Spilinek, the executive director, for permission to view and study the typescript of *The Shining Road*. The Historical Society received these manuscripts and typescripts (and many of Renfrew's personal letters and newspaper clippings) in 1978 from the estate of Lillian Rice, a leading member of the Hastings Woman's Club, which honored Renfrew several times.[105] Renfrew's unpublished work would have been lost to time if Mrs. Rice had not championed her friend's work, both in Renfrew's lifetime and after.

In summer 1984, Hastings College student Lori Cox received a grant from the National Endowment for the Humanities to research Renfrew. In addition to examining the archival materials housed at the Adams County Historical Society, Cox was able to interview people in Hastings who knew Renfrew and her siblings in the 1920–1940s. Cox's project, which is available from the Historical Society, was a valuable resource throughout the completion of this introduction.

Most recently, Dr. Jim Fritzler, now professor emeritus of theatre at Hasting College, revived interest in Renfrew's writing through his 2015/2016 sabbatical project, "Nothing Ever Happens Here: A Narrative Sabbatical Report." Hastings College Press would not have known about Renfrew's unpublished manuscripts and typescripts if it were not for Dr. Fritzler's deep dive into local Hastings history. (Hastings, Nebraska, really was the Wild West back in its first decades!)

The publication of this book took many years and the collaboration of students across many courses in the Department of Languages and Literatures at Hastings College. The project started in Fall 2016 when Leah Smith, an intern for Hastings College Press, photographed the manuscripts and typescripts of Renfrew's unpublished novels, with the help of staff at the Adams County Historical Society. Many of these manuscripts are in fragile condition—some typed, some handwritten on yellow legal pads. Dr. Fritzler shared his research with students in the spring 2017 English senior seminar at Hastings College and piqued student interest in this local author. Students in that class read several of Renfrew's unpublished novels and conducted initial research on Renfrew through online and genealogical sources. They recommended *The Shining Road* for publication by Hastings College Press. After reading and discussing the novel and reviewing the research conducted by students in spring 2017, students in a spring 2019 course on Midwestern women writers wrote the first draft of this introduction. Students in the 2018 and 2020 Book Production classes typed the text from the photographs, laid out the book for publication, and proofread the pages against the typescript images. In spring 2021, Publishing major Abigail Shaw copy edited the novel in an internship for Hastings College Press.

Dr. Patricia Oman, associate professor of English at Hastings College and the director of Hastings College Press, supervised the student work in all of these courses and internships and revised and expanded the section "The Renfrew Family and Hasting, Nebraska" in summer 2021 based on further archival research and newly available biographical information. In the last two decades, online digital databases have opened up astonishing opportunities for research into forgotten writers from the nineteenth and twentieth centuries. Between spring 2017, when we began research for this project, and spring 2021, when we were preparing to go to print, a new treasure trove of Nebraska and national newspapers became available on Newspapers.com and other online databases. Some of this information confirmed what we had surmised about Renfrew's life, and some contradicted our assumptions.

The following people participated in the creation of this book in courses and internships at Hastings College:

Research and Introduction

Alexandria Belitz
Kervin Brown
Jordan Colony
Michelle DeCoud
Lyette Erin
Nicole Havlik
Juliana Hernandez
Alex Holmes
DaeRon Jones
Kenzie Kolle
Tom Masters
Hannah Meeske
Patricia Oman
Josh Quinn
Rebekka Ralston
Katie Rice
Lydia Rodysill
Kyler Samples
Sally Stoltenberg
Kate Taylor

Layout and Proofreading

Agathe Baume
James Clapham
Dany Cook
Davianne Czarnick
Max Griffel
Kaitlin Grode
Jaidan Hanshaw
Jora Jackson-Brown
Madison Jagels
Ivan Linenberger

Taylor Lipinski
Dominica Lotmore
Milli May
Marcos Montoya
Lilly Nelms
Kyler Samples
Daniel Trevithick
Bethany Turner
Charleen Vesin
Jocelyn Wahl
Effy Widdifield

Archival Photography

Leah Smith

Copy Editing

Abigail Shaw

Notes

1. Public records differ on Renfrew's birth year. In fact, her birth year seems to have moved as Renfrew got older. Her death certificate and the 1920 U.S. census both list her birth year as 1868. The 1940 U.S. census indicates that she was born in 1873, the 1930 U.S. census notes that she was born around 1871, the 1900 U.S. census lists her birth month and year as June 1864. The 1880 U.S. census indicates her birth year as 1859. In the absence of a birth certificate, the most definitive sources are likely the 1860 and 1870 U.S. censuses, which indicate that she was born in 1858. 1860 United States census, LaSalle County, Illinois, population schedule, Town of Manlius, p. 256 (penned), dwelling 1839, family 1850, "Caroline Renfrew," FHL microfilm 803196, roll M653_196, digital image, *Ancestry.com;* 1870 United States census, LaSalle County, Illinois, population schedule, Town of Marseilles, p. 2 (penned), dwelling 13, family 13, "Carrie Renfrew," FHL microfilm 545742, roll M593_243, digital image, *Ancestry.com;* 1880 United States census, Adams County, Nebraska, population schedule, enumeration district 55, city of Hastings, p. 6 (penned), dwelling 50, family 52, "Carrie Renfrew," FHL microfilm 1254743, roll 743, digital image, *Ancestry.com;* 1900 United States census, Adams County, Nebraska, population schedule, Hastings Township, p. 112A (stamped), p. 5 (penned), dwelling 100, family 101, "Carrie Renfrew," FHL microfilm 1240916, roll 916, digital image, *Ancestry.com;* 1920 United States census, Adams County, Nebraska, population schedule, enumeration district 11, Juniata Township, Hastings City, p. 6B (penned), dwelling 138, family 144, "Carolyn Renfrew," roll T625_979, digital image, *Ancestry.com;* 1930 United States census, Adams County, Nebraska, population schedule, enumeration district 1-13, Hastings City, p.8B (penned), "Carrie Renfrew," FHL microfilm 2341000, digital image, *Ancestry.com;* 1940 United States census, Adams County, Nebraska, population schedule, enumeration district 1-14, Hastings City, p.7B (penned), "Carolyn Renfrew," roll T627_2235, digital image, *Ancestry.com.*

2. Birth years for Alice, Myra, Addie, Herman and Jennie are taken from the 1870 federal census; their death years are confirmed by grave markers and obituaries. Robert's birth and death years are taken from his grave marker at Parkview Cemetery in Hastings, Nebraska.

1870 United States census, LaSalle County, Illinois, population schedule, Town of Marseilles, post office Marseilles, pp. 2–3 (penned), p. 357 (stamped), dwelling 13, family 13, "Alice J. Renfrew," "Myra Renfrew," "Addie Renfrew," "Herman T. Renfrew," "Jennie Renfrew," FHL microfilm 545742, roll M593_243, digital image, *Ancestry.com;* Parkview Cemetery (Hastings, Adams County, Nebraska), Robert Renfrew grave marker, block B, lot 3, space 10; "Miss Renfrew Dies at Hospital Here," *Hastings Daily Tribune,* Jan. 23, 1941, 9, *Newspapers.com;* "Rites Wednesday for Mrs. Babcock," *Hastings Daily Tribune,* December 6, 1955, 11, *Newspapers.com;* Parkview Cemetery (Hastings, Adams County, Nebraska), Hermon [sic] T. Renfrew grave marker, block B, lot 3, space 15; Glen Abbey Memorial Park (Bonita, San Diego County, California), Alice Renfrew Batty grave marker, digital image, *Findagrave.com;* Mount Hope Cemetery (San Diego, San Diego County, California), Peter S. Burger, Myra R. Burger, and Clare C. Burger, grave marker, digital image, *Findagrave.com.*

3. Adams County, Nebraska, deed book 3, p. 105, Samuel and Harriet Alexander to Sylvester Renfrew, May 20, 1876, Recorder's Office, Adams County; Adams County, Nebraska, dedication of public streets, Renfrew's Addition to the city of Hastings, deed book 10, p. 159, Sylvester Renfrew and Mercy Renfrew to the City of Hastings, June 30, 1880, Recorder's Office, Adams County; "Mr. S. Renfrew, One of Hastings' Oldest and Best Known Citizens," *Daily Gazette-Journal,* May 20, 1887, 8, *Newspapers.com.*

4. "Mr. S. Renfrew, One of Hastings' Oldest and Best Known Citizens," 8.

5. "The First Theatricals—The Hall and the Companies and Comment," *Adams County Democrat,* Jan. 1 1904, 1, *Newspapers.com.*

6. Hastings, Nebraska, newspapers include several mentions of the Renfrew farms near Kenesaw and Doniphan in the 1870s and 1880s. See, for example, "Sylvester Renfrew Spent the Forepart of the Week in Kenesaw, Looking After His Farm Interests There," *Gazette-Journal,* Aug. 24, 1882, 4, *Newspapers.com;* "S. Reed Has Moved to the Renfrew Farm South of Kenesaw," *Gazette-Journal,* Sep. 21, 1882, 1, *Newspapers.com;* "S. Renfrew, of This City, Wants a Partner," *Adams County Democrat,* July 11, 1885, 5, *Newspapers.com.*

7. See, for example, "The Grand Opening: The Formal Opening of the Bostwick House in This City, Last Evening," Hastings *Daily Gazette-Journal*, Nov. 13, 1885, 1, *Newspapers.com*; "A Game of Loto: A Pleasant Evening at Mr. and Mrs. Frahm's, Last Friday," Hastings *Daily Gazette-Journal*, Nov. 30, 1885, 3, *Newspapers.com*.

8. "New Years Calling," *Adams County Democrat*, Jan. 1, 1881, 4, *Newspapers.com*; "New Years' Day," *Gazette-Journal*, Jan. 6, 1881, 5, *Newspapers.com*.

9. "We Don't Believe a Happier Time Has Been Had," *Gazette-Journal*, Feb. 2, 1882, 5, *Newspapers.com*.

10. "The First Theatricals—The Hall and the Companies and Comment," 1.

11. Francis Kennon McLaughlin to Miss Renfrew, June 20, 1945, Adams County Historical Society (Hastings, Nebraska), MS-64, folder 101. (The real purpose of this letter was to ask to buy the Renfrews' living room furniture. Perhaps the writer had heard that Carrie was ill and thought she would be more willing to sell than Herman would be after Carrie's death. Or maybe this was a kind gesture meant to help Carrie financially in her last days.)

12. "The New Church Choir," *Daily Gazette-Journal*, Sep. 12, 1887, 1, *Newspapers.com*.

13. "Art Exhibition," Weekly *Gazette-Journal*, May 18, 1884, 4, *Newspapers.com*.

14. "The Mikado," *Adams County Democrat*, Aug. 1, 1885, 1, *Newspapers.com*.

15. "Prof. H. Fairweather and Wife," *Daily Gazette-Journal*, Aug. 13, 1885, 1, *Newspapers.com*.

16. "Miss Minnie Thompson Has Taken a Two Weeks Vacation," *Gazette-Journal*, Oct. 17, 1884, 4, *Newspapers.com*.

17. Quoted in Lori Cox, "Carolyn Renfrew. Nebraska Author: A Literary and Critical Appraisal," unpublished manuscript, 1984, Adams County Historical Society (Hastings, Nebraska), MS-64, p. 5.

18. Adams County, Nebraska, deed book 11, p. 144, Peter S. Burger and Myra R. Burger His Wife and Gamaliel Burger to Sylvester Renfrew, June 18, 1881, Recorder's Office, Adams County; "Burger Bros. & Renfrew," advertisement, *Gazette-Journal*, Jun 15, 1882, 7, *Newspapers.com*.

19. Peter S. Burger and Myra Burger, marriage certificate, Nov. 2, 1876, State Library and Archives, Nebraska State Historical Society (Lincoln, Nebraska), digital image, *Ancestry.com*.

20. "Herman Renfrew, Who Has Been Confined with a Broken Leg," *Hastings Journal*, Oct. 23, 1879, 4, *Newspapers.com*; "Hastings in 1881," *Gazette-Journal*, Dec. 29, 1881, 1, *Newspapers.com*.

21. "Hastings in 1881," 1; "Burger Bros. & Renfrew Are Now Located in Their New Building," *Adams County Democrat*, Jan. 2, 1882, 4, *Newspapers.com*; "Benedict, Burger Bros. & Renfrew and Hawley," *Adams County Democrat*, Jan. 14, 1882, 4, *Newspapers.com*.

22. Adams County, Nebraska, deed book 16, p. 527, Sylvester Renfrew and Wife to Peter S. Burger and Gamaliel Burger, July 18, 1883, Recorder's Office, Adams County.

23. "Mr. Renfrew As a Candidate for Mayor," *Hastings Journal*, Mar. 25, 1880, 5, *Newspapers.com*.

24. "Municipal Elections—Who Have Been Mayors of Hastings," *Adams County Democrat*, Dec. 4, 1903, 1, *Newspapers.com*.

25. See, for example, "By Order of the Committee the Following Is the Program," Adams County Gazette, Jul. 13, 1878, 1, *Newspapers. com*; "Hastings Temperance Alliance," *Gazette-Journal*, Nov. 24, 1881, 4, *Newspapers.com*; "Temperance Convention," *Juniata Herald*, Jan. 5, 1882, 4, *Newspapers.com*; "Hastings Temperance Alliance," *Gazette-Journal*, Jan. 12, 1882, 7, *Newspapers.com*; "Alliance Meeting," *Gazette-Journal*, Feb. 2, 1882, 5, *Newspapers.com*; "The Large Attendance at a Meeting of the Temperance Alliance," *Gazette-Journal*, Apr. 18, 1882, 4, *Newspapers.com*.

26. "If the Hon. Mr. Renfrew Cannot Beat Fred Forcht for Mayor," *Adams County Democrat*, Feb. 12, 1881, 4, *Newspapers.com*.

27. "The Hon. Sylvester Renfrew, the Tall Sycamore of the Prairie," *Adams County Democrat*, Apr. 2, 1881, 4, *Newspapers.com*.

28. "We Understand That Miss Alice Renfrew Has Secured a Majority," *Gazette-Journal*, Feb. 16, 1882, 5, *Newspapers.com*.

29. "Once More It Becomes Our Painful Duty," *Adams County Democrat*, Apr. 1, 1882, 1, *Newspapers.com*.

30. "Miss Alice Renfrew Was Poisoned by Some Plant," *Gazette-Journal*, Aug. 10, 1882, 7, *Newspapers.com*.

31. "Alice Renfrew Is Rapidly Improving in Health," *Gazette-Journal,* Oct. 26, 1882, 1, *Newspapers.com.*

32. "Miss Addie Renfrew Is Very Sick with Erysipelas," *Gazette-Journal,* Oct. 5, 1882, 5, *Newspapers.com.*

33. "Miss Carrie Renfrew, Who Has Been Sick," *Gazette-Journal,* Nov. 16, 1882, 1, *Newspapers.com.*

34. "Mr. S. Renfrew's New Residence," *Daily Gazette-Journal,* Jun. 18, 1887, 1, *Newspapers.com.*

35. "The Contract for Heating the Residence of Mrs. M. Renfrew," *Hastings Daily Republican,* Aug. 31, 1906, 5, *Newspapers.com.*

36. Cox, 3.

37. The 1880 census shows that Peter and Myra Burger lived next door to the Renfrews. 1880 United States census, Adams County, Nebraska, population schedule, enumeration district 55, city of Hastings, p. 6 (penned), dwelling 50, family 52, "Sylvester Renfrew," FHL microfilm 1254743, roll 743, digital image, *Ancestry.com;* 1880 United States census, Adams County, Nebraska, population schedule, enumeration district 55, city of Hastings, p. 6 (penned), dwelling 51, family 53, "Peter Burger," "Myra Burger," FHL microfilm 1254743, roll 743, digital image, *Ancestry.com;* "Burger Peter S.," *Ballenger & Richards Denver City Directory* (Denver: Ballenger & Richards), 1891, 269, *Ancestry.com.*

38. "Burger Peter S.," *Ballenger & Richards Denver City Directory* (Denver: Ballenger & Richards), 1895, 222, *Ancestry.com.*

39. "Miss Carolyn Renfrew, a Noted Chicago Vocalist," *The Record,* Apr. 13, 1899, 2, *Newspapers.com;* see, for example, "Burger Peter S. rancher," *San Diego City and County Directory, 1911* (San Diego: San Diego Directory Co.), 1911, 714, *Ancestry.com.*

40. Newspaper accounts from the time report that Clare was found in his parents' barn having somehow shot himself in the side of the head with a shotgun. The Burgers did not know why Clare killed himself. He was apparently very popular in Chula Vista and was a promising musician. He had been working at a music store in Los Angeles before he came home unexpectedly and killed himself. "Young Clarence Burger of Chula Vista a Suicide," *San Francisco Call,* Nov. 24, 1901, 28, *Newspapers.com;* "Clarence Burger Commits Suicide," *The*

Record, Nov. 28, 1901, 6, *Newspapers.com.* See also "In Memoriam," *Hastings Tribune,* Nov. 29, 1901, 1, *Newspapers.com.*

41. "Mrs. M. Renfrew and Mrs. R. A. Batty Departed Last Thursday," *Adams County Democrat,* Dec. 6, 1901, 1, *Newspapers.com;* "Mesdames R. A. Batty and M. Renfrew Departed Friday," *Hastings Republican,* Dec. 6, 1901, 6, *Newspapers.com;* "Mrs. M. Renfrew and Mrs. R. A. Batty Returned Saturday," *Adams County Democrat,* Jan. 31, 1902, 1, *Newspapers.com.*

42. See, for example, "Mrs. Mercy Renfrew and Mrs. E. H. Babcock Departed Saturday," *Adams County Democrat,* Nov. 27, 1903, 1, *Newspapers.com;* "Mrs. Mercy Renfrew and Mrs. E. H. Babcock Who Have Been Spending the Winter," *Adams County Democrat,* May 6, 1904, 1, *Newspapers.com.*

43. "The Home Against the Saloon," Lincoln Evening Call, July 4, 1890, 4, *Newspapers.com.*

44. "Women Appeal to Hastings Voters," *Hastings Daily Republican,* Apr. 3, 1909, 3, *Newspapers.com.* See Roma Mary Grace's blog site, https://romamarygrace.com/breweryforhastings/, for a series of well-researched posts about the Hastings Brewing Company.

45. James G. Clark, "Carrie Renfrew," *The Magazine of Poetry II,* no. 2 (1890): 198.

46. I.L. Townsend Photograph Parlors was located at 224 N. Lincoln Ave. "Townsend I.L. Photograph Parlors," *Hastings City Directory, 1891–2* (Omaha: J.M. Wolfe & Co.), 124, *Ancestry.com.*

47. "Miss Carrie Renfrew, a Well Known Literary Lady of Hastings," Lincoln Evening Call, Mar. 6, 1893, 5, *Newspapers.com;* "Miss Carrie Renfrew Has Gone to Buffalo, N. Y.," *Nebraska State Journal,* Mar. 6, 1893, 2, *Newspapers.com;* "Miss Carrie Renfrew of Hastings Has Gone to Buffalo, N. Y.," Lincoln Herald, Mar. 18, 1893, 8, *Newspapers.com.*

48. "Miss Carrie Renfrew," *A Woman of the Century: Fourteen Hundred-Seventy Biographical Sketches Accompanied by Portraits of Leading American Women in All Walks of Life,* Frances W. Willard and Mary A. Livermore, eds. (Buffalo: Charles Wells Moulton, 1893), 604.

49. Cox, 5.

50. Quoted in Cox, 5.

51. Quoted in Cox, 6.

52. "Miss Carolyn Renfrew, Lately from New York, Has Decided to Stay in South Bend," *South Bend Tribune,* Feb. 9, 1895, 8, *Newspapers.com.*

53. "Miss Jennie Renfrew Intends Going to Chicago," *Hastings Tribune,* Jan. 7, 1898, 1, *Newspapers.com.*

54. "Misses Carry [sic] and Jennie Renfrew Returned Home Tuesday," *Hastings Tribune,* July 22, 1898, 1, *Newspapers.com.*

55. "Miss Carolyn Renfrew, a Noted Chicago Vocalist," *The Record,* April 13, 1899, 2, *Newspapers.com;* "Miss Carrie Renfrew Has Returned from California," *Hastings Daily Republican,* Jan. 23, 1900, 4, *Newspapers.com;* "Miss Carrie Renfrew Has Returned from California," *Hastings Tribune,* Jan. 26, 1900, 1, *Newspapers.com.*

56. "Misses Carrie and Jennie Renfrew Are in Kansas City," *Hastings Tribune,* Apr. 8, 1904, 1, *Newspapers.com.*

57. "R. A. Batty and Daughters Were in Kansas City Last Week," *Adams County Democrat,* June 30, 1905, 1, *Newspapers.com.*

58. "Renfrew Carolyn" and "Renfrew Jennie," *R.L. Polk & Co's Colorado Springs, Colorado City, and Manitou City Directory, 1907–1908* (Sioux City: R.L. Polk & Co.), 1907, 437, *Ancestry.com;* "Renfrew Carolyn" and "Renfrew Jennie," *R.L. Polk & Co's Colorado Springs, Colorado City, and Manitou City Directory, 1908* (Sioux City: R.L. Polk & Co.), 1908, 482, *Ancestry.com;* "Renfrew Carolyn" and "Renfrew Jennie," *R.L. Polk & Co's Colorado Springs, Colorado City, and Manitou City Directory, 1909* (Sioux City: R.L. Polk & Co.), 1909, 496, *Ancestry.com;* "Renfrew Carolyn" and "Renfrew Jennie," *R.L. Polk & Co's Colorado Springs, Colorado City, and Manitou City Directory, 1910* (Sioux City: R.L. Polk & Co.), 1910, 488, *Ancestry.com.*

59. "Mrs. Mercy Renfrew and Mrs. R. A. Batty Returned Sunday," *Adams County Democrat,* Sep. 4, 1908, 1, *Newspapers.com.*

60. "Fell and Dislocated Hip," *Hastings Republican,* Feb. 23, 1905, 3, *Newspapers.com.*

61. "Misses Carrie and Jennie Renfrew, of Casper, Wyoming, Are in This City," *Hastings Daily Tribune,* May 7, 1910, 5, *Newspapers.com.*

62. The wedding was announced in several Nebraska newspapers: "At 9 O'Clock This Morning," *Hastings Daily Republican,* Sep. 29, 1910, 15, *Newspapers.com;* "Renfrew-Babcock Wedding Today," *Hastings Daily Tribune,* Sep. 29, 1910, 1, *Newspapers.com;* "Wedding

at Hastings," Lincoln Star, Sep. 30, 1910, 4, *Newspapers.com;* "Married in Nebraska," *Nebraska State Journal,* Oct. 1, 1910, 7, *Newspapers.com;* "Thursday Morning at Nine O'Clock," *Hastings Daily Republican,* Oct. 1, 1910, 3, *Newspapers.com;* "Dr Fay G. Babcock and Miss Jennie Renfrew Were United in Amrriage [sic]," *Daily Tribune,* Oct. 7, 1910, 2, *Newspapers.com.*

63. "Married in Nebraska," 7.

64. Although this column was meant to be humorous, this description of Babcock as a dandy comes across as mean-spirited. We wonder if this impression might have influenced his decision to marry. "Elite Eligibles," *The Hastings Daily Republican,* Mar. 12, 1910, 2, *Newspapers.com.*

65. See, for example, "Babcock Faye [sic] G. (Jennie R), dentist," *R.L. Polk & Co.'s Hastings City Directory, 1913* (Sioux City: R.L. Polk & Co.), 43, *Ancestry.com* and "Babcock Fay G (Jennie), dentist," *R.L. Polk & Co.'s Hastings City Directory, 1924* (Sioux City: R.L. Polk & Co.), 88, *Ancestry.com.*

66. "Death Calls for Judge Batty," *Hastings Daily Tribune,* June 22, 1911, 1, 6, *Newspapers.com.*

67. R. A. Batty and Alice Renfrew, marriage certificate, October 9, 1884, State Library and Archives, Nebraska State Historical Society (Lincoln, Nebraska), digital image, *Ancestry.com;* "Marriage Announcements," *Nebraska State Journal,* Oct. 19, 1884, 5, *Newspapers.com.*

68. See, for example, "Batty R.A.," *Hastings City Directory, for 1891–2, vol. 1.* (Omaha: J.M. Wolfe & Co.), 38, *Ancestry.com* and "Batty Robert A (Alice J R), *R.L. Polk & Co.'s Hastings City Directory, 1910* (Sioux City: R.L. Polk & Co.), 1910, 41, *Ancestry.com.*

69. "Roberta, the Little Daughter Mr. and Mrs. R. A. Batty," *Hastings Republican,* Aug. 12, 1899, 3, *Newspapers.com.*

70. "Mrs. R. A. Batty Has Arrived from Lincoln," *Hastings Daily Republican,* Dec. 21, 1911, 5, *Newspapers.com.*

71. 1920 United States census, San Diego County, California, population schedule, enumeration district 237, Chula Vista City, p. 517A (penned), dwelling 105, family 105, "Myra R. Burger," roll T625_130, digital image, *Ancestry.com;* 1920 United States census, San Diego County, California, population schedule, enumeration

district 237, Chula Vista City, p. 517A (penned), dwelling 104, family 104, "Alice J. Batty," roll T625_130, digital image, *Ancestry.com;* 1930 United States census, San Diego County, California, population schedule, enumeration district 37-33, Chula Vista City, p. 3B (penned), dwelling 84, family 85, "Alice J. Batty," "Myra R. Burger," roll T625_130, digital image, *Ancestry.com.*

72. Mount Hope Cemetery, Peter S. Burger, Myra Burger, and Clare C. Burger grave marker (San Diego, San Diego County, California), digital image, *Findagrave.com.*

73. "Elite Eligibles," 2.

74. "Mrs. S. Renfrew Has Returned from a Prolonged Visit East," *Hastings Daily Gazette-Journal,* June 15, 1884, 4, *Newspapers.com.*

75. "Mrs. R. A. Batty Arrived Wednesday Evening from California," *Adams County Democrat,* Sep. 8, 1916, 1, *Newspapers.com.*

76. "Miss Addie Renfrew, Who Has Been in Ill Health," *Hastings Daily Tribune,* Sep. 3, 1921, 9, *Newspapers.com.*

77. "Miss Renfrew Seriously Ill," *Hastings Daily Tribune,* Oct. 17, 1910, 1, *Newspapers.com.*

78. "Miss Addie Renfrew, Who Fell on the Ice Monday," *Hastings Daily Tribune,* Dec. 31, 1926, 3, *Newspapers.com.*

79. Jim Fritzler, "Nothing Ever Happens Here: A Narrative Sabbatical Report," unpublished manuscript, 2016, Hastings College Archives (Hastings, Nebraska), 18.

80. Vida F. Watson to Carolyn Renfrew, undated, Adams County Historical Society (Hastings, Nebraska), MS-64, folder 101.

81. Marie Herrin to Carolyn Renfrew, Sep. 20, 1929, Adams County Historical Society (Hastings, Nebraska), MS-64, folder 101.

82. Mrs. Dixon to Carolyn Renfrew, undated, Adams County Historical Society (Hastings, Nebraska), MS-64, folder 102.

83. Cox, 7–8.

84. Cox, 7.

85. "Carolyn Renfrew Wins Poetry Prize," *Hastings Daily Tribune,* Jan. 11, 1923, 7, *Newspapers.com.*

86. The Briscoe Center for American History at the University of Texas at Austin includes in its holdings a 24-page pamphlet by Renfrew titled "Fragments," published around 1887. We are not sure who published this or why.

87. "'John Golding's Vision' Reviewed and Displayed," *Hastings Daily Tribune,* Dec. 17, 1938, 4, *Newspapers.com.*

88. Caroline Berg to Carolyn Renfrew, Oct. 17, 1924, Adams County Historical Society (Hastings, Nebraska), MS-64, folder 100.

89. "Program to Honor Carolyn Renfrew," *Hastings Daily Tribune,* Apr. 28, 1938, 2, *Newspapers.com.*

90. Edith H. King to Carolyn Renfrew, May 15, 1939, Adams County Historical Society (Hastings, Nebraska), MS-64, folder 100.

91. "Honors Come to Carolyn Renfrew," *Hastings Daily Tribune,* July 28, 1937, 2, *Newspapers.com.*

92. "Poetry Week Officials Tribute Miss Renfrew," *The Morning Spotlight,* June 27, 1939, 3, *Newspapers.com.*

93. "Miss Carolyn Renfrew Rejects Invitation," *The Morning Spotlight,* Aug. 30, 1940, 3, *Newspapers.com.*

94. Mildred Dewey to Carolyn Renfrew, March 12, 1940. Adams County Historical Society (Hastings, Nebraska), MS-64, folder 100.

95. "Special Notice Auction Sale for Jennie Babcock," *Hastings Daily Tribune,* May 6, 1955, 17, *Newspapers.com;* Adams County, Nebraska, report of receipts and expenditures, F. Carl Koch, November 16, 1955, probate file 6266 "Jennie R. Babcock," County Court, Adams County; "Rites Wednesday for Mrs. Babcock," *Hastings Daily Tribune,* Dec. 6, 1955, 11, *Newspapers.com.*

96. Carolyn Renfrew, "Editor of the *Hastings Daily Tribune,*" *Hastings Daily Tribune,* Sep, 17, 1927, 4, *Newspapers.com.*

97. "Herman Renfrew, Who Has Been Confined with a Broken Leg," *Hastings Journal,* Oct. 23, 1879, 4, *Newspapers.com;* "Sidesteps Auto; Hit by Another," *Hastings Daily Tribune,* Aug. 16, 1920, 1, *Newspapers.com.*

98. Sylvester Renfrew, "Whisky and Common Schools," editorial, *The Gazette-Journal,* Mar. 30, 1882, 4, *Newspapers.com.*

99. Kathryn Van Spanckeren, "Outline of American Literature," *United States Information Agency,* p. 26 https://usa.usembassy.de/etexts/oal/oaltoc.htm

100. William Cullen Bryant, "The Prairies," *The Poetry Foundation,* https://www.poetryfoundation.org/poems/55341/the-prairies

101. "Last Friday, a Terrific Thunderstorm Visited This Section," *Adams County Gazette,* August 7, 1878, 1, *Newspapers.com.*

102. Anthony Channell Hilfer, *The Revolt from the Village, 1915–1930* (Chapel Hill: University of North Carolina Press, 1969), 3.

103. Ibid, 4.

104. Ibid, 3.

105. Cox, 1.

I

The Shining Road. Over the earth it runs, here and there where human life, lifting its soul a tiptoe to gaze over the walls of the material, catches some gleam that lures it out of the broad highway of human purpose and endeavor into a spiritual trend that leads on and onward through sacrificial paths made compelling by that first spiritually suggested momentum.

It was a beautiful dream. Nadia Evertson had planned its shining way to goal after goal, each one athrill in her though only a vision as yet.

Bred in a western town that was set with the determination of growth in the midst of the wide spreading prairies, Nadia Evertson was molded to a great extent by the subtler influences of those wide open spaces to which many seem to be blind and deaf. Though so different from the mountains or valleys, yet they have a grandeur of their own, overwhelming sometimes, too, as the sea; the wild mad sweep of the winds is as though the ancient mystical gods were let loose in a frenzied ruthless rush, where the gentle breezes creep with tender caressings and whisperings.

And the meadow lark! Oh, how celestially it sang. Like something linking heaven and earth. God or the angels must have dropped it from a higher sphere to touch a mortal soul to some new key in the great yet undiscovered realms of sound. Its poignancy of beauty rifts the listening bending sky beyond, where only soul can follow and words cannot transcribe. Where speaks the voice of that pioneer past with its hardship, suffering, courage, patience, greatness, still so near in its brooding yesterday; and the voices of another past, far off, inaudible, ungraspable, lost, yet calling, unmistakably to the mind or spirit that is open to the unseen or unheard, that is alert to that which is poised behind or ahead of our little now. Where that pioneer spirit lives in its achievements, in the growth, expanding largeness of the inheritance, and its descendents still bearing within them traces of that strong courage and initiative though utilized in the different channels of a different age.

The burning sun and the hot winds of the drought time as well as the growing waxing grains and the luxuriant corn of the fortunate seasons, the soul inspiring grandeur and color music of its dawns and sunsets, overflowing the firmament with splendor like the opening of doors from some great heavenly beyond. In all the earth there is, there can be no dawns and sunsets more glorious or equal to those of the great plains west of the Mississippi or the Missouri in truth—that middle west— Nebraska.

To Nadia it was all an inseparable part of her life, of her individual being.

She breathed it not only in its material sense, as every one must, but also in its reactions on mind and spirit. Sometimes, if she could not ride, she walked perhaps miles out beyond the edge of the little city, where there would be an unobstructed view of the wonderful expanse, to see and hear and feel; to watch the sunrise or sunset flooding the sky with the depths and shadings of every color, a mighty inspiration and benediction by the Power of All, gripping the soul with longings of both the immortal and mortal.

In the family circle Nadia said little of this in detail, only an expression, in general, of the beauty and the greatness of it all. In that family circle she was second among six, three sisters and two brothers.

She could not help but people these plains with an ancient civilization, lost in an unrecorded past, whose phantom images and lives and builded walls, of homes and temples, still seemed to hover in a vague insistence over the land.

All this Nadia's poetic soul glimpsed in the shadows of shadowland, loving and suffering with them like flitting but living beings on a screen. She saw their cities and temples lifting to the sky, yet not the catastrophes or age decline that obliterated them and little by little wiped out all records but that which lives in the eternal shadows of What Has Been.

And always in the back of her mind, brewing in the depths of her quivering being, was the thought, the intent, if it could be clothed, armored with persistent purpose, "I want to do great things, be great. And I want to be a writer, a great writer, to do and to write what will add to the world's high and holy treasure. Oh, I long to do this and I must." And before her vision flitted the great ones of the earth, the wonderful spiritual teachers, ancient and modern, with Christ overshadowing them all, but the lesser lights shining like stars in the history of human struggle upward to the spiritual. Savonarola, Joan of Arc, and others took shape before her, thrilling her soul with the greatness of their souls, their sacrificial lives. The outstanding scientists, writers, artists and musicians, a radiant procession, developing, enlarging human intellect and soul.

In the childhood of the twentieth century, before that hideous presence of the Great War stealing, stealing near, had cast its cruel, jeering gaze over a supposed civilized world, out on the prairie roads, three or four miles from the city limits, late one afternoon in the first of August, though the hot winds, unwelcome and sometimes destructive visitors, where they had such a wide unobstructed expanse, were sweeping over the thirsting grain fields in the lapping waves of ruthless heat, Nadia and Oliver Raynor were riding in his new car. Before the war, automobiles were far more of a rarity and luxury than they were a few years later when, by 1923 or '24, even the common laborer must have his car.

Oliver had phoned for her to ride out in the country with him, where he was going on an errand, "That is," he had said, "if you think my companionship can offset the unpleasant day, as I know yours will make me forget it."

The had gone, other times, over these roads together, but today meant something different for both. It was depressing to see the drooping corn fields, two days ago standing up in luxuriant radiance of life, for a flourishing corn field says life, life, more than any other growing thing in the world of vegetation—and the wheat, ready, waiting to be cut but whipped with the burning heat.

"Oh, Oliver! do you think the crops are really hurt?" asked Nadia in alarm.

"Not much yet," he replied, "but another day or two of this, when they are already in need of rain, would be a great damage to the corn. The wheat may be shriveled a little, but I guess it will pull through moderately well."

"Oh, I hope so, I hope so," she said, "for beside the hurt to others it might mean more hurt than usual to me this year. If it lessened father's real estate earnings and income from his farm, it might interfere with my going to college or the university this year; and I have waited a year already as you know."

"Why do you say college or university?"

"Because I am planning somewhat, though as yet undecided, to go to an eastern college to get the friction of newness to me; new surroundings, new people, as one more element in a larger sided development. West and east rubbing against each other might be an added spur to development, though I love our west and our university, and may decide in its favor, but I cannot afford to take the whole course. There is too large a family of us, and I must be earning my living. I am going to compromise and specialize. And I have earned the right to one year at least. I have worked hard at home. I have done all of the sewing and saved many bills; and Oliver, I hate to sew. If I had to sew for my living, and especially when I am longing to do something different, I guess I'd jump into the river, only there isn't any river near us to jump into. It tires and deadens me, and my mind and soul are so far away from it. I long to do something so different."

"Give it all up, Nadia, give up college and marry me. I love you; I love you, Nadia. I have from the first. Give up your college year, and marry me now, and we will have a honeymoon trip wherever you say, even to Europe if you say so. And you won't have to do the things you don't want to do. Since I graduated at the university and went into the bank with father he gives me a good salary and says I have promise of becoming a capable financier. I have, too, a snug little sum of my own to start with—left me by my grandfather; so you see we wouldn't start poor and pinching. And also, Nadia, I am their only child; my interests are their interests, only I believe in working on your own merit, not counting on what others may leave to you. To be a real man one should stand on his own feet."

"That is true and right, Oliver, and the surest way to develop ourselves."

He had stopped the car; the sun, an immense ball of fire in an azure corona, was sinking toward the horizon in a grandeur that was soul inspiring; the voice of the infinite creator speaking in one great wonder chord to the souls of earth responsive to its wondrousness.

"How is it, Nadia?" His eager, handsome face, bending to hers in tender questioning, was a magnet that would have proved irresistible had Nadia felt sure of herself, sure that this was her prince, the prince life held in waiting for her; and she was almost won to the lure of himself and what he had to offer.

She looked up at him, her fair face shaded by a richness of gold tinted brown hair, and her eyes were softened to a more tender light, yet with a hint of troubled thought, also, in their depths, which he could not see. Nadia was charming both in looks and manner, though she was only partially aware of it herself, just enough to make her appear at ease wherever you placed her. As she looked up at him now, like a bright opening flower from the fairest of human gardens, Oliver longed to kiss her, as he often had before, but did not dare without some little weakening, inviting sign from her; for Nadia was proud, and held herself high, not allowing the personal liberties which some girls were lavish with. While some young men laid this trait against her, others, of a higher caliber, admired her the more.

"We are all glad to know that we are loved, Oliver," she said.

"Oh, you have known my feeling almost from the first; I've shown it plainly enough. You may as well say 'yes' now, Nadia." He grasped her hand and held it tight, "for I shall hold fast. Robert Merrill shall not have you."

"How do you know he wants me?"

"Oh, I know, and you know. You are a favorite too, as you also know."

"You flatter me."

"You are not blind, Nadia dearest. Say Yes!"

He lifted her hand to his lips and said, "I'd like to kiss your lips and hold you close if you will only give me the right."

"Wait, I am fond, very fond of you, but I haven't planned to marry anybody quite so soon. You are hurrying me, Oliver. Of course we all mean to marry. That is a part of life; and to those who don't something uncommon has happened, either for better or worse, as they may happen to look at it. Do you truly think one should marry quite so young?"

"Your sister Frances did, a year ago."

"But even that would give me a year of college. I am only nineteen yet. I have thought out what I want to do, whether I succeed at it or not. I want to be a writer; and one year at college might help to prepare me a little. Most of the girls and boys go to the university, and take the full course. We can't do that with our large family. Father cannot afford it. And I guess we are not made of that strong, self reliant stuff to earn our way. I wish we were. I have studied and read and kept ahead all by myself, though, so I don't believe I'd need to take a step behind any of them."

"No, you bet you wouldn't. You wouldn't ever," said Oliver with a decisive shake of the head. "But marry me now, Nadia, and we'll go to Europe for our wedding trip, if you say so. That will surely be as much help to you as one college year. You can get knowledge, inspiration, that way too."

"Oliver, you are a dear; and you do want to help me, don't you?"

"Help? All I know how; and I will feel I have one of the dearest brightest wives in the world."

"Wait till after our pageant, our sunflower pageant, is over; then we will talk over and settle it all. Give me that much time to think it all out. That is only a few days off."

"If I must, I must. But meantime I want to have a hold on you, and you can wear this ring so you will know who comes first if Robert Merrill or any other comes snooping around my garden."

"Oliver Raynor, how dared you be so sure of me as to buy that ring? How dared you be so sure of your fish, you arrogant fisherman? I haven't said yes, yet."

"I suppose it is a remnant of my caveman ancestry, and perhaps I would kidnap you if it became necessary." He laughed, and slipped the ring onto her finger, kissing both hands and ring. "Now wait until after the pageant, if you must, Sunflower Queen, but that will be a reminder."

"As if I needed one."

"It is just as well to be on the safe side," he replied and started the car onward.

"It surely is time for us to be returning home," Nadia said. "I have an engagement. Jessie Reed's party."

"With Robert Merrill, I suppose," he mumbled.

"Y-e-s! Of course you will be there."

"If only to keep you in sight."

There was only desultory talk on their way homeward, neither being able to take their thoughts from that which had just passed between them. When he left her at home, on turning away he said, "I didn't know of tonight's affair in time or I should have been in Merrill's place."

Looking over the family faces around the long dinner table that evening, she wondered what their future was to be; what was before them, of good or ill, success or failure, happiness or unhappiness. Seven of them, including father and mother and herself. There had been eight but Frances, the oldest of the six children, had married a year before. How dared any man and woman bring so many into the world not knowing what their fate would be. What a responsibility; and how few, if any, looked at it in that way. For the father the worrying unceasing question of support; for the mother the wearing daily care; and for both instilling of high principles. What a task it all must be. She looked at her father and mother; as such, the purest gold, their dear faces meaning to their children the best in fatherhood and motherhood; and she longed to help them more, to lessen their burdens. She meant always to be a helper to those around her, always a helper. That was a strong, deep element in her character. She knew she was a help, more than any of the others, in saving, lessening expense by the lines of her capability in the family needs. But she didn't want to go on this way any longer; she wanted to be doing something in the making of her own life, the road that stretched ahead beckoning shiningly. Yet she had done little toward its realization. A few worthy poems, and winning one slight prize, one little short story that had been very modestly paid for. Nothing more, except the beginning of the prairie epic, working in her longingly. Yet she felt the yearning within her, a yearning that was an inseparable part of her, whether it worked out into a visible success or worked only as an unseen leaven in the depths of her being. Would it be best to marry Oliver, unquestioning, lessening that family by one, and being so placed at once so that she could give her time to literary efforts, rather than follow her gleam alone, and teaching for a living see her literary efforts forced to take a secondary chance? And she was fond of Oliver. Otherwise it would be impossible to think of marrying him. But did she love him as she had dreamed of love? There were no rich quivers in her soul when she thought of him. She did not feel that life would be an utter blank without him; and her ideal said, "Do not marry until you feel all this." But maybe that was silly as well as impractical. Yet, what was a necessity for the make up of one, was not even recognized by another.

So, through the dinner, the general converse, and the hastened work, these thoughts, questions, simmered in her mind. During the meal she knew they had noticed her ring, a flashing beauty, which she would have fain hidden, and it did not surprise her when, after the secret and open glances of the others, her younger sister, Janice, said, "Oh, look at Nadia's ring. It's an engagement ring, ho! ho! Nadia and Oliver Raynor."

Nadia blushed slightly, but said, "Go a little slower, Janice, until you really know."

"But it's true, isn't it?" Janice, the youngest of six, was at the irrepressible age.

Then Laurel, next in line to herself, with only one year between, instead of the two between the others, and also an impulsive, said, "You better take Oliver Raynor, Nadia. He is a fine fellow, and if you don't, I will."

"Hear! hear!" exclaimed her brother Carl of sixteen years, and echoed by Jimmie, or James, the next in line.

"And how do you know you could get him?" asked Carl.

"Oh, I mean to get what I set out for. Nobody gets any thing by waiting for it to come to them."

"How truly wise," smiled the father, "and you think it even works in love affairs."

"Of course," Laurel answered. "That is not different from anything else. Perhaps a little more subtlety should be used; that is all."

"Think of a girl running after a fellow," sneered Carl.

"Oh, don't fool yourself," retorted Janice. "Boys and men are as vain as girls and women. They like to be fished for as well as to fish."

"And I wouldn't give much for a woman, or man, who didn't get a little thrill of pleasure out of the other's admiration," said Nadia. "But Laurel, we haven't much time if we go to Jessie's party. It is getting late and we must get the work done."

The mother spoke: "Janice and I will do the work. You can go and take more time to dress."

"No, mother. You are tired and we can manage it easily."

———————

It was a gay little company that night. Youth is the real owner of that quality of life, gayety, and only its shadowy counterpart comes down, or is projected into maturity.

Colored lanterns hung from the luxuriant boughs of the trees, those dear friends of life that breathe a benediction wherever they grow, enduring much hardship now and then when Nature's forces take on a mocking stingy mood, denying them their rightful moisture, yet clinging to life, smiling, waving, murmuring tenderness, singing orisons to the Creator of all beauty.

Laughter, and dimly formed hope, and cupid's darts, both certain and wavering, hobnobbed under those friendly trees that night, and builded crossroads of human destinies. The rich grasses whispered under the roving of careless human feet, grasses crisped a shade by the burning lips of the hot winds of the last two days, but youth hardly noticed this, intent in pursuit of pleasure.

Nadia and Laurel, whether together or apart, were centers of gayety and interest. Though sisters, they were as dissimilar as those of different parentage. Laurel belonged more to the world of the visible and its insistent calls, ready to answer and follow after them. Nadia, also quick to life's realities, had an inborn bias for the invisible, the spiritual, developed into a ruling power by a love for the literary and musical masterpieces of the world. Each one's atmosphere stirred a different chord in their admirers, yet they worked harmoniously together along the ways of every day life and their one special soul accord of music, for which both had a natural gift, achieving much on the foundational help given by father and mother, music lovers, without much from professional teachers. Music was one of the drawing cards of their home and one of its mutual bonds of enjoyment. But they never commonized their musical gift, never giving except where they felt the gathering was one that would individually listen in sympathetic appreciation. So this night with its combination of in and out of doors amusements, they could not be prevailed upon to go in and sing. When singing they were as two souls tuned to the same chords of life, to the same desires. Such is music's far reaching, harmonizing power—real music, not the jazz that has since, in later years, lowered human taste and emotion to the level of the savages' hideous dance and noise.

"Oh, let us have a serenade, a Spanish serenade," exclaimed Georgia Harris, one of the party who liked to see something new on the move.

"A serenade, a serenade," they all cried out.

"Jessie, bring out your guitar," said Georgia. "Robert Merrill, you're the tenor of this outfit. One of the girls go and lean from that window and throw him a favor. Go on, Nadia! You are the one, and sing him an answer."

"You want us to act foolish. No, thank you," answered Nadia, "but it would be a pleasure to hear Mr. Merrill sing a serenade out here under the stars, if he is willing."

"I will if you will answer it," he replied. "If only with two or three lines. Of course we all know it is done for fun and to show Georgia and the crowd that we can."

"Make it up as you go along?" cried Georgia.

"Yes, make it extemporaneous," added Henry Sloan.

"How unfair you are," said Robert. "Shall we gratify them, Nadia?"

"Yes, go ahead," she answered.

So, the guitar having been brought, Robert began to strum. He couldn't play, but he could make an accessory to his rhapsody, however poor a second.

Serenade
"Lean from your window, love, my own,
Lean from your window's height
And listen to the song I sing,
A song of love's delight.
You cannot know the thrill I feel
To see you shining there,
A human star that lights the dark
O love, my love, so fair."

Jessie held up her hand to stop the applause that was beginning and said, "Wait." Robert's smooth mellow voice, though dropped almost to a pianissimo, rode the evening, air with a tender appeal that caught them all. Then he handed the guitar to Nadia.

"I hear love's message floating up
On wings of song to me,
And lo! it wakens in my heart
An answering melody.
Out from my window high I lean
And waft a shadowy kiss.
There's fragrance on its petal tips
Brewed from love's flower of bliss."

Then the applause broke forth and "Bravo! Bravo!" swelled to the hand clapping.

"Too good for pretense," someone expressed. "What might the real thing be."

Nadia had also sung pianissimo, sweet and low, as though thrilling with emotion held in leash; and Oliver felt a wave of jealousy sweep over him at the possibility of Robert having awakened any thrills of love in her that did not belong to himself; and he was glad he had already spoken and placed the ring on her finger.

Then Laurel called out gaily, "Come, Oliver, let us give them another make believe"—he thought she stressed the "make believe"—"and a funny one this time."

"All right. I'm ready," he said, as he took the guitar from Nadia. "You know I don't play or compose verse or music, but here it goes." So, with great bravado, he began his mock serenade emphasizing manner, voice, composition, as mockingly as he could.

> "O maiden in the star,
> O maiden in the moon,
> Come sailing down to me;
> I am a love sick loon.
> I dream of you by day,
> I dream of you by night,
> O maiden fair, so fair,
> Have pity on my plight."

He did it well; and they were all laughing around him, captured by the fun of this, as well as by the appeal of the other.

Oliver handed the guitar to Laurel with a sweeping courtesy and she, with an answering exaggeration, began.

> "Ho! dreaming man of earth,
> Be not so deaf, so blind
> To other maidens fair,
> Pray, be not so unkind.
> You cannot guess where shine
> The eyes of love for you,
> O swain, O love sick swain!
> Ho, ho! adieu, adieu."

With a final swish of the strings she jumped up laughing.

"Well, we've done it, and not so bad for beginners either. Jessie, we charge you star prices for the extemporaneous stunt."

"All right, charge it to the unpaid social debts. But you four may find yourselves now on our city's vaudeville syndicate, the high brow and the comedy side by side."

"No, this is our first and last appearance in vaudeville staging," said Laurel as she grasped one of the girls about the waist and danced across the small green space of the lawn. In the jumble of youthful pleasure, Oliver had not had a minute alone with Nadia that evening. It seemed to be Laurel he was more often thrown with, or with Jessie, who was not averse to grasping every chance for his attentions. And it was only on the homeward way, a short distance that they preferred to walk on a summer evening, that Robert Merrill had an opportunity to speak since their little mock serenade and since he noticed the flashing ring on her little white hand.

"I want to tell you, Nadia," he said, "that my serenade was not a make believe as far as you are concerned. I meant it, and far more than was expressed in those few words. I haven't told you of my love because I felt I hadn't the right when I had nothing but that love to offer you. As you know, I am poor, with my mother and young sister to care for, but I don't intend to remain poor. I feel the power within me to conquer circumstances, to succeed. I love you, Nadia. I have hoped for favorable conditions before the blossom that is you was plucked by some other masculine hand. Tonight my heart jumped and sank when I saw the shining ring on your finger. It is Raynor, I suppose; but I have no right to intrude. It would be selfish of me to bind you to myself with my conditions as they are." It was a long speech for Robert Merrill who was seldom given to long sentences.

"I thank you for the honor of your love, Robert, the greatest gift one can give another. And we know this—nothing is sure till consummated in fact. What we plan or contemplate today may not come to pass however much our desire may be set on it. Neither you nor I can know what life holds for us. We can only hope and strive."

"And hope and striving can accomplish great things, even sometimes the seeming impossible," added Robert, with a decisive emphasis that self confidence gives.

"And we belong to the optimistic active west. We must prove ourselves its capable representatives. I am sure you will, Robert. And I—oh, I not only long but mean to do big things."

"You will, Nadia; you are gifted. I wish I could help you to reach your highest."

"Perhaps you will, Robert, and it may be you have already. The friction of our lives upon each other, on what we feel, think, do, and become, is never without its influence, and sometimes a great one."

They had reached her home and standing at the open door they said good night with a lingering sympathy. Who could tell how the clouds might descend or lift for either of their lives? As Robert turned away homeward he realized that Nadia had not given him any sign that she had any feeling for him but friendship, or that she was promised to Raynor. Well, his present conditions precluded marriage for himself. When the uptide came, which he felt sure would, and must come for him, where would she be? And where would he be? What views of life would have arisen and stulted or soured their present ones, instead of expanding and blossoming them? As he looked around on the world, life seemed such a lottery however much the struggle and the faith. Life, with all its fair promises and ruthless denials, its too often reward of evil for good, its lovelessness and sorrow and pain where love and joy should in righteousness have tarried. But he mustn't look at that side except to turn away and fight believingly for his own attainments.

Oliver Raynor had not earned his possessions and opportunities; and he had no responsibilities but to make good use of them, of what favoring Fate had given him. Well, he, himself, had to earn his own and climb the ladder of achievement carrying others in his arms; and if he missed one joy he would know and keep ever in mind that there were others, other joys, perhaps as great or greater still to be obtained; and he would attain them. Unceasing effort, watchfulness, confidence; they were the weapons or the tools that tunneled and hewed one's way through life's mountains of attainment.

For awhile Nadia's thoughts followed the same trend. Each was ambitious, each reaching beyond; and unless Nadia accepted Oliver and the help his money could give, each had only his or her efforts by which to climb the ladder of ambition.

Though having seemingly little in it to make it of more value than other social evenings, yet this evening made an unrecognized impress on the four characters standing out most prominently in its little drama, and possibly started little insignificant subtle growths, not to die out, but to live on unknown and put forth new growths in their small or great life dramas of the future.

The sisters chatted and laughed, before going to bed, over their foolish and yet enjoyable part in the evening's unprepared program.

"It wasn't quite a fair division though, Nadia, that both serenaders should have been your admirers," said Laurel. "You better not let Oliver Raynor slip off your string if you care for him, for if you do, I might catch him."

"You are not backward in warning me," Nadia answered.

"But that's playing square, isn't it? While he is yours, and I recognize it. But that is more because you are my sister; otherwise who knows."

"You are not very delicate, Laurel."

"Why should I be? From all I see, delicacy and looking out for the other fellow will not get you anywhere. Our big golden self sufficient sunflower can outlive the daisy. I observe and read the world better than you do, and truly, too, if I am a year younger and both of us young. I can see what this world is, if you can't. It's Self. And I don't want to be left by the wayside. So mostly I am going after what I want, I am going to be a pusher."

"Oh, Laurel, you make it seem good for our self desires but so hard and unbeautiful."

"Well, choose for your own life and I'll choose for mine. I'd rather be a flourishing, happy, common, yes, common human being, than a suffering saint you so much admire. They get nothing in this world and this world is all we know about."

"But how terrible if we didn't believe in any other."

"Yes, but I'm not troubling myself over what it may be now. Each world to itself, its own time. There is no end to what I want here and I am going to get it—all I can; and it looks as though I must get it mostly myself, by marrying it, which means marrying one with money of course; money—one of the things that brings other things."

"Laurel, you make me feel depressed."

"Well, I am talking wisdom, the wisdom of this world as you'll find out for yourself, some day. Good night. I'm sleepy."

The next morning at breakfast, Laurel gave the family a resume of the evening before, adding sharp little touches of her own to embellish the descriptions. Meal time was the family's experience meeting. They were usually all on hand ready to be social and to express themselves. The mother was the quiet one among them. In fact among so many of youthful exuberance her own more reserved nature would have had little chance except when she felt it wise to criticise or veto something, which was not often, as the father, though loving and indulgent as he thought wise, was the stern disciplinarian. These parents had not lacked in instilling high moral principles into their family, but it remained to be seen how broad and deep and strong their influence on the thought action, lives, of these diverse natures.

"How is the sunflower show coming on?" asked Carl. "Do you want us to go after sunflowers yet?"

"Not until tomorrow," Laurel answered. "The pageant is three days ahead yet. We only want the real ones for the advance guard, but even then you boys and others will have to scout and scamper to find enough. We've been making paper sunflowers, the girls and women of this town, till it seems the world itself must be a sunflower."

"It is in one sense," the father replied. "Otherwise it wouldn't flower, wouldn't blossom with plants, or animals; and great the potentiality of its seed. That is our dream, our hope, our faith; through toil and pain, through striving and achieving, through stumbling and falling, yet rising and struggling onward, becoming, who can say, the more wonderful seed of another and more wonderful sunflower plant."

"I like that thought, father," said Nadia, "the earth, our beautiful earth, a sunflower. The farmers seem to look upon the sunflower as an enemy to be conquered, wiped out, as the town people the dandelion, but I do love them both in one sense, for their beauty, their cheer and persistent life."

"Love the sunflower and dandelion!" Janice exclaimed jeeringly.

"Maybe Nadia loves the old thistle and even the tumble-weed, those unattractive denizens of our prairies," added Carl.

"Well," Nadia offered thoughtfully, "they, too, have some small virtue to speak for them if you hunt for it. Why! the tumbleweed, as it goes dancing, jumping, careening down the streets and side stepping over the lawns, driven by the carousing winds of the aging year, add an interesting element to the drama of the days. Alas for the blindness of him who fails to note and appreciate it as an almost attractive touch of opera bouffe in nature's operatic settings of the prairies."

"Very good, Nadia. Not so far amiss," her father nodded.

"Well," Laurel mocked, "somedays methinks I'd like to go adventuring even like the tumbleweed."

"Driven by the winds instead of by your own efforts?" her father countered. "No, Laurel, be not a wisp for the winds."

"Oh, I don't intend to be if I can drive my own chariot. I'm going after what I want so far as I can."

"Trust Laurel for that," Carl put in.

"Thank you, Mr. Carl Evertson. I'm glad I've impressed you with my ability, and hope I succeed in proving it."

"Oh, you're all right, Laurel. You're full of pep."

"Well," said the father, "pep is a good quality to have and I hope you all have a fair amount of it, but I hope also that each one of my children will win success in life with honor as a close companion. Would your mother and I could have given you great wisdom, but of what you have, make the most and strive to add to it."

"Oh, father, mother! That is what we all want to do, I am sure," said Nadia.

"Yes," he smiled at her. "And I am pleased that you and Laurel were chosen Queen and Princess for the pageant. It shows you have won the good will of your associates."

"Oh, it was Nadia's head of thick gold brown hair that made her Queen," joked Laurel.

"And you?" asked Carl.

"The power to make myself both heard and seen," drawing herself up in mock assurance.

"Ho! Ho! Conceit, conceit, thy name is Laurel," exclaimed Carl. "Nadia, speak up and assert yourself."

"She doesn't think she needs to; she is a budding writer whose voice may sometime be heard far and wide," broke in Janice.

"All joking aside, I only wish that would prove true; but the question is, have I that much within me? Who can tell?" said Nadia.

"As you say, Nadia, all joking aside, you have real talent but you are a dreamer; and do poetry and dreamers get there?" questioned Laurel doubtfully.

"Sometimes, Laurel, but better for them if they have the practical behind them to push and support," the father added.

"I wish, oh, I wish Nadia and I could make our singing voices heard over the country. I venture to assert if we had the courage and the push we could do it. I know we could if we would set aside that fool pride of ours and be willing to begin at the bottom instead of the top," Laurel jerked out the words.

"I confess to the fool pride, Laurel," Nadia answered, "though in truth I think it is more 'a don't know how to push.' Those who go to the cities and study with a big teacher probably develop the push or are prodded by others."

"Well, we can't, can we, father?"

"I see no way, girls," the father answered. "I couldn't risk the heavy expense and be fair to my family as a whole."

"Of course," said Nadia, "and we must work out our own salvation in some way. But Laurel, we must hurry and finish our sunflower costumes. We don't want to be rushed at the last minute."

So the breakfast ended, each one hurrying to task or pleasure as it might be, a happy family denied the opportunities and luxuries wealth might give, but lacking nothing in comfort or affection, untried as yet by the heavier and darker burdens of life.

I I

The gala day arrived. Nature smiled upon it. The burning winds hid away after leaving the scorched damaging reminders of their three day's holocaust. Youth troubled not. Maturity stolidly accepted the losses and planned to make the most of its depleted products as the middle west had many times faced its harsh realities and still worn a smiling undaunted mien and done its big share in feeding a hungry world.

A day of milder warmth and softer air stirrings. People gathered from the surrounding country and from the smaller towns in a wide radius; for this small city of Marshall was and had been from early pioneer days a central point, a center for a large section of the state. And while Omaha had its yearly Ak Sar Ben, this smaller city, while having its yearly County Fair, had given but one floral parade before in its history. And who ever heard of a sunflower pageant, a sunflower! one of the farm nuisances? Or thought of making this common coarser bloom among Nature's manifold blossomings a central figure for a public beauty pageant, even though Luther Burbank's genius had just given to the world his wonderful changes in colorings and size and usefulness, making use of nature's forces to add to nature's usefulness and beauty once more? Though these changes had not yet been utilized they had at least added to the sunflower's fame.

So the people gathered from far and wide, crowding streets and stores, making the holiday a sight seeing and purchasing expedition in one. All classes were jumbled together, rich and poor, cultured and uncultured. For that matter the west never had drawn distinctions of class, either financial or educational, as noticeably, decidedly as the older east. Caste is something that does not lift its head very visibly in the newer countries. And yet—yet there was a strong touch of it innate in Nadia and Laurel, and the family of which they were a part. That sometimes happens in families, or individual members of families, without regard to financial or other material lacks; an intellectual or cultural, or inborn social courtesy superiority.

Before the parade began, those who were not workers in its preparation found themselves wondering how it could and would be done to be an attractive and uncommon affair; but after it began to appear and roll its unique length they no longer wondered in doubt, but gave appreciative recognition to the feminine ability of the city that had projected and carried it through.

The procession introduced itself with a large green banner on which was printed a big sunflower in its richest stage of coloring and on one side in large white print, "THE PRAIRIE'S GREETING." On the other, "COURAGE! NEVER GIVE UP," "THE SPIRIT OF THE WEST." Then the band followed in uniform with a sunflower in each one's cap. And while as musicians they were not special artists yet they sensed the meaning of the day's tribute to prairie and flower and human courage and initiative, playing an appropriate rousing march, their own bodies aswing to the sonorous rhythm.

Then came six boys, two abreast, dressed in long tight green robes and wearing hats representing a big sunflower—the stalk and the blossom.

Following came six young girls in white, two abreast, each carrying a sunflower parasol made like one immense bloom.

Then the floats began to come; some representing the beauty idea; some the humorous, even with beauty not absent but a concomitant part. Among those dedicated to beauty the Queen's was, of course, the largest and finest. On a white float the Queen sat high on a gold colored throne under a sunflower canopy, wearing a sunflower crown and sash and with a green and yellow wand. Below her on the white terrace were her princess maids of honor robed in white, wearing head wreaths of sunflowers and green vine leaves, and sashes draped from the shoulder down.

Old King Corn's float was beautiful and interesting and his banner bore the words, "WE HELP FEED THE WORLD." One of the humorous, attractive and unique floats was a load of hay, a real everyday load of hay with here and there, scattered through it, a laughing young face, sometimes a girl's, sometimes a boy's face and head poked through a big sunflower. Their bodies were covered, hidden by the hay. This attraction gave forth amusement and happiness. So, with a varied and numerous representation, the parade wound its way. It was King Corn, and Wheat, and Oats, sheaves of each, with that claimant banner, that brought up the rear and won the last huzzahs of the onlookers. And truly Nebraska has the right to claim the glory of doing a big part in feeding the world though she has had many battles with the mocking Fates of drouth and hot winds. The parade was just long enough to give the onlookers a few breaths of delight, without wearying, and then it ended at the point where it began.

Oliver Raynor, and Henry Sloan, Laurel's friend, were on hand making mocking elaborate obeisance, sweeping courtesies, to the Queen and her ladies as they assisted them down from their white terrace.

"Oh, that is all very pretty fun," laughed Nadia. "Courtesy beautifies human life; and far better for the world if there were more of its reality in everyday life. I am glad this show is over for me; don't think I enjoy being set up just to be looked at."

"We don't need to be troubled over that," Laurel added. "We were only looked at as vague figures in a mixed picture— hardly as capital figures in a paragraph."

"Most girls like to be looked at, Nadia," Oliver remarked.

"You can bet on that," laughed Henry.

"Yes," agreed all the girls.

"But agreeing to that," said Nadia, "yet I'd rather be looked at for an additional reason, for some achievement, either done, or in the doing."

"Oh, come off, Nadia!" exclaimed Georgia Harris. "Take what you can get and be glad you get it; then get the other if and when you can."

"Well, come on girls, all of you, there's one more get now. We're going to have a luncheon party to end this show. I am the host. Henry, go find a couple more of the boys."

"But you will miss the mayor's speech at the Court House Square," Nadia reminded them. "And he will speak of what Burbank has done with the sunflower, added to his other agricultural and floral improvements on nature's productions; and he will also extoll the spirit of Nebraska."

"How do you know what he is going to talk about?" Henry asked.

"Oh, I just happened to be expressing to him my appreciation of the virtues of both and he said I was right and he was going to make that basic truth the subject of his few remarks at the end of the parade."

"Neither he nor the crowd will know we are missing," Oliver said. "There's Merrill and Will Osgood now. Not quite boys enough, but we'll do."

They came over smiling, congratulating the girls on the success of their appearance and of the parade, and after some little demur accepted the invitation to join the luncheon party.

Robert Merrill, though hurt by the hopelessness of his love for Nadia, and supposing that Raynor, with his material advantages had won her, was not the kind to give up to any hurt or loss, but to go onward making the best of conditions as they happened to be and looking forward to other possible blessings and gains in the future; so he exerted himself to be an agreeable companion and guest. In the small private dining room of the hotel they had a gay time.

Almost unaware, Nadia found herself comparing those two who had honored her with their special affections. In some of the foundational, dependable qualities Merrill was, she sensed, superior to Raynor, and though dependent on his own resources alone, and burdened from the start with the support of others, might yet attain a success in a worldly way ahead of Oliver, who had a more propitious start and who possessed the more attractive social power.

Wandering for a moment in this path of thought she was recalled to the chatter and fun by hearing one of the girls saying, "One of the committee told me just before the parade that the tickets for tonight are nearly all sold. The Opera House will be nearly, and maybe fully filled."

She was speaking of the concert for the benefit of the Red Cross which was to be the closing program for this day and evening. And of course Nadia and Laurel were to give their talent. They were favored singers gifted with the artist sense and unusually good voices. They had agreed to one number, one of the beautiful duets in which they were so proficient, as it was to be a mixed program in which the varied talent of the little city was to participate. But Nadia's and Laurel's offerings being artistic and stirring, in selection and rendition, never failed to stir their audience in the deeper, truer sense. Added to this number Laurel was to sing the solo accompaniment to a ladies chorus, while Nadia and Robert Merrill were to give the prison scene from *Il Trovatore*, with scenic effect, even though that opera had for some time been relegated to the background by newer fads in dramatic music. The evening's task having been called to their attention, it was suggested that the present gayeties be cut short that they might go home and rest a bit for the good of the evening's task.

Oliver laughed, "Of course I'm not one of the musical stars—only one unit in a glee club—and a slight tired flatting note from me might not do much noticeable damage."

"Good times don't tire me," said Georgia Harris.

"Right! Georgia, it's the lack of them that tires most," laughed Jessie. "Who wants to rest or work when one can have pleasure, a gay happy time?"

"Perhaps it is well for us that we haven't always the right to choose," added Merrill. "How much achievement would there be in this world?"

"Achievement is all right but I want the good times too," laughed Laurel with a toss of her dark head. "Both in their time and place."

With lingering chatter and fun, partly meant and partly mockery, the little party gradually separated, looking forward to the evening.

And the evening with its exhibition of varied talent was a success, bringing pleasure both to audience and performers, a success musically and financially. It happened that a musically cultured visitor from an eastern city was there and remarked of Nadia and Laurel, "Those girls are born singers, voice and temperament. In a musical center they would be able to win success."

But fortune as often favors the less gifted and fate worked unfriendly in this case. Sometimes our western towns, big and little, take pride in appreciating and recognizing their home talent; and then again, sometimes, there will be a begrudging that would, alas, rather see some rare gift and worthy personality clouded and crushed than to see them spread their petals and open their bloom in the expanding light and warmth of fame; but such are the smiles and frowns, the light and darkness of human good and frailty.

This was the end of this special gala season. Some of the girls and boys were soon to go back to the university, some to their already specialized tasks. It was the last of the untroubled joys and hopes of youth's budding April and May for Nadia.

The finishing of that bright page of youth which, turning in the Hands of Fate, shows another page where those Hands of Fate trace blight and frost and seem to linger long and pleasurably in that destructive tracing. It leaves no record, for the world, of the soul struggles, the spiritual heights and depths, the burning deserts through which one plods, with the "I Will" for one's only support, or the tiny oasis that springs up now and then, for the determined soul alone, that its dreams may not all die away.

III

With the earliest calls of dawn, though in need of relaxation
and sleep, Nadia heard decision, that grim presence, knocking,
knocking at her consciousness; that ruthless companion of
our striving human life, pointing at once in two directions,
sometimes more, into the unknown, with the one word—
Choose! And, right or wrong, we must make the choice that
will make or mar; unless that other and seemingly unescapable
presence, Fate, steps forward and says, "Nay, this other way,
which is one of darkness, I choose for you. And because you are
what you are, you cannot turn from it, you cannot escape it,
however great your longing."

Decision. One way—marriage with Oliver Raynor, a
trip to Europe with its opportunities, ease, a certain amount of
luxury and leisure to develop her literary talent and perhaps win
success with it. The other way—one pinching year at college,
with the technical and additional knowledge she might gain

33

there and the other merely possible lottery gains; teaching, who could guess how many years, with only the snatches between times for that part of her that yearned and called for expression and recognition.

Not many would ponder these two paths, but would turn in eager gladness to the sure and many gainful offerings of the first. But did she love him? Not with that deep, wonderful love her soul dreamed of. But maybe that was only a dream that could not or would not be realized in her life. Yet it was an innate part of her and that shining road stretching, beckoning onward before her soul's vision. Should she turn from it as an impracticable dream and accept this seemingly lesser love, with all its needful helpful gifts? How foolish it would be for her to refuse this, with its fullness of gifts, in this world of practical, harsh realities. What a fool Laurel would think her to be, as well as most others, if they could know about it. And her own common sense told her the same. Yes. If she said that yes to Oliver, from now on everything would be easy; and she could begin now and go on plucking the roses of life, and give full time, full vent to that creative literary talent. Yes, yes. She was more likely to be sorry if she turned from these offered realities to only the hopes and dreams hidden in that other choice. Yes.

The sun of a new day climbed up over the horizon and looked uncaringly upon their world again; upon the little scrambling humans, with their joys and pains, their small treasures and their unfed dreams.

"Girls! Nadia! Laurel! Girls, boys, all of you! Come at once," their father's pained voice came up the stairway. "Your mother is ill. She has had a stroke."

They bounded out of bed as though they had been struck, and a stab cut through Nadia's heart. Their mother ill. A stroke. Paralysis. No. No. It could not, should not be. Their mother! Always at hand, an unfailing support. Always helpful—now to be helpless? It could not, must not be. Why, they could not possibly get along without her at the helm, the dear, kind, gentle mother, unassertive unless necessity demanded.

They wasted no time in dressing, and in a minute were at their mother's bedside, a heart-stricken family before a stricken mother. No time to think of Self and Self's desires just now. Everything was hushed. The Doctor came, having been phoned for at once. What did they do without phones in those days long gone by? Almost as much a necessity now as the clothes you wear.

"Yes, a paralytic stroke," the Doctor said. "Not the worst. She may even overcome it after a while and be apparently well again. Time will tell, as it tells everything excepting what lies beyond the veil. Good care and good cheer will help immensely. Cheerfulness in one's self, and in those around one, is a great help. Mind is a big factor in the cure of this body of ours."

At first it was hard for the family to fit itself to its maimed conditions; but in a few days, with the mother sitting quietly among them in her wheelchair, a center of attention, they managed to make the household move on, smoothly and cheerfully without any apparent wrecking of their own lives, excepting Nadia's. She sensed from the first that Fate, ruthless, merciless, had stepped in and made another decision for her; and what lay ahead for her, outside of bleak denial and blighting of the buds of hope and promise, was an unbroken dark. She could not, would not leave that helpless mother now for either marriage or college. No. Self stepped into the background. She could not, would not leave that helpless mother now for either marriage or college. No. Self stepped into the background. She could not have brought herself to choose otherwise. More days went by yet she did not mention the subject though it stayed with her like a spectre of the dead that would not, could not leave her; clinging in soundless, moaning dead leafage to the blighted branches of her young tree of life.

Then, when they happened to be alone, her mother spoke. "Nadia, what about college? What about Oliver?"

"I haven't told you, mother dear, because it was a jumble in my own mind. Of course I wouldn't go to college now and leave you this way, mother dear, and the Oliver part can wait awhile until you are walking among us again. He will understand."

"But Nadia, I cannot bear to spoil your life. I hope you can go just the same. Couldn't Laurel and Janice manage, with the boys helping where they could?"

"You need me, mother, and I would feel wicked to leave you now."

"I love you for your unselfishness, Nadia, but alas, that may be the way your life will be spoiled."

"Let us hope, mother, that it will not be spoiled, but that in some now unforeseen way its threads will be woven into the pattern I want it to be. Do not worry about me now. I will have to work all the harder to achieve something without the college help. Others have done so before me, what one has done another may do."

But when she found out that all the others had taken it for granted that her plans would be laid aside, even though she felt that under the circumstances she could not blame them, yet she felt a little inner protest at their easy acquiescence. Ever since she was old enough to know about such things and felt the desire for expression she had hoped, looked forward to, and planned and worked toward it.

Of course if they all knew about Oliver's proposition they would look upon it as merely to be postponed for a while. And so it appeared, if she said yes to it now on that basis; but was it? Oliver loved her and might wait patiently for a little while but he was not one to go on indefinitely in denial and only hope. In such a test she could not help but think Robert Merrill was more the kind to be dependable and loyal, though he too would probably be able to turn elsewhere if too long tried. But then, perhaps that was best. Perhaps it would not be altogether right to bind another to your denials and say he should not seek and find happiness elsewhere. That might be asking too much of any man or woman. Well, time would tell the story. Her mother might soon be well and about again as usual. Oliver and his offerings had an even greater lure now, in the face of those darkened conditions. And in truth her darkened hope leaped toward it now in the possibility of its loss.

At the first opportunity they had talked it over and he had said, "Of course, Nadia. I couldn't expect or ask you to leave your mother just now. We will wait awhile. She will get better and then the others can take your place."

"We will hope so, Oliver. I know she depends on me the most, and would feel lost without me, until she can get about among us again. My college year has been taken away from me now anyway."

"Then you won't postpone me for that," he smiled, "only until your mother is better. Then Nadia, then Nadia, dear one, we will have a big time together, have our European trip, the knowledge and experience to be gleaned from travel. It may give you far more than your college year could give."

"Yes, Oliver, it might," she answered, "and more broadening and stirring. That is, if we are the kind to observe and absorb from the fullness of material around us. I hope I am."

"Nadia," said Laurel, one morning when they were alone, "you have given up going to college now, why shouldn't I go? Why should both of us be denied? And even that one year at our university might do much in making my life; and so many of the girls are going. Oh, agree to it, Nadia, and help to get father and mother to see it that way. They would, I am sure, if they felt you looked at it favorably."

A pang shot through Nadia, and for a moment she did not answer. All the denial, all the hardship would be hers, and Laurel did not want it for the same reason that she wanted it. Bright, quick, light-hearted Laurel whose desires were not deeply set on literature or higher education, but whose mind was set on "getting there" as she phrased it, in the direction her desires led. She, herself, who needed it most and for the higher purpose, must be denied; but even so, she would not refuse Laurel.

"Well, Laurel, I cannot deny it hurts me. You know how I have counted on it, worked toward it, not for any good time but for the knowledge that might help in what I want to do; but I will agree to your going though it will be hard on me here with no one to help with the work but the little that Janice can do."

"Thank you, Nadia. That is unselfish and good of you. I'll appreciate it. I'll have to rush to get my clothes ready. There are only a few days left to do it all in."

"You can have one of my new dresses. If I have to stay at home and work all of the time, I won't need many." There was some heartsickness and perhaps a hint of bitterness in this last sentence but any would have felt as much or more.

"It may be a little small as you are larger than I, but you can let out the seams some and probably you can make it do."

"Oh, Nadia, I thought of it but didn't want to suggest it; it will help a lot."

So Laurel had thought it all out for herself, without much sorrow for her, was Nadia's reflection. But such is this human world.

When the father and mother were consulted, both felt it would be unfair to Nadia, not only to give up her chance but to bear the burdens of the house work alone. But when Nadia persisted in the arrangement being made, saying, "Let Laurel go. It may help to make the happiness and success of her life. I could not leave mother now. And mother may get well soon so I can have my chances in some way."

Somewhat unwillingly, because of the burdens falling on Nadia alone, they agreed to let it be tried. If necessary she could discontinue and come home.

So, in a few days more, Nadia beheld Laurel, and several of their girl friends, leaving for her longed for goal, while she was left in the chains of uncongenial work and small leisure for cultivating the art she loved.

But she faced forward toward the shining road determinedly. She must move onward in that light though her progress, day by day, must be slight with time and energy stressed in these unfriendly ways.

Then Frances, who was living in Denver, came home to be with her mother for three days. With the visiting and extra work involved, there was no time to think along the lines of her desires or even to read those masters she loved and thrilled with. After Frances had gone, Nadia's Aunt Eleanor, of whom she was very fond, came for a few days.

Aunt Eleanor was her mother's oldest sister, the one who had been the sacrifice and burden bearer for that family and had therefore remained unmarried. One whose presence was a comfort and a help. Who gave more than she received, a quality not only natural to her character but also cultivated continually by the incessant giving and doing for others that life had asked of her. Before she left she gave Nadia a "shake up" or tried to. Though it made no visible effect on her life, yet she had unlimited cause to think of it often in the years that followed.

Aunt Eleanor had followed her to her room one day and closed the door so they could talk unheard.

"Nadia, I feel I must say something to you before I go away, for your possible good; they may not seem very beautiful to say but I feel they are truth, Nadia, you have begun wrong, unless you want my kind of a life, and I know you don't; no woman, or man, does, never to follow the desire, the call of your own life, always to turn your back upon them and give yourself in a drab, drab life for the desires of others. Much of mine could not have been escaped except by being selfish, out and out selfish, that quality we are taught and accept as the foe to all spiritually, the highest and immortal part of us. But I could have escaped some of it by forcing others to do a little of their part and seeing that I had rights, too. If you don't force them to see, acknowledge and act accordingly, they never do, never; for selfishness is foremost in this world. Only the few will sacrifice unforced, and only the few will trouble themselves over the thought that such as I have had desires, too, that, chained, continue to gnaw at the heart of me. Laurel shouldn't have gone. If you couldn't, neither should she under all the circumstances."

"But, Aunt Eleanor, I just couldn't bring myself to desert mother now, and it looked selfish for me to deny it to Laurel, though I confess I had some twinges."

"But why shouldn't Laurel have felt the same and stayed at home to help you bear the burdens. It is too much for you alone. Unselfishness is a beautiful quality but it doesn't always lead to beautiful results."

"Mother may get well soon," Nadia said, "and then everything will be all right again."

"Well, I surely hope so for her and for you. You know I am fond of you, Nadia, and I know your character, your natural make up is to give to your own hurt. If human beings were all that they should be, that quality would work in all for an equal adjustment. Another thing, Nadia, are you fond of Oliver Raynor? If so, marry him and don't wait too long either, for too great ideals, or for trial of his patience and loyalty. There isn't much of that in the world either, not much. I found it so. And Nadia, unless you are strong to stand alone, up in the clouds with your ideals, and be slightingly spoken of as an 'old maid or spinster' by the common world that puts sex relation above every other human attainment, then Nadia, marry anyway; be one with the herd who fail to remember that anyone can marry and propagate, that it doesn't require spirituality, or mentality, or character, only the animal instinct, and that is rampant over the earth, that the lowest never fail to marry and beget their kind while some of the greatest souls have turned from it and lived for the great things they could do, great deeds and great ideas. Messengers of the spirit, some of these are, and have shown mankind the spiritual—so far beyond their material vision and desire. But alas, Nadia, I am not one of those great ones and have often felt an inward protest and sometimes almost wished I had been selfish and followed the common ways."

"But you are one of the great ones, Aunt Eleanor, for the good you have done to those around you, even if not so recognized by the world," said Nadia earnestly.

"Or by those I have given my life to and for. Those are the ones who always credit one the least," Eleanor replied, "but let me warn you Nadia, take the safest way to happiness—or its mocking kindred—and marry without too high ideals blocking the way. One of the most selfish girls of my day married one of my fondest admirers and I think he has had to be mostly the giver between the two. She wouldn't know how to deny Self for even him, but she has had far more of life's blessings than I. That seems to be the unjust division of this world. I have given you warning, Nadia, but each one must follow one's own judgment however wise or unwise; but Nadia, dear, I hope you will escape my life of all denial and giving, and attain some of the desires before you, that still cry out in their dark chamber of denial in me; for I had talents too and denied them for others. I am through."

"I thank you for your affectionate interest, Aunt Eleanor, and believe you are not far from right; and especially in this, that each one should be required to realize his or her share of responsibility and obey it if possible. I must achieve some of my desires or eat my heart out. I couldn't be as sweet and cheerful as you under all denial. That is one of your great traits. Not every one accomplishes it. Do you think we can change ourselves if we are made to feel strongly for others and Fate puts the choice darkly before us? I don't believe you could do any different if you could live your life over, if you could waken and find what has been but a dream and your life still ahead of you. Your kind unselfish heart would still rule you, though the selfishness of human beings and the barren rewards that have been yours seem now to decry your sacrifices."

"Oh, I suppose that is true, Nadia, but how many, many there must be in this world, like me, who wish they could waken and find it all a nightmare dream and the trial journeys of life still beckoning with their hopes. Well, what has been has been. Yours is still beckoning; may it continue to shine."

IV

As the next weeks and months went by, Nadia had to plan and snatch at the spare minutes for reading, thinking, meditation, some of each so necessary for the birth of greater achievements. She found little time for pleasure, either, that other necessity for health balance of mind and body. She had an occasional evening and Sunday with Oliver—and once in a while with Robert Merrill—either for going somewhere or for a social time together at home; but the care-free feeling had vanished and she was sometimes too tired to cull the full amount of joy out of the recreations though ever glad of the companionships.

Laurel's letters showed that she was enjoying her opportunities whether the "advanced education" outlook was great or small. She was intellectually bright enough if she saw the special need and went after it. In that case she might outshine most of her classmates. She was not short in natural ability; it all depended on the goals toward which her desires were set.

Then the months slipped by and she with the other university girls returned home for the Christmas holidays. Naturally she was the center of new interest to the family; and Nadia asked question after question, her heart athrob with longing for not only all that Laurel was aquick to, but also, for that something big which only each soul, each life, could grasp for itself. The unfed longing ached within her but she gave no sign, though Laurel's untroubled gayety dominated the family interest and conversation. And so it seemed when others were present or when they attended an outside gayety; however quick or little her scholarship was improving she was at least gaining more and more of that "will to win" which places and holds one in the light where the gifts one has can be seen and appreciated. Sunshine and shadow. The laughing brook sparkles more as it ripples in the sunshine than when it smiles and murmurs its blessings in the shade. She could not be one of them on university affairs and was made to feel it, but she would not allow herself to give up to it or appear to notice it. Her tinkling laugh echoed with the others even though she felt a lesser exuberance; and Robert Merrill, at least, whose soul was deepened by burdens and trials, felt all the more the beauty of that laugh. He knew there was a soul strength with the ache beneath it.

It was on the way to their little holiday dance that Oliver said, "Nadia, let us give each other the greatest of gifts now and get married at once. Your mother is a little better, Laurel is home. Let her take your place. Love is knocking at your door; do not lock the door, Nadia. Let us consummate it now."

"Oh, Oliver, how can I just yet? Mother is better but not able to walk about. That will come after awhile. And wouldn't it seem a mockery to have allowed Laurel to go to the university at all if not allowed to stay at least one year?"

"Laurel has the sense, the wisdom, to grasp opportunity when it looks toward her," he said. "But you push it aside. Nadia, self sacrifice never gets anywhere."

"No," she murmured.

"Then don't be one. Look the way you're heading and turn about. It is the one who gets there, who succeeds, that the world admires. Not the one whom everybody can use and then forsake."

"Doesn't that sound very cynical for one no older than you are, Oliver?"

"It's a truth just the same, and you don't need to live long to see it. That is why you don't see many of them."

"Then Self is everything?"

"Oh, very nearly. That's what the world is," he answered.

"Then you are better than your code, Oliver; I know it. The growths of the spirit, the highest that human life has glimpsed, are in God's treasure house for this human life to gather. They may not be sought after much now, but their time will come."

"Long, long after we are gone, if ever," he replied.

"Two thousand years ago One taught it; and long before that others had visioned and sought after it."

"Oh, of course," he added, "it is all beautiful, but it isn't lived, lived much."

Wanting all the pleasure possible, Nadia tried to make and absorb it that evening as she always had, but, with shadows within and without, more effort was needed than should have been, according to the rules of right.

Some souls are born to vibrate to all the overtones of the scale. Even though such ones will enjoy more, they will surely suffer more also. How will it be in that realm of higher vibrations beyond the veil? Will they not find themselves more harmoniously attuned to the higher development? To this smaller number in life Nadia belonged; but because of this she was to suffer more and be denied more on the plane of this sphere of being. Even now the shadow was settling. It could not be touched or seen, but it was there. She was a little thin, a little pale, just a little quieting of the bright spirit as though fear's questioning had touched it and was waiting for the answer.

At this little dance, with mostly the usual associates, she felt for the first time she was not really one of them and in truth had never been; and yet she wanted to be. Even though favored, as she always was, she was almost relieved when it was over, yet knew she must not give up to the feeling or allow it to grow on her.

Afterward in the night, and the next day, she could not help but ponder a bit how she had been warned against the course she was pursuing by two opposites interested in her life; age and self sacrifice; youth and cynical self. Could she act on that warning in the future or would the chains that now bound her tighten and others come? God forbid. But she knew that for the present she must go on. She could not leave her mother yet or bring herself to say to Laurel, "you cannot go back." No, she would not deny her better, higher self, whatever destiny might bring her.

So the wheels rolled on.

The months slipped by with apparently little change, but the visible is always built up from the invisible, the noticeable changes from the unnoticeable.

Poetry and music, rhythmic twins, were both an ineradicable part of her. Her soul, she called them. And they yearned insistently for the growth and the expression that at present, under these family conditions could be given but a small amount of time and energy; but she managed somehow to keep them alive and active. She began her little story in verse, an epic, mind and heart athrill with it, with some lighter efforts thrown in according to her mood. Once she sang as soloist at a special concert, for a modest remuneration, but was forced to refuse an offer, in another town, given by one who had heard and admired her singing on this occasion. She wouldn't leave home even for a short distance and time.

Once when unable to accept an invitation, her father said, "Nadia, we made a mistake letting Laurel go and leaving all this burden on you, didn't we?"

"Oh, I hope not," she answered. "I surmise she is getting full value, for her at least."

"Well I hope she appreciates your part in giving it to her."

"But she doesn't," exclaimed Carl; the talk was at the dining table as usual when the family met together and were apt to express themselves somewhat unrestrainedly.

"Laurel is getting her fun and that is the principal thing. If I were a doctor to cure mother and a fortune getter, Nadia should have her chance too."

"Thank you, Carl, for the good desire that makes one feel better than indifference would. I'll get my chance some way."

"Well, Nadia, get the boys to help you when they can. Make them useful to you."

"Most honorable father, look at your oldest son with admiration for a new accomplishment; he has learned how to wash dishes, at a close pinch, in this house."

"Well, if the girls do that regularly, it won't hurt the boys to do it occasionally," the father said laughingly. "Help each other—would be a good motto for any family."

"But oh, how I hate dishwashing," Janice groaned.

"So does all womankind, I guess, Janice," the mother responded from her wheelchair at the head of the table, "but it has to be done."

"We all dislike the drudgery of our own special line of work," added the father, "but if we look upon it more as we should, like walking to get to a desired goal, it might lose some of its unpleasantness."

"Just the same I'd choose my drudgery in some other line than house work if I could," Nadia said decidedly.

"Ditto," from Janice.

"And yet, my daughters," the father said with solemn feeling, "in all your experiences as you go through life you will find that no other blessing can take the place of home, even though its upkeep may require, among its tasks, dish washing."

"Yes, father, you are right," Nadia quietly responded, "and even in planning for college the thought of leaving home seemed like the breaking of a string on a violin. And you and mother have made home dear to your family, dear to every one of us," she ended with a quiver in her voice.

"You bet they have," broke in Jimmie, "and I wish our home could last forever."

"Right, Jimmie," they all agreed.

"But that is one of the reasons to make it dearer; the changes come and break it up and it becomes but a memory that can never be restored to reality, however intensely we may long for it; while the faults and trials that went with it become as nothing beside its treasure. And also remember, my children all, that it isn't only what we do in life but also how we do it and the spirit in which it is done."

"I feel that truth, father," said Nadia, looking at him with deepened feeling in her eyes, "and it has a greater meaning than first thought might give it."

The telephone rang. It was Oliver asking for Nadia. She came back after their talk and told them, "Oliver has been to Omaha on business, and on the return stopped in Lincoln to see Laurel and the girls. He says they had a big time together. He is coming this evening to tell me about it."

"Well, you needn't help to do the work," said Janice. "Carl can have a chance to help with the dishes again."

"Ah ha! ah ha!" laughed Jimmie.

"Go slow, go slow, Mr. James, or we'll let Janice off, too, and set you at the game," mocked Carl. "No sarcasm, no laughing at another's misfortunes around here. See that you don't come to dish washing for a living sometime, young man. No one knows what's ahead."

"Oh, I'm going to be a sea captain and go back and forth across the ocean."

"Hear him, folks. And he never saw the ocean or a ship. And he isn't going to be a farm captain and command a farm ship on this prairie ocean."

"No siree," emphasized Jimmie, "you bet your life. And I have seen pictures of oceans and ships, and read and read about them. What you make up your mind to be and do you can, can't you, father?"

Thus appealed to, his father answered, "Probably if you try hard enough, James; but you are liable to change your mind ere long and want to be a big captain of business on land; but whatever you choose for your career, either one of you, go at it with determination to succeed. Never any half heartedness and dilly dallying."

"Right, father," agreed Carl, "and I am going to be that big captain of business. I am going to begin now, very soon, as a traveling salesman; learn how to influence people to see as I see, keep watch of affairs and be noticed for my extraordinary ability, and taken in as an influential member of some big concern. I can talk as a salesman even though I wasn't made to talk as a minister."

Oliver didn't realize when talking before the family or alone with Nadia that evening that he was making her feel more and more outside of the questionings, the gains, the pleasures. More as one afar off with the connecting link not yet broken.

"We had such a big time, several of us together, but Laurel was the shine of the crowd. She has the gift of not only having a good time herself but of inoculating others to have one too. And that's a good gift to have in this world, I guess. I don't know when I've laughed so much. We all did and couldn't help it. And laughter is good. I have always loved to hear you laugh, Nadia; you have such a pretty, tinkling laugh with an appealing note in it that catches at something deep inside of one."

"Thank you for the pretty compliment, Oliver."

"Oh, it's not mere compliment. It's truth, and I've heard others say something like that too. Well, those girls may be studying hard, but they manage to squeeze in some fun. I wish you could run down for a change."

"Oh, I'd only be an outsider, Oliver."

"It's a shame."

"It seems so now," she mused quietly, "but who knows? And who knows what is building soul? Not only fun, Oliver."

"But it's life we are living for now, Nadia. Let's get all we can out of it. Give me a song, Nadia. Sing that sweet little love song you wrote yourself. You ought to get that published. What a girl you are! a talent for this and a talent for that. You ought to make a success with them, sure. Laurel is winning with her music down there, too."

"Yes, she says so; and wished I could be there to sing with her for one special affair. We always did good work together."

"You bet you did. Sing that song for me now. It's getting late and I'll have to go soon. Even though the family have retired it will be a good song for them to go to sleep on."

So Nadia found this song of her own composition, words and music, and running her sensitive fingers over the piano keys with the little arpeggio prelude, she sang with her clear toned, tender, heart searching voice.

"If love should die
The stars would lose their light,
The sun forget to shine;
Day would be lost in night;
Despair would crush your heart and mine
If love, if love should die.

If love should die
The birds would hush their songs,
The leaves their murmuring;
The flowers would cease to bloom,
And blight would fall on everything.
If love, if love should die."

"Nadia," said Oliver as though lost in questioning thought, "you make one feel that it does lie at the root of things, love, even if seemingly overshadowed by the lesser. It would be a dreary world if there were no affection one for another. We see its leaven working its way upward among the birds and animals. Yes, I guess you are right; somehow it is the law of life though it may have its beginning in the material world as harmony."

"Why did you ask me to sing that?"

He was slow in answering, "Oh, for some unexplained reason it just took hold of me. Now sing one of your light airy things and then I must go."

She gave him one of her favorites of that type, and then, as he arose to go they went, strangely quiet, to the door.

"How strange and unknown it all is," said Oliver. "We desire and plan and our desires and plans go awry. They all get muddled. It is as though the Fates took delight in stirring and mixing and jumbling without regard to us, their seeming puppets."

"You seem to be in a wandering mood, Oliver."

"Can you wonder?"

"We do seem to be puppets," she answered, "and yet we are free will ones too. Were it not so there would be no meaning in anything."

"Oh, well. We choose in a way, of course, at times, to a certain extent, but not altogether."

"No, Fate and free will choice are fighting always but somehow I believe it is meant for growth. Do you realize it is spring again, Oliver, and the buddings are beginning to thrill in their cradles? The baby leaves are tumbling out of their cribs and spreading their arms out to us to notice their young sweetness. You can feel the wonderful life throb under your feet, in the air about you. The call of the prairies is clear and unmistakable, insistent, telling us over and over of the past that has been and the greater that is yet to be, though both are hidden from our time bound lives. It is a time when we feel that we are something real and that we too will keep on blossoming in new soul growth, and from sphere to sphere."

"Nadia, you dream into or out of these wide sun-burning prairies of ours more than most of us do. Most of us, set down here, seek and get only the material advantages. We'll take a ride to the Platte in a day or two, if you can get away, and see if you can teach me to hear that call of the prairies too."

"It will have to be on Saturday or Sunday, Oliver, for the others to be at home, you know."

"All right, we'll make it next Sunday and make of it a religious service, too."

"That can be easily done with an open and responsive spirit," she said.

But when Sunday came, a negative was given their proposed drive over the calling prairies and to that distinctively strange river, the Platte, where it seems to mock at restraint, at the usual law of running in one channel, and like a wayward wandering child, breaks into numerous runs to come together

again miles farther on. That strangeness once seen, and its
bridges crossed, clings to the fancies of memory and calls
one again with a different call than the brooding prairies that
surround it; though that too is a brooding river, not a hurrying
stream seeking joyously to reach its goal, the Missouri, but a
brooding laggard, looking untroubled on that other traveler of
earth, Time, so fleeting to the human visitors upon its shores.
Always, Nadia had taken that ride with strange pleasure and
when a few years later the autobus drivers made the trip back
and forth, at least two or four times day, she wondered if any
one of them was much responsive to the calls of the river and
prairie, or lost in the inhibiting rush and whirl of business, of
that human river of strife.

On this Sunday, Janice, having one of her headaches,
was unable to take charge of the house affairs, so Nadia could
not leave for the day and phoned Oliver to that effect. They
compromised on an afternoon hour's motor ride outside the city
limits, away from its shut in vision, into the spreading silences,
where the winter wheat dotted with green the otherwise bare
fields, that sure standby of the farmer in his battle against
possible drouth.

As they were winding along a stretch of road, where hilly
elevations dipped in depression to the road side, a flock of black
birds swept down and scattered here and there as though seeking,
it may be, for the seeds that might have been lost in the planting.

"Isn't that an attractive sight?" exclaimed Nadia. "And
yet, because of their color, I always think of them as predatory;
though I am ashamed to say I know little of their habits or
of bird lore in general. Someday I must cure that lack in my
education. But they do add a delightful touch to the scene

when, sometimes in the fall, at migrating season, they light in swarms on the lawn. What an emptiness there would be if all birds were shut out of earth's gifts of life. Oliver, would you believe Nebraska, part of the once supposed American desert, is one of the great bird states, one of their rendezvous?"

"Yes, I have been told so. What do you think I saw last summer? Two oriole's nests in the cemetery trees. Orioles are scarce; maybe they felt that would be the safest place. The inhabitants wouldn't interfere with their nests or young."

"They were wise in that. Oh, the birds, the dear birds! They waken all the raptures of sweet sound at morn and eve about our home all through the summer."

"It is a good thing you enjoy all that tied up as you are now, Nadia."

"But I could be tied up worse. I have some pleasures, Oliver; I have you at times and some of my friends occasionally."

"And the year is passing."

"There are months yet and wonders can happen in that time."

"Will they?"

"I hope and pray."

"But I believe, as Laurel says, you have to go after what you want if you get it. Climb over, ride over the obstacles. Letting them ride over you is surely fatal. How different you and Laurel are, and yet much alike in some ways, too; but not in that. I promised her and the other girls I would run down there soon again. They know how to make things lively."

Another pang of longing swept through Nadia, but she only said, "Yes, happiness seems to be in getting what you want. That is universal."

"And everyone has a right to it."

"As much as another, yes."

"But Fate and your own make up, your own point of view are robbing you. Look out, Nadia."

"I'm going to fight and win somehow, Oliver, but I can't do it by deserting mother yet, or father either, until conditions are a little brighter. They will be, oh surely they will be and, too, we are young and everything before us yet."

"But youth is the time you want most and must make your grab for it."

"I know that. I am thinking, studying for the now and the future. The storm is threatening, hadn't we better run away from it to safety?" asked Nadia.

Already the sunshine and the clouds were fighting for supremacy over the wide horizon toward which they were facing and the wind surging in gusts.

"I guess you were right. When it comes to fighting one of our western storms made destructive by savage winds, it truly is wiser to turn and run for shelter."

So Oliver turned slowly, carefully on the uneven road, while the wind grew and a thunder crash seemed to rock the earth. Here and there in the distance other cars were hurrying.

There is grandeur indescribable in a storm on the great western prairies; and sometimes, strangely, the greatest pageant of thunder claps and lightning flashes and roaring, rushing winds, as though the gods of Valhalla were at savage warfare, will end with a small amount of rainfall, the largest rainfall coming at times with the least fuss and parade. Is that not true also in man's achievements as well as in nature?

And then within a few minutes, on their homeward way, they beheld a strange happening, one that Nadia never forgot, one of Nature's ruthless, illuminated paintings burned on her sight, on her mind's vision, to come before her often, not only during Nature's chaotic strifes but also in life's questionings so unanswerable.

Not out of the angry, lowering, dark spots in the sky, where the thunder and lightning flashes came fitfully, but from a distant clear looking part of the sky, a lightning bolt flashed, like the sudden sword of some unseen angry god, and struck a barn not far from the roadside. They were close enough to feel altogether too near its blinding path.

Then they saw a woman run out of the house, wave her arms to them calling, "Help! help! the horses, the horses!"

The barn was on fire.

"Oh, the poor horses! Can't we help?" asked Nadia.

"We must save them if we can," answered Oliver, and stopped the car at once near the driveway. But even as he stopped, another car had rushed up behind; a man ran by them toward the barn, and they recognized Robert Merrill, who vanished inside where the woman had gone before him.

She was nervously struggling with the fastenings but had not yet loosened the straps that held the rearing horses, smelling fire and danger. Robert jumped in ahead of her, and being quick and sure of motion, soon released one and allowed her to lead it out snorting and rearing, while he hurriedly sprang to the release of the other. He was none too soon; instead of falling sparks there were burning fiery embers that fell on the horse and on him; and the now burning hay was a fiery furnace.

Oliver, and the man who had been Robert's companion, were in the barn now, and they helped to get the unmanageable horse outside.

Nadia and the woman breathed relief and a grateful "Thank God" as Robert followed. The barn was fast being destroyed, but there was no tragedy of life thereby, though but for Robert's quickness and efficiency it was probable that one or both of the horses would have perished. The last horse had a burn on its back and Robert had a burn on his hand. They were uncomfortable but not serious. As the wind was in the opposite direction and rain was now falling, the safety of the house seemed assured. While the other men looked after the horses, quieting and tying them in a safe place, Robert and Nadia went with the woman into the house, to dress with oil and bandage his burned hand. While doing this Nadia said to him, "You were more efficient than the rest of us all put together; but for your quickness I fear the poor horses would have been lost."

He smiled at her with a denial. When she finished the skillful bandaging, he bent his head and kissed her hand, saying, "It does not appear so now but some day I shall marry you, Nadia. Put that in your mental cabinet until called for and made a reality."

She made no reply except with a smile of friendliness. The woman had not heard his remark but had come near again.

Though thanking him appreciatively for saving their horses, she was bemoaning the loss of the barn, saying, "We had reached the point where we were going to pay the last installment on a mortgage and now we will have to go in debt again. We've had so much sickness and misfortune. God struck at us again, and not at our rich, fortunate neighbor just over there."

"Chance, madam; Nature's freak. We must not get it into our heads, whatever our misfortunes, that God strikes at us, or we will never achieve what we desire, or anything else," said Robert. "Let us be thankful your horses, you and your home, survive uninjured, or nearly so."

"Yes, of course that is the better way to look at it; but it is hard just the same, and my husband will feel discouraged when he returns. He only went to one of the neighbor's, and my son and daughter are out with friends. But take my thanks and my husband's with you, sir, and thanks to all of you," she added to the other two men who had stepped inside out of the rain.

"Though the freak of lightning was a misfortune to you, yet our coming at the right moment, another chance happening, was truly a touch of good fortune," answered the man who was Robert's companion. "Give me some oils, fresh lard or Vaseline, and clean cloths, and I will go out and dress the burn on the horse's back. It will pain less and heal sooner."

"Thank you, sir, thank you." Glad of the kind help she handed him the required materials. The rain which proved but a short downpour was already slackening, and soon he and Oliver went out and performed their deed of kindness for the horse.

The woman having phoned to the neighbor's and found her husband was returning, the four felt they could be safely spared to move on their homeward way, as the fire had subsided to not much more than a smouldering heap. He entered the driveway as they were about to leave.

"Too bad, Mr. Lenox," called Oliver, "but though your barn is gone your horses are saved. Thank your wife for calling us as we happened near and thank Mr. Merrill here for the quickest action."

"Hope you will have no more bad luck," Robert added, as their two cars drove on.

V

The days, the weeks slipped by with little change in the Evertson household unless an added lessening of diversions for Nadia. Summer blessed the earth. What if there were touches of drought and the burning kisses of hot winds here and there? What if there were telltale footprints of branding storms sometimes? Summer blossomed and fructified promising harvest again. Human life, and all life, lived and struggled and achieved, through gain and loss, joy and pain; and what it was all for in the great eternal harvest remained, as throughout the past, an unanswered question in the Great Unknown.

It was the time once more for the homecoming of college and university girls.

Then came the lightning bolt. It came even as that one of three months ago, out of the seemingly clear part of Nadia's sky; not a lightning bolt from Nature's elements, but one from the forces of human association; and striking, if not at life itself, yet at life's achieving forces, its foundational roots of affection and loyalty and truth.

A letter came from Laurel when they were looking for her. Nadia opened it, being addressed to her, while the mother waited near to hear the contents.

> "Dear Nadia,
> I ask you to forgive me before I tell you what I ask forgiveness for. Oliver and I are married."

For a moment Nadia read no further. Married! Oliver and Laurel! Those words, that fact, stunned her, held her attention. Not questioning, not analyzing, only as a stunning fact. Then she drove herself to read onward:

> "This may seem a great wrong to you, but is it? You do not love him as I do or you would have married him when he first asked you. We were married on impulse but the impulse must have been building some little time before. Oliver will, I know, feel embarrassed to meet you, though he said you never really said 'yes' to him; that it was taken for granted and that you have not shown any intention of overleaping obstacles to consummate marriage as he feels could and should have been done.
>
> I would feel a greater criticism of myself had I felt you loved him as strongly as I do, but you don't. I ask you again Nadia, dear sister, to forgive me, as I know your large forgiving soul will forgive. And I ask father and mother to forgive me too. I love you all;

but I felt I must marry Oliver or be unhappy. We are going east to New York, for a month's honeymoon trip, before coming back home. My trousseau is slim but that is of small import beside my gain.

Love to all, Laurel."

The waiting, watching mother knew something was wrong, but waited wordless. The two were alone. When Nadia finished reading the letter, she arose from her chair, handed it to her mother saying, "Laurel and Oliver are married. I am going up to my room for a little while. Don't worry about me, mother. It's all right."

In her room Nadia sat down by the window. Oliver and Laurel. Both untrue, disloyal to her. And not because of her unworthiness but too much worthiness. Why! it was something for the evil spirits to laugh at. Probably they were laughing, both the disembodied and the embodied. Very likely the seen and the unseen had them in plenty; for good, what is called good, does not seem to be supreme ruler, over the earth at least.

Laurel and Oliver. A sister for whom she had unselfishly overburdened and denied herself. And her lover, her one time lover of only a short, short time ago. The hurt was searing, searing to her pride, her affections, her hopes and plans for the future, the near future at any rate. Her college year of technical help and Oliver's offered opportunities gone; and she was stranded here, the head of a family, with only a little time for her longed for literary work, which seemed so large a part of her longing for expression.

Love—and then she realized it was not deep love within her that was crying out. No. That was not hurt. That had not met its own, and its own could never have been disloyal. Would it, this one specialized unit of the Great Complex Ideal, Love, meet that other one somewhere in the world, that would awaken it into living fullness of expression and joy? Ah, she knew that one was somewhere waiting if the wheels of Fate did not keep them apart. No. That part of her had not been given to Oliver, a lack she had surmised from the first.

Pride was hurt, but all the more need for pride to face it erect and unrevealing. Opportunity—she must work all the harder for that through her own efforts alone.

Affection?—one must often meet its disloyalties even to the cultivating of forgiveness, so greatly taught on Calvary, giving good and receiving evil?—that too He endured undisillusioned, and many lesser ones than He.

She heard the family come in, one by one, and knew her mother must have told them or let them read the letter. That was a necessary part of the episode, if episode it could be designated. It was lunch time. She must go down, take up her burdens, and appear outwardly undisturbed. That was the part of pride and wisdom, with her own family as well as with outsiders, and the first step toward overcoming.

She arose from her chair and went to the mirror, drove out the pained, drawn look in her face with several purposed smiles following one another, placed Oliver's ring in a little box and laid it away.

"I will return it to him by mail," she said to herself, "but will be forced to wait for that until they return unless I can know for sure their address. It ought to be sent at once, if possible."

That glittering symbol of a weak affection, one of the baubles that real, deep, undying love does not need for showing its expression or riveting its willing chains.

In the room below, where the mother sat in double suffering after reading the letter, more helpless in this new trouble that had flashed down upon them, and in her physical helplessness that had helped to bring it about. One by one the others came home and she knew it was wiser to tell them and have it over, not leaving it for Nadia.

Janice was the first. Astonished, she plumped down in a chair.

"Laurel and Oliver married! And Nadia, what did she say? How mean! And Laurel did this to her own sister."

Then Mr. Evertson came. When told, he looked at his wife wordless for a few minutes, and she saw the deep condemnation in his eyes; and her suffering grew not only for the wronged one but for the wrong doing, the selfishness of the sister; both their children, their own daughters.

"Well, if such disloyalty can be, better it should be at the early stage rather than the late. Less evil or harm would be accomplished. If that is the weakness of Oliver's character, his love and loyalty, better for Nadia to be rid of him and not be tied to, wasted on such unworthiness. I hope she will be able to see it so. Where is she?"

"Up in her room. Give her a few minutes," the mother answered. "She has a strong character and will make the best of it in the best way. I saw that at once."

When Carl and James were told, great were the explosions of condemnation and scorn, of both Laurel and Oliver, till the father stopped them.

"Remember what is done wrath will not undo. And Laurel is one of us even if she has done a wrong. We do not want to cast her off because of it, though she should know she has clouded our good opinion, our trust. And knowing now what Oliver is I should hate to see our fine souled Nadia bound in partnership with him. Laurel is different. She could travel unhurt over life's rougher ways and gather her own."

"You bet she can," exclaimed Carl, "but nevertheless it is Nadia who is getting the hurts, and who always will, because she gives and doesn't go after her own, rough shod."

And then Nadia appeared, composed and smiling, among them, ready to go on with her burdens as usual.

"Don't be troubled about this for me," she said. "I have felt from the first not sure of myself, feeling that I did not care for Oliver in the way I should for marriage, and I guess he knew it, for I so questioned in the beginning. Now I know that I didn't, for I do not feel any great hurt in that part of me, only in loyalty and worldly opportunities. The worldly opportunities I must hope to find some other way. And no unforgiveness from me shall strike at them. Let them prosper."

"Bravo, Nadia!" cried Carl.

"Hurrah!" exclaimed Janice, with Jimmie seconding.

The father and mother nodded approval, and Mr. Evertson said, "Nadia, you are to be both honored and congratulated in the way you meet this."

And even so she realized, intensely and with some heat of inward protest, that this, too, was easy for them; that none of their lives were touched by this added drought, that had fallen on her life—and that she knew was stretching ahead into her future. A drought of opportunity, and who could tell, perhaps a burning up of the fires within her, for, tied as she was with household duties, her own desires found but snatches of time or energy for their uses. Yet she must fight on, fight on, and believe that somehow, sometime, she would win.

A few days after, a short note from Laurel told where they would be, giving their address, for a fortnight. She grasped the opening and sent Oliver's ring to him, with her card, saying only, "Congratulations and good wishes." Could she have seen him, and read his thoughts when he received it, she would have known he was not altogether comfortable and was not likely to be for some time to come. He flushed when he saw the ring, and her card, and thought of the time when he placed it on her finger with eager assurance only a year ago.

"She is to blame," he thought, "and if she had loved me she would have married me then, at once, and not allowed anything to interfere. Laurel hasn't. She loved me and wouldn't let anything, *anything*, stand between her and winning me."

Thus shoving willing unconsciousness, like the large majority of the world, to the higher principles and ideals that are so liable to interfere with and deny Self, for those lesser ones that work in harmony with Self.

Afterward, when they returned, Laurel came alone to see her family. It took Oliver some time before he could come to them and act at ease. And Laurel said to them at once, "Of course Nadia and all of you felt I had proved a cheat, like a cheater at cards, only worse; but I just had to have Oliver, to marry him or be unhappy, maybe all my life; and I just knew, too, that Nadia didn't love him as I did."

No one made any reply whatever and she added, "And Oliver said, Nadia, that you never did really say 'yes.'"

"I think that is quite true, Laurel, as far as the mere word yes. The arrangement was merely understood, if that is of any comfort to either of you. Let it all rest. I am not complaining. Oh, no. I think you two are far better mated; and in truth I find I did not love him. Let us take conditions as they are and say no more."

Friends and acquaintances gave them a round of parties. Nadia went to some of them, forced herself to go, and felt aware, sometimes, of surreptitious glances at her to see how she was taking it when all had supposed that she was the favored one. But she ignored all, laughed and entered into everything as gaily as before, though no one knew or guessed the effort it cost her, facing the unpromising boundaries of her present.

Only once Robert Merrill spoke of it, in a way characteristic of him as well as helpful to her.

"One obstacle out of my way between you and me, Nadia. I don't know how the break came about between you and Oliver, but I felt it ought to come. He is a commonly good fellow, but you are worthy of one with a bigger mind and soul, who will want to be tender and helpful to you as one of his special joys. How is your literary work progressing?"

"Not very fast. I keep doing a little, but time and energy are heavily stressed otherwise."

"Nadia, I wish I had the power now to give you leisure for that, and money, and all other blessings. It will come. Neither of us is free just now, but it will come."

"That desire and the expression of it, Robert, is a help to me, and it strengthens my faith in human good," she replied.

Georgia Harris dared to say, "How did it come about, Nadia? Did Laurel get Oliver away from you or did you go back on him?"

"What does it matter," she answered, "so long as they are happy? I am satisfied."

"Well, I wouldn't be," she added, "for I would have taken him considering him a catch."

Two or three others spoke in a seemingly casual way, saying, "I thought it was you who was going to marry Oliver."

"Appearances don't always tell the truth, you see," she would say, in smiling rejoinder.

But little by little the newness wore off too, as the newness of all changes do, for individuals or even nations, and time, which never stops on this planet, where time and life are bound together, moved on.

VI

As autumn laid her varicolored garments over the earth the
world was stirred to indignation and horror, that swept into
fear, with its menace to civilization, by Germany's ruthless,
devastating war march through bravely, righteously, protesting
Belgium. The interest and the horror grew, as nearly all of
the European Nations and part of Asia were drawn into the
vortex of war. As the menace grew and grew, it became the all
absorbing topic for newspapers and individuals; and even before
America had been drawn into its grip, its poison had spread
over the United States' wide expanse and diversified radical
elements, developing traitors and traitorism requiring quick and
formidable action by the government to nullify their destructive
acts and purposes.

During the period before the U.S. herself was drawn into
this maelstrom, there was but little visible change in the Evertson
family. Carl had finished high school and started at once, with

eagerness, on his planned career of salesmanship, for which he seemed by nature fitted to his desire. The mother was slightly less helpless but unable to take charge or help with the work of the house. With the exception of a little added help from Janice, as she grew older, Nadia was still bound by the family's material needs. She had fewer diversions for the keeping of youth's brightness. She was a little more tired and pale, a little thinner, a little less animated, though as attractive as of yore, except to the most superficial, of which youth is mostly composed, yes, and the adult humanity as well. There was no added opening from the financial standpoint, for that maintained still only the comfortable not the luxurious basis, common expenses growing to keep even with any small added growth of the financial assets.

She went about often with Robert Merrill, and with some others occasionally, and entered in as much as she could with the gayeties and interests of her social crowd; but she felt that on the face of all her own fighting efforts yet she was losing, had lost much of her glad, eager youth and was older in every way than mere years should or could have made her—that in truth she was not as before—one of them.

She persisted with her literary work, though it had to be done always in snatches. That had to have some expression or mean unhappiness to her inner, higher self; and by the time the U.S. entered the maelstrom of war, as young as she was, she had achieved something of value, even though not promising much visible return in finances or even in merited fame.

She had finished her "Epic of the Prairies," a romance of a lost civilization, written in blank verse. It was not beyond criticism. It had faults as most productions have, even some by the great masters, but it also possessed great beauties, sufficient to overbalance its faults, in the judgment of any fair mind open to beauty and truth.

After some depressing failures she had succeeded in finding a publisher for this story in verse which, combined with some short verses had been brought forth as her first book. It was one touch of gladness in her so far denied life. And while its success was not great, very limited, as such books are, even when the author has already won fame, yet it was a beginning and a saving step onward and upward for her struggling hopes. Friends told her she ought to feel glad of that much, when only a small minority of book readers cared for the heights of poetry or of verse romance. She had also had two short stories accepted and moderately remunerated, though others had been refused; and she realized if she became self supporting through her writings it must be in the field of fiction. So she began to plan for a novel, not knowing for sure whether or no she possessed the long and drawn out story telling gift. And here too she made a wise decision for her years and time, to keep within moderate length any novel she might write, whether hers proved extra or only mediocre, saying to herself that only great worth, great value should be drawn out into a big volume.

And a few years after, when mediocre long drawn out "best sellers" filled the market, that opinion and judgment were confirmed for her.

When the Great War with its octopus arms reached out and caught the U.S. in its clutches, this little family in a small western town, like thousands of others, realized, at once, that the life of one of theirs was caught in its destructive grasp, whether to be blotted out or to go on maimed in body and soul, none could foresee but the Great Vision above all vision. Yet they knew it was inevitable; and in the presence, the call of the Great Right, they could not ask it to be otherwise. Carl would have to go.

With aching hearts, and fear beneath the excitement, they tried to keep at least the appearance of an optimistic outlook.

Being intently in favor of the Allied cause, looking upon its victory as the saving of civilization, and ardently loyal to their own country, they could do no less than give their own without protest, except against human evil and aggression that made it necessary, and whatever lesser help was in their power. Of course the hurt and strain would be harder on the father and mother than on brothers and sisters. Nadia could realize that whatever the outcome, her father and mother would be suffering inwardly, however quiet their outward appearance. And so it must have been with many, many others in this dark time.

And also with many as with Robert Merrill. He had just reached the beginning of his prosperity; the dawn of success was brightening the horizon of his life—earned by his own unaided efforts, when the call came, the lightning struck through that brightness and shattered the future, for the time at least. He could probably have obtained exemption, as the only support of his mother and sister, but he neither asked nor desired it. His sister was now ready to go to teaching, and be self supporting. She had chosen and prepared herself for it. He had so proved his capabilities and worth to his business firm that he had been made a member of the firm; and they were contemplating sending him with a big advance in salary to take charge of the firm's affairs in another city. They would have been glad to have him exempted; he had proved of such valuable efficiency. His efficiency of character not only went with him, but ahead of him, and made him an officer in this new field, as capable for the new duties that devolved upon him there.

Before he left, he came to Nadia for an evening of goodbye. That last evening together they felt a closer, more yearning, soul touching, comradeship than had yet been theirs. Both knew it might be their last meeting on this side of the wall of death. More chances of that outcome than its opposite.

During the evening he said to her, "Nadia, I would have loved to have married you and gone over there knowing you were a sure part of me; a comfort in the loneliness and horror; but for the fear that it might end for you with another burden on your hands, another helpless cripple."

"You know, Robert, you loyal hearted one, that fear would not be a deterrent to me," she replied. "You know I am bound here now and, who knows, perhaps for all or most of my life; and I would not want to marry any man, and carrying heavy burdens with me, be unable to give him but a part of my allegiance. I can only hope and hope and hope that conditions will brighten so that I can be free someday to choose a different and more broadening life."

"Broader, Nadia," he exclaimed. "Why, you are broader, wiser, with more knowledge and character now than any other of all our associates; you, with your burdens and home boundaries."

"Thank you, Robert, and as loyal as you are I wouldn't want to think your life was spoiled, narrowed from its happiness because of your loyalty to my denied one."

"If this war had not come, I was near to where I might have married you, providing you were willing, and helped to bear your burdens gladly. The Great Teacher said 'bear ye one another's burdens,' though I know too well only the few follow it. Most try to escape it; and even as your own sisters are doing, too; a lack on their part, even if they are married, as you might have been. Well, let me have your farewell song, Nadia."

And both wondered without speaking it aloud, where they would be, and how they would be when she would sing for him again or he would hear her in private or public.

She sang a tender love song and then an "Ave Maria" with which her tender appealing voice stole into the soul's deep longings and questionings with a touch of faith's soothing for their aching unanswerableness; and all Robert said was, "Go on, go on, Nadia. It hurts but it helps, too."

She did her own choosing and of her own accord chose for the last one her own little song, "If Love Should Die," with an ironical smile, inwardly, as she thought of having sung it for Oliver at his request, when he must have been already on the verge of turning from her because her loving, loyal heart had tied her to her mother's helplessness. But of this she spoke not to Robert.

When she had finished it and the last refrain—"If love, if love should die"—had faded away on the dying arpeggio he said, "Beautiful! beautiful, Nadia! But love can't die. Not while life endures; for as you say, all life would die then too. For love is the very foundation of life. That which sent it forth from the Great Mind and will lead it onward and upward to a realization of Him—the Father, Mother, God. We have weak examples of it truly, but the great undying germ is with us."

"How well you see and feel it with me, Robert," answered Nadia. "But for this individual love among humans—it turns weakly from one to the other sometimes. And what if you would meet and marry someone over there, someone you would love fondly and marry, knowing I was still in the bondage of unkind fate?"

"If that happened—which isn't likely, Nadia—if for some reason that happened, my love for you would not die."

"But it would be dead for me, wouldn't it? And yet I should want you to marry and be happy."

"Would you not be glad to know it was still there in my soul even though it might be given no outward expression?"

"Of course, Robert; but ah! does any one know one's self?"

"I know myself and I know you. And didn't I tell you I was going to marry you some day?"

"But sometimes one's own desires change, as well as conditions," she answered. "And by the time fate might allow it, there may be little left of me to marry."

"Nonsense! now I am going to kiss you goodbye. You will allow and give me that much to cheer me on. We will write each other often, of course, though mine may necessarily be irregular."

So they kissed each other and parted with a lingering handclasp.

"Goodbye, Nadia, and may success, prosperity and all good come to you."

"Goodbye, Robert; God bless and keep you and bring you back safely, to make the world a little better because of your ability, your honor and loyalty to the best."

And then he was gone; and Nadia stood for a long time leaning against the door through which he had gone, perhaps forever, and whose going had brought all the more a seemingly growing, extending desert to surround and engulf her life. And yet again she felt that the depths of that ideal love within her had not been stirred, though she cared much more for Robert than she ever had for Oliver. Probably that ideal was only a false dream. And was her shining road also? Yet all want to be loved and to love; youth, maturity, age; and the difference is only in manner, quality. And she loved Robert for his loyalty to her, and his high character. He had said farewell to the family early in the evening.

And then, later, came that other goodbye, closer, personal to the family, when Carl standing straight, tall, slender, young and fresh, erect as an offering, yet helpless victim to the shameless god of human warfare. Though he lacked two years of the draft age, Carl, seeing some of his friends called, was stirred by the spiritual excitement of the time to offer himself ahead of that age call, and enlist. His people felt they had no right to object, and though with aching fearing hearts, felt a thrilling pride in his courage and loyalty and fearless manhood. And could they have followed him through the testing experiences of that stressful horror they might have found their pride heightened by more than one proof of his courage and character when occasion called upon it. Though months were to be spent in training camp before going to France, yet the goodbye was now. They did not see each other again; and the book of fate was not held open to their gaze to read whether or no they would meet again in this world.

When the mother and father said goodbye to him, it was in one sense worse than death, for they could vision something of what he was going into; the hardship, horror, suffering, perhaps crippling, if not death.

Nadia could see them both age visibly before her eyes. Carl himself, though not hungering for such hideous adventuring, yet knowing he was called and called for the right, carried himself with a brave young manhood, an attractive specimen in his new uniform; and looking at him, Nadia did not so much wonder that some of the young girls and even some older ones were carried away to extremes by the glamor, the excitement or potential heroisms that those uniforms symbolized or prophesied.

Janice, not having finished high school, was one of them. Naturally of an impulsive character, the excitement, the emotions that ruled so strongly caught her at the crucial moment when judgment and common sense were in abeyance; and on the spur of that moment she married one of her boy friends, now surrounded by all of this enticing halo; though they had been for some time warm friends yet in a normal condition the feeling might not have grown to a fondness of sufficient power to have culminated in marriage. Not till the boys were gone, gone on that journey from which some were never to return, and those who did might come back either scarred in body, mind, or both, did Janice make known to her family what she had done. Somewhat frightened at what her avowal might mean to them, yet she could not feel truly sorry for her act. Time, and what it brought, might bring that about, but not yet. And little she realized of life but the little pleasures and disappointments of the present. It made one more worrisome burden for the father and mother just at this time. When she told them, all at once, for she felt it would be easier to have it done with that way, there was silence, a stunned silence for a moment, while an additional drawn pain settled over the father's and mother's faces.

"Oh, Janice, how could you!" breathed Nadia, almost too low to be heard.

"Janice, ha!" broke forth Jimmie. "Mrs. Ralph Eaton! Not Janice Evertson any more. Mrs. Ralph Eaton! how upsetting."

"I am sorry, so young," murmured the mother.

Then the stern but loving father spoke: "You have done wrong in this, Janice. You are too young to realize the responsibilities of marriage; and for that reason, if no other, you should have consulted the judgment and love of your father and mother. You have done apparently an unwise thing; impulse without reason usually is; but what is done is done, and we must strive to make it for the best."

"And must she go and live with the Eatons now?" asked irrepressible Jimmie.

They all looked at Janice, but she burst into tears saying, "No. No. I want to stay here at home with you all, until Ralph comes home anyway."

"Why, of course, Janice," said her father, "and you will both be older and more experienced by that time. We want you to remain here and be with us still."

"I bet you would get more here than at the Eatons', Janice. You didn't marry riches like Laurel did," Jimmie unwisely expressed.

"Nor a fellow who managed to keep on the safe side by getting exemption for some weakness of eyes or foot or such, as Oliver did, either," retorted Janice.

"There, there. We mustn't have any unpleasant flings. They never make any conditions better," remarked the mother in her quiet way.

"Money is a good thing to have but there are other good things to think of besides, and that come first, too, or should," exclaimed Janice.

"Right, Janice," approved the father, "and now have you your marriage certificate?"

"Yes, Ralph gave it to me."

"That is well and you better place it with my papers to keep it safely."

"And I don't want to go on and finish school now, father. It would be a constant embarrassment to me."

"But why? you chose to do this thing. Why be ashamed of it now. No. Would it not be wiser to finish school as long as you can't be with Ralph? The additional bit of education would surely be a help, not a hindrance. And you being under age, I could have the marriage annulled; though under the conditions existing now I am not likely to do so. Ralph is gone and we will let things work out the best they can; but better finish high school, Janice. Only a few months you know. I am sure it is best."

"Well I suppose, as you say it may be best, but don't annul the marriage. Let Ralph keep the knowledge, as a help while he is over there in hell, that there is one more besides his father and mother who cares. I am fond of him and honor him and our Carl. They are giving their lives, perhaps unto death, for their country and the right, while millions of others give nothing, unless a bigger tax, and remain in safety. I stand for the boys who have gone over there and may never come back, not for those who sought or gladly accepted exemption. I had thought of learning stenography and going into an office to earn and help and to have something to start on when Ralph comes back. Well, I will learn that while finishing school."

"That is not a reprehensible idea and purpose, Janice, but a commendable one," the father said.

"Working in an office isn't working in the arts to earn your living, but you can make any work high and honorable if you look upon it so, and are yourself high and honorable," added Janice.

"True, very true and sensible a view, Janice. A good one to follow always," Nadia agreed.

And Nadia, bound to her narrow and seemingly unbroadening way, with her shining road but a blurred, broken, untraceable line leading to its horizon splendors, would have counted it great gain, glad gain, to have changed places with her.

To choose and go out on your personal adventure in your own sail boat, though it took the chance and might founder on an alien shore. All were seeking their own and she was being taken for granted, but there was no outlet. If one chose to answer the call of other's needs, or the call of the spirit, and that must be by the denial of self, then Fate comes and, going before, marks out the paths with merciless austerity. And Nadia was to learn that more and more in the grim future. But, what you are you are. Heredity makes the trend, the sculptor's model; and environment, with her chance workman, carves it with more or less modifications, more beauty or more misshapen touches.

"Oh, human life! Oh, human soul! struggling, suffering, gaining, losing, yet ever upward, onward, only the Great Life of all life, the Great Soul of all souls, knoweth what thou shalt be."

The changed, depleted family circle moved on with the weeks and months, their heart interest, like thousands of others, held in the grip of the news from France, that stricken portion of humanity set upon and held in torture by the evil war gods, hideous reminders of man's still savage state.

Oliver had been exempted for poor eye sight; Frances's husband, as a needed helper in a business having some connection with the government supplies. At such times there is always much doubt with outsiders as to the rightness of some exemptions. Janice was not the only one who asked the best or most. Some will slide out if given the little chance, while some will make more effort to get in.

Those who gained exemption or, who for different reasons escaped or failed the call, did not go free altogether from chilling atmosphere of censure. But financial reward came to many of them afterward; and some of them were successful war profiteers, one of the rank injustices that no righteous government would make possible in such times of national stress and distress.

The honesty of Oliver's eyesight exemption, his money and position, did not prevent him from feeling some of this chilling doubt and censure and hearing a twitting fling at times. But it did not interfere with success or personal aggrandisement, for "Nothing succeeds like success" is a proved expression of common truth. As the Red Cross became one of the specialized activities of the whole country, Oliver and Laurel were among the most efficient, valuable workers.

VII

As the year 1917 moved to 1918 and the months of May and June, when these young Americans were among those swept on into France, that region overflowed with the lava of man's warring greed and lust; fear and heartache stalked with their families by day and laid down by them at night. That terrible year 1918 that, with its added horror and death toll, yet beheld the crippling blow given by America's righteous strokes to that mighty onrushing brute of warfare. While its various shameless offspring have continued to ravage here and there, yet that dinosaur of collective human passions feels, within, the prophecy of its own doom; if not through man's spiritual growth, at least through the striking back upon itself of the scientific powers and inventions that helped to make it so formidable.

This is not a story of the war, only some of its effects on life dramas, so we cannot follow these participants, these characters through their siege of stressful experiences. Probably, if we could we would have more love and honor not only for them, but for nearly all, who were caught in that net of the war fisherman, and proved that they possessed many of the higher human traits. Education, family, do not always tell the story of where these human gold nuggets will be found.

Sometimes, and perhaps often, they will be seen shining brilliantly behind the lack of all these worldly possessions and attainments. The gold mine of the human soul gives forth unexpected radiances as well as disheartening fumes.

During this year, one of the most conspicuous in human history, Nadia's everyday life went on in confined, circumscribed drabness. Only occasionally could she even be free to take part in the Red Cross activities and the little social element of its gatherings. Some of her special associates had married and their interests divided in different directions. Two of the girls—Georgia Harris, was one—had succeeded in gaining the chance to go to France as canteen girls; while someone she knew had been appointed on the amusement list in hospital camps; adventures and experiences many coveted here and there, and the latter of which she too would have been glad to have taken part in, with her singing gift, giving and receiving, for it surely meant both in these endeavors.

The warfare she, herself, was in, was the constant humdrum round and denial of all personal longing and brightness and change.

The battles she fought were in her own soul, where always, throughout life, the greatest battles must be fought by the greatest souls. No thrilling scenes here to relate or picture to the world. The battles fought, and won or lost, in the realm of spirit, are visible only in that realm of the One Great Spirit in which that little striving suffering individual unit dwells.

She and Laurel arranged and produced successfully, as one of their offerings to the Red Cross needs, a musical program that netted a good reward for their efforts.

Nadia struggled to do her best, determined in spite of her submerged life, to show her rare musical gift one of most uncommon worth, though Fate might deny it any wide expression. It was one of her spiritual outlets. As long as she could have a little of that, and her literary hope, she could go on cheerfully in her narrow personal life; and no one guessed her hunger for a broader more brightening one; moreover, no one troubled their own self seeking enough to care or question. As Time's wheels rolled on, even those who naturally would and should have cared, got used to accepting it and her as they were used to their three meals a day.

From three sources in the war zone came letters to this family—Carl, Robert and Ralph—and eagerly they were read and commented on. Each was as different as the characters were different, each reacting to experience from his own individual model. Even these letters were like three tragic dramas, enacted on a stage of lurid volcanic light and reverberating roar, between fearfully pregnant lulls. Their own beings responded with wearing intensity, and a fear ever clutching at them, though they tried to accept and endure with some of the philosophy necessity demanded, knowing their part as onlookers was easy in comparison with the actors.

The wear on the father seemed to be especially visible. He looked drawn. Business matters had been a little more trying but that had more truly diverted some of the otherwise overstressed thought and feeling instead of adding to its strain.

And then, one day late in the year, this father, first to scan the war news and the list of fatalities, looked for the second time at a certain line to be sure he had read aright.

"Missing: Carl Evertson. Company—"

"God!" he breathed, "perhaps death would have been far, far better. I'd know he wasn't suffering at least."

His heart stopped; then went on again; fluttered, quivered, and was still. If there were any more trials and tribulations for him, they were on the other side of the veil that human life has not yet lifted and gazed beyond.

Those trials were not only laid more heavily on the family, but on Nadia especially. They happened to be near at hand and saw him collapse. Knowing he was reading war news, they could make some guess as to the cause of this calamity. They were all in the living room for a few minutes, shortly after breakfast, to get the gist of the news, which was ever in the front of their minds, before beginning their routine of the day's tasks.

Between the three, Nadia, Janice, and James, who was now quite a good sized boy, they managed to get him on the divan; and while James phoned for the doctor, the girls worked over him desperately, in ways the mother suggested, in the hope of restoring him, with the heavy assurance beneath their efforts that he was gone beyond recall.

"Father! father!" Nadia and Janice called fearfully, over and over again, to the father whose heart had never before failed to answer to the call of theirs. There was no returning response; and the invalid wife and mother, who had strived to be helpful even in her helplessness, slid from her chair to the floor beside him, laid her head upon his breast and murmured, "Henry, Henry, my dear, why not I instead? You were so needed yet for our children. Oh, Henry, my dear, my dear, come back to us."

And so the doctor found them. Not yet had they taken time to look at the paper, "Missing: Carl Evertson. Company—"

That was it. That was why they had heard him say, "Perhaps death would have been better." Visions of torturing prison life, or lying badly wounded somewhere without care and kindness, so necessary to suffering human bodies, alone, without friends. Where? Their Carl so full of life and courage and joy and good will. Where?

"His heart was weak," said the Doctor, "and the pictured possibilities that word conjured before him used him as harshly, it may be more shockingly, than the word 'killed' might have done. Had he complained of his heart?"

"A little, just mentioned it a couple of times," Mrs. Evertson answered. "He wasn't one to complain, talk or think much about his own conditions. His thoughts and plans were always for his family. But I realize he wasn't as strong just lately. Of course the thought of Carl's fate and the horrors and sufferings caused by the war was a constantly wearing strain."

"Well, this is one more death the war has caused even though not on its own more intensive battlefield," mused the Doctor. "It takes its victims in many ways here and there outside its own zone. I mourn with you. Mr. Evertson was a good and wise man. The world needs more like him."

As he left the stricken, sobbing family, he heard Jimmie, the youngest, crying out, "Oh, what will I do without my father?"

They had all been good pals with their father and mother, both, though in the different way that each called forth.

There was comradeship of mutual faith and understanding and helpfulness, and James, or Jimmie as he was called by some, though never by father or mother, was coming to the age when that comradeship was most needed.

Janice phoned now to Laurel, and soon she and Oliver were there. In the midst of the stricken family, Oliver was ill at ease, though he cared as much as his type could outside of his very own; and he was relieved to be given something to do when asked, first, to send a telegram to Frances.

For an hour or more the mourning family sat together in their dark grief, before the still form, before the realization came upon them that death meant the undertaker, funeral service, burial out of sight, and then, little by little, to be forgotten— the Fate that comes to the great as well as the small; for only the living, brought into common juxtaposition with the living, are remembered, and even then if dark misfortune should shut them in and shut them out, they were left by the wayside as the savages left their aged ones to die when they could no longer keep up with the march.

So they, too, were forced to take up their burden with hearts heavy with the weight of the knell, the mysterious knell, that universal law has sounded since life came to this whirling earth. Does that same knell sound elsewhere amid the infinite stars? Or does life become then a something so wise and powerful that it bridges knowingly the gulfs from sphere to sphere?

Father was gone beyond recall. Was Carl also? Where is he? What has happened to him? Where is he?

VIII

Captain Robert Merrill sat writing letters in a rest camp back
of the lines. He was writing to Nadia; but even as he wrote,
she seemed to be near, so near he could almost see her; yes, he
could see her there close before him; the small figure, the dainty
spiritual face framed in gold brown hair, the deep blue eyes with
a world of longing in them. Was he visualizing her by his tender
memory thought alone? Or was there some psychic projection
brought to his own psychic vision because of some great need of
hers? Her eyes, her whole presence had that look, sent it forth to
him. She would not ask it in reality, of him or any one, she was
so sensitively proud. But in spirit, that big o'ershadowing part of
us that is veiled, hidden from the coarser, harsher outside world,
we call, oh! how often we call, to the kinder spirits we know
about us, as well as to the Infinite, for the help our proudly
garmented worldly self would not ask. The impression was so
strong he sat there, without writing, feeling, communing with

it, and when it passed no one could have made him believe it only an imaginary conjuring. He knew it was a psychic reality. She was in great trouble and among the most probable tragedies he thought of Carl. If the trouble was with those at home, he was helpless, he could do nothing; but he could make inquiries about Carl, in another part of the war zone, would try to find what had happened to him and give any little aid in his power.

All this he wrote to Nadia, a different letter than he had started with. And this he also added, "There is a girl here, an American girl among our entertainers, whose singing makes me think of yours, though the comparison is greatly in your favor. No one's singing ever appealed to me, to the inner deep of me, as yours did. But I like to hear her and we are also good friends. She is physically larger and stronger, and personally more self assertive, though not disagreeably so. She has given me some pleasant times, but I often wish for you, Nadia, to meet and talk with you. It would seem a touch of heaven in the midst of hell."

No psychic vision of the future touched him here. Did it touch Nadia when she read the letter after its journey across the ocean and continent?

After some persistent efforts Robert found that Carl was lying wounded in a hospital; at first he had been listed among the missing, not having been discovered at once, and some mix up in the identifications. His next letter to Nadia gave this information. Soon after this he received one from her telling of her beloved father's death, and the news about Carl that had helped to cause it. There was his first verification of his psychic visitation from her and the sorrow and trouble which made her soul call to him. Dear, spiritual, unselfish, gifted Nadia, whom life was likely to use harshly because of these very traits, but not if he had the power to choose for her and protect her. Would Fate work with and for him and her?

The news of Carl's safety, even in the hospital, wounded, though seemingly not seriously, was a relief to the family though it could not bring back the lost one, the prisoner of death, to them. Was he too lying in the hospital edges of that other realm, recovering from life's wounds before moving onward to gather the joys beyond?

Too well Nadia realized that life had dealt her another heavy, far reaching blow in the loss of the father, overseer, manager, wage earner, and so in the lessening of their living resources. Now there was no one to earn; they must live on the income from the property alone. It would necessarily mean more economizing.

Fortunately under the conditions, the helpless mother, and Nadia bound to her side, and James still in school, the will her father had made, left all in the mother's charge so long as she lived, to go on in the same way as now, if they chose to do so.

Janice had now finished school and was going into office work as stenographer and typist, but what she earned would of course be saved for beginning her married life with Ralph when he returned. Ralph was bright and sensible enough, apparently, to prosper in time, but they would have to start life with very little.

Frances had come and gone again after the father had been laid to rest. Not much had she to do with their daily lives any more, living afar and with her separated interests to fill her time and thought. Uncles and aunts, too, had come and gone, within a few days.

With several added to the family the time of mourning was, for Nadia and Janice, a time of continued house work with all the other demands; and when they were alone again, so overtired, with relaxation came a heavier heaviness of spirit. Why at mourning time, of death's dark loss, should it always be a time of harder work and anxiety, yet it may be even better so?

After the family had quieted down, alone again, one day, when Nadia and her mother sat together, the former writing to Carl and the latter trying to do a little sewing, this quiet uncomplaining mother spoke some of her heartache to this daughter whose life was being narrowed, shut in for her sake while all the others went free.

"Nadia, dear, I cannot but bemoan and question the justice, righteousness, for your sake, and for that poor boy of mine in France whose wounds we cannot help to heal whatever they may be. Yours, too, is a battle field with wounds that may or may not ever be healed. We cannot know ahead. Don't think I am callous to your needs and desires because I say little."

"Oh, mother dear, I know, and don't you worry," said Nadia looking at her with a tender smile.

But her mother went on, "To question the justice of things in this life is like beating one's head against a stone wall. I should have been taken instead of your father, for I am only a burden now and he was so needed."

"Not a burden, mother dear; don't think it. We are bound, you and I, of course; but we love each other and that lifts one above the word burden. And you are a help in many ways, too, even if it isn't physical help."

"Thank you, Nadia, for your unselfish loyalty. Nevertheless I should have been the one to go first. Why is it I wonder that the helpless so often outlive the useful!"

"But you are as I tell you, mother, useful, oh so useful, in some ways yet. Usefulness isn't all confined to the physical, you know."

Yet her mother went on as though to herself, but thinking aloud, "Yes, it seems so often, so often the helpless outlive the useful ones; even those most pathetically helpless of all. And the "no accounts." They live on to worry others to death. I have known of all kinds, and how much can any of us help our lives and choose? How much? We are the products of our heredity and environment and the reactions to that environment. Pawns, only pawns, upon life's chess board. The Fates, though they be called laws, play the game, and we are pawns. Your nature, played upon by your reading, your admiration of certain characters of history, and the love element, is to give and deny self; while another sees only for self, and gives where self will not be hurt but aggrandized thereby. We question the wherefore of all and get no answer. But I am interfering with your letter. Poor Carl! It is hard to have to send him bad news, tragic news, when he most needs cheer."

"And I am not enjoying the task, mother; would we could all be well again. What a little while it takes sometimes for Fate to enter the door and drive out peace, happiness, health, and often hope, even hope. But we must cling to hope always, mother; never let it go, whether for this world or facing the next."

"Yes, hope is the only spar some poor lives ever have; never realization's ships, so sure and comforting, to journey on to other goals; and while they listen, these denied ones, to the joy and laughter and dancing of those aboard the safety ships, casting only indifferent glances at their own suffering struggles, they only ask the—why—and get no answer; only the shine and laughter of the others through their burning unshed tears. I pray, God, Carl comes home not to face the world a cripple."

"May God grant your prayer, mother dear. Oh, how changed we all are, how changed," murmured Nadia sadly, "and war is so terrible you would think every human being, high or low, developed or undeveloped, would have reached a plane above it. I wonder if this blossoming earth will ever see mankind loving instead of hating each other. Yes, and choosing to live partly for the spiritual as well as the animal."

"It still has a long climb to reach that, Nadia," her mother replied.

And much more they realized this as they read, not only of the horrors, but of the depravity that went with the war.

And this waiting mother and sisters hoped and denied the possibility of Carl forgetting his manhood however dragging the strain and stress. It was pitiful, pitiful, for those tied and strained souls, but so it will be until mankind has realized his spiritual self strongly enough to feel its value so far above the animal that there can be no question, with the individual or the collective, as to which shall rule.

This letter of Nadia's to Carl was sent to the hospital address on the information from Robert's letter, but soon they received a short letter from Carl, written lying in his hospital cot with a badly wounded leg and greatly depressed mental condition. The depression permeating this short letter was such a bleakness, so unnatural to youth even in its misfortunes, and to Carl's own naturally optimistic temperament, that it came into their mental atmosphere as one more dark heavy cloud that they could not dissipate. His soul was wounded as well as his body. The insidious horrors seemed to have crept in and inoculated his inner being, overshadowing, perhaps destroying, its lightness and shine and its qualities of joy. Would it regain all its gladness or was this beautiful part of him gone for this life time?

"If only one of us, his own family could be there to encourage and help him," thought Nadia. "I wish now that Oliver and Laurel had gone. They could have helped some."

Oliver and Laurel had thought seriously of going to France, as part of the Red Cross staff, but at last decided against it because they would have to leave behind them their child, a boy of less than two years at the time they had contemplated going. Probably Georgia Harris would make the effort to visit him and give a bit of cheer. Nadia hoped for this, as slight a help as it might be.

And then, and there, came that cheering star in the midnight sky, the armistice. But even as it sent its glad message over the world, while it lifted above the horizon, that last battle on the groaning soil of France was fought, with its seemingly more hideously useless waste of life. For even while this tocsin of peace was sounded, at the eleventh hour of the eleventh day of the eleventh month, strange coincidence of time, before it was heard down all the lines, scattered skirmishes still wounded and killed; seeming even more needless waste, and touching to more bitterness, it may be, those crippled on this very border line of peace. And though those dead could not come back to express this feeling, it struck a deeper hurt in the hearts of their families.

Yet through the horrors of this most shameless, most uncalled for, most terribly destructive war in the history of man's

destruction of his brother man, in which 700,000 lives were
wiped out and which held devastation and ruin and atrocities
unspeakable, runs that golden thread of heroisms, selflessness,
gentleness, tendernesses, loyalties, one toward another, true
to the truest brotherhood while hanging over the abysses of
agony and death—the hidden blossomings of human character
springing forth in shine and fragrance, as often perchance from
those sprung out of the denials and poverties of life, as from
those bred in its houses and opportunities of culture; and with
a drawing loyal brotherhood between, eliminating all social
caste, that carried on into peace might serve to elevate the whole
rather than lower the plane of life.

Oh, the beauty of it! the stirring, thrilling soul beauty of
these outshinings in the stress of travail. All hail to the evolving
human soul! These sparks divine promising the divine destiny.
To chronicle these tales of human greatness that come to
our ears, from only scattered sources, would fill a volume or
volumes, but that volume would be more than a diamond mine
of human worth to inspire and upbuild.

Some wise great writer should arise and take up the task
as an inspiration and a help to all mankind. It would seem like
some sacred book, a teacher for this world and a promise for the
next.

Oh, what a strange, harsh, painful law of the o'eruling
mind that asks this minute human radiation of Itself to find its
growth, to expand and sparkle into gleaming greatness through
strife and pain, as well as through peace and joy.

This little Nebraska city caught the personal strokes of
these two last battles on the two shores of peace. One came
home crippled for life from one of those last fitful sputterings

of the war, and with that touch of corroding bitterness to carry within him, sensitive over his crippled condition, and as time went on resenting a selfish world's indifference to his handicapped life.

One was killed near that other shore of peace; was struck down on the twenty-third of October and died on the twenty-fourth; and among the instances of the ironies of Fate, of the two comrades who carried him from the field, twin brothers, one was killed outright five minutes afterward.

This one from home, a young officer, was one of their best; respected, honorable, as Nadia and her family well knew; while some of the unworthy were saved, unscathed, to carry on their unworthiness in progeny.

Life does not sift wheat from the chaff, and save the wheat on the fields of war anymore than on the fields of peace, on which are fought the battles of another kind of warfare almost as merciless and more subtly torturous. That seems to be life.

In this battle, too, when the armistice was preparing to spread its wings of peace over the slaughtering fields, the fatality lists included Captain Robert Merrill, seriously wounded. Thus striking once more deep into Nadia's heart, though neither this sad news, nor that of the death of the other home boy came to them for five weeks, probably owing to the more excited and overburdened officialdom.

All the more deeply now did Nadia realize how much he meant to her, his truth and loyalty in the narrow sphere to which her life was bound. Praying for his recovery day by day, she also longed to be one to visit him with cheer and helpfulness. What a blessed joy it must be to those who could do this for those wounded suffering soldiers so far from kindred

and friends who loved them. Great anxiety, for both Carl and
Robert, held her in wearing thrall; and she could only make
slow headway with any mental work. Still she knew she must
persevere. That was the work she wanted to do; and now was
the time she must achieve something, for she realized the time
might come, if her mother died, when she would, at least
partially, be dependent on what she earned for herself, unless
she married; and that, too, was one of the unknown quantities
of the future. She surely hadn't earned much yet but she hoped,
if she could finish her novel soon and find a publisher, that
would pave the way for her and perhaps bring some financial
reward; so she fought hard to hold her heart in subjection
and keep her mind to her task however anxious or worried or
exhausted by other tasks. That is no easy thing to do, under
a combination of trials, but needs soul courage and great self
control.

I X

As the year 1918 drew to its end, the siftings of a letter from
Georgia Harris to her family came to them. She had been to see
Carl Evertson, who would soon be sent home as a convalescent.
He had a lame leg and was one of the cases of shell shock. He
might get over that in time but was not at present the bonhomie
Carl of yore. How this struck home to the family who loved
him. Though they already knew it from his own letter, yet this
emphasized it the more and depressed them more accordingly.
Georgia had also made an effort to see Captain Robert Merrill.
She had only been allowed a few minutes because of his weak
condition. She spoke of a girl singer who had appeared to be
"stuck on him," her slang phrase, and she wondered if she
also followed him to the hospital and retained her noticeable
interest. So for the second time that girl was brought before
Nadia's vision, and, though she would not own to it herself,
with a touch of something like fear. Georgia also said she would

be coming home soon and Henry Sloan would be coming soon, too. They were to be married. She meant to have a bright church wedding, with bridesmaids and all the paraphernalia, as though this year of horror had not been. That was like Georgia, thought Nadia. Either the war had not crushed her desire for worldly glitter or this was a reactionary determination held to grasp and exhibit all possible shine from the good fortune held out to her. And it must have been the stirrings, the lonelinesses of that war zone which awakened or developed these mutual drawing together impulses which had not, mused Nadia, seemed to exist back in the old days before misfortune had swept down and obscured the sunshine along her own path. Those helpful, happy, sunshiny days that now seemed so far away and yet so near.

Oh, beautiful unclouded youth, unclouded hope, that has no prescience of the nearness of its creeping destroyers!

In a very short time after this, a brief letter from Carl told of his home coming on a certain hospital ship, so they watched for the news of that ship, with thought and heart traveling with it. Across that wide area of unfeeling sea, in their mental vision they followed with and pictured it ploughing homeward weighted with pain and cripplings and crushed hopes and disillusionment, and it may be despair, upheld by that soul courage, that heroism, a greatness that adds to one's faith in the potentialities of humanity's future and its onward sweeping survival. Those lives, bodies, minds and souls, had gone "over there" fresh, unbroken, unspoiled, as sacrificial offerings for the victory of right.

So they awaited the home coming of that ship and Carl's return to them. And, alas, what a shock to those who met him

at the train, and to those who waited for him in the home.
Thin and drawn and nervously touchy and irritable and bitter;
wearing glasses now, protecting glasses, over nerve weakened,
inflamed eyes; and using a crutch to aid his lamed leg. What
a transformation. James, now almost a man, with the fresh
wholeness with which Carl had gone away, seemed almost like a
mockery beside him.

Thus are all the ways and days of life filled with
mockeries, incongruities; the fortunate, side by side with the
unfortunate, the blessed and unblessed of destiny walking their
paths of shine or darkness within view of each other, yet so far,
so far apart; but with seldom as in this case, even the slightest
explanatory—why—to all one's protesting questionings.

But his disabilities, his present wreckage, unbeautiful as
all human wreckage is, opened the hearts of the mother and
big souled Nadia to take him in and embrace him with an
atmosphere all tender and protecting. Some there were, and
perhaps many, who had no such hearts to comfort and protect
them.

The shock of his condition was almost as a death stroke
to his mother; and in truth she grew weaker, visibly failed,
under the day by day wearing strain of his bleak conditions,
his melancholy and almost despairing protests. He was in need
of some spurring interest and hope to climb upward again to
something in life of value and achievement.

Janice and James were kind and sympathetic, as were
Laurel and Frances, who came home to see him, though they
were all of a different type that Carl seemed even to resent,
looking upon what he had become and comparing. So all
human wreckage feels though it may be unexpressed. He

seemed to feel, in an unanalyzable way probably, that Nadia was different in the ways that meant his refuge and his help in trouble; and one day when they were standing alone, out of hearing of his mother, he said to her with imploring emphasis, "Nadia, Nadia, don't leave me, don't desert me, ever. If mother should die, don't forsake me. Oh, Nadia! What would become of me?"

"No, Carl dear, I couldn't. Don't worry about that. But you are not always going to be like this. You are going to build up again, be happy and useful in the world; and maybe even your lameness will disappear. Keep up your courage and fight, Carl. Conditions, however dark, are never hopeless until we give up the fight."

"Oh, Nadia! it all looks so dark I can't help going all to pieces even before others, and sometimes hardly care how they take it."

"You will overcome it all, Carl. We will fight on. Even though Fate seems to cast us by the wayside, we will fight Fate all the more determinedly, you and I. Sometimes the most wrecked, burdened, and even forsaken lives, have won and given to the world the greatest greatness. And greatness, Carl, the greatest greatness is in not giving up. Take that into your mind, your soul, abide by and follow it. You are only twenty-two, and I am only twenty-five. Think of it, Carl, only twenty-two, not quite that yet. However black the clouds, there are great chances before us."

"Oh, Nadia, you are so true, so willing to stay by the other fellow."

And even as he said it, out of his need and faith in her, she felt the sweep of destiny enclosing her with its ruthless unprincipledness and could almost hear its mocking Fate's unfeeling laughter in her ears. And when up stairs in her room she murmured to herself, "Poor Carl! Poor me! The darkness is shutting down, down on my shining road. But I am still young; and I still have Robert's love and loyalty. Will I be shorn of that too? How lonely I would be. Oh, Robert, even as Carl says to me, stay by me; do not forsake. And yet, I am too proud to say that to him except in spirit."

How often our burdened, longing souls cry out in the soundless depths of spirit, unanswered and unheard, unless the Great One knoweth and making record thereof weaves some other good and gain out of the denials, in some other realm invisible, unrecognized by the narrow bounds of this.

She had received two short letters from him since confined to the hospital, only a few lines—"Owing to weakness," he said, "but Nadia," he assured her, "if I am as much in your thoughts and desires as you are in mine, we would surely meet often and often, perhaps halfway, or with an over distance to my credit, across the lands and seas of the spirit world. And that there is such a world waiting us, to which so many have been painfully, shockingly sent from here, the reflexes of this war's experiences, in spite of its horrors, have made me feel all the more assured."

How much good his letters always brought her. They never were empty of some value aside from that we are looking for. She also kept in touch with Robert's mother and sister, but apparently there were no special details for either to impart that the other did not know.

When well along into the year 1919, Henry Sloan and Ralph Eaton came home. Georgia Harris had arrived some weeks before and been the interesting center of several gatherings where they listened to her varicolored tales of experience and description, for which she undoubtedly possessed some talent, and made some a little envious of her opportunities.

The coming of Ralph, he and Henry at least physically unharmed, meant the great change for Janice, the real beginning of married life and also leaving the old home. While she was fond of Ralph and willing to go with him, yet the break from home, the dear known, to enter the unknown, hurt deeply all of the family left there in its fold; and she cried, unrestrainedly, even while she tried to laugh in the midst of it. If one's childhood home has been a happy one, with loved memories woven within it, can any future home, though filled with another's love or even open to wider world influences as sometimes is vouchsafed to this one or that one, ever, ever sever the longing love threads of memory binding one to that first home? Never, if that one has a developed soul. It belongs as one's very heartthrobs belong.

Ralph was bright and capable and so was Janice. They were more likely to "get ahead" and make some kind of a success together, perhaps more so than if they had not joined forces. Janice would keep on with her office work for a time, even though Ralph demurred, until they could buy and furnish a home and start that much in safety with the world. So again was the Evertson home despoiled, and Nadia more and more alone, and a little more severed from the outside world of affairs, general and social.

X

In the early part of the year 1919 in a hospital in France a
medical consultation had been held on the case of a young
American officer, Captain Robert Merrill, though unknown
to his mother or sister or sweetheart or friends at home, or
elsewhere. Instead of recovering or showing improvement from
the efforts made to restore him, he seemed to be slowly but
gradually weakening. Weakened originally by loss of blood, he
did not have the power to rebuild.

The decision of that consultation was blood transfusion.
But how could it be carried out? In this region, in this country,
at this time, that was one of the medical treatments hardest
to practice; to find the subject offering fitted, even if willing,
which would not be often, to give the required amount of good
healthy life building blood. And then when this was made
known to the hospital corps, to the surprise of the physicians,

the need, the call was at once answered by a young woman of his own country and race.

Rather slight of build yet rounded, with the pink glow of youth and health in her cheeks, her clear fair skin showing inside as well as outside cleanliness, her brown hair also showing life in its shine and abundance, she seemed a wise offering for the present need. But under examination she showed a slight heart weakness that might, under the loss of blood and the strain, be emphasized. They explained this to her, that it might endanger her life and for a little while lessen her own vitality; but she said with a determination they were not willing to refuse, "As I told you at first, Captain Merrill and I are friends. I am very fond of him. If a little of my blood can save his life or set him on his feet again, surely I am glad, willing, anxious to give it. I ask you to accede to my request at once, without delay. I came to France to give my singing to the soldiers. I have financial resources. My people are well to do. I am his friend."

They looked at her in admiration, assured there was more than friendship here though friendship might prove as true.

"And I ask you," she went on, "not to allow him to know who is doing this, if it can be prevented. Very likely he would refuse it, partly for the reason that he could see no way to repay, to make a return gift. Keep him in ignorance until after it is consummated. You understand of course?" She queried an earnest purposive look out of her dark eyes. They answered affirmatively.

"And please, I am ready now, at your earliest convenience; but let it be as soon as possible."

And it was. When Robert asked who was to give the offering and was told he should know afterward, see and talk with the person, he said, "But, what if it should be someone I would have an antipathy toward, or on a low plane of living. I am a great believer in the subtle, undiscovered properties in the invisible. You may call it foolish; even the blood may carry some of these unknown subtle properties, foreign to the accented health idea of good blood." He smiled at them, and they answered, or the physician who was for the time at the head answered, "You may be right. Science may prove it someday, but at present, with the knowledge we possess, we are not troubled with those, as yet, unborn theories. And be not afraid; even you could not question the worth of the one who is chosen to only help but to save you."

So it was done. Almost immediately he improved, with a ratio greater and more strangely life giving than the former experiences of blood transfusion would have foreseen. Was he right? This American from a land so given to the material quests, in his wild theory? Had this girl, in her fondness for him, projected to him through the mere blood of her body some subtler life gift of the soul also?

When, a few days later she was brought to him, after the nurse had told him they were keeping their promise that he should see the one who gave him the blood offering, he stared—stared—at her and exclaimed, "You!—my God!"

She went forward smiling, a little less pink tinted, a little pale in the lips, caused perhaps more by the strain of the stressful thoughts that had held her than by the loss of blood.

"Yes. I. Have you any objections, Captain? You surely would not deny a gift of friendship, or, my cleanliness of body and soul, therefore quite fit to enrich you with some of my blood." And she laughed with a lilting ripple of amusement.

"I would have refused," he said.

"I thought you might. Therefore, it was better you should not know. See how improved you are even in this short time."

"And you are a little pale."

"Only for a few days, and that was from the strangeness of the adventure."

"How can I repay you?"

"Repay me—shame to speak of it."

But when she was gone it troubled him. Being around her day by day, though he improved in strength, he knew little by little; the premonition was upon him. She was fond, more than fond of him. There was only one way he could repay her, the only payment she would accept. Marriage. He felt she would not reuse it, that she cared for him that much. But—Nadia! his love for years, who had been the pivot of his hopes, his plans, his efforts through denials and attainments.

Nadia. He would not only be losing her but also despoiling her just when all others were despoiling her in her sacrificial life. How he longed to lift her out of it and help her to bear her burdens.

Had black robed, black browed Fate stepped between them with ruthless, heartless decision, companioned by honor, asking the payment of a just debt? In truth his life now belonged to this other one, Ellis Marden. She had saved it, so they told him, doctors and nurses. He was as bound as though the marriage bonds had been signed. But for Nadia he might have been fond enough of Ellis for all that it meant. But Nadia was. And his soul cried out to her. Yet he knew it must be unless she refused him. He would tell her there was another one and she could choose.

After days, and even weeks, of this, in spite of which he continued to gain in health, he spoke when she was making one of her short run in calls, telling him to hurry now not only to walk but run about as she was contemplating going home. They had been strolling together a little and were now sitting outside, somewhat screened from any too intruding eyes.

"Ellis, I am very fond of you. How could I feel otherwise. In truth my life belongs to you. You saved it; and I ask you to marry me; but first I must tell you and let you choose. There is another one back in the home town who, but for her unselfishness in accepting and bearing alone the burdens of others, might have been my wife by now, the only one I have really cared for—except—you." He paused a second or two and then asked, "What do you say, Ellis?"

There was a silence for some moments, a silence pregnant with the Fate, the joy and sorrow of these lives hanging in the balance. Oh, those seconds, long and weighted, when decision hangs upon the verge before it sounds the knell for one, and the joy bells for another. While they lasted, Robert's own heart was like a dumbbell without power to give a quiver of this weighted present for the past or the future; then the silence, so filled with voiceless calls, was broken again by the voice of Ellis, stumbling somewhat, quivering with agitation, feeling its way to him in an almost pleading intensity.

"Robert—I—love you. I suppose you have guessed it long before this moment. You may think I am showing unworthy selfishness toward that other girl, but Robert," she laid her hand and her head down on his arm beside her and said brokenly, "I love you. I cannot give you up. You have become my life, my all. I want to marry you."

"Very well, dear Ellis. So it shall be, and very soon if you are willing without any show, any unnecessary preparations. Even under other circumstances that would have been my desire."

Thus it was planned and soon to be accomplished.

Then Robert took up the task of writing to Nadia. To him it was worse than writing a death letter. Would it be like that to her? Now that the unexpected and inevitable had happened, he feared it would. But there was no outlet. The sword might strike and leave its scar however the future might kindly heal it.

"Oh, Nadia!" he breathed, "would we might have joined our lives before the war and its following Fates could divide us."

XI

Nadia, her weakening mother and Carl's drooping figure, with
its atmosphere of resentful discouragement, sat together in their
desolated, heart heavy home. Each was trying to read, though
Carl's eyes allowed but little reading at one time, but Nadia was
doing more thinking than reading. She had done most of her
thinking, made her literary efforts in the midst of the family
circle with the talk and interruptions consequent thereto. It was
a family trait to do not only their reading but their thinking,
studying, writing, in the midst of the family circle. Some felt
they must go off alone to accomplish any consecutive thinking
or planning; but being creatures of habit, as all are, they would,
alone, have felt that loneness pressing down upon them as a
smothering blanket more than as a thought freedom.

Outside was a glad world happy in the new, ever wonderful
life garments it was spreading forth, untroubled, undisturbed
by whatever individual units within its smiling gaze might be

suffering. Nature is ruthless; it is only the mass that counts; to keep life and its life kingdoms going, going on—to what?—and to all appearances there is no Power watching in tenderness over the individual in vegetable, animal or man world.

Would we could find such a Power, feel it, know it. How unspeakable would be the comfort, the inspiration.

The beauty symphonies of May were ringing forth such glad tidings—for how many thousands or millions of years have they sent forth their raptures to the responsive and unresponsive—one could not help but dream that they were building for spirit however invisible, unknown. Is it only a dream? the shining young, young leaves of the trees, and the grass dear to the soul of man? The later blossoming trees holding the nearness of June still aloof? The glory of form and color and shine, of dancing motion and their silences of sound sweeping with lulling peace between sound's insistence, was as a soothing comfort and a whisper of hope even to souls heavily weighted and caught in the octopus arms of misfortune.

As these three sat together, saying something to each other now and then, the postman came. How little he knows or realizes it as he goes from house to house; the hopes, joys, fulfillments; the fears, failures, despair he carries, as their messenger, to the millions of waiting lives sometimes unconscious of the gift or the cutting blow that is to fall to them.

Among the papers and letters, Nadia found one from France in Robert's handwriting. For some unexplainable reason to herself, other than the feeling that her life had become the target for an unkind Fate, she said nothing of this letter, as yet, preparing to go up to her room and receive its contents alone, which she did within a few minutes. She opened it with a tremble of fear, a premonition. A short time before she had had a dream that seemed possibly premonitory at the time, but she had thrown it off and for the time forgotten it.

She dreamed of being wrecked on a reef on a desert isle, with help in sight, when, far off, but in a sight and hailing distances, she saw Robert sailing by; and as she called confidently to him, feeling sure of his help, a black ship with a black hooded, black robed crew came between them; and when she looked for him again, he was gone. With a hopeless cry for help she had wakened, but it clung about her as a premonition and now she knew it was that, a psychic, subconscious look into the future.

"Dear Nadia:
I know not how to write this letter to you. Can we choose words when we are weighted with suffering and know also that to some extent, great or little, we are hurting the receiver? You remember, while, we were saying goodbye, you said I might possibly find someone over here whom I would marry. And I said if such a thing should happen it would never be through any disloyalty to you. Well, it has happened. Fate has mockingly, and in a strange way, stepped in between us, but as I then said, through no disloyalty on my part toward you. I was weakened through loss of blood from my wounds and did not seem to have the power to recover. You remember I once wrote to you about a girl whose singing reminded me of you. Learning through a

nurse that a blood transfusion was necessary for my recovery, or it might be to even save my life, she offered herself and was the one who gave her blood, unknown to me. The identity of the giver was hidden from me until afterward, at her own request, guessing I would have refused the offering; for, she being financially well to do, I could not repay her with that coin. It weakened her somewhat, too. So you see, in a way she saved my life and it belongs to her. I laid the case before her; you, whom I have loved for years, but for unselfishness toward others might have been my wife before I came over here. Acknowledging your first right, yet she felt she could not give me up. Next to you I am fond of her; and now I must give her what seems to be hers. Do I see it right or wrong? Goodbye, Nadia, dearly beloved, goodbye.

Robert Merrill"

She read it through without a break; staring—staring at those black lines with their blacker meaning as though life had left her. Without a moan, a sob, she gave no sign for a few moments after. Then she broke into wild mocking laughter, threw herself on the bed and smothered her head in the bed clothes that those in the rooms below might not hear, retaining enough thought power to think of that. "Oh, thou devil of Fate that robs and robs my life," she cried; then as suddenly as she had burst into wild laughter, she broke into sobs, dry ones at first, and then with an overflow of tears; all smothered in the bed clothes.

Then, after a while she regained her self control, realizing that never before had she so rampantly given an outlet to her feelings.

Her music, her singing gift that was half of her, could not even be a side issue now. It would have no opportunity outside of home. It was a beautiful thing to lay away or bind to the confines of home, and this too hurt her in her inmost soul. She wondered if heaven's halls resounded to it through some universal forces yet undiscovered even though it be condemned to the soundless realms of this and its apparent waste.

Having regained self control, if not self poise, she bathed her face, redressed her hair, to erase the more visible traces of her break down; and to have more time for this she went about some extra household tasks before returning to the others. She was determined that no one should feel or suspect, so far as she could prevent, that she was in need of any pity or sympathy because of Robert's marriage; and in truth not any one really knew how close was the feeling between them, or of any real tie that bound them. They could only surmise; and as far as she was concerned they should all think she was unconcerned except on the basis of warm friendship, a warm comradeship which can sometimes exist between the sexes in this sex bound world, without any thought or desire of marriage on either side. She felt that even Robert's mother and sister did not know that there was any greater bond between them.

Is it truly greater? For a loyal friendship between sexes is one of life's greatest rareties.

Afterward the news of his marriage came to his people with the added information that they would spend a short time, perhaps a month, with her people in Cincinnati; and then he would take charge of the Chicago office for his home firm, which they were kind enough to still hold open for him. Just how much was said or thought in regard to her place in the drama she never knew. Of course there would be some; and the one who is left in the triangle race cannot entirely escape either notice, sympathy or censure. Now, Robert, too, was out of her personal vista.

––––––––––

The monotony of Nadia's life went on; the round of household drudgery, its ceaseless calls upon energy, planning for all its proceedings however wearied, exhausted, discouraged she might be; counting as blessings her loyal tender love for the mother never known to utter a complaint for self; and the drifting wounded brother in their great need of her; and the questings of her mind for truth, for the flowers of life, of the spirit and the hope of giving her garnerings to the world to help and bless. Would they be received, recognized and responded to? Whether or no, perhaps God would not let them waste, but go on filling the atmosphere of one here and there with the Oxygen of faith and hope and effort and courage. Her novel, a modest sized one, would be launched in the early fall. Would it sail or sink? And with the question she prayed to God always; she so needed the support of a little success, and the financial aid that success might bring to her.

James, having finished high school, was taking a short business course preparatory to going to work in the line he would choose. College or university had not been open to any of them unless they earned their expenses, at least in part, and the boys had chosen to go on without it knowing that many successful and great men had won, without that higher education, a help but not a necessity, even in this age when the poor from all localities, as well as the well-to-do, fill the halls of the universities. They realized, as it had been instilled into them by their parents, and reading, that not higher education but your own natural intelligence, faith, determination, persistence, are the real forces that make for achievement and success in these lives of human endeavor.

James was a kindly, good feeling boy, but showing a tendency to a little wildness that might prove troublesome if circumstances gave it too many opportunities. He needed his father. This, too, worried the mother, though she had faith in the natural good sense and capability of all of her children, though of such various mould. He and Nadia conspired together in the few ways open to them to make little brightening changes for Carl. They would have liked to buy a car, so common now, but they could not afford it with all the heavy expenses, doctor bills, and occasional unexpected outlays.

Nadia would not ask of Oliver and Laurel, nor would she personally have accepted from them, though that was unuttered outside of her own silent thought and feeling. It was just the one effect, the only one, left upon her by their now long ago disloyalty to her, though she would not wish that action of theirs done. They had taken the mother out a few times, but the effect seemed to wear on her, and she seemed satisfied when taken out on the lawn, or for a few blocks now and then, in her wheelchair, by James or herself. They had also taken Carl, but for some unanalysed reason, they did not bring him back apparently cheered, if anything a bit more depressed. They did not give him the right atmosphere.

How strangely different is our effect on one another even right intent be at the wheel; the crew behind counts big as to what realms you touch and how you touch them. Brushing aside her own affairs, Nadia in her efforts, with James's help and her mother's earnest cooperation mentally if not physically, tried in little social ways to stir Carl out of some of his brooding, effortless depression. They invited in some of his old friends and associates for lawn or house parties, but the present comparison between them and him clouded the other good. They were not sensitive and great enough to make his worth and sacrifice a bigger thing in the front of that black background. Also they had small picnics to the park where a miniature ravine, or gully, or draw, variously named by residents old and new, broke the level view of the surroundings, while the cottonwood trees, most often planted in the earlier days, fluttered their glad leaves high against the background of the blue sky, unaware of that opposition which arose in later years against them, that counted not their share in the beautifying and enrichment of the settling of these unbroken prairies. Where soft maples, walnut, birch and others mingled in life's beautifying companionship. As years went on and drought killed, wiped out so many of the trees without effort to replant, it became as a crime, a brand on the people of Nebraska in these despoiled sections. Trees—one of the greatest glories of nature and benefactors of mankind—and has its denial been proved to a certainty—a magnet for rainfall.

Here was a spot within their small city's radius that was pictured with a little dearer emphasis on Nadia's mind as a bright touch of variety. Where the stagnant water, better than no water, gloomed up at them here and there and the birds flitted and sang more plentifully. While not entirely lost in good effects, these idling times brought forth little visible good to the one they were most planned for.

The thought came to Nadia, with a slight breath of irony, for she was human after all, "Would blood transfusion, and that of some interested attractive girl, help Carl?" But she knew, while she questioned it, the thought came as a touch of ironical protest against Fate chasing and enveloping her and not any doubt of Robert's loyalty. While the body's wreckage was the cause, yet it was a medicine, a stimulant for the spirit, that Carl needed. A rousing of courage not to endure so much as to fight and overcome.

XII

The months moved on into symphonic requiems of the
aging year, wonderfully beautiful and filled with the prairie's
whisperings and prophecies above the greater undercurrent of
the invisible and soundless to which the majority of human
beings are blind and deaf. As Nadia's book, one of the more
moderate sized novels and the second child of her soul,
footsteps along her dreamed of shining road, came into the
world, the jazz degeneracy of the following year, in both music
and literature, was already beginning, and within a couple of
years was to become rampant. From now on the finer things
had a struggle to lift their heads above the horizon wherefrom
they beheld the lesser, the houdoo productions moving easily
on to victory by an advance processional acclaim. Nadia did not
even observe this; if she had she would not have dreamed that
its unworthiness could even affect her, her life, her work, in the
slightest degree.

Her mother was glad, glad to see these two offerings from her daughter's soul and life go forth from her outward confines to touch the larger world whether they rode the waves of appreciation and success or foundered on the reefs of the material. The truth and beauty and helpfulness within them would touch and be observed by some souls, here and there, and thus go on their shining way forever.

As the old year 1919 swept into the gulf of time and was lost in the past, so the ever patient ever uncomplaining mother, whose life record was marked only with the tracings of good, slipped into the chasm of unsounded depths and was lost, also, in time's division of the past. Without a murmur of protest, though a fear of the Great Silence was in her unexpressed, and prayers rose to her lips for all her children left behind to the mercy of a pathway she could not scan. How soon each one's special vacancy is bridged over however important and necessary they may have been in the sphere to which they belonged. Loved and honored and missed, by family and friends, another in that great onward sweep of the unseen eternal.

Nadia was again brokenhearted. The mother she had loved with an abiding unfailing love, whose going would mean another unfillable emptiness and an ache, that like her father's could not be cured. How glad she felt now, that she had been true to her, never failing that dear mother, gone from her; and she felt comforted when she remembered what that mother had said to her not long ago: "Nadia dear, I feel like saying to you what John Brandon's mother said to him just before she died, 'Johnnie, I want you buried close beside me, your grave next to mine, so I can feel, that by reaching out my arm, I could touch you, lay my hand in yours,' meant symbolically of course because he had always been kind and thoughtful and helpful. So you have been to me, Nadia, and to us all." Nadia had kissed and thanked her then, and the memory was a comfort now. More alone and feeling more burdened without her in the helpful care of Carl she accepted, because she must, this new desolation.

Aunt Eleanor had come again in time to see her sister pass on and give the last loving words each to each; again a help and comfort to Nadia for the few days she remained, after Frances had once more come and gone back to her own home in Denver. Even Carl liked to have her there with her push and assertiveness that yet gave and asked not but still put more life into the joyless atmosphere.

"You ought to have a rest and change, my dear," she said to Nadia, when they were alone, finishing some household task. "Those others—all—out to do their part and see that you have it. I feel like giving them a hint."

"No, Aunt Eleanor. They wouldn't see how it could be done, and if they can't see it for themselves they can't be made to see it. Though in all righteousness family burdens should be shared by all, as much as possible, yet I would not ask. Of course Janice is at work through the day helping them earn a home."

"I would stay and give you the chance, but just now I don't feel well enough to take the responsibility and do the work of the house; and neither of us, I surmise, feels financially able to hire a maid for any length of time."

"No," Nadia replied, "and I will have far less from now on, for the property will be divided with only a few thousand each, but Jimmie's held in trust of course. I will have a pinching time unless I can succeed with my writing, and I fear my kind would never be 'best sellers.'"

"What an unfairness!" Eleanor exclaimed. "Giving yourself, energies and time for the family and receiving no help."

"Mother was troubled about it," said Nadia, "and we talked it over. She felt I ought to have more, or the use of it, but feared the others wouldn't like it; and I guess I have some of the Luciferian pride for I wouldn't take it. I preferred to fight the harder and pinch more. But she did leave the home to me for as long as I needed it or wanted it. Of course, if free to go by and for myself, I wouldn't want it. If that time should come, which at present is dependent on Carl's recovery and self reliance, and James also, the home, too, shall be sold and divided."

"I see you haven't learned what I learned too late and warned you about from the first. Make others see and share the responsibilities. Few there are in this human world who do not have to be forced. They will all take what they want and can get, and alas, for the one who is the giver. The woman giver can give youth, good looks, ambition, hope, love, marriage, and all personal desires, the last shreds of her life, and no one will care; and in her despoilment and ruin, both the world and friends will think less of her and forsake her. But they will not forsake or forget to smile on and seek the flourishing selfishness. Oh! in such a life one needs the faith of all the sacrificial souls of human history condensed into one spiritual elixir to endure and go on, and also not to learn bitterness."

"Aunt Eleanor, I already see it, and face it, too much alas for soul sweetness; but, though we have inward protests and resentments at times, we are what we are, made for that purpose it must be, for we cannot make ourselves into something lower. The giver's heart responds to the call, the need, even as a magnet. You and I could not have done otherwise than we have."

"I hope your books will be a success and help you. They deserve it as well as you."

"That depends on the readers, you know. The verdict is not with me. My first, for the kind it is, barely lives. This second, being a novel, I hope for to a moderate extent at least. Whether they go on riding the waves and doing their work, or strike on the reefs of materialism and are stranded there, they, too, are a part, indissoluble, ineraceable, of my soul, mind, life; of that shining road I glimpsed and followed, and that lures me onward. Am I that shining road? I know not. I follow, follow the lure, the lure of the spirit."

As she said this her voice and her eyes were deep with longing, and the light of that shining road was in her eyes and face as well as in her soul. Eleanor knew then that only a kinder more propitious Fate, not any words of hers, could give her even a small share of life's rightful joys.

"But, Nadia, you ought to have a rest now or lose all of good looks. No woman can afford that. You have already lost your youthful glowing beauty, of which you possessed more than most. You must have a rest."

Little did she guess how Nadia realized this and how it hurt her, making her draw more and more within herself, but Nadia ignored this in her answer. "Then I must earn it, find it and take it, in spite of our misfortunes. Perhaps I can."

"Well, don't be too long about finding the way. You are allowing yourself to be nailed to the cross by Fate, your own sympathy and too high ideals, and the indifference of others.

Find a way, and I will help you all I can. In spite of his lameness and wreckage, Carl needs a stirring up of his courage, probably, as well as other curatives, before he comes back to self reliance."

Eleanor did not mean this in any hard sense but with kindest intent, and she was not altogether wrong. Courage, determination, are as great factors in overcoming, rebuilding the body as any medical treatments. Faith, according to many witnesses from Christ's time to the present, has accomplished wonders.

"If only his eyes would allow of regular work," said Nadia. "He could find something to do in an office or elsewhere and that would go far toward helping him back to be himself. I am sure that will come in time for his eyes are some better than at first."

Oh, eyes, eyes! blessed gift. Only those who have had and lost know the depths of loss. And great, great are the souls, that denied them from birth, still, with immeasurable courage and persistence, climb the heights of human knowledge and achievement

When Aunt Eleanor was gone again, they settled down to face the other vacancy, that aching emptiness of the beloved presence so helpful in the narrowness of their social lives.

XIII

Two years went by. Two years. It seems a long time to look forward to, even in a life of pleasure or activity in the fields of public achievement. It is longer still to look forward to, or to endure, in the denied, shut in, burdened, depressed, seemingly hopeless lives, however much they hold on to hope.

Carl did not improve, grew worse in fact. More and more in these two years he gave way to bitterness and even hysterical breakdowns. He wished he had not given himself just for what he felt was right and before he could have been forced. One minute he would express himself in this bitter way, and the next go back to his ideal of righteousness. Then again reminding Nadia of two young men of their acquaintance, who had come back unscathed and were leading unworthy lives, he would again give way to saying, "God blesses that kind. And the world smiles on them with indifferent forgetfulness of all the crippled and ruined."

Nadia could not deny the apparent truth of this, in his life and hers, but strove ever after that beautiful spiritual which was being so continually stabbed and clouded in their lives and which looked to them like a fading or lost dream in this world.

She sometimes felt if she should let go of one thread of self control she might do the same. Life with them had become a sickness in need of some drastic curative measures, but what and how? If they only possessed the financial reserve, she felt there were many helpful efforts that could be made for his rebuilding, saving, restoration, and the brightening, easing of her own life. How to gain it? As it was they were pinched much of the time. Their income from property left them was small; living necessities were high, everything being held to war prices. She would not allow what Carl received from the government to be touched for anything but his own personal desires.

But for the help from her literary work she would have been much worse off, though it was but a moderate help. Her novel, too idealistic for the prevailing taste of a more and more growing materialism, was only a moderate success, but she was thankful for that much. During this time she had held herself to her soul's ideals; driven by them she had written a literary drama hoping it would prove acceptable for the stage. The ideals and desire had seethed in her mind, for so long, like a soul striving to be born, that she determined in the face of many needs, and realizing that it could not, because of its idealism, bring in money returns unless accepted for the stage, to give it birth, finish it, make it a world offering whether appreciated or left by the wayside. It would, at the least, touch and help some few souls here and three who were seeking the heights instead of the swamps of being. But alas, so far it had failed of stage production and like her first was liable only to make a bare living.

The theatre was, like music and literature, sliding fast on the downward grade. Idealism, spirituality was passe in all of them; and how could the morals of the public be higher than what they asked for and patronized in these arts, supposed to be, even with their basic principle of amusement, educative, uplifters to the extent at least of the better morals to which humanity is supposed to have risen?

In truth, in the three years following, much of the fiction and drama had become as cesspools inoculating, degenerating the younger generations and adding to the lower tendencies of the supposed stronger mature element. These productions were spoken of as according to "the realities of life!" And she was told directly and indirectly to write "truer to life." They meant that she should choose her heroines or heroes from the sensual ranks; make sex, not in its high but its low sense, the very god of all thought and purpose and action, with money getting and self gratification the boosters, demigods.

That had become the outlook, so that even the harder, so called "freedom" enthusiasts and upholders began to feel there was danger ahead, that civilized humanity was nearing an abyss where even the right to the term civilized might be lost. Not till then did oppositions begin to lift the view.

Looking around on every side, Nadia beheld materialism, selfishness in the joy fields of life gathering its varied blossomings of desire, while she was shut in, bound to a narrow round of household tasks, of pinching economy, of aching hearts, and protest even if inescapable; and only the hidden

other realm of her own mind and soul seeking its outward
expression and recognition to help her to endure.

Then would come to thought, "Ah me! At present poor
Carl is in a worse plight than I. If only I could earn a small
fortune, I could hire some good man to take him to the best
specialists of the east, travel here and there for self forgetful
diversions, and I too could go somewhere for the change,
the interesting new, and a bit of my own rebuilding. That
wherewithal. How can I earn it? How?"

She sometimes felt she would almost like to run away
and be entirely forgotten. At this thought, she said to herself
ironically and with a smile in keeping, "It wouldn't take long
judging by the indifference of most of my old friends, or new,
either. Carl is right. Misfortune cuts you out from the lives and
thoughts of friends almost as completely as death. That you
have sacrificed for the right, or to help others, does not lessen
the surety of your being left alone in your aloneness and no
one troubling to seek or remember. You must be one of these
on active exhibition. Shut in, even the limelight of artistic
achievement will not help in friendship's close circle. How
disillusioned I am becoming," she mused.

All of the family but she and Carl were free to seek
their own interests, desires, pleasures, and they were doing it
according to their ability and opportunity. All possessed cars for
pleasure, not business. They did not need them for that purpose.
She asked nothing, and little was given. All were so interested
in their own affairs. Even James, who was now earning a good
salary in one of the banks, had probably preferred with wisdom
not to go into the Raynor bank, spent his money and leisure in
pleasure seeking without questioning his power to aid Carl or

Nadia though she held him by necessity to his third of household expense. He still was somewhat wild and careless though not to any bad extent. They did not mean, any of them, to be unkind. In their way they had always loved Nadia and Carl, but they accepted the conditions as an everyday fact. And the world only thought less of Nadia and Carl for being where and as they were.

Disillusionment was stalking at Nadia's side and sending sharp thorns into her soul. "How can I earn that needed money? It means thousands and thousands, and seems so hopeless. Poor Carl might be helped back to happiness and usefulness. Ah me! and I am so tired, so tired. How can I ever earn that money? How?" And then Mephistopheles, who follows Disillusionment, stalking his own prey, came and whispered in her ear, "Lay aside your idealism as a dream. It may seem a beautiful one to you, but does it win, in this world, anything but denial, suffering and even desertion? Write for realism, the realism the world wants. Come down from the clouds of spirit to the realities of earth. Make sex and its abuses the all absorbing center. In that way you might, might win success, success."

While these claims and suggestions seemed true to her disillusioned realization, they were horrifying to her real self. Yet they came to her again and again, and at last clung to her so that she found herself wishing she was the kind of being to do something akin to this, and perhaps win the success so needed for Carl and for herself.

Oh, Mephistopheles knows when and how to come to the tired souls of this world. He does not always win to the extent he purposes, but he touches them with his poison so they are never quite the same, whether it prove to their strength or weakness. With every new hurt that came to her personal life, or because of the slight success of her books beside the realistic "best sellers" and the glaring injustices all around her, she could imagine she heard Mephistopheles laughing, laughing. More and more she allowed it to come to her in this manner. Her body and life grew tired of it all and as more and more her soul protested, unheeded by humans, or that something Great we call—God.

"I have tried to give my best and my all," she said to herself. "I have tried to give the world beauty and truth and upliftment. They would rather revel in and gloat over their realism, not knowing that we become like what we look at and desire."

And then she remembered, recalled something of what she had read in an accepted first class magazine lately, by one in responsible position as editor and reviewer, who, in giving reasons why he accepted or refused stories for publication, had said, "I never have, I do not, and please God, I never will accept anything for the Messiah reason."

She may not have remembered it exactly but nearly so. She had been stunned as she read that horrible statement and sentiment, and had waited in vain for any condemnation to follow it from anyone. And now as she recalled it, she heard Mephistopheles's laughter, Ha, ha! ha, ha! ha, ha!

And as she looked at herself with her beauty gone, a beauty once undeniable, and at her narrow drab life, and then at the poor wrecked Carl, also, who loyally, nobly, had given his joyous youth, and to present appearance his life's usefulness and happiness, for the general good and righteousness, she could hear again that mocking laughter, Ha! ha, ha! ha! ha! ha!

Looking back she thought again of Oliver and Laurel, though with neither bitterness or regret, and again sounded the mocking laughter, Ha! ha! ha! ha! ha! ha!

Then she thought of Robert, with whom of course she did not now correspond but who had written appreciative congratulatory messages for each book that she had sent forth and who made it emphatic that she was only proving what he had always known was in her, success; though she felt truly he had not been to blame, yet she could hear it, that laughter, over and over, as though Mephistopheles had taken pleasure in this other, rarer, way of showing her what a fool idealist she was. Ha! ha! ha! ha, ha, ha!

She thought of her singing gift, a true gift, not only in voice but in its power of appeal, she had once hoped to go out into the world with, now pushed into the background so far by her narrow burdened life that it cried out in vain even to her now, too tired, too nerve tired, to give it an outlet. Came the mocking voice, in her soul this time, for her singing had been truly a part of her soul, "Ha, ha! Even that gift you allowed to be thrown away without a struggle because others shirked their share of responsibilities. It needed protection, push, a patron. Because you were not fitted to give these did the God you believe in give it to you, or any of His messengers come forward to see that it was done? This has happened with others but not for you. Ha, ha! ha, ha! ha! ha!"

She thought of her fateful experience in trying to earn this money she was so much in need through a story written for the screen and sent with strong hopes to one of the leading producers. She had respect for the screen's greater possibilities, for what it might and should be. Her story had a unique motif and a few unique scenes. After about three months or less it came back to her with the scenes underscored. About a year after, she had happened, in the effort to amuse Carl, but whose eyes could not bear the strain, to go to see one of this same producer's new pictures. There was the motif and two or three of the scenes taken from her story. It had not occurred to her at the time that there could be any redress. Only a year after that did she learn by carelessly, laughingly, relating the episode, that, had she kept her proofs and the name of the play, she stood a good chance, through the law, of obtaining damages; but even then was deterred, because she could not dare any expense in pushing the case. Again came the laugh, "Ha, ha! ha, ha! Did high purpose and honor help you there? Ha, ha, ha! ha, ha, ha!"

Money, money! what a power it is in this human world where lives, souls, are sold for it, degraded for it, that gleams and beckons as the all desirable lure and possession; and what a help and deliverer it could be for her and Carl, and for many more helpless and tired than they; and the mocking voice emphasized her thoughts.

"Money! the god and the opportunity and the deliverer. Money! with its baser and its higher uses but not forthcoming from your books written for the boundaries of spirit. Ha, ha, ha! ha, ha, ha!"

She thought how many friends she had in the joyous happy times before she took up the cross for others. How indifferently now they left her alone in her aloneness! a few even begrudging her a word of commendation for her books; the grudging spirit, sometimes, of those who cannot toward those who can. She had even heard of some saying of the sex bound novels much talked about and recommended, "I like them because they are so true to life."

Again the mocking "Ha, ha! ha, ha! High mindedness! Spirituality! Friends and they are church members! with that saintly soul for which the world crucified him, held before them as an example, an inspiration, to try to grasp and follow some of that uplifting teaching. Friends! Ha, ha! Friends are only friends when you are flourishing and don't need them. They desert the idealist when shut in and wrecked by misfortune. Even the criminal has his 'pals,' and are they any less true to each other than yours? Ha, ha! Oh, every human life needs friends, friends. Your sacred book told a truth filled with more than one deep meaning in that phrase, 'No man liveth to himself alone.' Ha, ha, ha! ha, ha, ha!"

The cold voice went on once more, "Unless you change, learn to look out for self, marry for marriage's sake, whether you have found that love you crave or not, which is more a dream than a reality, you will find yourself, when you are old, not only forsaken, but also slightly spoken of because you did not follow the herd. Having sacrificed your life for others and having spiritual ideals will not count. That is the height to which civilized humanity has climbed today. Ha, ha! ha! ha, ha, ha!"

Often these thoughts came to her and the mocking laugh followed, till it seemed to her sorry times that she could almost see the leering face behind the faces of those, who through self seeking and hard materialism were having the luxuries and blessings of life.

Already that jeering voice with its mocking reasoning had touched her. She felt it bidding, bidding for her future efforts and quests. And sometimes she wished, oh how she wished, she could make herself over into something more fitted battle with the realism of the world and be one with it. Could she write for the realism, picturing on printed pages the weaknesses, the sensualities, the sins, of human beings rather than, with the veil uplifted from these, to picture their heights, their weaving dreams, their struggles upward above the mere animal, and hopes by which the immortal soul is builded? Could she? She could try. One can usually accomplish a task if one tries hard enough. But oh, how hard, how unnatural it would be for her. Yet she must write something that would sell big, bring in the money she needed. Something with the sex lure. Yes, that was always wanted. Not love, only its baser counterpart. Yes, I will write a novel like that.

"God, oh, God!" she cried, "why is it all as it is? Why should others be rewarded and I punished? I have striven after Thee and after what seemed to me Thy highest. And I seem to have failed, failed in all. I am as an animal at bay, driven, cornered, by the hounds. I have prayed to Thee for help, Oh, God, and to show me the way. I have worked for Thy kingdom. Oh, God! I am so tired, body, mind, and soul. Wherein have I failed? Except toward Self?"

Day by day she thought about it, trying to write something on a different plane. Self was crying out for its own as it had been from the first, crying, crying out, but still it must be crucified. She couldn't harden her heart and desert Carl in his wreckage.

"And there is a way to restore him or help him. I am sure," she thought. "Writing is my only hope now; I must keep on. Yes, I will try that novel and fight to win this time."

Having decided, with a grimness new to her, she went to work at once knowing that time meant much for Carl and herself if their lives were to have the chance for any brighter conditions. Day by day, through the months, she grasped at all the long or short opportunities in the midst of her round of daily tasks and drove herself with an unabated, merciless fever of desire and accomplishment. She wove her plot and its various threads of human thought and struggle, of failure and success, of taking and giving, of climbing desires and falling weakness, and lived through them with her characters, till it seemed to her she had almost become one of them rather than herself. She found in the creations of her own mind, and its realms of imagination, that it is possible for a human life to even grovel in the mud and still get, perchance, the sunny glimpses that cause them to climb the mudbanks to the clean greenery and blossomings beyond them. So she went, in her determination and imaginary wanderings, with them, down from the spiritual heights into the swamps, and up again to the heights. Such is the real human struggle, more or less vivid and varied, with its variations only in comparison with the heights.

She never had failed in the giving of sympathy; and living day by day so intimately with these central characters of her story, instead of being made hard, uncharitable, she took on a wider garment, more outspreading, of understanding with its atmosphere of less chilling condemnation. And yet herself asking a living for the highest, she felt ashamed of the company she was keeping. They stayed with her about her household tasks though she might be too tired to think, were with her while she ate, when she went to sleep, persistent to be given this drama with her and then pass on, either into the fructifying fields of human harvest or the eternal waste of human thought. They walked with her when she went here and there in her efforts to amuse and cheer Carl, side by side with his limping, crutch supported form, drifting in between Carl's talk and hers, never really absent, only in the shade, the background, and yet insistent. Through the noise as well as the silences around her, the noise of talk and laughter when one of James's or Carl's friends was there, the radio alternations of this and that, for Carl had entertained and amused himself by making his own radio set, and had the amplifier to escape wearing the ear pieces. The radio had proved a great help and spur to Carl who had ideas and had already given a valuable suggestion that brought him notice and worthy recognition. These delvings into the radio field, where new gleanings were possible to the imaginative enthusiast, were like a saving medicine to his body as well as his mind.

Through all the days, and for six months she drove, drove herself mercilessly; and though deeply interested to the extent of keeping her own personal longings and sufferings in the background for this need, yet when the novel was finished and in the publisher's hands, gone forth on its adventurous quest, bearing beside its own cargo of unknown influences, her own hopes and prayers for her life's unchained future, it had left her worn and shadowy, more like an almost unrecognizable waif of the radiant creature life and youth had sent forth on the questing journey of the shining road. She was glad for the time being not to have a thought beyond necessity, too tired, body, mind and soul, even to lie out in the quivering friendly sunshine, amid the tender whispering green grasses, under the beautiful loyal friendship of the trees that never wavered in their helpfulness toward all life, and breathing their benedictions wherever nature and man's ruthlessness would allow them to spring forth and live and grow. How she loved them all. God's radiant garments robing this strange whirling earth ball. His beatitudes of visible and soundful beauty.

While she waited the verdict, the outcome, that dead peace settled down upon her, that strange quiescence which comes sometimes while waiting for the fiat over which you have no control, no influence, that comes even on the fields of warfare between barrages.

Strangely now, while hope and fulfillment hung on the verge both for Carl and her own future help, a gift of help came to Carl, and therefore indirectly to her also, brought by the unforeseen and unaccountable happenings of life's moving stream.

An elderly college professor on leave of absence for a year, to write a book which had been a long cherished plan, and seeking now a quiet place, had chosen their small city and had, with his young daughter, taken the picturesque cottage next to them on one side, with only a few feet of green laid between, thus becoming close neighbors in dwelling place, and eventually close neighbors in tastes and social comradeship. At once the young girl and Carl were drawn to each other, partly by a mutual magnetism and partly by her inborn hero worship, looking upon Carl as a hero with the hero's scars who gave himself not only for the right, for his country, but for every individual in it and for her.

After being thrown together a few times, alone or with others, they felt that mutual attraction that happens only occasionally in this world so bound to outward appearances, that attraction of the within more than the without, and they began to, in truth, love each other. Each stirred the deeper chords in the other and they soon loved knowingly, unwaveringly, with a measure not to be weighed by the surrounding or outward conditions.

Strange, strange that personal love, that vital elixir of the soul. What a tide of renewal it can send glowing through mind and body. What an upbuilding and growth it instigates and creates.

As Nadia soon beheld the transformation going on, the rejuvenating, restoring, even budding, creative power of this soul magnetism in Carl, she was not so greatly surprised, having a mind open to and ready to grasp at rare as well as common proofs of the great possibilities of spirit reactions. And she knew, oh she knew, such would it mean to her too, her tired soul, her tired mind, her tired body, spirit quickening spirit, aloneness, incompleteness merged in togetherness, and expansion. So she too, under such a fortunate, freakish gift of Fate, for a freak it would seem to her denied, robbed life, would have caught and regained in that quickening glow some of the freshness and radiance of her youth of which she had been so unfairly, ruthlessly despoiled, and the bloom of which should still in all righteousness be her now visible garment. Why had she been forced down from her height?

She felt she had lowered her banners of the highest, only the highest, only the highest, to the smudgy flags of so called "realism" which, even though true, is only the loud calling procession of the coarser elements even of that sex and material strife which they demanded, while denying their finer God given meaning. Some are born to carry good with them wherever they go; though quiet, unpretending, unassertive they make their presence felt as in sailing boats laden with life's more subtle gifts and perfumes. Professor Baird and Annetta, his young daughter, were of this unacclaimed but always most valuable type.

Professor Baird was of that intellectual cast of countenance that would appeal to the cultured but would not challenge the drawing attention from those given more to the materialistic conquests; and he had the slender form that goes with it. Annetta, slightly built, fresh and fair, was a bundle of quiet enthusiasms. They were not rich in worldly possessions. Few professors are. But they were rich with the ozone atmosphere of mind and spirit and brought helpful companionship to Carl and Nadia and even to pleasure roving James.

Nadia's book was on the market riding the waves, with whirling fortune at the helm, promising to bring her all for which she had created it, and it might be something more she would not want. We never know how far reaching or complex in effect will be our deeds, our words, our thoughts.

"The Crossroads." It stared at her from magazines and newspaper reviews, from store windows, from the glances of those she met on the streets. Her own advance copy had looked at her with unrevealing questioning, but it had won, was winning everywhere; why should she bemoan that little side of her own soul down the bank to pluck the lilies in the mud? Would others think she had ascended instead of descended because it had ridden into power? For such is the wide human world. "According to your success or failure be it unto you," book and author.

"The Crossroads." Often along life's journey we find ourselves at the crossroads and the choice awaiting us. The sign boards tell which way they lead but not always what awaits one on the way or the ultimate goal. Only human experiences of the ages give their gleanings and warnings to help determine the choice, whether it before the spiritual or material, right or wrong, success or failure.

This had been one of Nadia's crossroads. She had not realized it under those words when she chose to write this story, or its name befitting her heroine's straying from the path of conventional virtue. This realization struck her conscious recognition suddenly, and she felt that little ironical laugh inside, akin to Mephisto's. What an eternal battle ground is life confronted continually with the questions of good or evil, right or wrong, expediency or its opposites, great or small in all the ways and days of everyday. Is it so strange we so often choose wrong, make so many mistakes and wish we could go back over the road and choose the other path?

"The Crossroads." Her publishers were more pleased than she. They had found what was proving one of the extraordinary, talked about, widely read, popular "best sellers" of the times. Money, rest, change, something new, new; rest—rest—just a little rest; and the joy ways if only for a short time. Change, newness, brightness. Surely it would be worth it.

"Oh, God!" she cried, "it is what they wanted. Not the high ideals and dreams soaring alone and luring, beckoning like my shining road. They are only acceptable when companioned with the abused realism. Yet, oh, God! I hope I have not in this story touched with one drop of smirch any other soul or my own, but shown that good and evil, though bound together, can never merge, that good can send its quickening rays through chosen evil and light its dark with glimpses of heaven."

Money was to be hers now. That meant so much of what she was in need of. While now Carl was greatly improved, he and Annetta contemplating marriage, hoping his eyes would ere long allow him to go into some line of business again, perhaps his first chosen salesmanship. The limping lameness would probably stay with him through life, but it was lessened, and he could carry herself with more surety and poise. Well, she could help them now. Yes, and herself too. Could go forth and see the world, get new inspirations and make new friends.

She began to plan for this and for that, but was glad many times just to lie down without thinking and let the covering waves of peace sweep over her, cradled for a time in the undertow of nonresistance and forgetfulness which has its temporary virtues in helping one's recovery of strength for the unescapable, reactionary strife.

The weeks slipped by and all was arranged. Aunt Eleanor was there to take care of James and the Professor, with a maid to help her. Annette would not have gone and left her father alone, neither would Nadia, for the Professor had become one of them, giving a certain kind of helpfulness that only he could have given. He and Aunt Eleanor became friends at once, as Nadia was sure would be the case, though apparently such opposites outwardly. He appealed, unconsciously, to the best in women and thus caught and held her with subtle tentacles. Her high mindedness and willingness always to serve would have been recognized by him, even had he not been told before she cares.

"Go wherever you desire and stay as long as you want to," she said to Nadia after she had fitted in with the new friends. "You have earned the right. Stay a year or more. And don't worry about me, my dear; I'll get along splendidly. The Professor and I are already great friends and you can guess what a spurring man friend, even if he is such a quiet unassertive type, can mean of newness to a woman like me, nearing the autumn of life, yet much alive to gather the varicolored autumn leaves stream here and there. And just think of it, Nadia, we have already found, he and I, something that I can do to help him with that great book he is writing. Isn't it almost something to lift one's head in pride over, that I will have had a part in it, that book of solid truth to be given to the world? What if my part is only to hunt out certain material for the technical part, the weaving together? A kind of a secretary I will be of course, but I'll be interested and enjoy it. I'll keep watch over James, too, and look after his safety valve. And when Carl and Annetta return I'll have more still to interest me."

Carl and Annetta were to be married at once, and go on their honeymoon trip to an eastern specialist of high repute, in hope of a cure for his eyes. They were much improved, because of his general improvement, but not strong enough yet to bear the strain of any regular work. Neither he nor Annetta were afraid of the outcome. Faith, as well as courage and love, abided with them; and they beheld a smooth and smiling sea on which they were launching their companion boats together by one of life's greatest ties.

"Dear Annetta!" thought Nadia, "one of the pure pearls of this world. She and her father came as a blessing to us. What an influence for upbuilding forth, growth, or depletion and ruin, our human associations can be for us."

XIV

The age old earth was robed in its autumn garment of October when these changes came to Nadia's life. Time lags not for happiness or unhappiness, and, like nature, cares nothing for the individual, rocking them all in its cradle for a few jolts and then emptying them into the Great Gulf where perchance other jolts and other emptying, passings on, may await them.

Nadia had planned for a stay in New York, taking the journey in divisions, making a stop in the Illinois valley to see some beloved cousins for a day or two, restful characters always; and also to get the inspiration of that region's wonderful autumnal foliage, among Nature's grandest oratorios and rhapsodic symphonies, while the spirits of the calling river followed, followed, ever with its flow. A spot that no responsive beauty loving soul could pass through unnoticed, even on the railway train's swift and noisy passage. Visited once, in her very young girlhood, it had never left her or become a vague memory, but remained as a beautiful dream she had always hoped to visualize and enjoy once more. What an immeasurable, infinite influence nature has had in the making of soul. Yet we accept the year's four divisions of varied wonder, year by year, mingling complaints for their stress with our careless acceptance of their beauties.

Following this plan she had gained even more rest and interchange of affection and inspiration than had been anticipated, and she landed in New York with a glow in her eyes, and in her face, that had been absent for years. Tired as she was, and feeling alien to almost everything and everybody around her, from being so long shut in by the narrow confines of home, yet she had been as eager and alert as a child along this little railway journey to New York. Interested in and studying the faces and manners of her fellow passengers, of the train men and those gathered, and passed by in a few minutes, at the stations at which the train stopped; or the quickly changing pictures of the earth and sky that, calling to her beauty loving soul, vanished to give place to others as she whirled away. Coming up the Hudson too, by the New York Central, that wide, blue satin ribbon of Nature moving quietly toward the deep sea magnet, and brooding over its own age history and purpose, as indifferent to its historic association with man's history as he toiled along its shores, as the silver threads of tinkling water to the ants upon its banks. Do those, who go back and forth along that route, read or eat their time away, with but a careless glance from the car windows? Alas for those who, lost in the drying pan of Self's littleness, can take any of these journeys, often or seldom, and miss the quickening, broadening, coloring effects of mental growth thus gained, and count them as only interludes, necessary gaps between two goals. How many there are—they are legion—who take the journey to and through Europe with but little more gain; and that is the uninteresting kind to whom the most of such opportunities come, and they can give forth but little of value when you try to tap their mental springs. Unlike even the responsive wind bells they fail to tinkle to the zephyrs and the breezes that whisper and murmur around them but only to the winds and storms.

At first Nadia had considered a European trip, longing for all the gain she knew would be open to her gathering and harvesting. She could hardly escape the thought and contemplation when several she knew had gone, or were going.

Thinking it over carefully she decided she wanted her European trip, her Atlantic voyage, in the summer months when she could spend much of her time on deck, in comfort, and get the full benefit of the great ocean's characteristics and reactions on her own mind and body, not in the fall and winter when she was liable to be confined mostly to her own cabin or the public cabins like any hotel on land. And also she wanted to be out to observe and learn and know something of the ship's crew, as well as its passengers, heroes all in their own way on their fighting field of running a ship, with its cargo of hundreds of passengers, against the warriors of the mighty sea, and bringing it safely into port, when some little carelessness or cowardice might send them to destruction, even as with the crew of that land ship, the railroad train.

Now that Fate seemed to be smiling a little in the midst of destructive frowns, she would risk that advantage coming her way later. And, as to that, she could change her mind and go at some time after a stay and acquaintance with New York. What might be before her she could not guess; something for her growth, yes, for her happiness—who could tell? And even as she wondered, up rose before her thoughts those first three books of hers, and the last, with the bar between them. She was the instrument through which had come the springtime with its freshness, and the summer with the fungus forming at its roots.

Well, she would be able to see now, as well as read about some of man's big accomplishments; she would meet new people, some of the big minds in the various fields of endeavor; though they were not confined to New York, yet here was one of the centering points and she would surely touch the stirring atmosphere of some of them. She knew she was to meet some of the literary lights, the creative and business elements of that art. A dinner was already planned for her with some of these, at which she was to be the guest of honor. She had known of that before leaving home. And probably she would meet some musical people, and artists, and big business heads, with their helpers and followers, without whom they would be as waste in a desert, each one a link in the chain of endeavor and fulfillment, the smaller as necessary as the greater.

She meant to revel in opera and drama till her appetite was satisfied and in need of other condiments. Can we be filled to repletion with all the joys of the spirit as well as the senses? It may be so, for change seems to be not only a desire and necessity and destiny of life here on this small sphere, but of the universe. Change, one of the laws of life inescapable, and of all that is.

Coming into this immense area of modern cliff dwellers with its rush and whirr, its streets like canyon walls, its utter indifference to the individual unit, Nadia was filled with a lost feeling, a loneliness worse, in its soulless dwindling of one's being into insignificance, of helpless nothingness, than the overwhelmingness of the great open spaces, or the unfeeling desert. Without money in these great cities of men, money—that self driving vehicle that will carry one here and there wearing the crown and waving the scepter which man has given to it—money. How much safer, and richer, to be in a cottage by the green fields and the trees and the singing birds, with maybe a laughing brook, where you can feel the Presence of God and hear the Voice. Are they heard and felt as often and forcefully in the pens of city walls when even God's glories of sky are seen but through the rifts of those canyon streets?

Often this feeling came over her on the streets, walking or riding, at the opera or the theatre, or sitting alone in her apartment. She always drew a breath of relief, of freedom, when riding near the park, or Riverside drive and gazing out over the great harbor where that thrilling statue of liberty calls to all races of mankind with its dreams and promises. There are fulfillments and shipwrecks, but the masses knoweth not and careth not. Only the few could live in daily sight of any of these breathing places. The hunger of their souls could not be filled with their oxygen of life.

Like a spiritual oasis in the world's greatest material setting stands that historic landmark of man's lonely soul quest and aspiration, sacred Old Trinity, heading like a "Peace be still" that short famous "Wall Street" now the greatest money center and controller of the world, wearing the outward garment of the lamb, but hiding within the claws and jaws of the lion whose clutches and teeth are felt by rich and poor. At its head, sacred

Old Trinity, an undying, unfailing touch of help to many of
the striving, the tired, the lonely, the shipwrecked, the hopeless,
traveling by on their rough thorny paths of life toward the
unknown sea. St. John the Divine and St. Patrick's cathedral,
later dedications to the soul quest, though religion is not as
powerful as it should be in the world today, massive reminders
to the money seeking, the self seeking, the material bound army
surging around them, made their own differing calls to her
inner self as upon her outer senses. And the great universities,
beautiful in their setting and their meaning. How she wished
she might have been a student in their halls of learning.
No need to go to Europe for attainment of knowledge and
proficiency. The United States was rich in its centers of learning,
through all its length and breadth, the jewel pride of every state,
and she had missed it. But she had dwelt with the masters and
tried to draw in what she could of the atmosphere, the mental
exhalations of these projections of knowledge. How little most
of those fortunate in being given these opportunities realized the
worth of the gift and what its lack would have denied them in
the making of their careers. And in spite of these many centers
of learning and the wonderful discoveries and advancements of
science, at what an ebb are the arts and morals; fiction, drama,
music, the screen. Where is the remedy? A second coming of
Christ? Surely in the coming of some stirring spiritual leader—a
renaissance of the spirit.

New York! vast human maelstrom. Would she be glad or
sorry she had come? She, but as a grain of sand in the whirlpool.
A few might notice her today and forget her tomorrow. That
is the ceaseless ever moving tide of existence. The greatest
in the hall of fame and usefulness, even when living, are

unremembered, noticed but little more, are passed by in the whirling sweep.

Nadia had taken an apartment for the freedom and self reliance it would mean. In truth there was no other sensible thing to do. An intimate, dear friend of her younger days, married and living in the city, and with whom she had kept in friendly correspondence, had engaged the apartment from some of her own friends spending a few months in Europe. Then a girl, taking a course in the university and working her way, had been engaged as maid. But, being this kind of character, she became in part companion as well as maid to Nadia. Not wishing to be entirely alone, and also desirous of being freed from household duties during this vacation rest, this was a most acceptable and fortuitous arrangement. Sitting there alone, Nadia was not impressed that she liked to be alone. She never had been, from birth to now. Most of her writing had been done in the midst of the family circle with all its distractions; and she was not sure but it may have become, through habit, a necessary background. No, she was not one of these beings sufficient unto one's self. She could never become a willing recluse. To be driven into that would require destructive, black misfortunes indeed. But she was not, she told herself, in New York to accomplish much writing. That would only be a side accompaniment. She was here for some of the pleasures and broadenings she had been denied.

Her friend Julia, Mrs. Herbert Kent, had been with her on some of these little jaunts about the city those first few days and now she said to this friend, "I've now seen some of the outside of New York. I am ready to see some of the inside."

"You mean?"

"Personal contact with some of its moving spirits, to dip into its inner atmosphere and draw into my own some of its quickening radiations."

"It seems to me you have done extremely well without it, Nadia," her friend smiled at her.

"Thank you, Julia. But one can always grow and achieve more by friction with other personalities, by keeping an open mind and an open heart. It isn't healthy to sit down in a corner and depend on reading contacts alone."

"No. You are right; I realize fully in my own experience. Since Herbert's growing business success I have grown and broadened by being thrown more with others, and having better opportunities among them on that give and take basis success brings. Herbert and I want you to meet the head of his firm; Big Business, you know. While the big head, that all the employees and even associates are a little afraid of, yet he is not narrowed and dried by business and money. He is a lover of the arts, and you will be liable to meet him among those circles. You know, Herbert is also a lover of the arts and he casually spoke about you one day, during an interval's digression from business talk, and he seemed so much interested that Herbert invited him to dinner to meet you. I am going to be honest with you, Nadia. This interest and dinner association might react in a tiny bit more of interest in Herbert's work, though he has been fair, most fair to Herbert. We have no complaint."

"I will be glad to meet him in the way you suggest. A business genius. One of the moving minds of the times. You will be doing me a favor of course, Julia."

"Possibly you will meet him tonight. They all feel it to their advantage to know him. But with us it will be a smaller, less pretentious affair, and therefore a closer touch."

"What a good and helpful friend you are proving to me, Julia, like the warmth of our early days. What a rough barren road we would travel without a friend, a real friend, not the imitation, somewhere along the way. Julia dear, through these years of shut in forsakenness your letters and the thought of you soothed my wounded spirit as an ointment for the hurt loneliness. Take that into your heart as one drop in the chalice of your life's spiritual nectar."

"In that speech alone, Nadia dear, you gladden me immeasurably."

"You haven't asked, but I am going to tell you, how it happens that I am to be entertained and receive my first introduction to New Yorkers, mostly its literary element, by one of its society women, whom I had not known. Before I left home I received a letter from her, a beautiful letter that touched my heart. Those recognitions are not given one every day, by strangers, or acquaintances, or friends, unless to some specially favored one. She told me she loved my verse, had loved it from the first without influence from this novel that had given me more worldly fame, that some of it was a special help to her vision, her love, her life, that she would rather be their author, and poor, than dwelling as she was in material luxury. Perhaps a strange expression coming from one listed as a society woman given to seeking the material pleasures of life.

"Well, Julia, that stirred my soul, for my verse is dearest to me though it has brought far less success than the fiction. I understand it is so with some of the best known writers. She also said that having met my publisher, and spoken of my work and of me, she had learned I was coming to New York and not only wanted to meet me, but to be granted the privilege of giving a dinner in my honor and to introduce me to some of the other literary lights of the east. The way she expressed her love for my verse made it seem almost sacred to me, Julia, so much so that I have not spoken of it before to any one, content in myself to know I had so touched and helped one more life as I had longed to do. She has called upon me here, of course, and proved to be an attractive, interesting person to meet. Alas! I wish I could have gone among them looking more flourishing and attractive, too."

"Yes, Nadia dear, but you have something very appealing about you that will win always."

"That is consoling, but the world in general requires that you have the flourishing shell no matter how great or poor the character or being inhabiting it."

"I know, but you will win with some nevertheless, and a good long rest and a little happiness will soon bring back that flourishing appearance again. Now, coming down to woman's everyday matters, what are you going to wear tonight?"

This was to be the gathering, the dinner planned for her introduction to New York at which she was to be the special honored guest.

"Ought we not," Julia asked, "to have visited the modiste and bought a radiant gown for this introductory occasion?"

"Julia, I know too well how much dress counts, but I also felt it would count even more just now not to wear myself out and look more tired over the dress question, which has ever been a wearing task rather than a pleasure to me. I like pretty clothes, and want them as much as other women, but I want simplicity in them too, not the elaboration that makes your clothes you, but you your clothes. I am, this time, going to wear a simple black velvet dress touched with a brightness to soothe my tiredness. I am not worrying over it. Perhaps later we will go and take a modest dip into that expensive vortex of woman's affairs."

That evening, excitement tinted her cheeks in Nature's own inimitable way. She needed no rouge, for the time; and not having learned that art of the day, so prevalently noticeable in even the very young school girls, she would not have known how to apply it artistically.

"I may be driven to it," she laughed to herself. "Most everyone can be driven, more or less, to things distasteful if the pressure is hard enough."

When she entered among them on the arm of her host, Mr. Rogers, she at once felt an undefined stir, and in her extreme sensitiveness and shyness, traits which were not visible on the surface, thought at once it might mean disappointment in a probably preconceived picturing of how she might or ought to look. While this sensitive interpretation of hers had some bearing on the truth, it was not to that extent of adverse criticism; and her quick ears caught some words of comment by those, who of course thought she was out of hearing, and would have been except for that extreme alertness of all her senses and faculties to the new and undecided calls upon them.

"While she is little and frail looking yet she has a look of distinction."

"Yes, and as though she could rise to the occasion if necessary."

"It isn't always the big imposing figures that can do that," another voice had added.

And then Nadia was in the midst of the other guests, unaware afterward which ones of those she met at whose doors she could lay these unconsciously overheard comments. Though coming from a shut in life she carried herself with poise and graciousness, without any personal assertiveness, and with an expression of friendly interest that would have won the most begrudging spirits.

Surprisingly to herself, she proved equal to the calls made upon her in the conversation during the dinner, as well as before and after it was served. Necessity and pride stirred her powers and she came through with flying colors whether answering remarks addressed to her or vouchsafing her own share on the subjects at hand.

She liked the faces of those around her and the face of Mr. Ward, her publisher, whose approval she somehow felt she was winning. She liked his face more and more, though she had come prepossessed in his favor, for he had proved loyal to her books and to her, something more than a mere money seeker, and so making his service of greater worth to his own and future times. It was a brilliant gathering of brilliant people, not so many as to leave any one of them less noticed than another. Each had her or his special gifts of personality. One would expect to find that.

"They were all so alive, alive," thought Nadia, "and my aliveness has crept into a corner; what I have is sporadic, a stimulant of the occasion; I am so tired. Will it come back and stay under these stimuli, I wonder?"

There were three successful novelists, two women and one man. Success doesn't lay her laurels and riches at the feet of either sex to the exclusion of the other, but gives with an equal lavishness to both. Each had seen his or her work pictured on the screen. What matter, sometimes, to its defacement when money rolled in? Nadia knew that hers had been favorably considered and was waiting the contract settlement which would place her, as they were, beyond money worries. There was the special screen producer, who radiated material success as well as energy, sitting opposite at the dinner; and not far from him an acknowledged best scenario writer who cooperated with him. She was push and get-thereism, though in a well mannered way. There, facing her too, was an accepted masculine poet of the day, an exponent of the free verse order. Nadia wondered if he thought hers of little value because his had so far won more than hers. Probably because of his garden of success he looked on hers as only peeking through the fence at his, but sometimes the flowering vines trying to climb the fence have more beauty and meaning, more of God in them, than those coarser stronger swelling plants within the garden. But because he had pleased the reviewers, or some of them whose verdict was accepted, he had "gotten there" more than she. Strange are the freaks, the quirks of taste and so called success. For herself she cared more for her verse and drama than for her novel that had brought her success, even if she could have felt her spiritual heights had not been lowered or dimmed in the latter. She felt that novels, though most desired, are not the highest literary expression.

Next to her on one side sat a dramatist whose two plays had won in the city and over the country. He looked rather dramatic himself and his talk was somewhat studied for the stage of the social drama they were now playing. Not far away, on the other side, sat another successful playwright of the year, a rather young attractive woman. And the least heard, yet the most noticeable personage among them all, saying less but saying it to the point with culled meaning, was the man whom her hostess, Mrs. Rogers, had introduced to her as Mr. Raymond Dexter; and then she had added, "Neither a novelist or dramatist of the accepted terms, but a creator, a star actor in the world wide drama 'big business' and a wise generous patron of the arts. It is a privilege to know him, Miss Evertson, and a greater privilege to call him friend."

Nadia, smiling up at him, for he towered and loomed above her, said, "What a beautiful introduction for you, Mr. Dexter. I hope both privileges will be mine. The kind of an actor and drama I am most afraid of and feel the smallest with. The strength of mind, the bravery, the initiative, needed for 'big business'—it seems to me like sailing alone into the ice regions of the Polar Seas. Brave souls, they, who do that."

"Braver far than I would claim to be, Miss Evertson, and surely in knowing you, author of 'Epic of the Prairies' and your beautiful drama, as well as 'The Crossroads,' the greater privilege is mine."

"Now you have won my loyal friendship at once, Mr. Dexter, by appreciating those former children of my soul, dearer to me than the last."

Then they were interrupted and drawn apart. Glancing now and then at his strong, rather austere face, with the piercing, yet softly glowing eyes, among those other interesting faces, Nadia heard from somewhere in the invisible etherie atmosphere between them, a whisper: "You have met the one."

And to him, too, the whisperings came: "You have found her, but the 'bar sinister' is between you."

Yet neither knew nor guessed how close, how recognizable, that whispering voice had been to the other. Neither did it touch the border line of consciousness, so closely guarded by the senses, of any of those others meeting for a friendly exchange of greetings, before passing on their way along the narrow shore of time.

They touched, in their converse, on several subjects, elaborating on none, as customary at dinners. They talked of the present outlook for the arts and the moral principles with their lowering trend of the last few years, which was ominous for the future unless a something of the spirit arose to stem and turn the tide.

Some would have laid the whole original blame on the war, as war always leaves a blackening trail behind it for years. One asserted and others agreed, that the almost universal ownership of the automobile, and the moving pictures leading only to pleasure seeking, had been the great deteriorating first causes with the war. None of them wanted to lay the brand on the line of their own endeavor.

The screen producer would not allow his art to bear more than its share of censure, and spoke up in defense. "That the photo play has done its part in the general degeneracy, I'll not deny; but the creators, authors, must come first for that is where we get our material to work with. The same with the theatre, the stage. It has its cesspools. And the idealist, even the commonly decent life, could, by right, cry shame at all our doors. Before we produce, some of your various authors have created."

How true it was, and was anyone here free from some taint of guilt? Big business looked serene. Self interest may have not led in that direction for him. Nadia felt the blood creeping a little hotter into her flushed cheeks, and heard again Mephistopheles, "Ha, ha, ha! ha, ha, ha!" behind her. And she could see that spectre pass around the table touching and laughing, "Ha, ha, ha! ha, ha, ha!" more or less at each one, holding, waving the almighty dollar as he went. And he did not pass by Mr. Dexter. Nadia wondered how much they all looked upon her as guilty. She felt that she had at least touched the border line. In her disillusionment and need she had purposed coming down from her cloud heights to the frontiers of harsh reality, but if anything of hers should have a lowering influence she would feel ashamed to have it known afterward where her grave was; and yet, only since she had stepped down a little bit from her cloud heights to touch the everyday realities, had success, real success of the outward, visible kind come to her. Only a step down. Was she sorry? Not yet, but maybe she would be, and it hurt in her soul.

Feeling that she must put in a suggestion, too, she said, "Does it not appear that some of the newspapers, with their editions of illustrations, deserve some of the blame, as well as the pictures of the screen and stage novels?"

"Oh, Miss Evertson, I was hoping I was being passed by unchallenged this time," spoke up a newspaper man laughingly. "I fear I cannot deny your allegation and am constrained to count myself, for my line of productions, in with the rest of the mob."

"And what is the remedy when everything or nearly everything, is inoculated with the virus? What is the remedy that will bring the spiritual awakening?" asked Nadia.

"Yes, what is the remedy?" repeated Mr. Dexter. "You contaminate one part and you contaminate all. Jazz music, jazz dancing, both no better than the savages, and jazz morals, are all only a part of the general deterioration. The remedy must be Religion, the key always to the gates of the spiritual. Miss Evertson is right; it is a spiritual awakening that is needed. I may be looked upon as one in the hard money line of business, but I believe in Religion as a vital necessity to the world, its growth and upliftment."

"None of us will deny, altogether, the truth of what you claim, Mr. Dexter," said Mr. Rogers, "but the apparent variance, seeming opposition, of science and religion has been a factor in lessening religious faith."

"Seeming opposition, yes," replied Mr. Dexter, "and science has gone forward on its grand way, with wonderful progress, through all this materialism and spiritual depression, unhindered. I know and love science and the scientists who give their lives in denial of worldly pleasures. It is our ignorance, lack of understanding that sees science and religion in opposition. They are coming closer and closer together and will some day be seen as two branches of the same Spiritual Universal Truth."

"Mr. Dexter has voiced my view," spoke Nadia, looking toward him with glowing eyes.

"And the view of all of us as to its possible truth. Is it not so, my friends?" They all concurred.

"Yes, in theory," one answered.

"But at present," Mr. Ward went on, "the unthinking masses must cling to Religion in spite of science or cast it away as an obsolete dream, as some of both the thinkers and non thinkers have done."

"I prefer clinging to Religion," added one of the women novelists, while the free verse poet agreed.

Again Nadia spoke in her quiet unassertive way: "To me, faith is everything. The basis of growth, the spur to achievement, and the strength for endurance. It is the priceless gift of all gifts, for if everything else is taken away, and faith remains, one may still endure and strive and look forward. Looking forward, ever looking forward. That is life. Faith! Give us faith through all our ignorance and striving."

A generous applause and concurrence followed this earnest expression, and Mr. Dexter added, "So your books would show, Miss Evertson."

This subject had been carried farther than is customary on such occasions, but all had been eager participants and listeners, a very harmoniously mixed, though varied element. And then, in the general murmur of voices, Mrs. Rogers arose and said, "Let us give a toast to this last speaker, our new and honored guest. To the books of worth she has given us and to the hope for more to come. To Miss Evertson's past and future."

Others followed with expressions of appreciation. The feeling of all seemed to be kindly and true, and her own personality pleased them, throwing its outward visible aura about the inward light expressed in her books. Nadia arose and thanked them in a few well chosen words and wishes for good fortune to them all.

During the remainder of their evening, for a little while in the drawing room, they listened to a couple of selections by a dreamy faced violinist, with a shiny helmet of hair hanging low over his forehead, who played the best music with the touch and soul of the true artist. Also to an extremely good ballad singer whose artistry Nadia greatly enjoyed. But there was a hurt in listening to the singer, a deep hurt she could not help but feel with intensity and futile protest against the fateful shrouding of her own gift of song which, having been born and given to her, should by all righteousness have been allowed freedom of expression to a wide radius with consequent exultation, and exaltation, that would have come to both her and her listeners. Beautiful singing, that holds within it the soul appeal expressed, projected by soul, voice, personality, all submerged into one wonderful unit of expression, is a combination which few possess. There are varying qualities of artists in every field of art, and few, ah few there are who are gifted with the fullness of gifts, the whole artistic ensemble. That wholeness would have been Nadia's possession had destiny allowed wide fullness of its expression.

When most of the guests had made their personal adieus to her and were making lingering farewells on their way out, Mr. Dexter came, and waiting for the opportunity to speak unheard, said, "Miss Evertson, I am looking forward with great interest and pleasure to meeting you soon again at Mr. and Mrs. Kent's—friends of yours I understand. Looking forward, as you so earnestly and truly expressed a little while ago."

"Then it was you Julia spoke of today, without mentioning the name, as one they wanted me to meet. I am glad to have the pleasurable and, I am sure, valuable acquaintance extended."

Sleep was long in coming to Nadia that night. Her stimulated nerves did not easily tone down to quiet when so long denied their natural, rightful tonic of interesting social gatherings. She had enjoyed it more than anticipation promised. Though her hostess had, throughout much of the conversation,

somewhat effaced herself through courtesy in bringing forward
the personalities of her guests, her glowing social dominance,
a rare gift in itself, with the warm, friendly courtesies extended
to herself, made Nadia feel another wave of blessed human
response sweep over her as she settled down in her bed to rest.
Pleased as she was with each one of the group she met—she
was not out with the spirit of criticism—each one with a special
gift of message and personality, yet that one, Mr. Dexter, stood
in the foreground of her picturings and thoughts. Why? What
meeting ground for tarrying exchange of thought and feeling
could there be between a little, tired, partially faded suburban
specimen of femininity like her, just stepped into one form
of success, and this dominating worldly success, all masculine
personality, even though interested in her line of endeavor?

Yet she felt that some invisible thread held and was
drawing them together. One of the ruling financiers, he did not
possess that money hard face worn by some of the financiers she
knew. Money hard face. You see them sometimes, though the
wearer is probably altogether unaware of its visible possession.
She wondered if he was thinking of her before he slept and how
deep the thoughts went. It was pleasant to think she was to
meet him again in a day or two, and in closer association. At last
she fell asleep on the soft pillows of these new joys and because
of their comforting feeling and their prophecies of others to
come. A looking forward always even when dropped suddenly
into flowering gardens of ease and fragrance. She wakened to
the greeting of a shaft of sunlight falling on her through a rift in
the curtains as though calling to her, "Get up," and she jumped
lightly to the floor, at once alert to what the new calling brilliant
day might hold for her. How could anybody, happy or unhappy,

at ease or overburdened, ever talk of, or feel like "killing time," read trashy literature for that purpose; yet she had heard it said many times. With her time was always too short and fleeting. One can always find something beautiful and helpful to read, something beautiful and helpful to think about in this world of beauty mingled with its hardships and pain.

One who lived where even the dead leaf could be seen lying on the ground, on the still green grass where they have fallen from the disrobing trees, need not waste time without some good thought gathering. But how many nature starved souls might there be, in this immense cave dwelling place of mankind, who seldom had a glimpse of a living or a dead leaf, or of the dear green grass, Nature's glowing carpet of living beauty, of which one can never tire but loves with an increasing and ever welcome love, a friend that ever blesses and fails not. Poor defrauded souls yet unalive to the depth of their denial would perhaps even choose to go on living in these caves, shut out from these life blessings.

"Where shall I go today?" she asked herself. "What shall I see? I can't sit down within these walls yet, and write the make believes, or think about my realities past, present or future. No. They can wait. I want to see, see for a time; then sit down and let its worth, whatever it may be, work within me and germinate if it will."

Before she had fully formulated her plan for the day and evening, Julia phoned saying, "Our little dinner for you and Mr. Dexter is to be tomorrow evening; and Nadia, he has invited us and our friend, you, for the opera afterward. He will have a box; he always does; so look your very best. Don't get tired beforehand."

"I met him last evening and took quite a liking to him," Nadia answered.

"I thought you would do both. That accounts for the opera invitation just received," Julia laughed back. "You are getting on finely every way, aren't you? Well, you deserve it. We will have a fine time. Don't be late. Come early and be prepared to sing, and to shine, which I know you can do."

So Nadia put away all thought of the opera for this day, because it was the same opera, though she meant to drink at that musical stream to her heart's content while here at its fountain head. Once she had longed and hoped to be one of its star performers; and even though it had never grown beyond the stage of unfledged desire it remained as a part of her aching unfulfilled—as she had said once to Robert who had loved her voice—to spring forth into full glory of expression, it may be, in some other sphere of life farther on, a little farther on, who knows? Who can deny or affirm? But someday science will open the doors to the light that as yet only the spirit glimpses.

She spent this day and the next in ramblings near at hand, going to one of the theaters where a much lauded play was having a big run and bringing in satisfactory box receipts. She wanted to study these success dramas from the stage standpoint, wondering, in her reading of them, sometimes, wherein their great stage effects lay. The author of this one she had met at Mrs. Rogers's dinner.

How quickly success, fame, brought one to the front of life's stage, though usually but for a little while, unless success is founded on the true mastership of his art.

She felt this was not. Though it possessed some worthy qualities it catered too much to the cheaper trends of the day.

But she wanted to see and know the what and the why of each kind; and she wondered if, while enriching her, it might also contaminate her. Had she not already stepped down to obtain her success? And then arose before her the biblical advice of Paul, "Whatsoever things are true, whatsoever things are honorable, whatsoever things are just, whatsoever things are pure, whatsoever things are lovely, whatsoever things are of good report, if there be any virtue, and if there be any praise, think on these things."

She wondered how many thought of these bible commands, of those who chose and enjoyed the vulgar stage and screen productions and such fiction and picturings. Pleasure followed too closely leads into the mire to shake the thirst for change, and is too all content to stay there.

That evening at the Kents' was one of the happiest of her life. Why? Because he and she, brought together at last, as the magnet of souls meant them to be, were in close companionship, sponsored by mutual friends, and knowing, each to each, looking into each other's eyes, and soul into soul, that they were meant for the completion of each other. No need for a lavish outward expression to make it known. Though we live in a world of outward expressions yet our great, real, unmeasured life is within, in the, to this world, invisible and soundless. But it has its varied language projected from the silent unseen realm to this when the great magnet calls.

Julia and Herbert were cultured people, and good conversationalists, doing their part to the fullest in keeping the talk lively and interesting. When Nadia's rippling laugh broke forth after some of the humorous anecdotes the two men related, they drove each other on to more, just for that musical happy sounding laughter. Nadia had always had that rippling happy laugh, even in the midst of her darknesses. It was almost an inseparable part of her in friendly association, and was one other element of attraction among strangers, as well as friends, when it happened to come tinkling to their ears. That laugh seemed to sharpen their memories to recall funny things forgotten; so before they realized they were all so lost in the running pleasure, the opera ahead of them was almost forgotten and they had to make haste at the last. Julia said, "Nadia and I used to laugh sometimes for the mere pleasure and joy of laughing, and now hearing her again, I have the same feeling come back to me. But now, if we are going to the opera our time is short."

"I am not surprised, Mrs. Kent," said Mr. Dexter. "Miss Evertson ought to be paid a large salary to go among the gloomy ones of earth to cheer them with her laugh."

"I suppose that is to be taken as a compliment," Nadia replied smilingly, "but it would lose its spontaneity then and therefore its catching quality."

"Alas, yes," he answered as they moved toward the drawing room, or living room, of these apartment homes. "Joy is something that cannot be studied and practiced for a special purpose without losing its greatest quickening life force."

The women hastened to get ready, and the same maid that served at the dinner helped them with their wraps, for this was a small household run on a modest basis. Butler, valet, extra maids, belonged to riches not the merely well to do on a salary. As they hurried down the stairs again to the waiting men in the hall, Julia murmured low to Nadia, "You have a lovely evening wrap. Where did you get it? Not back home surely."

"Don't think New York is the only place where women dress finely, Julia. But I made this myself. I knew what I wanted and made it up to date, but to suit my desires. You know I always had to sew, to make ends meet, though I hated it. Sometimes it is convenient to know how."

"Well, it looks Parisian."

In truth with that wrap she would have looked distinctively well dressed whatever the costume worn beneath it. When Mr. Dexter took charge of Nadia, with a manner of gently protective appropriation, Herbert and Julia gave each other an understanding and pleased look, guessing that the tie between these two had at once gone deeper than mere liking. What his personal private affairs were they did not know, and of course any closer relations between him and Nadia must bring that forth. He was often seen with a widowed sister who lived with him. He had a young daughter in some girl's school, who at intervals came to visit him, to whom he seemed devoted.

They made a noticeable group even in the Metropolitan, that house where the star members of society, of riches, of fame, are on exhibit from year to year, with the change in personnel that the years must invariably bring. How many of those who have sat in these boxes, or been the stars on its stage, admired and envied, are now hidden in the grave and what may lie beyond, or in the obscurity of private life? Such are the ruthless garnerings of time. Nadia had longed for all of this and now she was here a part of it but not, alas, as the star singer she had once visioned, however vague the vision had been. She was steeped, lost in the music, the glamorous surroundings, her little draught of success and the presence of him beside her whom Fate had at last brought to her. Was it to fulfill or to mock? To give her the sight and fragrance of that flower of human companionship, to enjoy its bloom and fruition, or to take it away and leave an unfillable emptiness for the rest of her life? What did the mocking Fates hold for her?

Yet in the midst of these enjoyments she pushed these thoughts aside, would not let them abide near. She and he, content, both of them, to be together and knowing that the other knew. How sweetly peaceful, yet how deeply quivering, because of its richness, the content. Many in the audience wondered who she was. Only the few she had met at Mrs. Rogers's, who sat in her box next to Mr. Dexter's, and who had greeted them with a smiling graciousness, knew. Yet whisperings, here and there, informed many others before the evening was over and afterward.

How, mentally, she sang and acted with those radiant stars, following notes and phrases in their various expressions and meanings readily because she knew the opera and had studied it. Afterward on the way home, in Mr. Dexter's car, it was something of a relief to express how beautiful it all was to her music loving soul always; and then she added, "I suppose it is very presumptuous of me to dare to differ with successful artists in any of their renderings or interpretations, but it seems to me that passage"—she named it—"should have had more exaltation. But 'tis much easier to criticise than to do. I'd like to be one of, or rather with them, for we all want to be and remain our individual selves and be and do what we long to be and do."

"I must hear you sing soon, Miss Evertson," Mr. Dexter said.

"Of course you must, for Nadia was a born singer and didn't have to be made one," exclaimed Julia.

"We are in the same boat then, Mr. Dexter, I haven't heard her either," added Mr. Kent.

"Oh, don't expect much," Nadia said deprecatingly. "Among all the great artists you hear I would seem like a little sprig of heliotrope, not even the modest violet, among flaming roses. Only a little home singer, with all the dreams that came and looked at me passed by, sailed away into the clouds of 'The Might Have Been,' where more ghosts dwell in their eternal requiem than ever have peopled the 'Has Been' or 'What Is.'"

"Ugh! Nadia! the way you put that gives me the shivers, even though it is a tragic truth with all of us," Julia declared.

"A truth most aptly expressed," both men affirmed.

"We must insist on her singing for us, nevertheless, Mr. Dexter," Herbert Kent added as the car stopped in front of Nadia's apartment building.

Without even an insistent gesture to Herbert, Mr. Dexter went with Nadia to her door, saw the door opened, and both ready to say their goodnight, after she had expressed her thanks for his part in the evening's pleasure; then he said, "May I call on you Sunday afternoon? Will you sing for me? I am looking forward to it. And then go with me for a ride, oh, anywhere, through the park or along the riverside?"

"It will all be a pleasure to me that I too will look forward to, Mr. Dexter."

"At three o'clock then and we will dine at the Ritz."

Afterward, in preparing for bed, she felt such a happiness sweeping through her whole being, her movements were slow, very slow, because of the nerve tingling excitement her self control was a long time in quieting. What a wonderful evening she had had after all these years of "shut in" and denial. It held something of almost every good. "Oh, if it would only last," she said to herself. "If it would only last and merge as it should into more and more good." And at last she went to sleep on those waves of happiness closing, closing her around with gratifications of the present and promises of the future.

The next day she spent, in a desultory way, in a preliminary search for something to wear. She didn't want much; didn't want to be bothered with too many clothes, just enough, no more. Julia would want to be with her for the decision on a new gown. She enjoyed that task like most women, but to Nadia it was a necessary task, not a pleasant one, even with the required money at hand. This day which, in her present state of nerve excitement, seemed but an interval between two wonderful chords, she beheld a tragedy, or the tragical end of a tragedy, that never quite left her memory and left its mark, its perhaps unrecognized influence, on her afterward.

She saw an elderly woman, rather forlorn looking in person and dress, stop, while crossing a street, to grab and push another woman out of the clutches of car wheels that were about to catch and crush her. In so doing she was caught herself and broken beneath the wheels. Though a stranger, yet unlike the careless strangers around who gave a glance at the tragic figure and went on, Nadia could not go on. That crushed figure with its look of aloneness called to her so that she went in the ambulance with it as though she had been a companion; and soon afterwards she saw the last of that life breathed out, without a struggle, on a hospital cot, almost as soon as placed there. When asked if she had any relatives or friends to be sent for, she answered slowly, "Relatives—yes; but don't bother them. I am alone—and no—one—cares. I gave my life—from youngest girlhood—for others. Since I am old—the way they look upon me—I don't—want their help. God—you have done this well. It is a fitting end. I gave my life—in loving service—hardship. Love? I—longed—for it. I have not seen any. Love!"

Then after a few minutes she lifted her hand, waved it feebly above, with her eyes looking upward as though the blue sky was looking down on her, and spoke the last words she was to utter on this side of that visible sky, saying, "I am so tired. So tired. Write it across the heavens in letters of flame. I—am—so—tired."

That was the end. Nadia was crying, and even the long hardened nurses had moist eyes. But the cities, and even the small towns, have no time in their rush, rush, and Self, Self, to give to the unfortunate individual left by the wayside, whether the one that is caught and stranded be one who gave for the kingdom of Christ or God, or one, who, forgetting that call, followed the lure of Self. If caught and stranded and broken, the crowd, the separate units, move on with less than the most careless thought, not even to be recalled as a shadow again.

"And in a little while," thought Nadia, "I too might have been in her condition, forsaken and alone. Whatever you do, whatever you are, it seems a ruthless Fate cares not. Or a ruthless humanity either. And when one turns from, denies Self to give one's life for those whom others have brought into the world, is she not far greater than the mere physical mother, which even the lowest can be and are? But is she so looked upon? No. Because spirituality appeals only to the few but materiality to all.

Handing over to the head officials the money the anticipated new garment would have cost, for the righteous disposal of that silent form so that its end would not be the dissecting table, last but unknown sacrifice, she went sadly home. Nadia went back to the apartment and tried to read herself into a more peaceful mental condition knowing the world was full of such sadness and tragedy beyond her control.

She was glad to go to bed early that night and sleep the reviving sleep of forgetfulness. And she had been comforted, too, to know that Edith, the student maid, was close at hand, and to talk with her a little.

XV

The next morning, Sunday, after this tragic episode, even though looking happily towards the afternoon's blissful associations, she felt a more than usual strong desire to go to church and pray where others were gathered in His name. To kneel in some sacred precinct and pray not only for her own and herself, but for the forsaken, the suffering, the unhappy, too often the sacrifice for human selfishness; that selfishness with which the earth is darkly branded after almost two thousand years under the banner of Christ's teaching, "Love your neighbor as yourself," "Do unto others as ye would that they should do unto you." That poor wreck of yesterday, forsaken, dying alone, after giving unto others to the last. Oh, ironies that lie between human teachings and human living.

She went over to the Old Trinity, one of the beloved prayer places of many who feel the stir of the unworldly beneath their worldly, a hallowed shrine from which you must gather some touch of comfort, of strength, of restored faith. Kneeling there she felt the influences of those long ago brave and suffering lives mingling with those of today as a call to continue courage and faith, and her day seemed the better for it. When, glancing over the morning paper, she saw staring at her in a headline an account of yesterday's tragedy, and its pathetic ending, with the philanthropic part taken in it by a famous novelist of the day, how glad she was that her name was not given. They had sensed her right to privacy there. But the story was beautifully, appealingly told, and could not fail to touch and enlarge the good in the hearts of its Sunday morning readers.

Three o'clock. It hung before her and him like the golden sunrise of a glad day, and when it rang its arrival and they were together again, the doings of the world were lost to them, merged for the time in their own completeness, their own joy, as complex notes that travel through discords and minors into a beautiful, wonderful chord.

"I am waiting with great anticipation to hear you sing," he said after a little talk, and he settled down in an easy chair ready to forget everything else.

"So you are not content to know me through my books, like most of the world?"

"I want to touch and sound all the strings of your beautiful instrument of life as is made possible to me."

"Thank you, but I am somewhat afraid, Mr. Dexter, when you have heard all the best artists. I will sing, however, and hope you will forget the greater ones."

She went to the piano—she had rented one, at once, on entering the apartment, feeling too much the deprivation of its denial—stood for a moment's consideration of her different songs and chose some little old ballads of past composers of finer type than most of the songs of today. "Were my songs with wings provided" by Hahn.

> "My songs would fly all unaided
> Toward thy garden at a word
> Were my songs with wings provided
> Like to a bird.
> Unto the air so confided
> Would thy chamber be its goal
> Were my songs with wings provided
> Like to the soul.
> To thy hart anon 'twere guided
> As to her nest flies a dove
> Were my songs with wings provided
> Like unto love."

"Your songs are, with wings provided and reach their goal," said he from the depths of the easy chair. "Go on. Do not stop."

She sang "Four Leaved Clover," one of the old record songs, because it was always a favorite in any time or place, then "After Sorrow's Night" by Rotoli.

> "After sorrow's night
> Dawned the morning bright,
> In dewy woods I heard
> A golden throated bird,
> And love-love-love-it sang,
> And love-love-love."

It faded away like the last call of a bird sinking to rest at night. After the dying cadences, both were silent for a moment, then Nadia said, "Those have always been favorites and I have given you enough for once unless I end with the old, old, but dear, 'Last Rose of Summer.'"

"Do sing it," he answered, "but I wish you wouldn't stop."

"After this, yes."

She sang it with the heart appeal and true artistry that is seldom heard, and he gave her that recognition.

"You are a born singer," he said slowly as though coming regretfully out of a golden cloud. "Singers, true artists are born not made. But I am selfish enough to prefer you as you are, rather than on the stage, though the public is the loser."

"I am glad I pleased you."

"Please isn't the word. You have conquered and won me had you not already done so. I want my sister to hear you and know you. We will attend the opera sometime this week and I will bring her to call on you on the way. You will go, will you not?"

"Gladly."

"And now, if you will not sing anymore, we will go for a ride, I make a practice of it on Sundays, as a rule."

While she was gone for her wraps his attention was drawn to some strange decoration on the mantel and he went close to examine it.

"How odd," he mused. "What does she mean by it? A crucifix over copies of her first books—the three of them—the verse, the drama, the first novel; and over a copy of her last book, the successful novel that brought her here—a mocking figure of Mephistopheles. What does it all mean? Those two opposites? And overlooking copies of her books, being in sight of anyone who enters the room gives one the right to ask."

He stood there, looking at them, when Nadia reentered.

"The oddity of combination and unguessed suggestiveness of this mantel decoration constrained me to ask you what it means."

"Can you not guess? Have you read my first and last?"

"I have. After Mrs. Rogers invited me to meet you, we had a bit of a talk at the time. I read your last and the first, the book of verse. Since then I have read the others, though my time has been limited. I congratulate you on their beauty and value. I cannot see why the Christ and Mephisto should both be considered as hovering over them."

"Here then is the explanation," Nadia began, looking at him with an earnest, imploring gaze. "Those first books I wrote, brought forth from the high and holy temple of my soul, hoping to add to the good, the beauty, the truth and helpfulness of the world, they only exist. I would starve on their sales. Christ is in them, and therein is crucified again in my own hurt soul, though some here and there have loved them and sent me such recognition. And I learned, lately, that a greatly respected judge had chosen one of the poems as his best beloved verse; and so it was read and quoted in his obituaries a short time ago. But the world, at present, hasn't been wanting high and holy and beautiful in literature but the stirring tawdriness, the crawling slime of sex abuse, of cheap pleasure seeking, of all lack of high purpose. I understood that the 'best sellers' were of that kind or had some of it in them. Giving my life for others I was in need of money to help them and me, so I listened to the voices of disillusionment, Mephistopheles, I call them, and tried to step down from my heights; you understand me? I *tried* to step down, and that is falling into sin, isn't it? Though the downward step be but a slight one, you have fallen nevertheless. I brought that stepping downward into my last book. Though I lifted the characters back again to the heights, having them choose to climb back by sacrifice of Self, yet there was the picturing of sin, however vague, that made the book a 'best seller.' So, Mephisto won, alas! In this success and money help and social acclaim that has come to me I keep myself humble by keeping this reminder before me. I don't believe I went far enough to do any harm to any human soul or life—oh, I pray to God—but I listened to that disillusioning voice and darkened my own soul for the sake of what it would help to bring me and mine. Now you know, Mr. Dexter. How do you feel about?"

She waited, looking at him with that frail, spiritual face and shining, imploring eyes, for what judgment she knew not.

"How do I feel about it?" he repeated after her. "That you didn't and couldn't step down. You weren't even dragged down. Your disillusionments, your great need, your longing, only gave you another strength, another courage, another vision, to touch the world's lower side and show it can be lifted up to catch the gleam and make the struggle to obtain it. Why, Nadia—can I call you that?"

She nodded shiningly. He went up to her and took her in his arms. "Call me Raymond," and she murmured it low with head on his broad breast.

"Nadia dearest, do you think it could be any shadow of Mephistopheles who brought us together? Any shade of wrong doing? It was that book, or the success it brought to you, that brought you here, wasn't it?" She nodded. "Well,

I love it for that and I love it for its self. And I love those
others as deserving a big success for their beauty and truth and
helpfulness even though it may not have been accorded them.
You have done good work. You have given the world something
of value. Your books shall not be crucified. They shall live as
a gleam, a help to many a starving soul. Little followers of
Christ, you might call them. And no sinful influence, though
you name it Mephistopheles or only disillusionment, can
follow or has followed your last book the 'The Crossroads.'
Neither can it touch you. We belong to each other. Thank the
forces, seen and unseen, for that blessedness whatever comes
to us in the future. I have longed for you, beloved. I knew you
from the first."

"And I, you, Raymond. That thought came to me, though
vaguely of course, for I am quick to feel personal magnetisms or
negatives."

"Bless you, beloved. And you will marry me as soon as it
can be arranged?"

"Yes, Raymond. You are a widower, I surmise; or are you a
bachelor? Strange I don't know, while drawn to this closeness."

He felt a chilling hurt pierce him at the thought of what
lay between them.

"I have at least lived alone for years, longing for the right
one. I will explain all while we are out riding, out in God's free
air and sunshine, an expression universal in thought and feeling.
God's free air and sunshine always helps to endure, to overcome,
to achieve. I shudder, Nadia, at thought of those shut out from
them in prison cells. Let us go and breathe it in while I tell you
what you ought to know, though unpleasant in the telling and
the hearing."

As they entered the car he said to the chauffeur, "Riverside," and to Nadia, "Today we will take the ocean breeze. Another Sunday we will go down the river. It is late for that today. Your singing was to me like riding down another river, the river of sound with the foliage of the spirit."

"Oh, Raymond," she hesitated on the name, smiling at him. "You too, have poetry in you. I didn't suppose it grew and blossomed very profusely among the so called 'hard business men.'"

"Some of us get a harder name than we deserve, but no one can achieve anything in any line of endeavor in this world and be a jelly fish. You must have stamina, back bone, to endure the rush and strife of its harsh waves."

In the car as they swept along through the fresh insweep of air from the ocean, moving on its purifying way over that vast swarming human nest, they told each other what each should know, talking low, though the chauffeur in his compartment could not hear.

"Tell me, Nadia, something about yourself first," he said. "I want to know just how you began or started on your career, the phrase in common use, what denials, hardships, were yours. What was the one beckoning light that lured you on?"

"Taking a general, cursory glance there wouldn't be much to tell, Raymond. Born and growing up in a western town, where there is little of what is looked upon as adventure or stirring deeds outside of the common daily associations, it might seem like a mild unthrilling tale one would have to tell. Outwardly all of my later years look like, what is spoken of as, drab. But were they that in the eyes of the spirit? The outward, visible, is not the seal of reality. I grew up in the midst of the open spaces, wandering, feeling, questioning, out on the edges of those vast calling prairies, for they called to me with a language and brooding knowledge all their own. Alone I went sometimes out on the prairie roads and among all those strange wordless whisperings around me the lark's song, born of the paradise of sound, would soar up into the vast blue of the skies like a heavenly call to the listening spirit. I loved everything in Nature that environment showed me; even the searing droughts and hot winds had their virtues with their destruction, as a forced spur to thought and overcoming. I delved into the literature of the old masters, lived with them from early childhood—poetry, drama, fiction—very little of the modern drew me. That was mostly a dim candlelight beside the glory of the old masters, and it is a murky candlelight today. Those masters were my only school, outside of common high school, which now has far more advantages than a few years ago. Why do the great majority of people care only for novels, only to be amused, and turn from poetry, the best, those short, pithy, beautiful expressions of truth that can remain with you, live with you, day by day, a comfort or spur?"

"Because," he answered, "most people are only after amusement and don't want to think or gather mind pearls as they surge along the coasts of life."

"Our parents were high minded, high souled, no better anywhere, but they had a large family, six of us, and could not afford to send us to college. Today nearly everyone manages to go to the university, yet we do not hear of great scholarship or of many of the great achievements. Why? Is it all for pleasure only? Early I glimpsed what I called, "The Shining Road." It stretched ahead vague, yet dimly shining, with glory as the goal.

To be, to do, to achieve something for the mind, the spirit, the upward striving humanity. When I was nineteen, just beginning my work, my mother was stricken with paralysis. I gave up my plans for the time to stay with and care for her. When the war came my young brother Carl felt the call for right and for his country, and, though under age, volunteered. One by one through all of this strain my three sisters had married, my beloved father died, and then the brother came home lame, with damaged eyesight, broken in body and in spirit. I had him, the mother, the house to care for, no time for pleasure, snatching the time I could for writing down my thoughts, my visions, my creative fancies, within the prescribed bars of literary expression. Then our mother died and the property was divided. I could not desert the broken brother, and also leave a younger brother without a home. Then I began, as I told you, to listen to the voices of disillusionment and necessity. There is the outline of my life. Not much is it? Not very shining." Then she told him of Annetta's coming, and the Professor. Of Carl's interest and gradual improvement. Of their marriage, of their courage and hope once more. "Here I am for a rest, change, something new and bright. I have found it all and far more, haven't I?"

He drew her close and she was glad to rest her head for a moment on his shoulder.

"I thought twice, once especially, that I loved, but felt it was only a part of me, not the real depth of me that responded, and now I know it. Those family misfortunes came between us, prevented consummation."

"Thank God for that," he murmured. "As dark as the Fates made it for both or us they brought us together at last. We will not rail at them but thank them now. I shall take care of *you* now, not you of others, and I will help those others. They shall be mine as well as yours. My heart is with the soldier brother, broken, disabled for his country and the rights of humanity. I was refused as an active soldier through a physical defect that might have made me useless, but my heart and efforts were with them. I was on the advisory board of the government and went over to France once in that capacity.

"Here is my dark story, but without the sacrificial shine of yours. In my ignorant youth I was won by and married a pretty face, not realizing that a pretty face, bright with the glow of youthful spirit, pictures very little of the being behind it. Though considered one of the precious jewels of a woman's life, you want something more and better than that to live with. It didn't take long to discover I had made a mistake but felt I must make the best of it. She was an insatiable, rampant, pleasure seeker, with apparently no other aims in life. No high purpose, desire, or thoughts, seemed to lead her in many other directions. I was so different she soon lost pleasure in my companionship. There must be some similarity of taste to hold two individuals, married or single, in bonds of friendship. They may be bound together but it will only prove bondage. I loved all of the arts and sciences, though without creative gift in any of them that I had discovered. I had shown successful business qualities from the first and aimed to make myself a leader in that line of endeavor and keep alive and open to the influencing greatness of those others, and to me, greater advancements of human striving. I meant to succeed in the business world but to be something greater and better than a mere money seeker. After our little daughter was born I thought, surely, motherhood would develop better, worthier, qualities. She was not bad. She had not been taught that life has its duties, that work is more and greater than pleasure. That is wherein most parents wrong their children and are wronging them today to a degenerative extent. Without work and interest in that work human beings would soon degenerate into savages. Again she was lost in the pleasure seeking, and the child left neglected in the care of a maid. Pleasure, a good time, a 'rousing time' was all she cared for. I decided she should be my wife no longer, except in name. No other child of mine should have her for its mother. If one is going to bring children into this world he or she should give them the best in heredity and environment."

"Oh, how right, how right that is and how few live up to it or care," exclaimed Nadia.

"Of course we drifted more and more apart. At last she went to an extreme that I could not tolerate, and I succeeded in obtaining a divorce and the custody of the child, a girl, whom I placed in my sister's charge, and she has known no other mother. Thank God, she is promising far better than her mother, and is doing well in a girl's school. I provided fairly for my divorced wife until she should remarry. We were living in Chicago then. Influences that were working in my business affairs brought me to New York soon after, where I have made one of the large financial successes. That was twelve years ago. For some years I lived at a club. Then, my sister being left a widow, I bought a home, and she and I, with my daughter in vacation times, have made our home together. Though lonely I have not married again because I was waiting for the one mind and heart would recognize. It began to look as though she would not come; but now you are here and my loneliness, with its long waiting, is a sad life that is gone. I am forty years of age, but since I met you, only a few nights gone, I have grown younger with the surge of the happiness of the now, and the promise of the happiness ahead. But dear heart, here is the 'bar sinister.' I must tell you, but do not be afraid. I am not."

"Afraid with you?" she looked at him trustingly.

"Twice a year, since the divorce, she has sent me the same threatening letter, on the anniversary of our marriage, and when the divorce was decreed. And this is what she says each time: 'You shall not marry again. If you try it you shall rue the day. I both love you and hate you.'

"That is all. What she thinks she could do, or attempt to do, I do not guess. And probably she thinks she has had me scared the reason I have not married. How little she knows me or has ever known me. I have paid no attention to it, and have ever seen her since the divorce was granted. Now beloved, you know all. Are you afraid to marry me now?"

"No, Raymond. We are doing no wrong to love each other or to marry. It is only through God's holiest that we love or consummate that love. We have waited long. I am yours now."

"I could employ a detective to watch her movements, for a time, but my inclination is to go on ignoring her threats as far as possible."

"Yes. That seems the better way to me also. Poor deluded woman," answered Nadia.

"Being known, personally, we cannot keep it out of the papers, but we will have a quiet wedding. You do not mind?"

"I much prefer it."

"Let it be within a fortnight. Why should we wait to know each other for a year, or six months, or six weeks? We knew when we first met."

"How good it sounds to have you so earnestly sure," said Nadia.

"Are you not just as sure? And that is good to me. Make your arrangements. Think of where you would like to go for a little honeymoon trip. Just now it would be hard for me to leave long enough for a satisfactory European trip. We can take that a little later. How would you like either a boat or train run to Florida for a few days, then up to your Nebraska home, plan and make conditions right and satisfactory for those you still feel a responsibility for, and then here again to our home together? Our home together. Doesn't it sound good?"

"It is a beautiful love dream coming true," she answered. "Yes, we will follow that plan and then my mind will be at peace in regard to the others. How thoughtful and good of you."

Interested in each other, and their affairs, time had flown. It was growing late, and, ordering the chauffeur to drive to the Ritz, they were soon a part of the brilliancy, showing their own distinctive personality without regard to place. It was all a pleasurable study to Nadia. In rich or poor places, city or country, human beings had both mental and heart interest for her, and she had learned through her own experiences, as well as reading, that neither position or possessions told the measure of their spiritual, or mental, or character values. She had found heartening soul greatness in both, and its disheartening lack. Tonight there was nothing lacking for her own inspiration and enjoyment either in the spiritual, mental or material. She was being blessed with it all. Blessed! Blessed! And while material luxuries had not visualized or called along her "shining road," yet how acceptable they were except when she thought of the sufferings of poverty that darkened this struggling world, so often unmerited. Being a small eater always, at these times and places interest so enthralled her that whatever the viands placed before her, she ate so little it was noticeable to those with or near her; and Mr. Dexter spoke of it after their dinner was half through, saying low, "Nadia, I imagine you need someone to watch over you in material ways. Judging by the amount you are eating no wonder you look so frail. The body cannot live on the food of the spirit alone."

She laughed back at him, "Remember it wasn't food for the body I came to New York for. Almost every other kind but that."

"Nevertheless, I don't want to see you fade away before my eyes like a ghost."

Her laugh started to ripple forth, but she caught it back on its first little tinkle, remembering in time where she was. A couple of his business friends came to them for a few moment's greeting and she was as glad to meet them as those along the lines of her own career; and she met them with that expectant interest seldom noticed amid the indifferent courtesies of strangers either in the rush of the metropolis or the enveloping self interest of the smaller cities and towns; so it could not be mistaken or provincialism but was at once understood for its own sake as an innate friendliness of character. These same friends took the liberty of asking Mr. Dexter afterward, "Who was the friend with you that evening? The lady with the frail face and the shining eager eyes set like stars within it?"

That was the way he too would have expressed it, and his love went out to her all the more, with that enveloping desire to protect as well as to possess. That is one of the beautiful traits in the good man who truly loves—that desire to protect. And does real love come to any but a good man unless its coming makes him good? They had decided that the Kents, her friends, and Mrs. Rogers, having brought them together, had the right to be taken into their confidence at once; and Nadia requested him to take that initiative, feeling a bit shy of doing this herself.

They couldn't have found more interested friends than these who had been the agents for their introduction, and who now entered helpfully into all arrangements for the happy consummation though the principal reason for quiet and simplicity was not mentioned. That was a private unpleasantness to be kept, like the skeleton in many a family, hidden from sight and sound, taking the chances of prayer and righteousness that its claws would not be stretched forth in the dark, or the light, in an effort to harm. Oh! this beautiful day with its beautiful ending, that had poured out a full chalice upon her longing, denied life. Its goodnight had given her the first kiss of her long dreamed of real love, and how full was her cup of joy.

XVI

At once Nadia wrote to the home folks. What a sudden surprise it would be to all of them. She, their standby for all these years, to be taken from them, not by death, but by a fullness of joy that had been so absent from her life for long, so long, while dwelling among them. How noiselessly and quickly the doors had opened for her. Those close, hard shut doors of success and joy and love; of love—"And the greatest of these is love." Of course the love of that quotation is not personal, but that greatest of all love, the All. Yet how beautiful is that personal love, in its richest reality how enthralling to the one to whom it comes. She had only been gone a month and those doors were set ajar, had opened wide and let all the sunshine of life flow into her. She wished the dear father and mother could come back and share in her joy. With Carl recovering and happy, there would be little to hurt them. The last letter from these two had said their hope was being partially verified and the oculist

expert had set them farther along the road to recovery, so that
Carl was expecting to be very soon back on his pre war job.
The lameness, though a detriment and inconvenience, would
not, in its lessened state, be much of an interference. And Aunt
Eleanor's letters told, so far, that all was well. Oh, life! so full
of beauty and pain, of blossom and fruitage, and of blasted,
withered hopes. While with all our struggling, Fate seems to
step in and make the choice for us, regardless of our offerings,
whether of righteous merit or of glaring unworth.

Without waste of time, the next morning, Monday, Mr.
Dexter phoned her and arranged for the opera together, saying
he would bring his sister to meet her before the hour. When
the time came, Mrs. Burgess, Helen, he called her, met Nadia
with sufficient warmth of greeting to dispel any shyness or
questioning sense of anxiety she had felt in the prospective
meeting.

"Raymond has told me all about you," she said at once,
"and I am glad for his sake. Now that I see you I think I am
going to be glad for your sake also."

"I trust so, Mrs. Burgess. And I hope that not only he and
I but all of those around us will be, in some way, benefited and
made happier by our happiness and union."

"We sometimes know more by what we feel when we meet
a person than what we hear about them," added Mrs. Burgess.
"I want to know you better, at once, and you will dine with
us tomorrow evening, will you not? With perhaps one or two
friends. You must know Raymond's and your future home."

"Of course," Nadia answered. "I am looking forward to
that and to knowing and being fond of those Mr. Dexter is
fond of, his sister and daughter. I am sure we will all be happy

together. The more hearts that beat with and for each other the happier and broader and greater they are. Not those who, with one or two of their own, build fences around them, shutting out the rest of the world's hearts and interest."

"How right you are, Miss Evertson; that is the way my brother and I feel and try to live up to."

"We are all infinitesimal drops in the ocean of the infinite mind and each one, however poorly developed, has a necessary part in the symphonic whole," added Mr. Dexter.

"How truly alike we see it," Nadia smiled at him, "though you are in the hard business world and I in the home and dream world. We cannot all be stars in the same environmental drama, but even the lesser ones of the Now may become the stars sometime, somewhere. That is my faith in the human soul, with all its weaknesses, its limitations."

Again at the opera. How she loved it, that glowing drama combination of life's varied colorings of which she had tasted so little. She realized, of course, that like the sweets of the table she wouldn't want this all of the time; one could become satiated. But now happiness had opened wide all the doors of her being and every key of her soul's organ was quivering. She wondered how many in that brilliant gathering came for the sole love of the music drama, and how many for the pleasure of being one with the fortunate scintillating life throng. So many types of faces, so many types of souls met hers here, like the touching of the waves from passing ships. How strange is life, so filled with fulfillings of beauty or denied like desert hungering.

"Can it be," she asked herself, "that I am the same being transported from that small western city, from a shut in, denied life, to this of which I have dreamed? Will it last?"

Between curtains these thoughts recurred to her in the midst of the low voiced converse of their party. Tonight was an opera with which she was less acquainted, belonging to that school of musical composition that appeals more to the mental than the emotional, but she was alert to the differences of meaning. And the bridge that now connects them will in time grow shorter and shorter until they are merged as they should be, into one more satisfying whole. In the audience she had caught sight of the Kents and smiled at them happily, at the Rogers and some of their friends, again near them; and afterwards she met some more of Mr. Dexter's friends, making their way out a pathway of pleasant greetings.

Always after these evenings of nerve excitement she was long in quieting to sleep. She did not try to separate, dissever, the different elements of pleasurableness. Only the one blessed fact stood out always by itself, refusing to be submerged with the others, the blessedness of being loved, watched over, protected. Was there anything in life's personal joys to stand beside this? Of course that soul attainment, the sacrificial spiritual that gives all and asking not, receives not, is above and beyond all else, reaching over the heights of this life into the heights of another sphere. That was beyond all personal.

Often as she waited for sleep to come and enfold her in its soothing arms, she wondered what all this inflow and newness would do with her future writing. Could she, born, bred in, used to the open spaces, be shut in this great crowded tenement called a city, write for better or worse? Did any of the great writers do their greatest work in these jumbled cave dwellings, or out in the clean free, breathing spaces that God, not man, had made and given? Here she could not go out on her own little green lawn and sit down under some grand old tree that spread its waving arms of benediction over her, its leaves like so many whispering, loving spirits. Nor could she sit down in the lush grasses, running her caressing fingers over and through their bountiful friendliness, all of them brothers and sisters along the highways and byways of an impenetrable, unexplained life. She could not watch the sunset—or sunrise at early hours—dip its wonderful brush to an unseen wonderful palette of unforgettable colorings, and spread its majestic, inspiring, painted glories above and below the horizon, deeper and deeper; and showing golden rivers with vague little cloud ships riding down them, making one feel that the boats of angels must be gliding there, with waving pennants of greeting at their bows. But love, love was here for her. Not love's sacrificial altar with its burning consuming fires, but love the beautiful giver; and here was her abode henceforth in that love's arms. Henceforth. With what beauty and blessedness it enwrapped her. God grant it to every lonely human soul.

The following days and evenings were full to overflowing. The days were given, in part, by herself and Julia to seeking the required outfit for her trousseau. Nadia would not go beyond her own present enlarged finance, though small as it was in the calls of New York's riches; and she said, "I want just a few beautiful but simple garments. I do not want to be burdened with things, things. Life itself is too valuable, and the seeking growing mind that is life, to waste too much of it on a round of things. Enough, and no more."

Julia being sensible also, and a woman of both style and good taste, they managed to obtain a wardrobe of beauty and simplicity and distinction not always seen even among those of accepted qualifications and opportunities and finances. Nadia's well formed slender figure had a grace and style of its own; her well poised head stood on its slender stem like a proud calyx enclosing the flower of her mind and soul. She was not beautiful in the sense of mere physical beauty. She was too frail looking for that. It was a beauty far above, beyond, that which is common everywhere and dependent on physical health alone, a beauty that wins the unperceiving eye always and rules the material perceptions. Yet even that common element, so in the majority, looked at her, and looked again, feeling something stirred deep, deep in their being but which they did not understand or seek to analyze. It is so much easier to take what comes to us from the touch of life's passing breezes and not trouble ourselves with thoughts analysis. To think deeply is work. The many shun it.

That first evening in Mr. Dexter's home she had anticipated feeling shy and sensitive but the atmosphere thrown out around her was so like a delicious June morning that opens the roses, that she, too, found her own petals expanding to an extent that surprised herself, so given to holding back, waiting for others to make advances and touch the key notes. The rich surroundings, the service of butler and maids were luxuries that fitted her taste and needs, though her life so far had run on a simpler plan of Self and family service. How much easier are the reactions for the person of refinement when dropped into luxury than into poverty, like walking in dainty, well fitting shoes or rough, heavy clumsy clods. The friends invited were few but among those of prideful pleasure to meet. The Kents, though not in the swim of society, or artistic spheredom, were invited for her sake and proved themselves capable, agreeable additions to the conversational entertainment.

When asked to sing, by the hostess and host, she could hardly refuse, as they had made the request beforehand also, telling her to come prepared. She made little effort in choosing her songs, almost at random, from a varied selection. She sang "The Nightingale" by Alabieff, a sad, minor, bird song with trills but no other showy artistry. It was one she was fond of and equal to doing, not only well, but according to the rare higher renditions.

This she followed with two short heart ballads among her favorites; one, "The Dawn" by d'Hardelot and then, because they didn't want her to stop and she felt like giving it, she sang "Home, Sweet Home" with more beauty and stirring power than is often heard from the musical stars. Nadia had truly the gift of ballad singing, the lyric poetry of music. Her hearers loved her for the gift of expression that made their own heart strings quiver, soul speaking to soul, through these two avenues of words and music at their best.

She could not have asked for more appreciation. When the last tender tone faded away there was as a silence for a moment, and then her hostess, Mrs. Burgess, came forward and kissed her without any apology; and Mrs. Kent, Julia, did the same. Then Mr. Dexter said, smilingly, "Why shouldn't the masculine hearers be allowed that privilege also? We have no such effective way to express our appreciation of the rare pleasure Miss Evertson has given us. It is not quite fair to us."

That broke the spell with laughter, and talk followed. Mrs. Burgess was as a church woman, and among the guests was the head pastor of her church. He voiced his own appreciation by saying, "That is better than any sermon. When you sing, Miss Evertson, I will have to step aside."

"Oh!" laughed Nadia, with the flush deepening in her cheeks and the glow in her eyes. "You dear people will spoil me with such high compliments here in the country's musical center. I was afraid, but you have turned my fear into gladness. I thank you. The poet, the composer, the interpreter, the listener, when all meet on the same plan, make a combination that bridges the gulfs between them and reaches into the immortal and unknown. You make me glad that I sang for you. That is the singer's greatest reward."

And a few evenings after, when Mrs. Rogers gave for them a large elaborate prenuptial affair, though without stating that fact to anyone, as she had been requested, Nadia had scored a triumph that, now too late, might have meant a great help and joy to her had it come a few years earlier, or before this love fulfillment had mapped her future into different channels. She would have preferred to hold aloof from singing this time, as fear was never far from her, gazing at her with disquieting threatening possibilities, but they had persuaded her to a half promise beforehand, so she felt the call to fulfill it. She had asked to have Julia for her accompanist, as it would be easy to rehearse with her and to explain her interpretations.

"Of course," Mrs. Rogers had answered. "I should invite them for your sake anyway." And she did. So that night dressed in a gown of white satin simply made, with Julia at the piano, though at the smaller house affairs Nadia preferred to be her own accompanist, she sang, first, Henschel's "Spring," rendering it with that fullness of beauty which made it almost unrecognizable as the same song as interpreted by most singers who skimmed it more as a bird in hastening flight. Nadia's rendering made it, as it should be, so overrunning with joy and wondrousness one was reluctant to let go of that first golden outcry of "Spring," but at first, full and strong, holding on, and merging into the next, as though the words "sweet Spring" must be made to carry the glory and joy behind them in full measure; and especially when the glad song ends with that lingering, lingering, "sweet, sweet spring."

No need for applause only, to tell her that she had made it beautiful for them. She knew. Following with a little ballad fraught with sadness, and then ending with the old ever favored "Last Rose of Summer," with its never failing heart appeal. After the moment's silence, and the applause that followed and passed, one of the more celebrated guests spoke for all to hear, "Miss Evertson, you have proved to us once more that not only real poets, but real singers, are born, not made."

"In truth they are one, are they not?" she asked. "At least the soul that brings forth is the same though the voice might be lacking."

Another said, "You have stirred the deeper, richer being in us, tonight. Not often is that done, and we owe you more than gratitude."

Afterwards another came to her, one who was in some way connected with directors—had she known of him she would have, in fear, refused to sing—and offered to contract with her for a series of concerts.

"You have no fear that they might prove unsuccessful?" she queried.

"Not any," he answered.

"But I am not a showy stage performer, Mr. Hamilton."

"You suit me very well as you are."

Mr. Dexter standing beside her heard and wondered, a bit deprecatingly for a moment, if she thought of accepting. Surely not now. He would not wish it.

"I thank you for your appreciation and your faith, Mr. Hamilton; I cannot make a final decision at once. Let me consider the advisability of launching out on two careers at the same time."

"But don't fail me. The public needs your kind."

She had begun in fear, but fear was not at the end. Here was another of her longed for "dreams come true," in part, but apparently too late. She sensed Mr. Dexter's adverse feeling and, added to that, she also realized too well her physical frailty and, more negatively than that even, how fear bound she always was. But for the success of her book and love's fulfillment, with its amplitude of finances, she would have been almost sure to have launched on that trial trip. At any rate, how her dreams were all coming true after the drought of years.

"I must do more for God's kingdom," she said to herself then, "to show my gratitude."

And when a large check came to her from one of the evening millionaire listeners, with the message, "In grateful appreciation of your singing, to keep for your own use or any charitable desire of your heart," her heart almost ached with its fullness of gladness, and love, and thankfulness, and desire to do and to give—give—all of the good within her.

Oh, the poor denied suffering souls that are forced by ironical circumstances to go through life with only drought, to a famine end.

And she told herself never would she forget, in self enjoyment, the lack and pain of the world. She could not have done otherwise had the drought remained her portion. How unjust life and its forces. In all righteousness everyone born into this world should have the right to happiness, love, growth. Do they? No. All are the creatures of heredity and environment and their reflexes, coming, unasked, without choice of either, victims of forces and chance, with only struggling self modifications for their own chosen sculpturings. What is success? Merit doesn't always receive it, unworth sometimes does. This world ranks it as money, fame, position. In the next sphere what will it be? What is success in the sight of God? Probably that success would be laid at the doors of many unknown, suffering alone in obscurity.

Going to and fro the lovers had their little private communings, for Mr. Dexter always went after Nadia and took her home, to what she temporarily called home, and each time they said goodnight with the comforting realization that they were a few hours nearer when they would be together, without those interfering separations. They not only loved, but each was proud of the other, which gave an added zest to their attained togetherness. Yet that same quality often brings about jealousies and separations where love is not deep and strong enough for an unquestioning loyalty.

On the way home from this social evening, Mr. Dexter did not ask Nadia if she thought of accepting that concert offer. Though he hoped she would not yet he felt that was her own affair, and her own right of decision. She spoke of it however and said, "Do not be troubled about that concert offer, Raymond. I felt you would not want me to accept, but I also felt that was not the time and the place to give a settled decision and any detail of why."

"Thank you, beloved; for now at least let it pass into the future possibilities. I am relieved. I want you to myself. Selfishness, of course; and now I want to ask something of you on another matter. An important matter has arisen that makes it both inconvenient and unwise for me to leave for a week or so. Would you be much disappointed if we spent our first honeymoon week at home?"

"Surely not, Raymond. Arrange it as you desire."

"Then, after that matter I speak of is settled, we can go as we planned. We will have one golden bright quiet week together, maybe two, before we go. Only three days now, Nadia, and the binding words will be said. I will feel safer then, more sure that you cannot slip from me. Goodnight beloved, and God keep you."

"And you," she breathed in return with his lips seeking hers, and then the night and its dark had separated them again.

They had planned a quiet unadvertised wedding in church. Nadia's religious spirit caused her to desire that additional feeling of sacredness. Then they were to have the wedding breakfast or luncheon in his home with a few special guests. That was all. It was enough. No spreading show, but simplicity and happiness. Until it was all consummated, that fear, that bar sinister, would be facing them with its unknown threatening evil.

XVII

The day before the wedding Nadia sat quietly reading in the little living room of the apartment. The packing of trunks, for removal to her future home, was in part finished and the rest, Edith, maid and companion, was to take charge of after she, herself had departed. She was trying to quiet the excitation of mind and nerves by various devices of make believe interest and random reading material. It was early afternoon. The sun was shining in at a southwest angle of the front windows and made a cheerful drape across the corner of the room. The telephone rang. She was not sorry for the interruption, resting as she was on the surface of the present hours looking forward to tomorrow. When she answered, a voice asked, "Do you know who is behind this voice, Nadia?"

"The voice sounds like Robert Merrill. Is it you, Robert?"

"It surely is, for it isn't my ghost yet, even if I haven't seen you since I went off to war. I want to see you, Nadia. Can I come to you at once, as soon as I can get there, within a half hour probably?"

"Yes, I am alone at present. Come as soon as possible."

"All right. In a few minutes, Nadia."

How strange it seemed that he should come just at this time, she meditated. After those years of separation and that last parting as lovers, the bond of which had so strange a breaking, and helped in its mocking wreckage of Fate to bring to her those mocking voices of disillusionment, of weakening faith in the firmness of good.

When he came, and she met him face to face once more after these years of many changes, her heart warmed to him, this lover of her youth, and their hands clasped, both at once, in a tightening grip.

"Nadia."

"Robert."

He would have kissed her at once had he dared to act on that impulse. There she was once more, the one he had loved from early boyhood, changed, of course, by all the burdens she had borne, the first freshness of the shining youth gone, but in its place that deeper meaning and beauty that draws one unconsciously, forgetful of the mere physical youth call. And in his well remembered face she saw at once the continued fulfillment of that strength, character, loyal dependence, helpfulness, he had proved in their earlier years.

"Nadia, I have found you again. You have never been far from my thoughts. No one could ever take your place in my heart. I was fond of my wife. She was good and true, worthy of any man's love. Had I not been fond of her, returned her affection, I would have proved myself an unworthy specimen of manhood. She died eight months ago."

"And I had not heard of it. I am sorry," said Nadia.

"She left me a baby son who is now a year old and at present with her parents."

"I am glad, Robert, you have that joy to comfort you," Nadia responded. "You are not left all alone and despoiled."

"I was going back to the old western home to seek you when I heard you were here; so I came in search of you, and with a business purpose added to keep me busy for about ten days. I understand you have made quite a success and I glory in it. I knew it was in you."

"That is what made it possible for me to come here, after my dear mother had passed away and Carl was improving and in good hands. Without it that terrible money question would have held me, too," she smilingly rejoined.

"I hope your success and fame will not lift you away, separate you from the old friends and admirers, me especially, Nadia."

"It was misfortune, giving, that did that Robert, not any success of mine," she answered soberly.

"I know; oh, too well I know, in part, even if not in all. But you do not blame me, Nadia, for my seeming desertion? I tried to make it plain to you, so you would understand."

"I understood."

"She saved my life, by the gift of her blood; and I gave her the only payment she wanted or would have accepted. Strangely, as healthy as she seemed, she never quite overcame what physicians would have expected to be but a temporary weakening; and it, in the end, helped to bring an early death. I could not have done otherwise and been just, righteous. Could I, Nadia?"

"No."

"As long as she is gone beyond the desires and hurts of this life, I hope I am not too late to regain what I lost—you, Nadia—you—always my shining star. Am I too late?"

They were still standing, as when he had entered and she had greeted him. Neither had yet thought of being seated. The sunshine sent a ray across the room passing between them and falling on the wall, more like a friendly listener desiring to ease the tension growing, growing between them.

"Am I too late, Nadia?" he repeated as he again clasped her hands, gazing yearningly into her eyes, in whose depths he saw something that seemed a denial of him in some unforeseen way.

And then she answered, "Too late, Robert. Tomorrow is my wedding day. Tomorrow I am to be married to another."

He stood as if dazed for a moment.

"Tomorrow! married to another. Oh, my God!" He staggered a little, then sank into a large chair that he groped for near at hand, and put his hands over his face. She stood sorrowfully watching him at first, then went up to him and took those hands—firm, helpful, kindly hands—in hers and looked him in the eyes again.

"Do not. Do not, Robert dear! you almost break my heart with your suffering. You will get over it, dear. Time lessens and sears over the raw sores of every hurt, every loss. That is what life is, isn't it? Over and over. Dare I say it, Robert, dear friend, you may find another dearer far to you than I have ever been."

"Never, never," he groaned. "From early beyond I have seen only you among them all. You were my star, though you never seemed to know it."

"You have done me a great honor, Robert; far greater, I fear, than I deserve. And I honor you in every sense. I was very fond of you when you went away. I do not know how deep that love would have become had Fate used us differently, but it was different than this I now feel toward this other one. And when that black message came to me from you, my one hope in a denied shut in life, you, my one touch with the outside world, that strange message telling how a leering Fate had robbed me of that, too, I did worse than you are doing now, Robert, though no one saw or heard or knew my hurt and loss. I laughed at first, like a crazed woman laughing back at a crazy Fate, and then I cried as unrestrainedly, all smothered in bedding, so others would not hear, until sense and self control came back and I again assumed once more my everyday face and demeanor; and I took up my tasks with fight, and endurance, and determination again, in spite of that last despoilment. So may you, Robert, for you are not shut in, or altogether denied."

"Had I known you cared that much, Nadia, I could not have gone on with the other. No. I could not. Oh, Nadia, my love, my love."

"But you owed it to her as you say. It was a debt that you could pay only as you did. Regret it not."

"No. No. She was worthy, to be honored and loved. But I cannot lose you again, Nadia. Do you love him, this other man? But, of course, you wouldn't say no."

"We knew and loved each other from the first."

"Then you think it is more real than ours, but it isn't; it isn't."

She knew it was, but answered mildly, "In that the Fates were kind and kept us for each other."

"I wish I had gone back to the old home, to you, before you came here. Respect from her held me."

"There is a destiny that shapes our ends."

"It looks that way. As though we are the puppets of unfeeling, soulless forces. Who is this fortunate man, Nadia?"

"You probably know, or know of him, through business ramifications, in some way. One of New York's financiers, Raymond Dexter."

"Well, there must have been some unseen magnet to bring you two together. He, well known in this great metropolis, and you, just let out of a far western town. Strange!"

"It was my books that brought us together, and mostly my last book that brought me the money to come with, and his interest in and patronage of the arts."

"You have right to happiness, Nadia; you have earned it. Yet you cannot blame me for wishing to be in his place with you."

Time slipped away as they talked on various interests, though the hurt of loss was a weight on Robert that prevented any lightness of talk or feeling. They had many tastes and subjects in common, aside from the old home associations.

"I suppose it means goodbye again when I leave you today."

"Not unless you choose it so. It would always be a pleasure for me to see you. I shall count you as one of my dearest friends. If you care to see me married, here is the invitation that will admit you," and she handed him one of the invitation cards.

"It is in church." She told him the one. "We have chosen to have it very private, unheralded, with only a few special friends to be with us. Then we go directly to Mr. Dexter's home for the wedding luncheon. We had planned a short honeymoon trip, which would take in my old home, but that, owing to some pressing business matter, is postponed for a week or more."

"In the midst of loss and hurt, I truly say—God bless you, Nadia. Will you now sing for me one of the old songs? And then I must go."

"Oh, Robert! I don't think I could, now. There has been so much tragedy since I sang for you last. It would weigh my every effort, every tone. Let it still remain that time we both remember so well and so poignantly."

"'If Love Should Die'! As I told you then, it does not die. Only its false mask dies. Sometime, somewhere it moves on." He arose to depart.

"Come and see us, Robert, at Mr. Dexter's home, which will be mine, too, then. Within the next few days you would find us there."

"I may bring my self control to bear that, Nadia, not only to see you again, but to meet and know the man, personally, into whose arms you have given yourself. My heart aches, Nadia. After all my longing and hope to lose you again. Why did it have to be? To go again, on and on without you who have always been my star. Goodbye, Nadia dearest." He went up to her, took her in his arms and kissed her. "Forgive me," he said.

And then he was gone again. Dear friend. She hoped he would find another who would make him happy, as was now promised for her. Strange ruling of life that one shall find joy at the expense of another's sorrow. The commandment says, "Thou shalt not covet," but we do, over and over, and not in material possessions alone.

Robert Merrill went from her that day, coveting the love and possession of her that another man had won during his own seeming negligence; and the sight of her and contact with her unconsciously magnetic personality made that longing—covetousness though it might be named—a consuming fire within him. Why could not some other strange freak of Fate come between these two and give her back to him. Yet even as the thought arose in him he despised himself for it and knew he could not be happy, in its higher sense, if that happiness had to be obtained through any robbery and suffering of others. He must accept this dark decree again. The unforeseen forces shake the dice and we win or lose, now here, now there, with choice too frequently an ignored factor. And he too felt in sympathy with her expression of a little while ago, of the Mephistophelian disillusionments which had driven her to that last literary effort to obtain success, money, freedom, happiness, and the self condemnation for the unspiritual thought and desire. But it was Nadia's spiritual personality that made him love her and probably drew this other man, too, though marching the hard, material roads of the business world.

"And yet," he said to himself over and over again, "how small the chances of the spiritual in this struggling, fighting material world." You must love it for itself and be satisfied with that; and, it may be, left by the wayside forsaken, uncared for, as that poor woman Nadia had just told him about, as one of her New York tragical episodes. Not for anything it can bring in a material sense; in the face of the claim that the material is founded on the spiritual. What a strange, seemingly contradictory conglomeration. It would be more than a sword through his heart. It would be a suffering and protesting bitterness in one. What hadn't that war done to mix and jumble the currents of human life. But for that, he and Nadia might have lived their lives together in love and happiness. Yes, life is made up of disappointments, of unfulfilled longings and striving after the unattainable and non understandable.

Walking on and on, questioning, brooding, the ache deep and sore within him, hardly realizing how far he had gone without calling a taxi or cab, choosing the partial outlet of physical exercise, and time to collect and connect his forces; coming near to a crossing, away from the more congested points, he happened to look up at a passing taxi and his attention was caught and held, in that moment of its passing, by a girl's agonized face leaning forth with a cry of "help!" that seemed meant for him especially, more than any other passer by, who, perhaps in the rush of self interest, had missed that fear bound, pleading face, and even the faint cry of "help" which had been strangled at once.

Quick as a flash, with Self forgotten at that cry for help from face and word, he signaled another taxi and jumped in with the order, without waste of seconds, "Follow that taxi, quick," pointing out that tragedy hiding car hurrying on, in devious ways, as though knowing not only its destination but the ways of escape by which to reach it. Here and there, in and out, they followed, but at last lost it, almost as soon as they had started. They had no clue, he or the driver, its number having been defaced, blurred, so it could not be made out, unless at close range. "God! that face, that cry." Yet he might as well hunt for a mustard seed in a sandbank as, without a clue, seek for that unknown one being hurried on to a hell, he could surmise, beside which death would be a saving mercy. And it was a devil animal in the shape of a man, who carried on, caused these horrors in this realm called human life, with sometimes the devils of the other sex to help them. How much of that horror goes on in these great seething cave dwelling places of mankind? And the blue, shining sky smiles down unheeding, and no angel comes forth from the clouds, or the haunts of men, in answer to that crying need, "Help! Help!" While out in the great void the star systems move on, unheedingly also, to which the agonies of these pygmies of humankind are inconsequential. And that we call God, called these stars into form and sent them on their courses, made this fragment earth a world of other systems we call life, moving on in their courses from the fiat of birth to the fiat of death, made this human, both the good and the bad— explain as you will—that God made them all. The innocent suffer for the guilty. Why? After billions of years of his striving, climbing existence, man has only glimpsed that something high he calls spiritual. Some see it and try to follow it. Some see it and turn away from its unfulfilled far offness at the call of the material Now.

For the time at least, Robert was lifted out of his own trouble. He told his driver, went to the police station and told of the occurrence. The police promised to set a search in motion but it seemed a hopeless, impossible task. "Would they be true to their duty and this call for help?" Robert went on his way at last asking himself, "What is my trouble, my loss, to such a tragedy of ruin and horror that must be going on within that agonized face that vainly looked out and called to me in its desperate need. And I failed her. Oh, God! open a way to safety and happiness and for all such as she. Oh, God, hear."

These are some of the tortures and sacrifices on the battlefields of peace, more shameful to the life and soul of mankind than any made on the battlefields of war.

Never could he forget that face, that call, that heart breaking episode, in the quick passing of his human ship by another, not if he lived far beyond the alloted span of years; and it was to be a factor in his thought, his action and purposes throughout his life, not only to make him more helpful toward others, but a power in striking at evil conditions and the inefficiencies of law, in fighting for the moral upgrowth of humanity, that in these last few years seemed to have stepped deeper in the mire. A thought and assertion, that was made more positive to him when going to the theatre that evening, more in the effort to forget, to lose himself than any other purpose, he saw a successful, much praised, and advertised drama, by a well know dramatist. It was well written, had power, good points, but catered to the abuse of sex; its vulgarities, instead of its heights, meant to grow by shadows through the ages, as the foundation of companionship, then affection, then family love, then the individual love which can sometimes glimpse and attain self sacrifice casting off all sex bonds and seeing the spiritual beyond, above. He saw how the drama is lowering the human, with the moving pictures, the fiction of today, all a part of this jazz age—not mind or spirit—but where love means only sex.

XVIII

To the deeply religious, or to many who would not claim to
be religious, there is something about the inside of a church,
with its stained glass windows, its chancel, its imposing organ,
a building dedicated to the service of God's kingdom on earth,
that adds solemnity and sacredness to a marriage solemnized
within its walls, and the accompaniment of the organ's
diapason. So it was with Nadia, and Raymond Dexter was not
averse.

Flowers, flowers, those beauty wonders of life, in its
determined efforts to produce its kind, greeted the beholders
with a joyous communion. Expense had not been spared to
make the chancel beautiful and fragrant for Nadia's wedding.
He would not have had it otherwise; and he had ordered also,
that after the ceremony, the flowers were to go, in her name,
to the hospitals where the poor and friendless look toward bare
walls, without a brightening touch for the lonely spirit or lonely

eyes. The small gathering of guests had been chosen, of course, from the friends of Mr. Dexter, his sister Mrs. Burgess, and the Rogers, including those Nadia had met at their homes. The Kents and Robert were her only old time friends, and Robert was there.

"I will go," he said to himself. "I will see the last act in the love drama between Nadia and me. I must face it and go on again without her, thankful she goes to happiness."

And that tortured, pleading face of yesterday came again before him, branded on his mind, never to be erased while he and life walked the earth together. He would have been sitting among them in that church an absolute stranger, in his heart echoing aloneness, but he had known Julia Kent before she went away to school and married elsewhere. Nadia had phoned to her, after Robert left the afternoon before, and asked her to keep watch for him at the church and give him friendly attention. So he was sitting with the Kents, awaiting the entrance of the wedding party. Simplicity marked that: coming up the aisle together with few attendants, just one little flower girl, Mrs. Rogers's daughter, one bridesmaid chosen by her, one groomsman, friend of Mr. Dexter, then the bride and groom walking together. The organ sang its joyous many toned wedding march which always stirs the heart mysteries of feeling in the silent deeps. It was a beautiful service, and the minister made it seem even more than usually impressive. But to Robert Merrill it was as though he were bound and torn upon a rack in spite of all his self control and determination to accept Fate's decree with a philosophical spirit. And when the ceremony was over and the wedding party came back down the aisle facing the onlookers, the sight of Nadia's face brought the choke into his throat that even the stern masculine cannot always keep down. No one but Nadia knew there was a tragedy in the midst of them, a minor submerged in the major of love fulfilled.

As a bride Nadia was not showily beautiful in the radiant physical sense; but only in that higher sense, to those who can see and feel beyond that fleeting material beauty which is worn by the commonest human types of femininity as often as by the higher type. In truth Nadia's frail, spiritual face had not yet lost its tiredness, gained in those years of overburdening and sorrow and denial, even though all these golden fulfillments had come to wipe it away. She had known and felt it coming, in fear and protest, when, if that life had gone on much longer, her facial beauty would all be gone and she would be thought less and less of by others; and even Raymond who sought not that, having learned its small value, but something higher, might not through its loss have recognized her. Too well she knew the world's unfairness on that point. She had observed, heard, read it everywhere. A beautiful, strong soul would not save her or help her in the eyes of others. Yet now she was glorious. The deeply glowing eyes alone would have caught and held even the shallow observers, though they spoke a language beyond their ken. The soft brown hair climbed over the white forehead, as if in tender protection, as a green leaf shades a dainty, delicate flower. Her head erect but modestly poised, with no veil, only a wreath of tiny white flowers to match the white beauty of the shimmering satin and chiffon gown, and the white flowers in her hands.

The sob in Robert's throat was the sob of admiring boyhood and deprived yearning manhood, in one; a double portion, the choice having grown with his growth. But he, too, was learning, as many more denied, more darkly weighted than he, to say, "what is *is*." What we can't change we must face and endure with courage, if not with stoicism. And then she was gone from his sight. Well, the man she had chosen, and to his credit had chosen her, had proved his worth in the world of honorable achievement and, so far as he could hear, of clean, worthy manhood. He looked all of that, if face and bearing can tell the story, even in part, of the life behind them. A man physically well made, strong face, dark haired, quiet, rather austere looking, but with a pleasant smile, and of distinctive personality. Yes. No doubt Nadia was in good hands. One who would do some of the giving and caring for her, surrounding her with tender care she so truly deserved.

Before leaving, Julia asked Robert to dine with them the next evening, and he accepted knowing he must go on as before, and adding to, not cutting off, diversions and friendships. Also, Julia used to be a pleasant companion. He had been asked to the little reception at the Dexter home, but that was more than he could bear today. It was over.

He went for his lunch but could not eat much more than the pretense of a meal. Then he went forth once more to attend to business matters. Work. Work of some kind is the making and the saving of mankind. Without it we would, with no great lapse of time, drift back to the animal stage which is not left very far behind. Work and thought together born of each other, though a seeming paradox, by which we climb the ladder of progress. Work, our making and our saving, though too often looked upon with disfavor and abhorrence, as an enemy or unpleasant companion. Put a man in a desert with nothing to do to amuse or occupy his mind and he will soon go mad. Give him something to do and he will not only live but is more than likely to find his way out. Pleasure as pleasure should be looked upon only as the oil that greases the machine to keep it running smoothly.

XIX

For the next few days happiness immeasurable dwelt in the
Dexter home. Calm and peaceful before, now that peace had
come alive, almost as the seed lying in the ground unknowing,
when touched by the awakening forces springs into life's activity
and bursts its enclosing shell and moves, moves upward to
an unseen warming, developing light, growing, expanding,
blossoming, fructifying.

Each one of that household was a different being, taking
on a brightness they had not known before, the servants as
well as the heads of the home. Nadia had brought to them
the quickening impulse, while the love and responsiveness
caused her personality to blossom more and more. Though the
first day shyness held her in a loosening grasp, it fell away in
the warmth of love and happiness. She went about the living
rooms, the stairways, the halls, as an embodiment of joy, of life's
fulfillments. Her laugh, which was music in itself, was always

a melody awakener in other hearts, and brought forth special
efforts from those others to make it ripple forth again. She sang
not only songs with the piano accompaniment, but snatches,
phrases, trills, without any instrument, like a bird that has lived
long enough to know the fullness of life and of its own gifts of
song, flitting from branch to branch, letting its soul forth in
song with its love nest beside it. Her life and brightness were
never expressed in a loud or frivolous way, unbecoming in one
beyond youth's earlier years, but just that living joy which is ever
beautiful, even in the aged, which can be seen, strangely enough
at times, here and there, in the very face of that oncoming
visitant who bears each one away into the gulf of the unknown.
And Nadia was only thirty.

"Getting on," she thought, "and success did not come too
soon to bring me into all this dear love and attainment."

She made the house a garden of life, of color and sound.
She and Raymond did not miss a moment of being together
that his affairs would allow them. If she went anywhere it
was planned so that she was there to greet him when he came
hurrying home. She and Helen Burgess, drawn to each other
at once, were like closely twined sisters who did not want to be
separated and were glad to go on together.

Achievement—something of worth given to the world—
success—recognition and its rewards, gladness of appreciation,
financial return that lifted her out of shut-in-ness, shut-out-
ness, and household drudgeries. Love—the beautiful personal
gift—added like a golden glory and benediction to that love
of all which God had implanted so deeply in her. Her shining
road had lead her through the sometimes haze and cloud and
threatening dark, onward to this goal of glorious, fulfilling love.

Her shining road. And she mustn't stop satisfied, lost in this attainment, but follow still that call to be, to do, to give. Only so one could respect one's own soul and grow, grow, answering the divine urge within by which human life age by age, aeon by aeon, attains. In the midst of all the blessedness that chilling question did persist occasionally.

"Did I step down and touch the mire? Did that Mephistophelian voice of disillusionment cause me to swerve from the highest and purest to gain all this? Can any shadow of impurity bring good, real good?" Her soul revolted at the incongruousness of its possibility. "No. It must be as Raymond says, even though I stained myself with the thought. No. Mephistopheles may have tried to win me but my own strong, clean soul was the victor."

And then she would sing again. Each to each, she and Raymond told their soul desires, those that were not too vague for expression. He told her though he had made one of the greater successes in business, having apparently been born with the gift and forced to earn his way, and in this success and effort he had opened the way for other men to earn and care for their families, he had been cautious, sure, perhaps stern but never unfair or unfeeling but wanting others to profit by his profit; though he felt he had been of service to the government and to his country during that terrible war, even if not suffering and dying on the battlefield where so many, many had been tortured and sacrificed, yet there was within him a something else, something greater it seemed to him, undeveloped, a germ, an idea, that had lain questioningly on his mind for years and years, aroused to greater intensity by that war, and which brought forth, developed, might have proved of great benefit to the world.

"I am not what is called an idealist. I have too much practical reality for that, but I have the combination of the two, that is more likely to succeed in what I undertake with interest and purpose." That was one of his dreams. Her coming had given it another quickening. If he lived on perhaps he could accomplish it, give up a part of the strain of business and bring that idea forth into usefulness.

"I will explain it to you some other day," he had said, "when our time is not so broken in upon. Perhaps your own vision and faith, Nadia, will add to mine. It may be you will add the spur I have needed all these lonely years and I too will see, in its achieving, that part of my 'shining road,' as you call it, come into its own, even as you have brought in its golden glow of love. 'No man liveth to himself alone.' We help or harm. I want to help. Your coming makes that desire stronger."

"Oh, I am sure we can help each other, Raymond. I feel I can do bigger things now. Surely our coming together must have been meant for a higher purpose than our personal enjoyment alone. I am longing to know what that great idea of yours is. I know it will come forth into action now."

"Yes, when free from interruption we will talk of it. But what about your Mephistopheles foolishness now?" he asked teasingly.

"I begin to think as you say, beloved, nothing but good could have worked to bring us together, and so I couldn't really have followed that voice and stepped downward."

"We all have times of disillusionment but when we are on the path, call it the 'shining road,' or whatever name given it, we cannot leave it and travel the lower way not even at your

'Crossroads.' We may glance down but the pull of the Voice recalls us."

They did not speak of the "bar sinister" that had stood between them threateningly. Had they forgotten it in their fortunate fulfillment, the richness of their joy? Yet even now it was on the way, on the way. They were sitting side by side, hand in hand, before a grate fire in the library, after dinner, waiting for the opera hour. A new opera was to be given that Nadia was anxious to hear.

"I'd rather sit here and listen to you sing some sweet song especially for me than go to that opera," he said.

"Far better for you to have changes, my dear sir," she teasingly rejoined. "I don't want you to get too much of mine."

"Why, beloved," he drew her head to his breast, "I think if I were slipping down into death, and had truly died, passed to the frontier of the beyond, your voice in song or loving speech could call me back. It reaches to the soul of me."

"Oh, Raymond, how beautiful that sounds."

"It is true, beloved. I feel it would do just that marvelous thing."

"Don't try it, Raymond. As beautiful as it sounds I don't want to test its possible truth for fear it would fail me and I would be left without you, here alone," she shuddered at the dark picture.

"Oh, I don't expect to, dear heart, until we have had some happy years together. But who is this friend of yours, this Mr. Robert Merrill? Kent tells me he is a fine fellow, made a fine record in the war as a captain, and was one of your special admirers, that he is not backward in saying so, and was greatly disappointed when he lost you. Shall we invite him to dine with us soon?"

"Aren't you afraid to invite an old lover of mine then?" she asked smiling.

"Not if she is willing to come to me with him already here on the ground between us. No. You can't arouse my jealousy. I only think more of a man or woman who appreciates you. Did you love him?"

"Not as I do you. I was fond of him, but it wasn't the love that knew its reality when I looked into your eyes."

"You dear! What separated you?"

"Ask him."

"You tease. You know I couldn't."

"The war brought it about, brought forth the cause."

"Well, whatever it was, invite him to dine with us, and the Kents too. We must return that courtesy of theirs. A good fellow, Kent. A good worker too, to be depended on to do right, what falls to him to do."

Coming unasked, this appreciation of Julia's husband by his austere business head pleased Nadia, and she guessed the pleasure it would mean for them if they knew. Then Mrs. Burgess appeared, saying, "You wanderers in paradise, if Nadia wants to hear that new opera it is time we were on the way."

"Nadia, why did you plan for it?" he asked lingeringly.

"But you, too, are fond of the opera," she answered.

"Yes. But I like this better."

She arose first, leaned over and kissed his forehead.

"We must keep in touch with the world of beauty around us, not hold aloof because of our love, and that very love will take on greater beauties, don't you think? The larger the flower, the greater amount of fragrance it can send forth."

"Right, beloved. But sometimes the big flowers don't have any fragrance and the little ones have much, like you." She laughed her happy, tinkling laugh.

"To tell the truth, there was something I wanted to learn in their rendition of this new, to me, opera. It all has a bearing on my knowledge, my own singing, and my literary work. There is a reflex we cannot measure between us and our work, whatever it may be, and all our experiences."

"Will you sing it for me tomorrow evening?"

"There are selections from others I like better. I will choose from them. You will have much of my singing, and of me, in the years to come."

"God grant it," he said fervently. Nadia ran up the stairway, to the rooms they had beautified for her, and came back with her wrap, without waste of a moment. The three congenial ones hurried off, to pick up a friend of Mrs. Burgess on the way.

———————

That same day Nadia received a letter from home, the old home, now she had another, from Aunt Eleanor. Of course she had received letters from each, now and then, but Aunt Eleanor having taken her place, in part, her letters were most important, under these conditions, and this one held a surprise and gladness. The letter told all were in good health, and doing well, and would be happy only that they missed her.

"But you have a right to all the good you are receiving. I don't think one of us denies it or

begrudges it to you, Nadia dear. The Professor and
I are surely glad because you brought us together.
And now what do you think of you having set the
wheel of marriage going among us? Don't think you
are the only one the marriage fisherman has snared
for your wedding day either. When the word came
from you that you were to be married on a certain
day, the Professor and I, having decided that we need
each other, decided to quietly yoke together on that
same day, a double wedding though separated only
by a fence of distance, a fence which science seems
to be threatening to tear down. Don't think I was
driven to marriage this late hour in life just to escape
the slighting term of 'old maid' or 'spinster' for I
am used to that, which is only a survival of human
coarseness and cheapness, like the survival of the
remnants of the tail, ha! ha! No. Even elderly people
can fall in love. And isn't it more beautiful and true
than the surface loves of Youth? We think so. We are
truly, deeply happy together. We bless you, and that
so rare smile of the unseen forces that brought us
together, even though our life span is moving into its
autumn. Is not the foliage of autumn, its wondrous
soul expressions, beautiful beyond the power of
language to tell? I say, soul, for Nature has a soul,
a part, even as we, of the Great Soul that is tireless
in its putting forth of varied wonders. Now there
is only James left to be introduced into the double
yoke. He is too young yet. When you come we will

plan for his home life, until he too finds, as we will hope, the 'right one.'

> *Your affectionate Aunt Eleanor"*

Nadia's heart leaped in gladness over that letter. She was the more at ease in regard to them all. "Dear Aunt Eleanor. How true and good and wise without pretense, all gold," Nadia said to herself.

She was on the watch for him, when Raymond came home from his office a little earlier, and she drew him and Mrs. Burgess into the library immediately, and told them about Aunt Eleanor and the Professor, both lovable personalities, showing their humorous points, telling of her witticisms, so they enjoyed it all with her, and felt it would be a pleasure to know them.

"Oh, you will like them all, Raymond. So would you, Helen, as true, good, bright people, the 'salt of the earth' as the old phrase goes. As a family we never have had riches in the money sense, also so necessary at times, but we have had a fair share of the more valuable riches of mind and spirit; and a father and mother who shed that atmosphere around us."

"I will be glad to meet and know them soon, Nadia darling, as a part of you, and your environment, to prepossess me in their favor from the first."

"Will I ever meet them too, I wonder," mused Mrs. Burgess.

"Someday, ere long I hope, you and Raymond's daughter, Luella, whom I have yet to know, and love too."

"She is a lovable girl, Nadia, like her father," Helen laughed back at them as she left the room

"Helen is lovable too, Raymond," Nadia earnestly added.

"Yes," he responded. "She has been a true, helpful sister to me, and a true, wise, foster mother to Luella. It would all have been much harder for me without her. God bless her," he said fervently. And Nadia repeated it, as fervently, after him.

The next morning, after Raymond had gone to the office and Nadia to her own special private room to write some letters, Mrs. Burgess answered a telephone call that caused her to seek Nadia at once.

"Nadia, I have taken the liberty to make an engagement for you early this afternoon, answering that you would be willing and glad to do what is requested. If you object, I am to phone your refusal at once.

"What is it, Helen?"

"My pastor, Rev. Dr. Sargent, who presided at your marriage, and heard you sing here that first evening, you remember, and told you your songs were better than a sermon?"

"Yes."

"He wants you to sing for a friend of his, a young man badly crippled in the war, and shell shocked, who continues so depressed in mind and body that there seems to be little hope for him. His college days had promised much, but he looks upon himself, his life, as ruined beyond any redemption. He loved music but hears it seldom, would not go out publicly to hear any now if he could. Dr. Sargent wants you to be so kind as to sing for him this afternoon, and he, himself, will meet us there as early as 2:30 o'clock."

"Willingly," she answered. "If the little I can do will help any suffering soul, that little is theirs whenever possible. Of course they would have a piano."

"Very likely. Everybody has, or most everybody."

So, the hour named found Nadia and Mrs. Burgess at the home of Mr. and Mrs. Charles Norton, where Dr. Sargent met them at once, as arranged. Just moderately well to do people, Mr. Norton, a lesser member of a small banking firm, with his son, Warren, their only child, in whom their hopes had been centered. As they entered the room they had seen him, this son, rise, somewhat awkwardly, as a cripple must with one false leg, from his big easy chair to greet them with due courtesy, as Dr. Sargent introduced them.

"Warren Norton, one of our brave soldiers, Mrs. Burgess, Mrs. Dexter. Warren, I have asked Mrs. Dexter to come here and sing for you that you might share in what gave great pleasure, something more than pleasure, to me. She is a born singer, Warren. Not one of these whose singing is a fuss and fume, not a lot of vocal sounds with words set to them, but the prism of the voice set to the prism of word meaning sent out from the soul. After you have heard her you will not only be grateful to her for coming but to me for having asked her."

Warren, a courteous gentleman, never forgot to wear this beautiful decoration of human life, courtesy, so lacking in the majority, bowed with graceful salutation, and said, "I am truly grateful beforehand for the pleasure of meeting the ladies and for their kindness. Dr. Sargent and I are in friendly nearness on the music question even though he does have an irritating time with me on the religious." He didn't smile, as one would naturally have expected, only a shadowy glint as its courteous representation.

"I haven't given up over our coming together on that either, Warren," Dr. Sargent replied. "Wait till you hear Mrs. Dexter, her song sermon, with mine, may work effectively."

"You set me too high, I fear, Dr. Sargent," said Nadia, as she went to the piano, open, and facing her with its invitation. "Please don't get your hope too far up for I fear it may tumble, Mr. Warren Norton," she said smilingly. She placed a couple of her songs on the rack before her, sat down on the piano bench and sounded a few preliminary chords to test it, and prepare herself also. Choosing again one of her dainty heart ballads, she sent it, like a celestial messenger, into the hearts of her listeners. The appreciation she had received in the few weeks here, among so many strangers, had made her original song gift blossom as the rose from its bud, and even she rode upon its winged petals beyond her former flights of youth, which is ever supposed to be the glory time of song, as facial beauty.

Warren Norton, in his monotony of despair and disillusionment, had begun to listen perfunctorily, not expecting much out of the ordinary; but as the song moved on he lifted from his reclining position, sat up and leaned forward, listening, gazing intently, yet with a yearning softness as though following an invisible flight a panorama of sight and sound in a more shadowy realm. Without appearing to notice his attitude, yet they were all aware of it. Interest, not mere pleasurable acceptance, but interested response in the within of him. The Reverend Sargent sat opposite him where he could observe his manner and expression, and he surmised at once that this song movement was not all going to be in vain. When the first song was ended, he, speaking for the others, said, "Don't stop. Don't wait for us to say anything. We only want to listen."

Looking around with a smile, Nadia turned back and began again. Choosing two songs she loved, she was able the more to express their meaning with a rare fullness. When the second was ended, like something dear floating away into the unknown, she turned and arose as if with the implication that she had finished. But, no. They would not allow that.

"Please don't stop," Mrs. Norton said persuadingly. Nadia glanced at Warren and though he did not speak the look he gave her was enough.

"Well," she said, "I love the old, old songs. Call me old timey if you will. Which one do you want?"

"All," they agreed.

"No. Only one more this time. Too many might cause satiety so you wouldn't want to hear me again. Which shall it be? 'Home, Sweet Home' or 'Annie Laurie'? Mr. Norton, I guess you and I should feel much alike about music. Which shall it be?"

"Both."

"Not this time," she smiled back at him. "Only one, and the other some other time."

"Will you come and sing for me again?"

"Yes, or you to me. We will turn and turn about. Then, you see, if you get tired of it you can stay away," she laughed.

"Oh, don't place me in that bad plight, Mrs. Dexter, for I might be unable to come, you see," but he didn't smile back at her, only that glint more like a smile being born.

"I will leave 'Home, Sweet Home' for the next time when, perhaps, you can come to me. We love it more than ever when we are away from home, you know." So she sang "Annie Laurie." They had never heard it rendered with such unexampled, appealing interpretation. There was a silence, a pause, while its old time beauty and yearning love loyalty sank into their hearts, old and young. Then Dr. Sargent asked where she gained that specially beautified rendition.

"Oh," she laughed, "by its frequent singing and as the favorite, most loved of all songs, of a lovable Aunt of mine who seemed to have much of the Scotch element in her, mixed with English and Irish. There were traits of each visible in her, and then she was married to a Scotchman also; and they were so truly yoked together that each was restless and miserable if separated for longer than office hours required of him. It was a bit laughable but beautiful too. That kind of union, whether among the so called cultured or uncultured, the rich or the poor, makes marriage beautiful."

"If only we could have more of it instead of so many divorces," he said, "which are only the ravelings of the general lowered principles."

"Mrs. Dexter, I love your singing. That is all I can say," said Warren, as Nadia left the piano. "Will you please come and talk with me?"

"You could not say more, Mr. Norton," she answered as she went over and sat beside him.

"You see," he went on talking, "I am crippled, one leg gone, and scarred." He pointed to a sore on the left side of an otherwise handsome face, "and wrecked generally. I am only part of a man. I couldn't be a gallant to any woman, however attractive she might be, or helpful to one, however old and helpless and in need."

"Oh, don't say any of that. It hurts," she replied, "and it isn't altogether true. And you can overcome most of it, I am sure. I know it. Oh, I know it. The real man is within, and can do more wonders in overcoming and achieving than we would dream possible. I can see what you have been and what you will yet be and achieve through the real now of you, Mr. Warren; let me call you Warren. I like to say it, after hearing Dr. Sargent say it, and we are to be friends, not mere acquaintances."

"All right. What is your name?" he asked.

She told him and he repeated it twice, to himself.

"I want to tell you about my brother. He had not lost a leg but one was crippled, so he was very lame, and was very sensitive about it. His eyes were badly injured so he could use them but little at a time. He had to wear protecting glasses. His nerves were shattered by shell shock, and he was extremely despondent. We made every effort we knew how to make, and he improved a little, whenever his interest was aroused. He had been of the bonhomie type of man, friends, everywhere a favorite. He had succumbed to where sensitiveness over his conditions, and despondency, made him brooding and self hiding, almost solitary. When he had improved a little, and began to take just a little interest in one or two things, fortune brought the Professor and Annetta to live next door. And what do you think happened, Warren? At once they took to and were interested in each other; and then they learned it was love— love—Warren. And visibly, rapidly, Carl, my brother, improved, improved, so we all realized he was going to overcome those physical disabilities and the despondency, and go back to his work as a traveling salesman. Though of course he will always be somewhat lame. That is what interest and love did, Warren. And they were married just before I left for New York. Therefore, fall in love, Warren. It may do wonders for you too. We are all much alike. Fall in love, Warren, and try it. We have to live, you know, go after what we want and get all we can get righteously."

"I have fallen in love already."

"That is good. Is she in the city?"

"Yes. In this room." She looked at him bewildered.

"You," he said. She broke out into that glad rippling laughter that all loved to hear; and Warren laughed with her, really laughed. And he hadn't really laughed since he came back from the war, a wreck. How glad they all were to hear that laugh. His mother could have almost danced for joy, yet all pretended to take it as a natural, everyday occurrence.

"Me?" exclaimed Nadia. "Me!" She arose and made him a sweeping curtsy. "Thank you, Mr. Warren Norton. I am crowned a second time, and I thank you. Why, Mr. Norton, Warren, I am not beautiful, and the world is full of beautiful girls."

"The shine of youth and health and inexperience," he replied. "Not that inward shine that stands for soul and greatness."

"Ah but don't you realize," she answered "that only the few see and appreciate that kind of shine if the outer shell of a woman, not thus of a man, is defaced? I lost my youthful beauty through shut in years of sorrow, hardship, overburdening, and grew sensitive too but couldn't and wouldn't give up."

"I am glad you didn't. I wouldn't have known you. I used to think those plump, peppy girls were it, as the slang goes, but not now. Your kind beats them all to smash."

Nadia laughed ringingly again, and he with her, for the second time.

"Oh, you flatterer! Don't tell me you can't be a gallant anymore. Well, I'm not a young girl any more. I am getting quite mature." The others listened and laughed with them, only occasionally saying something to each other, too interested in these two to even pretend interest elsewhere, under the circumstances.

"What kept you from giving up?" asked Warren.

"Partly that I couldn't shift the burdens on others, I suppose, and what I called my 'shining road.'"

"What was that?"

"Through those years it seemed almost lost or hidden in darkness but it lured me on. The desire, deep within me, to give something of value to the world, to leave some little— shining trail—because I—had—lived." She ended slowly, questioningly, as though looking on—and on—along a calling road, with its goals yet unattained. "An idealist, impractical by nature, but forced by Fate to be in part partial, which is better for all of us."

"You are on your shining road," said Warren thoughtfully, tenderly. "You have trailed it here today. Wrecked as I am—I must again find my own—that I have lost—or—die. For I had one, perhaps not fully defined, but it was there." He too was talking slowly as though pondering, finding his way back through a jungle wherein he had been lost. "I must find a way out or die. And—I—will—find it."

"Bless you, Warren, my friend."

"Bless you! Nadia, my more than friend."

"Bless both of you! my children of the Lord," added Dr. Sargent, in a voice deeply affected, while Mrs. Norton and Mrs. Burgess surreptitiously wiped the tears from their eyes.

"I guess we all have a shining road in life's fresh youth, even the least of us," continued Dr. Sargent, "however far we wander from it and forget its call in the hard struggle; and it is pitiful how few of us attain its goals. Yet, greatness of soul is in the striving on, and if we lose sight of it, finding it again, never forsaking it—the God call within us."

"There he goes again, Mrs. Dexter, Nadia. He calls it God. So do you, of course. But where is God? And what is God? However you theorize. I sit here in my wreckage and ask over and over, 'God, where are you? God, what are you? Help me, help us all, God.' Over and over. As I say to this dear, loyal, patient friend of mine, so true to his profession, and whom I am very fond of, though I've never told him so, was God in that hideous war that sacrificed, tortured and ruined millions of innocent lives? Do we see God in all the suffering and denial over this struggling world with its many horrors in the midst of its beauties? Where selfishness more often wins and unselfishness goes under? Where the innocent suffer for the guilty? Yet I can see humanity climbs to knowledge and greatness through man's inhumanity to man—he is forced to, there is so much of it—though he also climbs by that beautiful something we call love—and—God, if you will—but which, so far, is only showing its glory like the early gleam of sunrise before the spreading glorified dawn. The love of a true mother and father, like mine, who, perhaps, have suffered more over my wreckage then even I. The love of a loyal human friend like Dr. Sargent, one of these God's messengers, if such there be; the human love that, like yours, sees and feels and gives to friend and stranger unassumingly. Greatness of soul. Love. They have a lure you cannot turn away from though their way may lead you long through darkness and pain."

They had let him say it all uninterrupted.

"Yes, I know many of the world's greatest souls have achieved through heartbreaking conditions, with heavy burdens. And if that God *is,* if that other world beyond *is,* they have traveled far on the 'shining road' of the spirit; and it may be that all of them received some impetus from some other life or circumstances, the right touch at the right time. For we are all built up of reflections from and on each other. I am glad you have given me that thought and phrase. It helps. Strange, isn't it, how two or three words put together right can hold for us a world, a lifetime of meaning? Forgive me for holding the floor beyond the dictates of good taste."

"I too have asked, over and over, in my almost give up hours of disillusionment, 'God, where are you? God, what are you?' And even with bitterness shadowing me, when I have asked that, silently, hungeringly, desperately, I have felt, seen God. Not with the outward senses, but a something infinite surrounding me, enfolding me, like an atmosphere tender beyond the word tenderness; enveloping warmth, love, beauty, wisdom. I have not only felt but I have seen, though with the spirit, not the eyes of sense, and I would go to bed comforted. Then, strangely, get up in the morning to the wear and tear and hardships and denial, looking upon that beautiful experience as more likely only my imaginary longing. So material bound are we."

"I am sorry to say I haven't read your books, because I have read very little of the literary output of the last two or three years. One or two I read palled me. But I will read yours now."

"When you do," Nadia said jokingly, "if you don't say you care more for my verse, that has only managed to live, than for the novel which brought success, and brought me here, I'll drop you down the scale of literary appreciation."

"And of friendship, too? But you make it hard when you ask us to place secondary the novel, which you say brought you here."

"Well, I love the verse best though it is not a seller. Verse you know is not a money making book, a big seller, for publisher or author, even when sent forth by one who has made a name, though if it has salacious qualities it series to be more on the road to success. But if God puts into you to love it, to write it, to send it forth for his kingdom, why? Why? does God not make it flourish for His Kingdom's sake? And put the quietus on cheap degeneracy? Why? Why this? Why that? I keep asking God and my own soul. But comes no answer to any of it. Why? Why? If you think of a literary career don't begin with verse unless you have a known name, a position, or influence, or a good advertising publisher. You may suffer a monkey and parrot time over its sales."

"What is a monkey and parrot time?" they all asked.

"Well, it isn't a refined sounding story," laughed Nadia, "but it 'hits the nail on the head' as the old saying goes. A family owned a monkey and parrot. They went away one day and left them in a room together. When the family returned they found that room covered with feathers and fur, and the parrot called out, 'We've been having a hell of a time.'"

They all laughed heartily, and Warren as heartily and unrestrained as any of them.

"I've forgotten how that story came to my knowledge, but it expresses one's feeling so pointedly and fully, sometimes, it would seem folly to discard it altogether, because of the use of the one word which surely must be common in Dr. Sargent's vocabulary even though for different reasons."

"Right. That is so good and to the point it thereby loses its roughness to a great extent," returned Dr. Sargent. "And why should it be looked upon as any worse to use it that way than

'Some will go to heaven and some will go to hell,' which has been said for more than 1900 years. Of course we don't believe in any lasting hell for anybody now."

"And it is my observation that we have had enough of it here without having it in any other world," Mrs. Burgess slipped in quietly. "And yet too well we all know that growth is not attained by ease."

"In seeking the why of what goes on in this human world," went on Nadia, "here is one instance that came to me here a few days ago." And she told of the elderly woman who had given the last of her life to save another on the street, after having given all her life before, its own desires, hopes, longings, for the brothers and sisters, and then made to feel 'not wanted' when she was old—looked down upon for being a foster, a spiritual mother, instead of a physical."

"Alas! for human selfishness," said Dr. Sargent, "and yet it must be that such a golden spiritual thread, woven in such a sombre setting here, will, in God's own unreadable weaving, find its own shining pathway."

"You realize," said Nadia, "that a slave, whether forced or self given, never receives any appreciation, any good words, but is only thought less of, and perhaps forsaken when no longer able to give. Not only a second coming of Christ, but common moral principle is needed more and more in the world."

"It is all a problem beyond our solving, and blessed is he who is willing to trust however called upon to endure. And just now, Nadia, I think it is time for us to be going," said Mrs. Burgess.

"Please wait till I have served tea," hurriedly broke in Mrs. Norton. "The maid is bringing it now."

At that moment the maid appeared with the refreshments. A little longer they stayed, out of courtesy to Mrs. Norton. Through all, Warren had tried to keep the scarred side of his face turned aside from them, not being able to quite forget his disfigurement even though interest and laughter had again, strangely, unexpectedly, after long, long time, bleak years, come in their own immeasurable friendliness and riches to greet him. Would they abide with him? Would those mighty helpers come, again and again, until he had yoked his disabilities and despair and, binding them, said, "I am master! I am. I rule. Get thee behind me, Satan"? How his mother and Dr. Sargent hoped and prayed before they left.

"I have no right to ask it, but you will come again? And soon?" asked Warren.

"Yes," she smiled at him. "But you are to come to me too, remember."

"Can I, I wonder?" he said half to her and half to himself, as she made her adieux.

"I'll have to take that as a measure of your desire to know me and to hear my home singing again," she laughed at him.

"Never, my dear friend. Never."

Taking with them Mrs. Norton's and Dr. Sargent's warm earnest thanks, they left.

"Another innocent victim," said Mrs. Burgess as they rode homeward. "And they are many. While the rest of the world goes by with indifference. But then very few care for the sufferings of the other fellow, only for their own. They may give a little money, now and then, to the Red Cross or some charity, but they don't want to be bothered any other way."

"And so many, so many look upon and use those in misfortunes as only derelicts to be deserted as the savages desert their old, their aged ones," Nadia responded. "Oh, God! whatever you are, wherever you are, help us all. Come into our consciousness. Help us to know, to understand. To be what we ought to be. To do what we ought to do."

"Amen!" breathed Mrs. Burgess, fervently. "And it was you, then, the novelist visiting in the city, who went with and stayed with that poor woman till she died. If I had known you then, I might have guessed it. I happened to see the article, in skimming that Sunday morning paper."

"I just happened to be standing there and saw the accident, and her effort to save the other woman, thereby being caught herself. Through the beauty and joy around us there is so much, oh so much of the opposites. Why? And we all make so many mistakes. We are all guilty of commissions and omissions. All are in need of a guiding spirit about us. All are in need of a Divine forgiveness and tenderness. I am, I know."

Over and over, within herself, she kept questioning, "Could all of this good, this success, this beautiful appreciation, the affection, the great love have come to her because she bowed to and stepped down for the Mephistophelian voice of disillusionment? No. No. Had she not always loved the Christ and those other beautiful souls of history? Surely this was as Raymond had said; she had only come nearer the blinded crowd and laid her gifts at their feet and at the feet of Christ. That was it. But would all this beautiful, beautiful, continue for her? She must make some of that good and beauty overflow into other lives. Otherwise she would have no right to keep it, and for those who do not share, their blessings become heavy, stagnant, flavorless, *things*. No giving forth, no cleansing, receiving renewal from the leaven of spirit. Unconsciously she had made the dreary, despairing one laugh. So much to the good. And laughter, that is born of and meant for good, is vivifying. The kindly, humorous, upwelling, laughter is a help to strengthen and build."

And the bar sinister was drawing nearer.

XX

That same day Robert had phoned to Nadia asking when it would be convenient for him to call and see her, as he expected to leave the city in two or three days more. "Before I go I want to see you again, Nadia, in your own home. A picture of you, in your happiness, to carry in my memory." She had invited him to dinner the next evening; so, she and Mrs. Burgess consulting, a few others were invited to make it something more than a mere family evening, and that her marriage would not be so strongly emphasized to the destruction of all enjoyment for him through the evening's associations. They must strive to make it pleasant and have some interesting people. Would that she could make Robert, and everybody in the world, as happy as she. Why did it have to be, so often, that one person's happiness was gained at the expense of another's unhappiness. Why? The severing Fates had surely kept watch between them from the first, to strangely bring only good to her in these beautiful consummations that had seemed so far off, so improbable, just a little while ago. Yet was she not traveling that shining road far more truly in those shut in years of self denial and loving service for those in need, than ever could be possible in the realization of Self's longings? Ah, yes. For the shining road is of the spirit, and if the need at hand calls first, and calls for the sacrifice of Self, that is the true "shining road" though the world sees it not and cares not. Only is it seen and realized by the Great Spirit of All, like a gulf current running through the ocean.

When Robert entered the Dexter home that evening he was impressed, as he would have expected had he thought of it beforehand. Luxury, affluence, not with the commonly visioned meaning of those terms, the costly glare of wealth, but of that higher sense, the soft glow, the interest of innate good taste with richness behind it, the artistic furnishing with yet the home quality with them, the paintings, large and small, adorning the walls, of the type that were like recognized friends, though unseen before, with whom you felt like sitting down to rest and communing, receiving and giving your own interpretations, in return, to the artist and his ideal. A piece of sculpture that spoke to you from its appropriate setting, not in the language of the dead cold marble, but as though, like Galatea of old, ready to come alive and speak in answer to your call. Not the common show place of mere riches this. No. Just enough of the best, but that best that only riches can buy. Only the riches of mind and soul, and only genius can produce them. Also, only riches can own them. And this was now Nadia's setting.

He could not help but think and question in the midst of the converse, "Here are love and riches dwelling together," with the talk going on around him and yet ready to do his part. "Love and riches dwelling together. Does that combination, which we all desire and strive for, reach out, spread its shine, shed its fragrance and bloom to the help of other lives anymore than when love and poverty dwell together? I wonder. Yet love, true love, wherever it is, cannot be selfish; it must give, give, not to the one beloved alone but in its overflowing, a part of itself to all around it.

He knew as Nadia knew because his soul was keyed to some of the same spiritual notes. While he could not have given her quite this much yet, still, he could have given her enough now; ease, comforts, and perhaps travel. And he felt, within himself, he and she would have lived lovingly and happily together. And his heart had turned to her from the first to last. Fate willed otherwise; first in the need of his mother and sister, his first call; then in the calls that held her; and in the war, that hideous evil; and then the strangeness of his marriage. Well, that little wife had given him her love and her life. Her memory was sacred, though in the exchange between them he had lost Nadia.

When they had stood together to give him greeting and welcome, there was a hurt deep within him he could not keep from rising up to stab at him, but he downed it again, having learned, in these last days, to accept and face the inevitable and make the best of its decrees. Their guests were well chosen. They had a jolly and interesting time. He was glad he had come. At the dinner table, and afterwards as well, the jests and varied expressions of opinion went around, causing each one to feel that he or she was as noticeable a factor and personality as another. How was it done? Could it always be done whatever the combination of guests? Through a power of courtesy dependent on hostess and host? Yet it must also be able to beget that quality and its response from each one of the gathering. But it was a gift that brought from each one some of his best and made for him pleasure and happiness. Are we all not happier when our best is brought forth and appreciated by others of our kind?

Courtesy. Beautiful courtesy. As far as Robert could see there was no lack of it here in this household, this evening, and he could easily believe, accordingly, it would not be lacking in everyday. Beautiful courtesy, which, wherever found, beautifies this common life of ours, with all its defacements, some of them necessary, or unescapable, because of our common animal heritage, but others alas, unnecessary and easily effaced but for the indifference of selfishness and ignorance.

Its lack today is one of the most visible and greatest lacks in this human world.

Self seeking, indifference to others, money getting, self aggrandizement, have driven this lovely quality, beautiful courtesy, into a dark closet and laid it away on a back shelf. Robert could not but recognize it here in its rarity. And he loved it. He remembered there had always been more of it in Nadia's old home than among those around them. He remembered it was one of the qualities of the highly developed cultured human, of the soul, that she loved. They had once spoken of it and agreed that it was an attainment all should seek for. And she had then said truly, "Courtesy, beautiful courtesy. Its foundation is in the heart. There it must first be born; and cultivation but adds some of its outward graces of expression. The true soul, the kind heart, beautiful courtesy, will make even the humblest, the most wrecked, the most forsaken, feel that he is of value wherever brought into contact."

He remembered it all, partly because it was so deeply true, and also because she was so young then to have so fully realized it, without much worldly experience to have had a development of truth like that woven so completely into her life and character.

The talk skimmed subjects general and special as it must skim at dinner parties. They talked of art and literature, which is one of the arts, of course, as illuminatingly as though they had been a company of artists and litterateurs instead of a mixture. Sometimes some of these outsiders are better informed, broader, better judges than one who follows some special path in one field. They talked of the value of poetry, true poetry, the height of literature, that, standing on its lonely peak, receives the homage only of the few, who, looking upward from the jazz around them, see it in its beauty and soul worth and take it unto themselves.

"Not the crowd," said Mr. Dexter. "Only the few. But the crowd does not follow the highest, finest music. Only the few. The crowd does not follow the finer, soul lifting drama. Only the few. The crowd did not follow Christ. Only the few."

"And yet, even then, those few seemed to differ so completely in their tastes as to what is the highest poetry today," said one who had occasion to feel the adverse differences.

"And the dictum of the reviewers goes forth, and whether worthy or unworthy, capable or incapable, their verdict turns the wheel of success or failure, for the time at least," said another.

"Success or failure. How they hang by a thread, like the sword of Damocles, and true value is not always the deciding factor whether it be in the realm of poetry or any other field of endeavor," another added.

"So it seems to me," spoke Robert. "Success or failure seems, as far as we can analyze conditions, about as much a matter of chance, of conditions and circumstances, as of ability. I have seen some men of very minor abilities make a big success, if we may call money success, and that is the accepted definition though not a high and commendable one—and some with greater abilities fail, mostly because opportunity or circumstances worked in favor of the first and at the right time. And some of our great scientific discoveries have come by chance, though always the thinking, seeking are back of them, if not for that particular discovery. That is what we must always do: think, seek, work. Yet as I read life, while we are ruled by law we are also, to a great extent, creatures of chance and accident. Even heredity, that says law, has its chance factors. We are innocent victims of those who have gone before us and of the chance happenings to them and to us. It is chance that two meet and mate, whether beautiful characters are drawn together through chance meetings, or defective characters meet thus and unite. And—and—is it not that very chance element that in spite of its bad developments makes also for progress in heredity and in ourselves?"

"That is a question still somewhat unsolved; and in part, I might take exception to you if we had time and place to talk it out," said one of Mrs. Burgess's friends.

"Anyway," added Robert, "we are the innocent victims of our heredity and environment, having no choice in either until old enough to choose, and then our choice is made by what those two have made of us."

"You would do away with free will, with choice then?"

"No. For, by choice, we can modify. If we come in contact with the good, strong enough to touch us, we can compare, reason, and choose, between influences pro and anti. It may be the truth of my observations might be easily shaken by any one of you; I am not a scientist. But I love them. They are greater than I."

"Mr. Merrill is not in the least a pessimist, my friends; I vouch for him on that score," said Nadia, smilingly. "He and I have known each other from childhood and we always, he and I, saw the beautiful vision ahead and believed in, sought its attainment. We both believe in eternal progress of the human, however creepingly slow it may appear and whether by law alone, or law, and chance, advanced."

"And science, great friend of mankind, walking side by side with religion, however dissimilar and unfriendly they may now appear, will step by step give us the truth by which we prove our faith and walk onward and upward, making its fiat of fact, someday, the proof of faith's glimpsed immortality," Mr. Dexter had added.

"I believe it."

"I believe it," each one exclaimed.

"May the day hasten," said one of the company.

"And when that great uplifting, inspiring truth is given forth by science also, mankind will rise with it."

"Amen!" murmured solemnly one of the women guests most given to careless surface enjoyments. For none are so careless, so lost in the common realities of every day, as not to feel the stir, the quiver of longing to know that vision of the spiritual made a mathematical fact.

"The wonders of science, great as they are, are pointers of the way to greater wonders, greater discoveries yet to be, I fully believe," said Nadia.

"And," said another, "who dares deny, that someday, science will enable man to communicate with beings on other planets; though it has failed so far, we may be on the verge of that attainment even now, as some of the wise ones believe."

"But there may not be any other beings," someone reminded them.

"That is inconceivable," Mr. Dexter replied, and Robert agreed with him, "inconceivable that weak, faulty man, as great as we feel ourselves to be, should be the only conscious beings in all the stellar realms. I believe in our great destiny—a faith that helps to spur mankind upward—but I also believe there are others moving onward and upward with us, perhaps in all those shining universes, and much higher on the path Godward. And that thought should also be a spur to us, to our aspiration and effort."

"And this," thought Robert, "from one of our so called hard business men. The financial world has its high gleams as well as other fields of human struggles."

"I wonder how it will come," he said aloud, "through the electric or light wave or some new cosmic ray."

"Or something altogether different, hidden still from man's groping search," he answered. "Like Mr. Merrill, the scientists, though some of their gifts to man have been misused, used for the advantage of evil, yet the ultimate is for good, knowledge, helpfulness, spiritual uplift."

"Yes, for the basis, the sum of all, is spirit," added Nadia.

"Is it? Who knows? Or the duo, spirit and substance," one of the guests replied.

"Anyway," Nadia added, "feeling the leavening germ of the Godhead within us, it is for each to seek and strive to do his part, add his bit to the great weaving, bright with trying, though unrecognized by all but the Infinite Weaver; for each life is a unit needed in the whole."

"Yes, we may feel that our lives are wasted," added another "but they cannot be entirely, though but as the drop to that water volume that makes the ocean, we are, in the infinite ocean of being."

"But it is all such an overwhelming, unsolvable problem," exclaimed one of the younger feminine guests, "one almost wants to run away from it, and just take what comes without much heavy thinking and vain questioning, making the most of what little joy one can get. It does seem, as Mr. Merrill says, that however you look at it, trying to explain it, we seem to be, to a great extent, innocent victims, and also, to some extent, creatures of chance."

"Let us eat, drink and be merry for tomorrow we die," the old slogan—moving on with every race and age—"is again the slogan of today," spoke up another guest, "the degenerative slogan that always precedes and brings decadence of a race. It is doing this today, yet one can't be blamed very harshly for feeling that way at times."

Afterward in the drawing room they were having a happy time with jests and laughter, each seeming to draw out the bright humor, the mysticisms of another, when, in the midst of it, the butler brought a card to Mr. Dexter. He looked at it. It read:

Martha Rand
The Times

Supposedly a newspaper reporter. He didn't notice that it didn't say "New York Times." "Tell her to come again, that I am occupied at present."

"Begging your pardon, Sir, I took that liberty," the butler replied low. "She says she is heavily pressed, and asks your indulgence and courtesy."

Mr. Dexter rose, and excusing himself to his guests, followed the butler from the room. As he entered the entrance hall, with the card in his hand, and advanced toward the figure of a woman, standing partially turned from him, she turned and faced him. Almost at once he exclaimed, "You!"

"Yes, I."

"Ah, he had known her," flashed through her mind bitterly, "in spite of the years between." He was improved, grown more handsome and impressive, while she was faded, coarsened, far from the beautiful girl he had married and deserted. But this thought didn't take but a second or two to flash through her.

"You got ahead of me, but I am here."

"What do you want now that you have attained this meeting through deceit?"

"To show the world that divorces can't always divorce, that marriage cannot be undone except by death."

"I endured everything from you with a patience that became a weakness, a fault. This cannot go on. My guests will hear. What do you want?"

"I warned you, you should not marry or you would rue it. Neither my love nor my hate will let you live with another woman."

"Love and hate never abide together. You mean your hate, which is your selfishness."

"Call it what you will, then."

"Enough of this. I cannot listen now. Some other time, if there is any good to be gained by it. As the mother of my child, I wish only good for you, and happiness." They had talked low, but he feared their voices might reach the others.

"There is no other time. You shall not live with her. Rather—this."

She lifted her hand, and a shot rang out ominously through the rooms. A pause. A hideous pause. Everybody, everything, animate and inanimate, seemed to hang for one moment, breathless, moveless, waiting on that one prophetic sound, prophetic of evil hanging on the fearful unknown. That pause, that gulf of silence, crossing which meant to come upon tragedy.

Then the rush. The whole household, and the guests, were on the scene, with frightened faces and staring eyes. Mr. Dexter was lying on the floor in a crumpled heap. Nadia was first, and sank down on the floor beside him, barely seeing the woman who stood a few feet away with the revolver still in her hand. Nadia had lifted Raymond's head into her lap and was murmuring low to him.

"You cannot have him," the woman watching her said. "He is mine. I sent him on before. Now, I follow," and another shot rang out. The strange woman, like a diabolical figure in this diabolical scene, fell to the floor, groveled there where she fell for a moment; then—crawled—crawled—inch by inch— painfully—in a stricken, desperate, hideous effort that held all eyes spell bound, inch by inch—to that prone, silent figure of him she had come there to kill, and—reaching his feet at last— laid her hand upon them, her head close—close to them, and with a satisfied gasp, a relaxing of the torture drawn features, sank into that unconsciousness which, temporary or lasting, blots out all miseries as all joys, all loves as well as hates, all longings as all gratifications.

What the onlookers had seen had happened so quickly, it seemed but a moment to their surprised, horrified senses, that they were like an audience held in thrall by a dramatic scene, on a stage, that was not to be interfered with, not a reality of which they were a part, though an accidental ignorant part. Then they stirred to some show of action. One of the men hurried to the phone to call a doctor. Then they questioned Mrs. Burgess as to who was their nearest. She was down on the floor beside Raymond now. Was he dead? Was the woman dead? Strange how you can be a living, breathing, thinking entity—how you can be—and then not be—in the mere fraction of a second. How so much can hang on so little is one of the paradoxes of the unsolvable universe. Raymond was not dead to Nadia when she sank down beside him. His heart was still beating, though jerkily and feebly, but he was unconscious. He did not notice her caresses, her kisses. To all appearances they might as well have fallen on a marble statue. Then, for a short time, the doctors were there, two of them. After the first tentative examination they said, "We fear he is gone, Mrs. Dexter. There seems to be no heart action."

"Gone! No. No. He will come back," Nadia cried out. "He said if I called, he would come back to me. Just last night he said it! Or was it years and years ago? He said, if he had gone suddenly to that far off shore, and I called him, he would hear my voice and come back to me. I will call. I know he will come. He will not leave me. We love each other. Raymond!

Raymond!" With heart breaking intensity the cry went forth, "Raymond, come to me. I need you. I need you, Raymond! Raymond!"

Tears were in the eyes of all who were looking on, and a choking sob of sympathy in their throats.

Then Robert Merrill, who knew love's loyalty, and those others—did they know it too or only its weak symbol?—beheld what they would never forget, hanging breathless over that unknown; with that call of love's intensity and faith sounding, sounding over the gulf to that other shore unrefusably, as unrefusably as Christ's own call to Lazarus, "Lazarus, come forth!" and he came, so Raymond Dexter heard that call on the edge of the other frontier, and—and fought his way back— back—breasting the heavy tide that held him—back—back—to that yearning, calling love in need of him. The heart stirred. Slight as a faint breath it caught its beat. His eyelid quivered. He opened his eyes to those yearning starry orbs looking into his and said in a faint whisper, "Nadia!"

"Raymond, beloved! Oh, my beloved! you did hear me. You did come back to me. I knew you would. You wouldn't leave me here alone, Raymond dearest. Raymond dearest! You have come back to me. God, I thank thee, I thank thee, God," and she laid her head down beside his saying over and over, "I thank thee, God."

Once more had been witnessed one of those miracles that lie poised between the mysteries of life and death, the miracle of spirit calling to spirit, overcoming with its yea the nay of the material bondage. Love, "the greatest thing in the world." Not body love. Love, the magnet of spirit. Not often it is called forth in this unbelieving self bound realm of being. Yet it is there potential, deep in the germ of the human soul—the leaven of the Godhead.

Those who beheld it went afterwards to their homes and about their daily tasks strong with an abiding faith, and looking upon their fellow kind with more of that wisdom and charity and love taught by the prophetic vision of One, two thousand years ago, called The Prince of Peace, the Prophet of Spirit.

The other actor in this drama of death was gone. The doctor who had worked over her trying to revive or restore the spark of life stated that further effort was useless. She was gone. She had reached the other, unseen shore. That love to bring her back did not call from this side, or in her own weak, uncontrolled being, though it was there self bound, in bitterness, from which it would emerge, in its own radiance, in some other country of the soul's adventurous journeyings. Not in one sphere do we gather all the growth, the truth, the beauty and the bloom of the soul. But over mountains and plains, over rivers and seas, from world to world, in God's infinite creations of being, we travel on; and God loves us all.

Hanging on the verge, Raymond Dexter was lifted to a cot and carried to his private room, Nadia holding his hand and occasionally speaking, to keep hold of the dangerously drifting consciousness.

To Mrs. Burgess had fallen the part of directing mind in what now remained to be done. She had thought quickly what should be done. She must be charitable, fair and honorable, toward this dead woman, who had once been one of their family associations if not one of them in the truer sense that would have held them together. And she was the mother of Luella, her foster daughter, whom she loved almost as her own. She could guess what Raymond would want done now. He had provided worthily for this woman through all these years of separation, undeterred by her unworthiness. They knew little of her life but that it was a continued seeking of the cheaper pleasures, and she had not remarried, some of its looser characteristics which naturally would follow with these lives no higher developed than to make pleasure their only purpose. She would telegraph her people and while waiting their expressed desires, have the body cared for at a capable undertaker's. Both must be attended to at once. But she felt if Raymond died she wouldn't care much where the murderer's body was cast out.

If only there could be found a way, she thought, in her horror and shrinking, to prevent loud publicity of this tragedy, of its family affairs. Was there a way? An accident? An accident whereby a woman was dead and a man dying or near death. Could it be made to sound plausible? Hardly. Guests and doctors and servants might possibly cooperate with her but even so there might be no sure way. There would have to be a police investigation and perhaps a quizzing of all the guests. There was no way out as she and Robert saw it. No. If such notoriety had to be faced they must face it courageously. And better the real facts than the distorted ones. No. She could see no escape.

Before leaving, each one of the guests offered their help in any way possible. But, thanking them, there was nothing they could do, she answered. Yet, almost unexplainably she found herself accepting assistance from Robert Merrill and consulting with him, even glad, though also unexplainable, that he remained with them, quietly helpful in an understandingly efficient way, that made it more possible for her to endure the nerve trying conditions, as also to think and direct.

There are some people who are helpful, always, under almost any conditions, among friends or strangers. That was Robert's nature to begin with, and his life experiences, with its long service for others, had developed and strengthened and also given it a fineness that not only made it more acceptable but welcome and soothing.

The cot on which Raymond had been borne upstairs to his rooms was brought back and the dead woman placed on it. All effort to restore her had been in vain. Poor mistaken being led by wrong impulses to the waste of life's better opportunities. Poor deluded woman! Poor weak, groping souls, each one of us.

She would send for Luella, because of both father and mother. She was old enough, fifteen years of age, to accept with understanding and poiseful courage, the unpleasant, unhappy ways of life as well as its better.

So Luella came. She leaned caressingly over her beloved father, murmuring love words with tender pattings and glinting smiles. She wept over the dead, wayward mother, when she, with Mrs. Burgess, went to look upon her face, where her body lay in waiting for its last journey, and to be the mourners at the little prayer service of farewell.

When she and Nadia met, each looked at the other with strange feelings. Each beheld that outer shell which tells so little, so little of what dwells within, yet which rules far beyond its right, and acknowledged to herself the outward attractions the other possessed. Luella was a blonde with some of her mother's beauty added to some of the stronger characteristics of her father whom she much resembled. She saw in Nadia's frail face and form, in her glowing eyes, the finely poised head held aloft by the unconscious pride of character, not that inferior false pride of Self, that something which she had not yet learned to know and name—that something of personality called—charm. But there had arisen within herself, at first, the personal self opposition in combat with this woman who had won her father's love and been the cause, though an innocent one, of this tragedy and unpleasant notoriety. Had caused some more shadows to fall upon her young life and leave a blot upon her family and name.

Yet even as she felt this, she knew she was unfair, and tried, at least for her father's sake, to put it aside, to suppress it. If it had not been this woman, naturally it might have been some other. She was old enough, at least mentally, to realize that. And what was done, was done. One must accept the good. She had won Aunt Helen too. They were fond of each other. And she, herself, must not, could not be an outsider in this small family group to which she belonged. She could not bear that. And this woman drew her, drew her against her will. Nadia, surmising the presence of this feeling and how natural it would be, was patient and unassertively kind, liking the girl for herself as well as for the father's sake. It was not long, as the days slipped by, till their attractions each to each, as well as their mutual interests in the other two of their family group, drew them together; and their own natural spontaneity of good feeling helped and hurried the attraction. Then also, as Luella, thinking it over dispassionately, accepted, the poor mother was at rest now, and it may be, looking back upon them with more kindly feeling than when she had left them. Surely that must be a part of God's invisible plan, that we see with clearer vision, not self bound, the unclouded sight of the spirit, which is of God.

Before Luella went back to her school, after the father was well on the way to health, and the holiday season over, she and Nadia were more than friends, and the latter had become to the former a source of help, of growth, of inspiration. She, too, began to glimpse though shadowily, that something beautiful in life that Nadia called "the shining road." She felt a more tender, loving interest in her associates, and strong stirrings of desire to be and do according to the deeper, worthier valuations, not mere self seeking.

For many days the fight went for Raymond Dexter's recovery, and Nadia was constantly beside him. His eyes rested on her, followed her, and she knew, without the words, that he wanted her near him and in his sight. His other Self, he told her afterward, that he must hold to tenaciously, yet trustingly, or lose it never to find it the same. He did not talk much. At first he asked anxiously for knowledge of "her"; of what had been done. When told that "she" was dead from the first—he groaned a little—and that Helen had had the body well cared for and sent home to her people in answer to her own telegram and at his expense, and a care taker with it, thinking that is what he would have said to do, he merely said, "She did the right thing. Helen knows." Then, after a moment, added, "Poor lost life. Why do we all make so many mistakes." He made no comment then, not until afterward when he was getting well, as to the threats that had been made and carried out. When they did speak of it they also spoke of what they realized must have been, that "she" had a hired informant in the city keeping watch of his, Mr Dexter's movements, but that he had kept under cover and could not be known.

When told of Robert's assistance and helpfulness through that trying time, he said, "We must not forget it then, in times to come. And I took from him the treasure he wanted. Such is life. But few would have put their hurt aside, stayed near and faced it, and given Self in helpfulness. We must keep the friendship of such a man, Nadia."

"That loyalty, that helpfulness is a part of his 'shining road.' He gave himself for his mother and sister and for his country. He follows the vision," added Nadia.

He would have worried about his business, but his head assistants came to see him and declared everything was moving on smoothly. That he had left it where they could "carry on" and he must not be troubled in the least.

Through these days of convalescence he would ask her sometimes to sing; and with gladness in her heart that he was going to live and be well again it came easy to sing, low and sweet, some tender verse, or ripple forth some phrase of a bird song, whatever struck her mood and fancy at the time. Or she would read to him snatches of things she loved, from the poets of her favored garden of poets, little quotations of thrilling beauty, each one a spur to any awakened soul, each one around on the upward ladder of human growth. And he loved it all, this man of the big, hard, business world, for he too had the awakened soul, and had seen the vision of the shining road; and one of its unfollowed goals, that had long shone in the hidden chamber of his soul, was calling, calling stronger and stronger to him as he lay there in his own room, shut out from the rush, the turmoil, the insistent calls of every day. Aside from an honorable industrious life he had always wanted to help, in some specialized way, his struggling, suffering human kind. He had always given his "tithe," more than his tenth, for the kingdom of God! The Red Cross, the Salvation Army, were favorites of his bounty. He believed in and loved them. Probably they too, like all organizations and effort, had their faults, their weaknesses, their failures, but at their foundation they were good and invaluable, and he loved them for their purpose and the good they accomplished, a helpful and uplifting element in human endeavor. But he wanted to give himself with his money. Though he had given himself in the earning of that money, he wanted to give himself with its giving, at least in part. "He who gives himself with his alms feeds three; himself, his hungering neighbor and me." "Accordingly as ye have done it unto the least of these, ye have done it unto me."

Speaking of this to Nadia one day as they sat there alone, he said, "Added to all of this, Nadia, I also feel that no one should live or die hoarding, hoarding. It is soul withering."

"I am with you in all of this, Raymond," said Nadia with intense earnestness.

"I knew you would be, dear. One should give of one's surplus and one's self while living, and make what is left behind in death work to some great good."

"After a comfortable providence for those connected with one personally, and who should ask more, I want to endow a college for scientific research, with medical specialties, which must include the cure of diseases that cause mental disorders, the most pathetic of all human diseases. I had a friend, whom I was very fond of, who went that dark road, Nadia, and ever since, that has been one of the ways in which I have longed most to help. And think how many there are on that long dark road. Some of our best, our best, and the number sadly increased by the war's shell shock victims. The world casts them aside, their friends put them away, and the wheels roll on. Who cares much what happens to the other fellow, so he or she can escape. Institutions of confinement are not enough. Love should follow them and help. The heart of the world should be with them. Untiring research for cure."

"Oh, Raymond!" breathed Nadia tenderly, "it was all of those desires to help others, those greatnesses of soul in you, that won me unconsciously to love you from the first."

"It may have been that magnet in us both, Nadia, that drew us unknowingly, as you say, from the first. And we will work together, Nadia, you in your way, I in mine, supporting each other by understanding sympathy and love. We will seek the unfortunates and give them a touch of happiness now and then. One would never need to seek far. They are all about us. And I wish we had the power to strengthen our own and others' faith in God and immortality. That faith would be one of the greatest, yes, *the* greatest gift, and would make all mankind better, richer, and wiser, in all that means true riches."

"Raymond, how beautiful it all is. How beautiful that God has blessed us that we may work together, you and I. We must not fail to do our best," Nadia said with clasped hands and glowing eyes, with the prophet's light in them. And then she quoted,

> "Not God himself can make man's best
> Without best men to help him—
> 'Tis God gives skill.
> But not without men's hands.

He could not make
Antonio Stradivari's violins
without Antonio."

How beautiful it all is in our souls, even though the outward may have hardship and denial.

And whether in that unsolvable Why of things, it be your lot to pick the blossoms or the thorns along the way, the shining road is—Giving; the shining road is—Love.

And the wheels roll on.

XXI

When Robert Merrill left New York this time he left it a lonelier man than he had come. Life with its strange, weavings had again denied him one of his most longed for possessions. Love, desire, had lured him on and on with his vision fixed on Nadia. No other had ever lessened the steadfast loyalty of his desire. And each time Fate had unexpectedly woven a web and forced them apart. We plan and plan and however sure we may be of reaching our goal some mocking Fate may step in sometimes, even at the last moment, and say us nay with an inexorable ruthlessness as to how great, how devastating may be our despoilment. But Robert Merrill was a strong minded, strong souled man, one of Nature's noblemen. He tried to make the best of what life allowed him, what he could distill and draw from it by his own earnest, steadfast strivings.

Once more he went forth to his work wherever it might lead him, whether along rough unshining ways or where perhaps some new blossoms of affection might at last spring forth and say, "Come breathe my fragrance. I am not that one but I am another with different beauties with which to bless and companion you. Though you loved one flower for its special attractions and it is lost to you why should you not find and love another among all life's uncounted blossomings?" That is the common practice whether love enters in or the mere human or animal desire for matings.

So, absorbed in his work, life and time moved on for him with their visible and invisible tracings, the latter more important always in the great weaving, though that truth is seldom realized as the great power behind the throne on which the crown of attainment wears it halo. In the next three years, his name was recognized more and more in the business world and he had climbed high on the ladder of success but always hand in hand with honor, high principle.

A few times during those years he heard of Nadia indirectly through others and when another book from her pen came forth and added to her fame, he wrote her of his gladness and appreciation. She answered with the warm friendship and earnest interest and faith in him as of old. Once he had again visited New York on calling business matters and, making his presence known, was invited not only to call but to dine at the Dexter home as a welcome and cherished friend. He found them with the shine of happiness in their eyes and glowing over their faces. Such a happiness. Could life hold anything more beautiful and alluring? How he yearned for it. Did achievement of some great truth discovery for the world, or some great spiritual vision, in the harsh grasp of sacrifice, pointing the way to a wonder height for the attainment of the human soul, bring a deeper more beautiful happiness? It must be he felt when thinking of the struggles, of some of the world's great scientists and spiritual pointers of the way.

"Oh, Robert! how good to see you." Nadia had greeted him with welcoming, outstretched hands and warmth in voice and face. "How good. Your coming makes the dear memories real and present with me again. May they never fade from us. And may we always be much, much to each other. However happy we may be, and I am happy Robert, oh far happier than I had hoped to be, if one dear one is taken away there is an ache in our lives that cannot be cured on this side of that ever enclosing Unknown."

"I don't need to tell you my feeling, Nadia. I have done that in the past and I am unchanged in that regard, though life and time has brought other changes, of course."

"And you are not married?"

"No. I have thought of it as making life more comforting and satisfying, but I am still unmated, with my boy, a dear child, and my mother and sister with her husband whose work takes him much away from home, to make my home for me. Life is a strange mixture and delights in juggling with us. No one can know what each day's distilling may bring forth."

"No. But I wish you all the good that is possible to human life, and you deserve it, Robert."

"I do not know as to that special merit of mine, and life does not always give according to merit, though I have much, much to be thankful for. I often go over and over, in my mind's vision and bearing, those horrible war scenes and their hideous sounds. I cannot wipe them out, though the world is forgetting those who suffered and laid down their lives. It goes on in its

careless self seeking on a lower plain, with lower aims than
when those lives were called to their sacrifice, while their spirits
hover over that once war torn land, over our land, over all lands,
and cry out unheard to all who are living or are yet to live, not
to so desecrate their sacrifice or throw it away into the waste
of human strife, but to make it what it was meant for, a great
turning point for more and more uplift, more and more human
good. No. I cannot wipe it from my mind even in my busiest
times. It is ever there in the background."

"Oh, I can understand all, all. And Robert, I honor you
the more because you feel that way and were one of those who
did his individual, commendable, share in that great struggle
and sacrifice now, as you say, being desecrated by a lower moral
plane of living when it should be a higher. I, too, can see those
hovering spirits and hear them calling to all the lives of earth.
"Be true. Be true to high ideals," and alas, the world seems not
to heed the calls. Away and away it rushes on its self seeking,
pleasure following, unspiritual way. Well for my comfort of
mind that I wasn't there in that maelstrom of war to behold its
visible horrors. Like you I would never be able to forget." She
too rubbed her eyes as though to brush the conjured visions
away.

"But I didn't mean to make this meeting together again
a sad one. No," he said and at once changed the subject. They
were in the midst of an animated talk about home folks and
doings in the onetime home town, when the others of the
family made their appearance, ready for the dinner hour.
They had thoughtfully allowed these two old friends to greet
each other and go over old times together alone before being
disturbed and interfered with by the new friends.

Robert's impressions of Mr. Dexter were heightened by that additional meeting together. They came upon points, matters, on which they were sympathetically responsive. The others, the sister and the daughter, pleased him more also. The daughter was a beautiful young lady now, but not so beautiful in his eyes in her fresh girlhood as Nadia in her blessing achieving womanhood.

It was a happy family dinner. There seemed to be a harmonious spirit pervading the household. More so than might have been commonly expected under past conditions and diverse elements. As the evening wore on in pleasurable converse he told Nadia he could not go away without hearing her sing again, one of the songs he had loved in the years gone by. She could not refuse him, and in truth that spirit of the old time came back, swept over her and made her, too, prefer for that evening their sorts of long ago. So she sang two of them, those she knew he had loved. Her gift of song had not lessened in the atmosphere of happiness and fulfillment, but was as appealing and perhaps even stronger than of yore. Robert, leaning back in his easy chair, said nothing for a moment after she finished and left the piano. Then he spoke as though coming up, up from a long distance out of another world.

"Thank you, Nadia, friend. You sent me down into the world of dreams that is ever at the center or this real world of ours, and who knows, perhaps far more real though apparently remaining for us but shadows. And yet, and yet, shadows that live and work and influence us to do their will, or a part of their will, though invisibly so, making us more like puppets than we dream of. As you know, Nadia. I suppose I should say Mrs. Dexter, but I can't."

"No. No," she demurred.

"Your singing was always a dear inspiring pleasure to me. And now I am going with that as another remembrance, like a hovering presence to follow on with me to do its good work. Mr. Dexter, I envy you," he said turning to him in farewell. "Ladies, I have had a most enjoyable evening and companionship not to be easily slipped into the shadows."

And soon he was gone again, traveling his separate life journey not knowing when it might meet and touch theirs or never again. But those he had left had a feeling, even expressed openly, that he was to be linked with them once more in the bending future, though in some now unforeseen, unguessable way. And he seemed almost as one of them going forth unaware to meet that something unknown which might mean blessings or despoilment to one or all. They fell spontaneously into quietness after he was gone. Nadia said little.

"Dear big noble Robert Merrill." And she went and sat down on the arm of Raymond's big chair, into which he had settled when the guest had left, and put her arm about his neck, leaned her head against his.

"All right, Nadia," he said. "I am not jealous. I want you to love your friends; just so you love me more, most."

"More, most, selfish man. But you know you have that more, most, or how our happiness would be shattered. And I am so happy, Raymond, in spite of the sorrows, losses, of the past. I sometimes wonder if it is possible to last. If Fate itself would not become jealous and send a lightning bolt to break and destroy."

"No. No, dearest. Don't let imagination even hint such possibilities. Dark changes come often in life, but let us not help them, open our doors to them by even a thought, and lessen the shine of our happiness by even their possible shadows."

"Right, Raymond." And she nestled closer and set her lips in a loyal, loving kiss upon his brow.

"Mine. My own," they murmured together when the other two were talking together before going up stairs for the night.

And the wheel of life, the wheel of Time, the wheel of Fate, went rolling, rolling on, making their tracings that no man can discern and separate because he does not know what they are, and could not altogether if he did.

And the wheels rolled on.

XXII

More months had gone by and another summer was nearing the autumn. Not since her marriage had Nadia been back to her old home. Of course Raymond must go with her, meet and like each one of her family as she knew they must like him. How could they help it? Business matters had continued to interfere. Through the hottest parts of the summers they spent just a short time at their country home in the mountains or at the sea shore. They had not even taken a real sightseeing trip to Europe. Raymond having cause to go once on a hurried business trip, she had gone with him, but had only time to take in some of the special outstanding points. Someday they might take a "round the world" trip, but neither was in such need of something interesting to do to fill their time worthily as to feel that round the world pull to any great extent. Life was full of interest to them, where they were and as they were. Sometime, too, they meant to go sight seeing over their own country, their beloved United States, so full of famed interesting sights, and over the whole western continent. But they didn't need any of this to make them capable worthy citizens of their country or the world. She kept in close correspondence with her family, desirous of and striving to be of help even at a distance, especially with James, the youngest whom she had felt might for a time be most in need of another's careful interest. And now he was to be married. So young. She couldn't make that purpose seem quite right. To take upon oneself such responsibilities when apparently too young to realize the greatness of those responsibilities. But neither he nor the girl could be persuaded to postpone such a consummation of their desires. With this occasion a family reunion was planned and hoped for. If only Raymond could get away for ten days, just ten days, they would go. She couldn't bear to go without him. He was planning for it for her sake. Coming so soon, as an addition to the hot weather vacation, made it a bit harder rather than easier to manage. Mrs. Burgess and Luella didn't care to go on so short and limited a trip. They would rather wait and go on to the Pacific coast, and up and down its varied length to see how different it would appear in comparison to their old acquaintance, the Atlantic. During the same week of their planned reunion and James's marriage, their little city, with the cooperation of a large number of towns in the surrounding region, were to have a regional celebration of the sixtieth anniversary of the founding of the city. Indians from the reservations were to be there. Imitation Indian battles, pioneer hardships and such outdoor staging were naturally to be a part of the celebration, though they have been made a common exhibition of the screen, and now would offer far less novelty; and auto races of course are the great interest of modern days at all outdoor celebrations, and even on this occasion, would add its incongruity to the representations of those old brave, lonely, pioneer struggles. It was set for the middle of September which was not far away. Yes. They were going.

And then they were on the way. Nadia was going back to the familiar faces, the familiar scenes and her heart was aquiver; with all the happiness and success that had come to her since she left them they had not taken a back shelf in her interests. They were still dear. They were all a part, an integral part of her, whose influence in her molding, in making her what she had become, could not be measured, could not be guessed. The hurts and denials too, with all the good and attainments, who could say—perhaps were a part of that necessary rough chiseling of the farm, the likeness, the expressed idea, the statue from the waiting unfarmed stone.

Chicago. So much nearer, nearer. The very name sounded like the opening door by which she could walk in and greet those familiar and dear. On rolled the wheels visible and invisible, audible and inaudible. Those we are cognizant of, and those we can only vaguely pray to with hope and fear as we wander unknowingly our way, blind and deaf to many of the forces that will influence our destiny. Those wheels were rolling on.

After leaving Chicago they were enjoying their dinner that evening early, in the dining car their attention and interest diverted, more than diverted, by the passing scenery the larger windows gave to their vision. The autumn glories were only beginning with the pianissimos of their great, their mighty color symphonies of October, but they called to the artist eye and soul bringing them, as all Nature's beauties will, into a nearer touch, a nearer consciousness of the Infinite Soul. In the midst of these digressions they found themselves unexpectedly and gladly greeting Robert Merrill, who had, unseen by them, boarded the train at Chicago and who, they soon learned, was also on his way back to the old home for the celebration and friendship renewals. His family, mother, sister, boy, had gone on a few days ahead of him.

"Nadia is looking fine," Robert thought. "She goes back wearing even more of that inner beauty of soul, as well as that of the physical, or, probably only made more visible by overflowing happiness, and the improved physical expression that cannot fail to give. I wonder if she would be showing as much of both of these outward expressions if she had married me. I like to think so. They are a distinctive looking couple. Anyone should be proud, and benefited, in knowing them."

And still there was a sore spot in his heart that had not healed. A void, a space, it seemed to him, even yet as he looked at her, that no one else could quite fill and make into a well of content. He could not but feel that he would have fitted into her needs and growths if only Fate, Destiny, call it what you will, had brought them into the marriage bonds. The three shortened the trip for each other by their responsive companionship. Not all individuals, characters, could have done so under those mixed personal conditions hiding in the background, yet of which each being cognizant they could not keep entirely submerged in the depths of memory. When they bade each other goodnight they little guessed it would be the last time that Nature's night would descend upon them before another night, that so far has a given us no wakening dawn, had descended upon one or more of them and other travelers, strangers to them, but who were rolling along with them on these audible and inaudible, visible and invisible wheels. Unaware they rolled on.

Next morning the three met at an early breakfast, but didn't linger long. And then they found themselves going west from Omaha, whirling wheels rolling nearer, nearer home. The dear old prairie state, new in history, but old to Nadia—with its strangenesses, its virtues and its faults—the state that has known many of the living and the dead tragedies of life, human and animal, tales that stir one's admiration and love of the great qualities of life. The state has added its share of glory in its short existence to the country and the world, its proud share of impetus to the advancement of the world on its upward trend.

Omaha was behind them. The rolling wheels of audible called, "We are going on, on, to your goals." The rolling wheels of the inaudible, invisible, called, "You do not know, but we are rolling on and bearing you—whither?" No answers from the riddle of the future near or far.

Each one in his Pullman seat had his thoughts on the everyday things of life's appreciations, not on the unknown that fenced them in on either side with its unsolved denial.

Suddenly—jar—jolt—crash—crash—chaos. Chaos outside and chaos inside. A pandemonium of fear and shrieks and horror.

Robert Merrill, after the first shock, pulled himself together, and through the fear crazed jumble around him found himself outside. The shrieks and groans of the conscious living, the silence of the unconscious and the dead in that chaotic jumble of the nonsentient and the sentient smote him with an almost paralyzing force. Then his human will to help, to serve, came welling forth and gave him what seemed a superhuman efficiency. With surprising strength and wisdom to overcome, he tore the debris imprisoning, crushing those human forms, drew them forth, sometime unaided, from their death pens.

Somewhere in all this chaos of horror was that one he loved and the one she loved. Where? He would come to them. Would it be too late? Rescuers were doing their best. When he thought of her, fear and will battled with each other but always will was the victor. And then he saw her. Saw her pale loved face staring up at him unknowing, unconscious. Like a madman in strength, but tender, oh such a tender one, he liberated the unconscious form, lifted it in his sheltering arms, and carried it out on the soft bed of the wild grass beyond the road bed and laid her down. She was still living. That was plainly apparent. There was a gash on her head that was probably the cause of her unconsciousness, and bruises and cuts on her body as blood splashes showed. He bent over her once more and kissed her, oblivious, uncaring if that terrorized, stricken humanity took any notice. Probably they didn't. Then once more he went back to find and bring to her that one she loved. He was there, near where she had been caught and penned, his face twisted to one side and blood smeared, but recognizable. He was rather a heavy man in physique, but Robert managed stumblingly to lift and carry him to that same spot, and laid him down beside her. And oh, the tenderness of sacrificial love—his own love denied, twice, yes, even thrice denied by arrogant Fate after its springtime growth and cherishing. He laid her hand in the hand of the one she had chosen and found happiness with after many of life's vicissitudes. "Did they recognize each other, those hands?" he wondered. "Did the subconscious call each to each, and say, 'Here am I. I am with you beloved.' Ah, who could say yes or nay." Dexter was not dead, but Robert realized he was badly injured.

And in the ache, the suffering within and around him, breathed a prayer, not for her alone, but for both. Why should he at such a time dare to think of Self? Self has no right even against its victors in a fair fight, when stricken helpless by other forces. Leaving them thus he went once more to the help of the helpless.

Among all the noble rescuers and workers of that hour or hours filled with suffering and death, not one was more efficient, tender, self forgetful than Robert Merrill. Another record of heroism though unrecorded, added to that already, so soon, time forgotten one of the world war on the shattered, death strewn soil of France. As soon as possible help had come, a hospital rescue train from Omaha, and back to that city and its hospitals they went. Robert went with these two. He could not, would not leave them until he knew they would not need him. Once he had the gratification that made his heart quiver when kneeling beside them just before they were carried to the hospital train, he saw Dexter open his eyes for a moment only, heard him say, "Nadia," heard her lips slowly whisper in answer from the depths, "Raymond," saw the eyes of both open and look at him for but a moment's consciousness, while Nadia murmured, "Robert," and Dexter's voice brought forth, "Merrill, don't leave us." Then both slipped off into unconsciousness again.

In the hospital in Omaha, there was no hope for Raymond Dexter, the doctors agreed. It was only a question of a few hours before Death would summon him. When he was told and given restoratives to help him to say what he wanted done, he said to those around him, "What must be must be. My will is made. I must manage, if you can help me, to write a few last lines for my wife to read after she has become—accustomed to—the feat—of this horror, and loss." With Robert beside him, helping him, while Nadia still laid unconscious in an adjoining room, he scratched those few last lines with his own hand, sealed them in an envelope addressed to his wife—"Not to be opened until six months, or a year, as desired by her, after my death." And then asked to see and bid her farewell, even if it had to be with her unconscious.

"She will have to be brought in to you," they told him. "She is not as badly injured as you. She will recover."

So she was brought in to him not fully conscious, but on that side of the border. Close, side by side those narrow cots were placed. His hand went out and lifted hers and brought it to his lips.

"Dear hands," he said, that have worked in many ways to help others and made me one of their blessed recipients."

"Raymond! Oh, Raymond!" came her voice in yearning.

"Dear voice," he went on, "that has spoken always the words of kindness and love and gone forth on inspiring song. Dear face of my own—beloved—beloved—goodbye."

"No. No. Raymond." No borderland of consciousness was hers now, but its fullness. "It is not goodbye. No. No. See, we are here together, talking, looking at each other, loving each other back, out of this sudden dark into our shining happiness again." She had struggled and lifted herself, with the arms of a nurse behind her; she lifted her head across the little space and laid it down beside his, her body stretched across that separating barrier of the divided beds. "See, we are together. Both of us will be alright again. And there is Robert, dear, kind Robert to help us."

"Yes, beloved, he will help us," Raymond answered, as he caressed her face with one hand, still clinging with the other to hers. So they were allowed to lie for a while, neither the doctor or attendant or Robert, who had been requested to remain as a possible help, wanting to interfere and hasten the end of their last goodbye. A goodbye which is a sad, devastating thing to see and hear whether they be friends or strangers. And lying thus after a time the veil spread by those physical injuries began to fall over them again and wrapped them once more in its silencing blinding folds. So they did not know when they were drawn apart, and for the last time, never again to meet knowingly each to each on this side of that river of death whose other shore beats back to us, unanswered, all our questionings and theories and yet has never killed for us the tireless winged bird of Hope.

What mattered to them, or many, the cause of the wreck? A spreading rail, a misplaced switch, a misread or wrong signal or some other weakness in the material or the human forces except that one more tragedy caused closer investigations and more watchful efficiency throughout railroad transportation, to the credit of which there is a far smaller ratio of casualties to its amount of freightage than the appalling record of the automobile with its careless drivers.

For all that now devolved on Robert Merrill it was well that he was equal to the needs and had no shadow of the spirit of the shirker, no indifference to others needs because of the calls of his own. He was alert, in the midst of all this shack and sorrow, to the needs to be attended to here and at both ends of the journey of these two friends. "Well for them that I happened to be on the same train," he thought once and then was again lost in the doing, the helping. Friends—when they are friends with the true meaning of the word—never fail one in misfortune. That is when the test of the real, the branding of the true and the false comes. And alas, the brand, the gleaming writing, "True goes like a lovely, but shining star in the thronging dark of the False." Misfortune is the test, especially long continued misfortune. It sifts the wheat from the chaff.

East and west Robert sent telegrams. Her home folks so near and yet afar. His home folks so far, halfway across the continent now.

The first brought the answer, "Coming. Carl and Aunt Eleanor."

The second, "Shocked and grief stricken. Bring Raymond's body back to his home, and bring Nadia if she is able to come. Mrs. Burgess and Luella."

He had Dexter's body taken charge of by an undertaker awaiting further orders. Not knowing, and hardly able to guess what Nadia's desires would be, he decided after consultation with doctors, to have her told of Mr. Dexter's death whether that task be his or another's. The doctors claimed that Nadia's impurities were more of the nerves than of other bodily organs. The gash in the head had come near hurting the brain and helped with the nerve shock to cause the spells of unconsciousness, but this would all now be overcome. The bruises on the body while uncomfortable were not serious ones. So, at Robert's insistence the doctors told her the next morning while he hung in the background feeling not only unhappy, but miserably out of place because he was here and the one she had loved most was taken away.

"Mrs. Dexter, we have decided to tell you something without delay, that your friends may know your wishes and act accordingly. You will need all yourself control to receive what I am going to tell you. Call it forth now, for it is futile to break our spirits by beating them against the inevitable." Her eyes were staring wide and solemnly at him now. "Your husband, Mr. Dexter, has passed away, into that other world where we must all follow, without choice of when or how."

"Gone. Oh, God! And I wasn't with him," she answered. "If I had been there—if I had not failed him, he would have come back to me again. I would have called him and he would not have left me," she groaned. "He would have come back."

"Oh, no, Mrs. Dexter. He could not. He was too badly injured. The spirit cannot always overcome physical injuries. Sometimes they tear too deep for even that strongest conquerer's overcoming." And then he left her to the nurse and Robert.

"Take me to see him again, Robert. Just once more."

"It is too late, Nadia. He died in the night without coming back to consciousness. You heard his last words and spoke the last words to his consciousness. That is something to comfort you, Nadia. When you are able you can go and look upon his unconscious face before his body is sent home if that is what you desire."

"Of course he must be taken home and I must go with him. Back to his own home which I wish I had not caused him to leave and come on this fateful journey for my pleasure. Oh, Oh! Regret, regret, how vain you are, for your very meaning is 'too late.' Oh, Robert!"

"I would bring him back to you if I could, Nadia," he said, meaning it to the depths of his truly sympathizing being.

Carl and Aunt Eleanor came with the expectation of taking her back with them, but she was determined to go back with Raymond's body to his own home, the house where they had been blessed with the great happiness of their lives. She could not be moved from that decision.

"But Nadia you cannot go alone, now, even if you are able to travel back there," Carl reminded her.

"But you or Aunt Eleanor, or both, can go with me. You need not stay any longer than you feel you can, and of course you know I would bear all the expense. I do not have to hesitate over expense in this hour of my need, which wouldn't have been the case in the old day, would it, Carl? Thanks to him, the loved one just gone."

Afterward by themselves, Robert put before Carl that it was his duty and in grateful recognition of what she had been to him in his own time of need, to go with her, and Aunt Eleanor also, if she could.

"If I offered to go in your place it would look strange, and hurt her too, that not any of the family she had sacrificed herself for could give in return just a little of themselves in her time of need." So he placed it before Aunt Eleanor who, of course, saw it as he did before he expressed it. Within a couple of days these three took the train for New York, Nadia fighting the inertia of the body's hurts and her crushing loss with its heavy dejection. Folded next to her heart was Raymond's last written message to her while she wondered why it was not to be read now instead of six months or a year after. Robert's parting words to her as she left him behind had been, "Remember, Nadia, I am always to be called when you need me or want me. Do not forget that."

"Thank you, Robert, dear friend. Who can say when that loyalty might be my one support again."

He did not know, nor she, that the last words of the one who was gone had recognized that loyalty in an uncommon way.

Though her willpower ruled, and drove her onward, yet Nadia needed help for the body on the way home and after, for a time. The bruised shocked body and nerves revolted without regard to the preponderating mental blow. But they reached home and she went through the last rites and tributes to her lost one. Being a man of prominence in the business, philanthropical and social worlds, the tributes of the press with their laurel wreath of appreciation were many, but like all who die, he having passed on, others were filing in. No matter how great you are, or your achievements, your day is over and the world moves on without you, apparently undisturbed but in those little corners of your nearest and dearest.

Carl and Aunt Eleanor stayed just a little longer to grasp a surface acquaintance with America's vast city and its pleasures, but, by themselves, unaccompanied by any of the stricken family, of course. Nadia felt now that never again would she want or seek anything of the kind for herself. Her great light of happiness had gone out. She felt that she and mere pleasure were ended so far as companioning together in this world. That is what deep grief says to some at first, until the washings of time and life's continual stresses force one to make the best of what is, and lift oneself above the gulf of despond to the more natural level of normal life that offers here and there some little soothing fruitage for the willing gatherer.

XXIII

For a time Nadia succumbed to her grief and aloneness, though
two others, in their own special way, grieved and felt the
loneliness. Then rousing all her faltering faculties she forced
herself to an active interest not only in her own work but in the
philanthropies they had planned and initiated together—he and
she—the upreaching for good that each strengthened in the other.

And now she felt, ah knew, that he was still with her,
comforting, supporting, exalting her. Not in any psychic vision,
but the within of him, that could not die, close to the within
of her. They had been too responsive to each other, too closely
intertwined, to be entirely dissevered though the bodies through
which we meet in this world were forever separated. So her
work went on and sometimes it seemed to her she could almost
talk to him. Often she thought of that treasured letter, but when
the six months were at their close she felt a hesitation, a strange
touch of reluctance unexplainable, in opening and discovering

its contents. Once, she opened its treasure case, glanced at the missive within but closed and locked it again from sight. Then one day when the others were gone for the afternoon, she decided to read it and know, knowing well that only love was there in some expression for her good. She locked herself in her room and drew the letter forth. His own hand had written it when Death was already bending over him, saying, "Never again. Leave now your last words. Hasten." And here they were:

> "Nadia, dearest, having been told that I must die very soon, I am wondering what message I can leave that will tend to make life easier, not harder for you, not deny but add to its comfort and joy, and this thought has come to me. Knowing that Robert Merrill and you were once fond of each other, I suggest that if that feeling revives and he asks for you again in marriage, that you consummate it. Do not make your life sad and lonely to the end mourning for me. Knowing your love is mine now, if I were still there I could not bear it. But the book says, "in heaven there is not marrying or giving in marriage." In spirit we will love and be near and help each other always, always. That I believe is a part of the Universal Purpose. Merrill is, I am sure, a worthy man, and he has stayed with us in this tragedy. Repay him if you can. If not that way then by some other expressed appreciation. Goodbye my dearest, dearest. I don't want to go, but when our time comes we have no choice. Dearest Nadia, Goodbye.
>
> *Raymond*"

Strangely moved she read on to the end. How like him to put Self aside for her sake, even in death. And what a strange last message to the one beloved.

"Oh, but I could not do this. How could he? The love thoughts of you, Raymond, would be coming between me and Robert and I could not prevent them if I would." She murmured aloud, and somehow suddenly she felt he was there, truly there, with her. She could almost vision him with a wonderful look upon his face.

"Oh, Raymond! Why were you taken from me? It seemed with your going, my light had gone out too." She sat there a long time lost in a maze that was only broken by the homecoming of the others.

"Well, the mystery of the letter is disclosed. You gave me six months to overcome the first harsh stroke of your death before venturing this suggestion. It seems a sacrilege now, too. Raymond. Raymond."

She did not mention this last letter to the others. They had not known of it.

"Raymond," she said again as though talking to his presence there, but low, almost inaudibly, "with you gone, gone, I now begin to yearn for a sight of the old home, the home faces. I am going to them now for just a little while, and then to my work, our work, again."

She went. The wide open spaces once more. The little city a thriving human nest on the bosom of the great prairie that stretched so far and so voicefully with its many languages of Nature's creating. She loved it all, all. Even its faults seemed, to her, almost as a decoration to its virtues. She went in to meet the members of the family not quite the Nadia of old. The same yet not the same, for all the varying forces sweeping against us in absence or together mould us day by day into something different. They were all happily glad to be together again, but her place of old was gone. It was not very long till she began to feel all the more that aloneness that was now to be hers. Each one was married and interested particularly in his or her own affairs. Their need for someone to serve for them was not as necessary as in the old days. They looked upon her as one who had succeeded far beyond them and therefore a bit strange and outside. In the town she was honored and feted as much and far more than she could accept. Her heart was not in these things yet. Once they would have meant more, than just now in her heartache. And yet the recognitions, appreciations pleased her and her family.

She wondered if she might be happier here now than in the great human jungle of New York or any other large city. Does the where you live have much to do with what makes your happiness?

Then she was back there again, and hard at work, not only to achieve but to hide from herself some of that terrible aloneness.

Another six months went by.

The wheels rolled on.

While Robert Merrill had written her twice during the year to learn how she was faring, and she had answered his letters, she had not seen him since the last tragedy, which took Raymond from her. Then one day when October was glorifying Nature's garments a telegram came to her signed by Robert's sister.

"Robert is dangerously ill. In his delirium he keeps calling for you. Can you come to us? It might help to save him. Will you come?"

She answered, "Coming at once." She named the train.

The sister met her at the station in Chicago.

"It was good of you, Nadia, Mrs. Dexter, to come. He seems a little better, but still delirious and calls for you often. If he comes out of the delirium, he may not remember he has done that."

Then she was in his room bending over him, while the nurse stood by and the mother and sister pale with wearing anxiety stayed near, but out of the sick one's vision, to see what would happen.

He looked at her with that roving far away vision and suddenly grew quiet, while a gladness spread over his face. Oh, such a gladness, it brought the heart leap and the tears to each of those in the room.

"Nadia, it is really you. Not just one of my dreams. You have come to me at last, at last. I have longed for you, Nadia. From—boyhood. You—were—one of my goals. Strange wasn't it that someone came between us twice. Much as I wanted you, longed for you, Nadia, I wouldn't have separated you from him you loved. No. I wanted your happiness first. But when— when—he was taken—through no fault of mine—that good big brained, big souled man—then—after a time—when the shock was—being lessened by time—I began to think of you again in that old longing way—as I did through all those horrors—on the battlefields of France. Is there hope, Nadia? Is it necessary for both of us to walk alone? Is there hope, Nadia?"

He half lifted himself toward her and stretched out his arms. Both pathetic and beautiful it was. The naturally reticent, self-poised, strong, helpful man, still on the verge of delirium, opening the doors to his proud soul. She could not have said no to him. Could not deny his hope under this plea and all this revealed stress and love. And truly even as a soldier, a brave, faithful soldier in war, and in peace, he had earned yes, righteously earned what he asked for. Otherwise, had he not asked at such a time and in such a way, she might have held aloof, have denied him.

She bent her head lower and lower, with tears clouding the brightness of her eyes, and laid it against his as he fell back exhausted on the pillow.

"Yes, there is hope, Robert, hope. Get well and we will walk together. Even he, Raymond, would smile on us over there. I know."

And she buried her head in the bed of clothes and tried to hide and keep back the sobs. Then while others were almost sobbing with them, in their loyal human sympathy, she looked up again with a smile trying to soothe or cure the tears and the sorrows behind them.

So it came to pass at last, came to its fruition, that love, and its hope, which had its birth in early youth and traveled on, past high fences of denial, to its bruised, wounded, but perhaps greater affirmation. Afterward she told him of Raymond's last message.

"Big even in death," Robert said.

And the wheels rolled on.

The End